Chief Executive

"As his readers know, Alexander Fullerton tells a very good story; his *Chief Executive* fairly spanks along. *The Power Game* was never so good."

Daily Telegraph

Alexander Fullerton served in submarines during the Second World War. After the war he learnt Russian and was employed in Germany as a Naval Liaison Officer with the Red Army units. In 1949 he resigned his commission and emigrated to South Africa where, after five years in shipping, he then sold books. He returned in 1959 to live in England, and has since been a director of two publishing companies. He now lives entirely on writing.

Also by Alexander Fullerton
in Mayflower Books

THE PUBLISHER
STORE
THE WAITING GAME
SURFACE?

Chief Executive

Alexander Fullerton

Mayflower

Granada Publishing Limited
Published by Mayflower Books Ltd 1971
Frogmore, St Albans, Herts AL2 2NF
Reprinted 1974

First published by Cassell & Company Ltd 1969

Made and printed in Great Britain by
C. Nicholls & Company Ltd
The Philips Park Press, Manchester
Set in Intertype Times

Chief Executive

I
Sixties

CHAPTER ONE

When the door-bell rang, Nick Morrell laid his pen down and turned the letter which he'd been writing face-down on the blotter: then he stood up slowly and went out across the hall to let his chauffeur into the flat. Burton was exactly one minute early.

"Good morning. sir."

"Morning, Harry. I'm not quite ready. Come in, will you?"

"Right, sir."

Burton stepped into the hall, and removed his cap. Morrell said, pointing, "You'll find coffee in the kitchen, if you want it."

Morrell went back to his desk, turned the letter over and picked up his pen again. He'd had two days to think about writing this; two of the most unpleasant days he'd ever lived through. To be trapped, so completely helpless; to have to take it lying down; he gritted his teeth, and the last words he'd written stared at him from the sheet of white, headed paper: *under all the circumstances, and for private reasons of which you are aware, I must ask you . . .*

He wrote, now, slowly and carefully, hating every deliberate stroke of the pen, *to accept my resignation as from the date of this letter*. He signed it, *Nicholas Morrell*. Then he wrote on a white envelope, *Sir Charles Briscoe, Chairman*, and sealed the letter in it.

So now it was done. Or it would be, in a couple of hours' time when the board met and Briscoe, as chairman, accepted his chief executive's resignation. What a great day this must be, for Sir Charles! Months of planning, probing, and attacks: now he had what he wanted, and probably no other member of the board would have the slightest inkling of how the trick had been worked. Like – when you thought about it – a sudden, murderous knife-thrust in a dark alley; and in the one area where they'd had him cold, unable to defend himself or fight back. He couldn't even tell anyone about it – now, or ever.

Morrell stood up, and headed for the door.

"Let's go, Harry!"

"Right, sir." Burton came out of the kitchen. Looking at him, Morrell thought, To him, it's just another morning. Nothing different about it. His guts aren't tied in knots, like mine. The lucky bastard! He walked into the lift; Burton shut the door of the flat and joined him. Riding down into Eaton Square, he murmured, "It's a beautiful day, sir. Really lovely. Summer at last."

"Good." Briscoe, he thought, will certainly be thinking it's a lovely day. He probably sang in his bath, this morning. The bloody old queen.... My God, if I ever meet him alone on a dark night, they'll have to scrape him off the pavement!

As they came out of the building into the square, Burton passed him and opened the back of the Rolls. Morrell climbed in. The way Briscoe has fixed me, he thought, I have to do it politely, discreetly, as if I'm doing it because I want to. *Want to!* McLennan Ridgeway hasn't only been mine, it's been *me*. I've worked and fought, sweated blood, built it and trimmed it and powered it, put it up there with the leaders: not with them, *ahead* of them! I took a lousy shambles off the scrap-heap where that disgusting creep Briscoe was content to let it lie – where he belongs himself – and I gave it shape, strength, and purpose. They'll drag it down again now. A business of this size and complexity, all you need do is stop driving, and it stops. Or simply fail to understand it: the effect's the same. They couldn't achieve that without pulling me down first. But now they'll be happy doing it, that shower of ignorant, stuffed shirts.... God, they should be drowned, like a litter of unwanted cats!

The shares will drop suddenly this afternoon, when my resignation's announced in the evening papers. He thought, if the Germans have sold their ten per cent, they're lucky; they'll have unloaded just in time. That stock has to drop, and it won't climb back. Not for a long time, anyway. The business world knows damn well this has been a one-man job; and it's a fact that if you take the mainspring out of a watch it's unlikely to keep good time. That's how it'll be with McLennan Ridgeway. So I'd better arrange to unload my own stock before the word gets out. I'm losing the biggest battle of my life, but I don't have to lose my money as well.

Burton stopped the car outside the McLennan Ridgeway building, opposite the central, plate-glass doors. Robinson, the commissionaire, came hurrying down the steps to open the car door: but he wasn't too fast on his feet, particularly on steps, and Burton got there ahead of him. Both men looked surprised that Morrell hadn't moved: he was still sitting in the back of the car, staring fixedly out of the offside window.

"Sir?" Burton peered in at him. Robinson's craggy, ex-Army sergeant's face showed concern.

"Morning, sir."

"Eh?" Morrell looked out at them. He was thinking, *I'm not as green as I was twenty years ago, but by Christ, I wouldn't have thought a Minister of the Crown would stoop as low as . . .*

"– and a very nice morning too, sir."

"Oh. Yes." He climbed out. *Not even,* he thought, *a four-letter man like Elliot Hooper. . . .*

Well, you live and learn. He asked Robinson, who'd lost a leg at Arnhem, "Is the chairman here yet?"

"Yes, sir. Sir Charles got in 'alf an hour ago."

Morrell nodded. Sir Charles would have been up bright and early, to be in at the kill. He'll manage to look sad when we meet, though. "Stick around, Harry. I may be needing you."

"Very good, sir." The chauffeur nodded. Morrell went up the steps quickly, shoved back one of the glass doors with the heel of his hand, like a rugger player fends off a tackle. The girl behind the reception desk got up quickly, tripped to the lift and pressed the call button. Morrell recognized her legs – she wasn't hiding much of them – but if he'd ever been told her name he didn't know it now.

"Good morning, Mr. Morrell."

"Morning – er –"

"Jean Fawks." She had a nice smile.

Morrell nodded. "Of course." Markwick, the personnel stooge, was certainly competent at picking receptionists. Well, he had to be good at *something*. Morrell smiled at her, hearing the crash of the glass door as Robinson stumped in behind him. The lift doors slid apart and he stepped in, pushed the button for the top floor, the penthouse suites that were his and Briscoe's offices. As the doors ran together he saw both

Robinson and the girl watching him, their eyes on his as if they were trying to read his thoughts. The doors met, flattening their rubber edges together and shutting out the girl's smooth face and the man's, creased like a ploughed field: but facing the mat-painted steel Morrell frowned, still seeing those intent eyes, realizing they must know already – those two and all the rest of them as well – that there was something in the wind.

He watched the light travel up the indicator panel: thirteen, fourteen, fifteen. The lift stopped, its doors opened, and Priscilla, his secretary, said "Good morning –"

"If you tell me it's a lovely one, I'll brain you."

"I won't, then." She followed him across the ante-room, through the office where her two assistants worked, then past the door of her own room and into his. It was big, and impressive to anyone seeing it for the first time. French doors led to a railed terrace, and the panoramic view of London, south across the river as far as Crystal Palace, made it seem even bigger. On each of the two walls flanking the windows was a Montague Dawson seascape – tea-clippers, flying spray and moonlight. The only other picture, which hung on the wall behind Morrell's desk, was also of a ship: but it was a photograph, not a painting, of a small warship almost buried in a great driving weight of sea.

Morrell crossed to the french windows, opened them and stepped out on to the terrace. He thought, Whatever I do, I won't get a nicer office than this to work in. Well, perhaps I'll stop work, just look after Inge. . . . He stood with the tips of his fingers on the railing and looked down across the corner of Berkeley Square and the roofs of Shepherd Market to the green smear of Hyde Park beyond them. Closer down and to the right was the roof of Crewe House, headquarters of the Tillings empire, its lawn emerald in the sun.

Behind him, Priscilla said, consulting her notebook, "The board meeting is due to start in one hour and ten minutes. Sir Charles has been asking for you, and Mr. Crane of Hawthornes telephoned for a luncheon appointment. Most important, though, Mr. von Mettendorf called from Hamburg just a few minutes ago. He'd like you to ring back urgently, before the meeting. He was extremely insistent it should be *before*."

Morrell nodded. "Yeah."

"Shall I get him for you?"

"No. Don't bother."

"But –"

"I said don't bother." He came back into the room and sat down at his desk. He told her, "Too late to call him now. He doesn't know it, but it is. Get him when I come out of the meeting – remember, will you?"

Priscilla had perched herself on the end of a sofa. She looked anxious. "He said it was most important. He did sound very – well, excited. Still, if you think it's –"

"I know it is." He looked at her thoughtfully across the room. She'd been with him more than ten years: ever since he'd been appointed a vice president of McLennans in New York. She was an American: but she'd wanted to stay with him when he'd come back here to run the combine formed by McLennans taking over Ridgeway. So she'd come along.

Morrell drew a deep, slow breath. "Priscilla, you'd better know it now. I'm resigning, this morning."

She jumped as if she'd been stung.

"You're joking!"

"The hell I am."

"But you can't! You simply *can't*!"

"I can, Priscilla, and I'm going to." He took the envelope out of his pocket and showed it to her. "It's in here. Formal. 'Dear Sir Charles, I regret to inform you', etcetera. Don't ask me why – I've reason enough. Officially, the only reason I'm giving is that I'm getting married and I want to ease off. But in fact I don't know quite what I'll do next: all this has come up rather suddenly. Whatever I decide on, I'd like to have you along with me. How d'you feel about that?"

"Awful. Terrible."

"Well, thanks."

"Nick, you can't be serious –"

"Never more serious in my life."

"It's so unlike you. To give up. I can hardly *believe* you'd –"

"That I'd let these bastards win? Well, there it is. I've – well, I've had enough. . . . You'll move on with me?"

She nodded.

"Fine. And if I decide not to take another job, I'll see you get fixed up. Maybe you'll want to go home to the States?"

She shrugged. "Let's see what happens."

"All right. Well, now: anything important I should look at?"

"About fifty things. Still – under the circumstances, I suppose they'll keep. But I wish you'd call Mr. von Mettendorf."

He shook his head. "Hamburg doesn't come into this. Not now. And I can't explain to him what I'm doing. So forget it, will you?"

The intercom buzzed. He pressed a key.

"Yes?"

"Ah, Morrell."

"You want something, Briscoe?" He spoke roughly, hating even the sound of the man at the other end.

Briscoe's voice, dry and wafer-thin, asked him, "Did you know Gilbert McLennan was attending our meeting today?"

"McLennan? Is he over here?"

"I thought I mentioned, he's attending the meeting this morning. He *must* be here, mustn't he? I thought perhaps you had invited him."

"Why should you think that? He's a director of the company, he doesn't need any invitation."

"I find it difficult to understand why he should have arrived in London without having let any of us know he was coming. Can you explain it?"

"How the hell can I explain it? Where is he now?"

"He telephoned half an hour ago from the Hilton. Asked me to delay the meeting, if necessary, until he gets here."

"You'd better do that, then."

"The Hilton is hardly so far away that we should have –"

"If he's just flown in, maybe he needs a shave, shower. Even some breakfast."

"H'm . . . Morrell, I'd like a private word with you before we start the meeting. Will you come in here?"

"Sorry. I'm pushed for time."

"I happen to be your chairman –"

"That's a temporary situation. And you also happen to have my total contempt."

"Now look here, Morrell –"

"There is one thing. Regarding our conversation yesterday. I want your signed offer for my shareholding, at this morning's price. Signed, witnessed and given me before the meeting. Get that?"

"I see no reason to –"

"What you see doesn't matter. This is what you have to do if you want my co-operation."

"Are you in a position to state terms?"

"I wouldn't push too hard, if I were you."

"Well, as it happens, I can't see any objection to that proposal. No.... Very well –"

"I want it before the meeting starts, remember." Morrell switched off the box. He muttered, "At least I don't have to pretend to love him, now."

Priscilla's eyebrows rose. "Have you ever?"

"Well, not lately.... Rustle up some coffee, will you?"

She nodded, and went out. Morrell thought, Gil McLennan being here makes no odds. No more than whatever Karl von Mettendorf has to say could make a pfennig's worth of difference: this is personal, and it's me that's on the spot: those bastards have got me by the short and curlies – the only way for me is out. He switched on the intercom again, and spoke to one of the girls in the outer office.

"Yes, Mr. Morrell?"

"I don't want any calls, inside or outside. No visitors either – nobody, d'you understand?"

He thought, At least I'll cost them something. If they buy my piece of the equity at this morning's price, they'll have dropped a packet by the evening.

Priscilla came in with the coffee. Setting the tray down, she murmured, "No calls or visitors.... Pause for reflection?"

He nodded. She said, "I hope you'll decide to change your mind."

"No, I won't do that. D'you realize it's been damn near twenty years?"

"*That* long?"

"Sure. I joined McLennans in 1946, but I first ran into Gil when I was still – hell, doing *that*." He jerked a thumb at the photograph of the little ship battling through Atlantic rollers. Priscilla glanced at it, and shivered as if she'd felt the coldness of that heaving sea. Morrell thought, stirring his coffee, I've known it rougher. Like now, for instance. *My God, those prime bastards! God, if my hands weren't tied –*

But they are. And getting in a rage isn't going to help either. But this is what's so damned hard to accept – this *impotence*.

"Coffee all right?"

"Eh? Oh, yes, it's fine." He leant forward, poured the rest of it into his cup. To be at the mercy, he thought, of that bloody old queer.... He told his secretary, "You go along now, Priscilla. Give me a bell when it's seconds out of the ring, will you?"

He watched her go. The door shut quietly behind her, and he thought, Gil McLennan – Karl von Mettendorf – hell, forget them! I'm on my own. I suppose I always have been, really.

Time like this, though, you get to notice it.

He glanced up at the ship on the wall, the corvette in the Atlantic gale, and he asked himself, I was on my own then too – wasn't I?

"Come back five degrees to starboard."

The air seeping up the pipe stank of tobacco smoke and vomit. Morrell heard the helmsman's acknowledgement of his order, and straightened. He was thinking that the next turn would be due in a few minutes. When they were settled on the new leg of the square search and young Dean was back on watch he'd go down himself, strip and dry off, take in a mug of hot cocoa. There wasn't any damn U-boat. They were doing this for the hell of it, to make things look right in the record just because some bloody pilot had spots before the eyes. Some tired aviator breaking the monotony of a routine patrol by *imagining* he'd seen a diving submarine.

Up until yesterday morning, they'd been part of a convoy escort. Then there'd been this aircraft sighting report, giving a position fifty miles south of the convoy's track and astern of their own position at that time. The escort commander had been satisfied that he had enough ships to get his charges safely into New York, and he'd detached *Dunnock* and *Wildoak* to search the area. Well, that was the policy, now – aggression. You didn't wait for the wolves, you sent the dogs out to find them before they could form a pack. There were enough ships, at last, to do that.... So many ships, he thought, that they're sending half-weaned kids to sea as officers. At twenty-nine, Morrell was young for command; but when he looked at his ward-room officers he felt like a grandfather.

He had his glasses focused on *Dunnock* when the torpedo hit her. He'd been keeping a close eye on her because it was coming up to the time they'd turn on the southward leg of the box search; he had her in his glasses, and for a split second after the impact he couldn't realize what had happened. Or he knew it, but his mind rejected the knowledge, wouldn't allow it.... But the sudden leap of what looked like a giant wave, abreast her funnel; there was water in that leaping plume but the water was already falling back and the top of it was smoke, hanging, grey then black and its outer edges orange-tinted; he'd realized what it was, then, reality and horror clicking, dovetailing in his brain a moment before the sound of it reached his ears, one harsh thunderclap by way of confirmation. At the same moment he thought he saw green water, a hump of it, where *Dunnock*'s funnel had been a second ago: green water, between the corvette's fore and after parts. His thumb was on the alarm button under the overhang of the bridge screen and bells were strident in every compartment of the ship, sending his own men to action stations. But *Dunnock* had gone. She'd broken in two and gone.

"Starboard twenty, full ahead!"

The fish had hit *Dunnock* on her starboard side: somewhere out there to the north was the U-boat for which they'd been probing. Or another one. Christ, what a hope! A million acres of broken water, and one rather slow, outdated tub.... The tub, *Wildoak*, was swinging to starboard, rolling very much like a barrel.... He thought, She'll pitch less on this course. Just as well. With maximum revs on, in a sea like this her screws would be out of water half the time, and racing. A breakdown now would put the bloody lid on it. Worton, his First Lieutenant, was at his elbow. He'd yelled some question.

"*Dunnock*'s fished. Sunk –"

"Survivors –"

"Not a hope.... I'm going after the U-boat."

Small hope of that, too. But one thing certain: you couldn't stop to look for survivors, with that thing there. There'd be no survivors anyway: blown in half, gone down in less than thirty seconds, and in this sea ...

"Midships.... Steady!"

"Steady, sir. Oh-one-five –"

"Steer oh-two-oh." A guess, no more, that the U-boat had fired from abaft the beam and not from ahead. Morrell turned to Worton. "Number One. Clear away charges, shallow settings. I want a very sharp lookout from all hands on deck.'

"Aye-aye, sir."

"Bridge!"

He bent to the other voice-pipe. At the same moment *Wildoak* flung herself to port and he cracked his face hard on the rim.

"Bridge."

"Gun's crew closed up, sir." That was Dean.

"Very good. Load with S.A.P. and keep your eyes skinned."

"S.A.P. and – aye-aye, sir –"

"Asdic!" His nose was bleeding.

"Sir?"

"Sweep red three-oh to green three-oh. And *find* the bloody thing!"

A fat chance, he thought. It's a miracle I'm looking for as much as a U-boat .... *Wildoak* thrashed through heaving, leaping sea where *Dunnock*, five minutes ago, had sunk. There wasn't anything but sea.

"Haines, Martin, Stewart! You, too! Get up there, look out for a periscope." A telephone buzzed: he grabbed it. "Yes?"

"Depth charges ready, sir, shallow settings."

If there'd been any survivors, they'd be gone by now. Even if there were some, the odds against finding them in this sea would be a million to one. Even if we were that lucky, it'd be nothing short of criminal lunacy to stop.

Haines yelling, pointing –

"U-boat surfacing, starboard!"

Black, shiny, slimy: like a whale's back – no, a snake's, vicious, deadly.... It was like a great hand in your guts, suddenly twisting: hate and excitement like an explosion in the head....

"Starboard twenty!"

"Starboard twenty, sir. Twenty of starboard wheel on, sir –"

"Steer oh-four-oh!"

The gundeck voice pipe: "On target, sir!"

"Open fire!"

He heard Dean's high wail, "Fire!", heard the first shot go, small and sharp, the sound whipped away in the wind but cordite smell across the bridge: he thought, It's either hit or miss, you can't see fall of shot in a sea like this so you can't bloody well correct.... God knows where that one went.

"She's going down again, sir!"

He checked the bearing on the gyro repeater in the starboard wing. "Steer oh-three-eight. Have I got maximum revs?"

"Yes, sir.... Steer oh-three-eight. Course oh-three-eight, sir!"

The gun had fired again. Morrell made up his mind. "Gundeck –"

"Sir?"

"Cease fire. And hold on. I'm going to ram him."

A cable's length: only the U-boat's tower and periscope standards visible now. *Christ, I'm too late....* Half a cable. Well, then, depth-charges, that's the – hell, try this first – He grabbed the microphone of the tannoy broadcaster. "Stand by to ram! Wherever you are, hold on to something!"

He dropped the mike. "Starboard five!"

"Starboard five, sir –"

Diving steeply, the U-boat's stern had showed for a split second, black, wave-washed white and green. He wouldn't have seen it if it hadn't been for that sudden frothing above the screws.

"Midships."

"Midships.... Wheel's amidships, sir."

At the last second, just before they hit, he saw the whole of the submarine's afterpart clear of the waves: his mind registered the thought that in this sea, diving athwart it, surface turbulence would naturally have made it tricky to get under.... Then he was on his back: he'd warned everyone else to hold on but he'd forgotten to do it for himself. Thrown off the bridge step backwards, he'd cracked his head on the binnacle as he went down. Now he pushed aside helping hands, staggered to his feet, grabbing the voice-pipe to haul himself forward.

"Slow together! Port fifteen!"

Wildoak had recoiled as she'd hit the U-boat, her forefoot biting into the pressure-hull; then her screws had driven her on, crunching a wider gap into the submarine's stern as she rode over it, driving on, her stern swinging to starboard as the two ships broke apart. There was no sign of the U-boat now.

"Stop port. Midships."

"Port engine stopped, sir. Wheel's amidships."

"Gundeck!"

Dean answered.

"Keep your eyes skinned, Sub. Open fire on sight. On the port beam somewhere, probably, if it's coming up at all."

"Aye-aye, sir."

God, he thought, I'm wasting time. Over the bastard again, a pattern of charges to finish him or bring him up....

"U-boat surfacing, sir!"

Wallowing up, bow first: sixty-degree bow-up angle. No, not as much: but she's finished anyway. Conning tower just emerging now, water streaming, waves beating, breaking right over: Morrell heard the four-inch fire and saw the flash and smoke-burst of its shell bursting on that long, defenceless bow. Defenceless? It hadn't been defenceless fifteen minutes ago, when *Dunnock* had been a ship still, the home of living men. Another hit....

"Check, check, check!"

A German on the conning tower with something white: a table cloth? More men coming up. Waves were breaking right over them but they were still there when the sea had swept past: their submarine lay sluggishly, nearer now to an even keel. That conning tower was packed: as Morrell watched, Germans began one by one to dive off into the sea. He thought, watching, They can drown outside that filthy thing as easily as in it.

He stooped to the voice-pipe and told the quartermaster, "Slow ahead together. Starboard ten."

The telephone buzzed.... "Yes?"

"First Lieutenant here, sir. We're holed for'ard. Cable locker and forepeak flooded. I'm shoring the for'ard mess-deck bulkhead now, but –"

"Wait, Number One," Morrell moved quickly to the voice-pipe, ordered the starboard engine stopped. He put the telephone back to his ear. "Right. I'm going slow ahead on one engine now, and I'll be stopping that shortly for about five minutes. Long enough for you?"

"I'll try, sir –"

"Well, get on with it, and report when the bulkhead's secure."

"Aye-aye, sir. But – Captain –"

"What?"

"It's leaking quite a bit already. Even when the shores are in, it won't stand much strain."

"Do the best you can."

He thought, as he shoved the phone back on its hook, I'll go down and see for myself, presently.... He could visualize the look of that messdeck, the deck itself running with scum, and the timber shores with rolled hammocks to pad their ends where they'd be jammed and chocked against the thin steel of the bulkhead. Of course it'd leak: it was never intended to resist the strain of hundreds of tons of water. He wondered, suddenly, why on earth they didn't build strong bows into anti-submarine craft, when ramming had so long been accepted as a method of attack at close quarters.... He thought, If I have to, I'll take her in stern first: hell, be like trying to steer a drunken cow! Unless the weather eases.... I could stream a sea-anchor over the bows, though. That'd help a bit. He went on thinking about it while he conned *Wildoak* round in a wide, slow circle to come up abreast and to leeward of the foundering U-boat. Then he stopped the ship and sent for the bosun. At least that hole in the bows had solved one problem. . . .

He told the bosun, "Get a scrambling net over the starboard side. Any of those swine who're good enough swimmers to reach us, pull 'em up. You've got about five minutes, so make it quick."

"Ay-aye, sir." The seaman turned to go. Morrell stopped him.

"Bosun. I don't want anyone risking his neck. D'you understand?"

Four knots, heading for New York with wind and sea to port between beam and bow: revolutions for four knots, but it wasn't safe to steer a straight course, and zigzagging reduced true speed by about fifteen, twenty per cent. Morrell knew they'd be doing well to make good three and a half knots. With a hundred and twenty miles to go, that meant thirty-six hours' steaming.

If . . .

If that bulkhead held up. It was leaking badly, in the worst places actually spurting. They'd used every timber shore in the ship, and Worton had rearranged the watchbill so that gangs of men could work non-stop baling out the messdeck.

If the weather didn't blow up again. The sea had gone down a bit, now, but the forecast was uncertain. Limping slowly towards the American coast with her shattered snout almost totally submerged, the ship wasn't in any state to cope with bad weather. Even now, with the waves lower than they had been and the wind down to force four, every sea raked her, sweeping up the ramp of the fo'c'sle, smashing like shrapnel against the superstructure, flooding aft and swirling a foot deep around the throwers. Morrell had considered trying it stern-first, but that way they'd be lucky to make as much as two knots, and with the difficulty of accurate steering there'd be no question of a zigzag. *Wildoak* was enough of a sitting duck already. If the bulkhead got any worse, though, that was what he'd have to do.

"Haines."

"Sir?"

"Find the First Lieutenant, tell him I'd like a word."

"Aye-aye, sir."

Every time a bigger wave hit the gun-mounting, which was immediately below the bridge, the bridge itself was drenched. Not just spray, but green water dropping on their heads. There wasn't any point, now, trying to keep dry. Morrell remembered that just before *Dunnock* had been torpedoed he'd been planning to go below and change his sodden clothes. Just to think, now, of the feel of a dry shirt was to imagine untold luxury.

"You wanted me, sir?"

"Yes, I did." He grinned at Worton as he lowered the binoculars from his eyes. "How's it going down there?"

"No change, sir. Not good.... Damned hard work for the lads, on top of watchkeeping. The stokers are grousing like –"

"Stokers *always* grouse.... Number One. Any of the prisoners fit enough, d'you think?"

Worton's face lit up. "Why didn't *I* think of that?"

"See about it. Any that are up to it, put 'em to work."

Morrell raised his glasses, resumed his sweep of the broken, grey horizon. He thought, The bastards were strong enough to swim fifty yards, and they've had an hour to get their breath back. Let 'em work for their living!

"Does he talk English?"

The First Lieutenant nodded. "Amazingly well. Fluent, in fact."

"All right, I'll see him. Up here. With a gun in his back."

"Aye-aye, sir."

Two minutes later the U-boat captain was standing on the bridge. He was wearing a sailor's oilskin over a blanket, and his feet were bare. Leading Seaman Hennings stood behind him with a .45 Service revolver nestling in his ham-like fist. Worton had led the cortège up the ladder.

"Take over, Number One."

Worton stepped up into the front of the bridge. Morrell moved to its after end, and stared at the man whose submarine he'd sunk. Young: about his own age, maybe less. Fair, blue-eyed, and all of six foot – in his bare feet he stood an inch or two taller than Morrell.

"I am the commanding officer of this ship. I understand you wish to discuss something with me."

The German inclined his head. "Kapitän-leutnant Karl von Mettendorf. I have to state a complaint –"

"You have, have you?" Morrell's face hardened. "Well, state it."

"My men are prisoners of war. I am told you are forcing them to work in this ship with your own sailors. This is contrary to the rules concerning treatment of prisoners, and I must request you to –"

"All right, that's enough!" Morrell's fists were bunched in his pockets: it was an effort to keep them there. He told the U-boat captain, "Your complaint is trivial and utterly ridiculous. I've no time to continue this interview." He glanced at Hennings, jerked his head towards the ladder. "Take him below and lock him up."

"Aye-aye, sir –" Hennings stepped forward.

"Wait." Morrell told the German, "Perhaps you don't realize how lucky you are to be alive. I'm trying to keep this ship afloat: I should imagine that's in your interests too?"

"It is a matter of principle –"

"The hell it is! I'll tell you something about matters of principle, shall I? Couple of hours ago you sank a warship. One of my own flotilla. You'll appreciate there were a large number of our personal friends in her."

He was finding it difficult to keep the tremble of anger under control: he could hear the shake in his voice: in the effort not to shout, he was almost whispering.

"That ship's captain, for instance, was a friend of mine. I'd have liked very much indeed to have stopped and searched for survivors. I couldn't, because if I'd stopped this ship I'd have provided you with another easy target. It's been your habit – since 1916, I believe – to sink ships without warning even when they're engaged in saving lives. So I couldn't: I had to leave my own countrymen to drown. Can you imagine how that feels, you with your bloody piffling complaints, your damned impertinence?"

Wildoak rolled as Horton turned her to a new leg of the zigzag: the German staggered, grabbed the head of the ladder for support. *Natürlich* – of course ... I – regret this. But I do not believe there could have been –"

"What you believe or don't believe is of no consequence whatsoever. The fact is I couldn't stop for my own countrymen, and I *did* stop for you. You can thank whatever God you worship for the total injustice which has resulted in your being alive. I assure you, personally, that it's not an outcome I'd have wanted. D'you understand me?'

"I understand, but –"

"No!" Morrell was tired, wet, hungry. He shouted in the German's face, "That's *all*! Now get off my bridge!"

Dawn, June 5th: twin echoes on the radar screen, then a flashing lamp, exchange of recognition signals. Light spreading from the east across a sullen but tamer sea revealed, as they closed in from dead ahead, the narrow bow-on shapes of two United States destroyers. The rendezvous had been arranged in the radio'd reply to Morrell's signal reporting the loss of *Dunnock*, destruction of the U-boat and damage to his own ship.

An hour later *Wildoak* was under tow, stern-first, making six knots for the Hudson River. That evening Morrell had the Statue of Liberty in his glasses when the phone from the W/T office buzzed: he walked over and grabbed it.

"Yes?"

"Just had a news flash, sir. We're in Rome!"

"We're *what*?"

"Rome, sir. Italy. The Eighth Army. It's –"

"Oh. Good...." He dropped the phone, turned to his signalman. The leading destroyer had been flashing. "What was all that about?"

The signalman finished scribbling down the message. He read it out: *Intend to stop off Brooklyn Navy Yard while you disembark your prisoners to Military Police launch then enter North River to dock at McLennans Hoboken stop United States 88th Division is camping in Piazza Venezia Rome Italy how's that for a day's work?*

CHAPTER THREE

Morrell stood sweating between puddles of oily water in the bottom of the McLennan dry dock, staring up at *Wildoak*'s crumpled bow. Beside him Hank Smith, who'd introduced himself the previous night as general manager and vice president of the yard, watched his engineers erecting the framework from which they'd start work. It would be a cutting job, first, burning off a twisted mass of lacerated, knife-edged steel. The Asdic dome had gone, along with that slice of bow.

Smith, somewhere in his forties, five-foot six and built square like a heavyweight wrestler, was in his shirtsleeves. Morrell wished he was too: it was a baking hot day, and down here in the wet, stinking bottom of the dock the heat and humidity made for greenhouse conditions – a greenhouse that reeked of oil fuel, dirty water, garbage. Morrell thought, trying not to breathe too deeply, They must pee in it.

"I'd say three weeks. That's guessing." Smith rubbed a hand over cropped, grey hair. "Tell you better in a coupla hours. Course, there's maybe –"

"Be nice if you could do it in two." Morrell shifted to a drier patch: he looked around for rotting fish, but there didn't seem to be any. "I'd like –"

"Sure you would. Me too. Plenty more jobs waiting, believe me." Smith glanced at the Englishman. "But what's your hurry, Commander? Don't care for New York? You have a wife back in England? No, you don't, you told me –"

Morrell shook his head. "No wife."

"For a single man I'd say this is not such a bad town. I'm married twenty years, myself, four kids –"

Morrell knew it. Smith had shown him snapshots of his family, last night in *Wildoak*'s wardroom. The captains of the two destroyers had been present, too, enjoying Plymouth gin in almost unbelievable quantities.

Smith growled, "My head hurts. Let's get outa here." Morrell followed him up the narrow, slimy steps, stepping carefully and trying not to touch the dripping wall of the dock. At the top, Smith turned to him.

"Better, huh? Well now, Commander. You met Bill Short. He has charge of this job and you'll find he knows his way about it. One of my right hands. Any troubles, though, you're welcome to come to me. Right?"

"Right. And thanks."

"Hell, I almost forgot. Taking you to a party tonight." He jerked his thumb at the impressive skyline across the river. "In Manhattan."

"Nice of you, but –"

Morrell had half promised to visit one of the destroyers whose captains he'd entertained last night. Not a definite engagement, because they hadn't been certain about sailing orders.

Smith shook his head. "Please, none of that 'But' stuff. I got orders from the boss. You know, McLennan?" He pointed a thick forefinger in Morrell's face. "You don't wanna miss this one. I tellya, Nick, the guy uses champagne to wash his goddam feet. You just see that apartment! Well, two apartments, he has now. The other's the one he keeps his –"

Smith shut his mouth like a trap. "I must be sick. . . . Pick you up here, six o'clock. Okay?"

The second he stepped into the McLennan apartment that evening, Morrell felt the air-conditioning wrap itself around him like some magic hand soothing, lifting his spirits: the heat of the afternoon had been appalling, deadening, and while the whole of New York – three-quarters of the world, for that matter – was delirious about the day's great news he'd found it had little effect on his own feelings of frustration. In fact it made him feel worse. Since early morning, Allied troops had been swarming across the English Channel into Normandy – and he was stuck here with a ship that wouldn't float for at least a fortnight, quite like three or four weeks. After years of longing for his own command he'd got it – and what the hell was he doing with it?

The room he'd come into must have been sixty feet long and twenty wide, and it was crammed with people. Uniforms, dark business-suits, crewcuts, pretty girls. . . . Hank Smith lifted two glasses of champagne from a passing waiter, pushed one of them into Morrell's hand.

"Get this down, 'n we'll find Gil." He jerked his head. "Be up that end, where the bar is."

On the way over from Hoboken, Morrell had discussed with Smith the work-programme on *Wildoak*'s repairs, and he'd explained some of his own anxiety to get back into the war. The McLennan vice president had grinned sourly, glancing sideways at his passenger. "Out there killing Germans, that what you want?"

"I wouldn't put it like that."

"What I'm mending your damn ship for, I guess. . . . Okay, let's get this war over. That's the only way to do it, yeah, let's do it. So maybe I'll be out of a job, who cares? You know my name – Hank Smith. Know what it used to be?"

Morrell waited for the answer.

"Hans Schmidt, that's what. Hans Schmidt, Hank Smith, see? Might as well tell you before some other bastard does. McLennan, now, he likes telling it. Well, I say, who cares? I'm American, same as he is. Hank Smith sounds better, that's all – an' it was *his* lousy idea I should change it. Now he tells 'em like I'm a card, done somethin' funny. Jesus, *he*'s the character!"

"What makes you say you'll be out of a job?"

"Not would. *Could*. Well, we're busy, you seen how damn busy we are. More'n we can handle. McLennan saw this coming just like it has, that's when he got in. Didn't know th' first thing about building ships, mending 'em: hell, he doesn't now, either. I'm the know-how, he's the money-man, the fixer – you know, politics. So, come peace again, not so many holes in ships, not so many ships either, the yard don't make these profits and what'll old Gil do then, eh?"

"Sell out?"

"I guess so. Cut down, sure. Then how's about Smith alias Schmidt?" He shrugged his bulging shoulders. "Maybe worse off, maybe not. Won't shorten McLennan's sleep."

Morrell saw McLennan now, across the room. The crowd had parted temporarily to let a swarm of waiters through with trays of snacks, and through the gap Morrell saw a tall, silver-haired man, immaculately groomed. Perhaps fifty years old: he'd have looked less than that if it hadn't been for the colour of his hair. To Morrell's eyes he looked the Hollywood prototype for a U.S. senator or State governor. He was chatting to a group of people which included an American general and a British commodore who couldn't have been a day under seventy: he'd been an admiral, retired before the war and joined up again as a commodore of convoys. Morrell had met him once, at a convoy conference in Liverpool.

"Let's go, huh?" Smith had Morrell by the arm and he was trying to shove him through the pack towards McLennan. But they'd started too late: that cleared path had filled again. Morrell found himself suddenly jammed face to face against an attractive chestnut-haired girl in a clinging, rainbow-hued silk dress. Their impact had slopped her drink, but she didn't look as if it concerned her much: he used his free hand to mop at her wrist with his handkerchief.

"I'm awfully sorry...."

"You're awfully British...."

"You sound English yourself!"

"That's because I'm such a *brilliant* actress."

"Well, good heavens, of course! Well, I'll be – I mean, you're –"

He was trying to look as if he never could remember a name when he really needed it. The girl decided to help him out.

"Martha Scotland."

"Who else?" Smith's face at his shoulder: he'd grabbed his arm again. Smith winked at the girl. "Honey, you can have him right after he's met the boss. Okay?"

"What boss is that?"

"Mine, dammit!"

"Oh. *Gil*...." She smiled at Morrell. "Tell him I said not to keep you long, huh?" He nodded, yielding to the powerful drag Smith was exerting on his arm: the girl called after him, "Hey, what's your name?" A dozen people laughed: he yelled, "Nick Morrell!" Some hand patted him on the back, and a woman he was passing at the time murmured absently, "Hi, Nick." Then he was shaking hands with Gilbert McLennan, and the commodore was observing drily, straight-faced, "You seem to have quite a number of friends here, Morrell."

"The natives do seem friendly, sir."

Gilbert McLennan laughed. "Delighted you find us that way, Commander. You've given my yard quite a repair job, they tell me. Rammed a U-boat, is that right?"

"Yes."

The commodore's pale eyes flicked up to Morrell's face. "Was that necessary?"

Morrell nodded. "Very close quarters, he was diving and I was alone."

"Alone?" White eyebrows rose. "One corvette alone?"

"There'd been two of us, sir, detached to investigate an aircraft sighting report. The U-boat torpedoed –" he checked, just short of the ship's name, remembering security: "– the other one."

"Survivors?"

"No, sir. None." He took a breath. "I picked up a dozen Germans, that's all."

"Not much fun, that."

"No, sir." He turned to his host. "I'd like to thank you for the treatment we've received in your yard. Your vice president has been extraordinarily hospitable and co-operative. Makes a lot of difference, I can tell you, and it's certainly appreciated."

"Fine." McLennan smiled. "Nice of you to mention it, Commander. Mind you, I'd be extremely disturbed if you found any other kind of welcome. Hank Smith, now – well, I wish I had a dozen more like him.' He looked round. "Now where the hell is he? Why, Len Carlsson! You just got here, Len?"

"Yeah. Five, ten minutes."

"Let me introduce Commander Nicholas Morrell, my friend Lennart Carlsson. Thinking of making a bid for my yard, so they tell me."

"Who in hell tells you lies like that?" Carlsson, as tall as McLennan but heavier, shrewd eyes in a wide, bland face, seemed mildly amused. He told Morrell, "Maybe he'd like me to want his stinking yard. . . ."

"Heard there was some fishing around, that's all." McLennan rested a hand on Carlsson's shoulder. "Tell you what Len. When you want a piece of my yard, you call me and we'll discuss it. Say five, ten years from now?" He turned to Morrell before the big man had time to do more than open his mouth. "Commander, will you explain to me what you told the Commodore about having to ram that submarine because you were on your own?"

"Certainly." Morrell drained his glass. "The German was in the act of diving. For one corvette alone, particularly a slow old tub like mine, the odds against a depthcharge attack being successful are pretty long. If I hadn't rammed, he'd probably still be out there sinking ships."

"Well, that's very clear. Yes, thank you." McLennan's smile was as warm as his handshake had been firm. "Always something else to learn. You are a regular Navy man, Commander?"

"No. I was a Merchant Navy cadet when the war started. I could go back to it after the war, I suppose, but –" he shook his head – "I've seen enough salt water. Will have by the time the war's over, anyway."

McLennan beckoned a waiter, and Morrell took more champagne. Carlsson drank his down, too, and got another: he asked McLennan, "Elizabeth not with us tonight?"

"Couldn't make it, unfortunately.... Commander, you said you brought in some of the U-boat's crew?"

"About a dozen." He told McLennan and Carlsson, and a group of new people who'd just joined them, about the German submarine captain's complaint: they listened with interest, and expressed astonishment.

"Can you beat *that*?"

"They had a nerve, all right." McLennan glanced round. "Why, I'm sorry, I didn't introduce you. This is Mrs. Hamilton, here's Senator Durlach, and this is Mr. Hamilton. Commander Nicholas Morrell. Hey, wait a minute. *What* did you say that German's name was?"

"Karl von Mettendorf."

"Von Mettendorf.... *Karl* von Mettendorf?"

Carlsson, the big man, was watching McLennan's face. "That name mean something to you?"

"Could be. But I guess not." McLennan smiled, dismissing whatever thought he'd had. "No, it's just I used to know a man called – well, it wasn't that name. Something *like* that, but – no." He glanced at his watch, and started. "Good Lord, I'd clean forgotten. Have to call Elizabeth. Mrs. Hamilton, will you excuse me for just a minute? Gentlemen, make yourselves at home."

Carlsson muttered to Morrell, as they watched their host leave the room through an ornate door set in the wall behind the bar, "Calling someone, sure. Not his wife, though. See his eyes pop, at that Kraut's name?"

"But he said he didn't –"

"Sure," Carlsson chuckled. "Could you use a piece of advice, Nick?"

"If it's free."

"On the house, boy. Just never play poker with Gil McLennan."

Morrell was talking to Hank Smith when McLennan came back. Nick had started by looking for the girl, Martha Scotland, but she'd been so heavily involved in a tête-à-tête with the general who earlier on had been talking to McLennan that he decided to leave them to it. When Smith showed up beside him, Morrell felt all the pleasure of meeting an old friend.

"You're in luck, sailor." Hank had a full glass in each hand. He gave him one of them. "Disembarrass me, will ya?"

"Thanks." He put his empty glass on a passing tray.

"How d'ya make out with McLennan?"

"Fine." Morral nodded. "I like him."

"Yeah." Smith sipped champagne. "Expected you would."

"Who's Lennart Carlsson?"

"One of a lotta small-timers who'd like a piece of what McLennan's got. Len around here?"

"Over there somewhere. McLennan told him he'd heard that he – Carlsson – wanted to buy your yard. Carlsson denied it, and McLennan said he'd been told someone was sniffing around, but if Carlsson did want to bid for it he should come and see him about it in five or ten years' time. But it seemed to me – for what that's worth – Carlsson really didn't know a thing about it."

"Yeah. Well, thanks, Nick." Smith was lighting a cigar. He peered at Morrell through the smoke. "Tell ya how it looks to me. Knowing McLennan, I mean. Carlsson and others like him are watching him to see what direction he's heading. McLennan has his moves worked out, all right. Carlsson never wanted the damn yard, see? But he gets this idea now from McLennan *somebody* wants it. Not him, he knows that: some other guy. Well, who? So now there's talk, ain't there – who's trying to buy McLennans? Then Carlsson and his buddies get to wonder who started this goddam story anyway. Why, McLennan did! So they think, feeling pretty smart about it, McLennan's flying a kite, he wants out. See? Now they're thinking what McLennan's wanting 'em to think. Get it?"

"Not as clearly as all that."

"You figure it out, Nick."

Morrell shook his head. He thought, It's not my world. I supposed I'd get the hang of it, in time. If I had to. God forbid.... He asked Smith, "Tell me about Martha Scotland?"

"Not bad, huh?"

"Not bad at all."

"Calls herself an actress. She is, too. But she models, mostly. That's what they say – how should I know? Used to run around with McLennan, then there was this story she was gettin' married, some other guy." Smith sucked on his cigar. Expelling smoke, he asked Morrell, "You rich?"

"Christ, no!"

"Martha won't love you, then."

"Like that, eh?"

Smith looked at him. "Maybe the uniform'd do it. That'n the Limey accent. But, Nick, doll like that one burns a lotta gas."

Morrell laughed into his champagne. "Hank, I'm more than grateful for the advice."

"Advice?" McLennan, smiling, loomed beside them. "What kind of wise counsel has my vice president been imparting to the Royal Navy?"

He looked even more urbane and cheerful than he had ten minutes earlier. Morrell thought he looked as if he'd had good news: his eyes had smiled before, but now they were positively sparkling.

"Covering certain aspects of the New York social scene." McLennan raised his eyebrows. Morrell added, "Girls."

"That's a subject I doubt we have to teach the Navy much about." McLennan reached sideways, scooped a glass from a tray. "Though I do believe it's one respect in which this town might be regarded as kind of a world centre. Eh, Hank?"

Smith puffed smoke. "You'd know, Gil."

McLennan's eyes turned cold. "Mr. Smith's observations tend at times to be less subtle than maybe they're intended."

"Meanin' I never been around like you have. One town I know – this one. An' married to one woman more 'n twenty years – damn sweet woman, but hell, I'm no connoisseur."

"You're a truly fortunate man, Hank." McLennan turned to Morrell. "Nick, I was just talking to my wife, and we've been wondering if we could persuade you to leave that ship of yours in Hank's extremely capable hands for the weekend while you come and visit us at my little country place. It'd be a real pleasure for us both to have you along. How about it?"

"It's most kind of you."

"You'll come, then?"

"Well, yes, thank you, I'd be –"

"Fine! That's just – why, Elizabeth'll be delighted, and so am I. Nick, that's great!"

Morrell thought, It's amazing. He looks as if he really means it.

"Someone can tell me how to get there?"

"Don't worry about that. I'll send a car. Pick you up at the yard, Saturday eleven o'clock?"

"Make it the Barbizon Plaza? I'm moving in there tomorrow."

"Better than that hot little boat, eh? Well, fine, that's settled. Now I guess I better walk around a bit, talk to some of these people. But you need a fresh drink, Commander."

Hank Smith was staring at Morrell over his glass. When the tall man was out of earshot, he muttered, "That 'little country place' ... Greenwich, Connecticut. It's a palace. Two pools –"

"What's he want two for?"

"Maybe Elizabeth McLennan don't like mixed bathing. Who knows? I only saw it once. Seeing as I lack the social graces –"

"Nonsense!"

"Not to McLennan, it ain't. Hi, Martha."

"Hello, there!" She smiled at Morrell. "Gil said I should look after you."

"Must be the best idea he's had in years."

She smiled. "I like it, too."

Hank Smith muttered, "Jesus. I shoulda joined the Navy."

But I can't remember where ...

"One of my favourite songs –"

"Bit long in the tooth, now –"

– or when ...

"Well, that's me too."

Martha laughed, close against his ear. "Why, you're just a baby!" He thought, stung for a moment, If she was running around with McLennan, I suppose she might see me like that.... Her body was close against his as they danced, and he wasn't having to strain any muscles to hold her there. She asked him, "Thirty, thirty-two?"

"Thirty next month. You're – no, I won't guess. Tell me."

"Twenty-five, give or take a little."

"I'm in a taking mood."

She moved against him. "I'd never have guessed. I like you, Nick."

"Now that surprises me. That cold, formal manner, I'd never have imagined –"

The clothes you're wearing you were wearing then ...

"One thing I don't like is those goddam buttons!"

"Can't take my coat off in a ritzy place like this. Well –"

He moved her away from him. "That more comfortable?"

"Silly." She slid close again. "Ritz, hell. We're slumming." Her arms were soft around his neck. "I'll put up with the buttons on your sailor suit."

"Martha the martyr."

"That I'm *not*. I'm strictly a pleasure-loving person, Nick. I love it enough to put up with a little pain, even."

"You want me to beat you?"

"Why? D'you like –"

"Oh, no! Well, I never tried –"

"Nick, take me home?"

"All right." He looked at her. "If that's –"

"Then go on over the river, get your stuff and hurry back. Huh?"

"McLennan's orders go that far?"

He felt her stiffen and pull back. He said, "I've been wondering why he'd have –"

"It happens Gil's a conscientious host and you're a stranger at his party, so he asks me to talk to you. *Talk*, that's all. Okay, go on back to your stinking little –"

"Martha, I'm sorry. It's just that –"

"Noticed the music's finished?"

"Christ, has it?" Morrell looked round. They were alone on the dance floor. The band were resting, smoking, having drinks, and all the other customers had gone back to their tables. He followed Martha to theirs, beckoned a waiter for the check. He told her quietly, "I don't need to fetch my gear tonight. There's no – look, I'm sorry –"

The waiter, with the check. Morrell paid it, thinking, If that's what it costs just slumming, God knows how I'll last a fortnight. I'll need to hock my pay a year ahead. He looked into Martha's warm, wide eyes, and he thought, Hell, why not do that? Then he was slipping her mink cocktail jacket over those perfect shoulders, and he thought, When this war's over, I've got to find a way to make some money. *Real* money.

What for? Because it's around and I want it. Other men can get it, why not Nick Morrell?

The thought wasn't entirely new, but certainly it had never struck him as forcibly as it did now.

When he tried to put his arm round her in the taxi – a natural, almost formal gambit, under the circumstances – Martha swayed away from him. She whispered, "Save it, Nick.

Home first, huh?" She pushed her hand into his, watched out of the window while their taxi skirted the top of Central Park and headed south-west towards Martha's address in the seventies. Neither of them spoke again until they got to her apartment.

She went in ahead of him, moving swiftly into the big, dark room. Morrell shut the door and heard the lock click as she switched on a single lamp on the far side of the room. She'd dropped her fur across a chair.

"I know what you think I'm going to do now, Nick."

"You do?"

"You think I'm to say, 'Well, I'll just slip into something more comfortable,' and leave you here gnawing your fingers while I make myself accessible and all that. Isn't that what you expect?"

"I suppose it's more or less the form."

"Christ, aren't we *British*!" She put her arms round his neck. "Nick, I just want you to fix some drinks. Scotch for me." Between phrases, she kissed his jaw. "It's over there under the light. Scotch for me, you have what you want. I'll be back."

"Good."

"Well, go on, then." She stepped back from him. He went to the table where the bottles stood: while he was pouring the drinks he heard her hurrying about the room – moving things, by the sound of it. He turned with the two glasses in his hands, and in that second she'd gone, through the other door.

He put the drinks down on a low table by the sofa: then as he looked up he saw what she'd been doing. All around the room were mirrors: two on walls, two more standing like big photo frames, and another, much bigger and reflecting all the others, on the front of a corner cupboard. She'd opened that mirror-covered door to just the angle that it caught all the other mirrors and also his own reflection as he stooped in front of the sofa, not yet straightened up from setting down the glasses. Whichever way he looked, he saw himself reflected from every angle. She'd known exactly where to arrange her props.

"Hi." The door clicked shut behind her. She'd taken off everything except her shoes and makeup. Now she sat down in the centre of the sofa, straight, almost prim, and turned her head slowly, looking into one mirror after another. She was studying her own reflections, but in one of them her eyes met his. She asked him, "I have good breasts, Nick, don't you think?"

He touched one of them. She shivered, and put a hand over his, pressing it against her. She was still looking in the mirrors, not at him. She said, speaking apparently to the long glass on the open cupboard door, "That uniform looks nice beside me, when I'm like this. Don't you think so?"

He didn't answer, and Martha moved suddenly against his hand.

It was partly that he'd avoided dying for such a long time, now, with the risk or even likelihood of death a kind of barrier which had made the contemplation of any post-war future an academic, pie-in-the-sky exercise. Now suddenly he could think about it. The future was almost here in front of him: in the last twenty-four hours it had come rushing towards him like an object coming into abrupt focus in a telescope.

He lay on his back in the half-dark of Martha Scotland's apartment. Her head was pillowed on his shoulder, her left arm flung across his chest and a leg crooked over his; his own left arm was round her, its fingers resting on the side of her breast which he could feel soft, warm against his chest. She was breathing deeply, evenly, and he lay absolutely still, enjoying this peace, her closeness, the scent and femininity of the apartment: and in sum of all that, the total unexpectedness of everything that added up to this present moment.

It was the future he wanted to think about. In a way, it led straight out of it.

D-day, the fact that the Channel had been crossed, meant the war couldn't last all that much longer. You realized that, and the fact that you were, after all, alive. That with any kind of luck you'd still be alive when it was over. Right on top of this revelation which in itself took a bit of getting used to, you found yourself peering into a world where men made fortunes quickly, spent them lightly, controlled the destinies of other men through the possession of that wealth: where a man like McLennan must earn in a week – even perhaps in some days – enough to support five Nick Morrells for twelve whole months. You saw the glitter and you wanted the feel of the gold: at least, you wondered what its feel was like.

Those apparently casual remarks to the big fellow – Carlsson – those were aimed, according to Smith, at some chosen target: you dropped a few words into a crowded room, an alert ear, three lemons came up in the back of someone's mind and in a month or two you'd hear the cash bells going like castanets. God knows, he thought, how or why. But to be in a position to do this: build, influence, manipulate....

He sighed, and Martha stirred in her sleep. He thought, It's way beyond me. All this is another world; I'm a guest in it, an onlooker. There are men like McLennan, and men like me. I don't have that – that touch, that flair for – for whatever it is he does. Well, for making money. Although I can't see why, if he can do it on *that* scale, I shouldn't be able to work out at least some kind of –

"You awake, Nick?" Martha's voice was sleepy. He felt her hand slide down, rest on his belly.

"Been awake for hours." His fingers stroked her. "You've been out cold."

"Not cold. *Warm*." She snuggled against him. "What'll we do today?"

"Work. Remember, I've got a ship?"

"Oh. Well, I have a date tonight, Nick."

"I thought you might have. And on Saturday I'm going out to Greenwich, Connecticut, wherever that is. McLennan's place."

"I know. I'm going too."

"You are?"

"Sure. Aren't you glad?"

"Of course."

"We'll have fun, Nick!"

"In *both* swimming pools?"

"Heck, no." She rubbed her face on his chest, a cat-like motion. "The small one's for the servants."

"How many of them?"

"Five or six, I guess.' She laughed. "Should make you feel at home."

"It should?"

"They're all English."

Morrell closed his eyes. "That's nice."

Martha told him, "Not the chef. He's French."

CHAPTER FOUR

"Pretty bad out there, I guess?"

Charles McLennan, Gilbert McLennan's nephew, had been bombarding Morrell with questions about the Atlantic battle. Charles was a cadet at West Point, a lithe, husky lad with a crewcut and a consuming interest in all things military. Morrell's interest, however, was more in the boy's girlfriend, an eighteen-year-old Australian who, in a minimal white swimsuit, lay between them now on a yellow sun-chair. Her eyes were hidden behind dark glasses: Morrell was finding it difficult not to watch her while he answered Charles's questions.

"Nothing like as tough as it was. Year before last was the worst. We were losing, then. Since spring 'forty-three it's been turning our way."

"Yeah? What swung it, Commander?"

"More ships, new methods, weapons." The girl, Toni, had a deep, even tan: in that white costume she was really something to look at. Soft, dark hair, its fringes on the golden skin of her shoulders. Morrell lay back and closed his eyes: he told himself, She's just a kid, and she's *this* kid's girl. What's the matter with me, anyway? How many women do I need at once? Besides – he told himself again. She's just a schoolgirl.

Looks remarkably like a woman, from where I'm sitting.

"– in particular, I imagine, it's techniques of detection more than actual weapons of destruction?"

Oh, Lord. . . . Morrell nodded. "You could say that."

Elizabeth McLennan – in her bedroom now, resting – had told him during lunch that nephew Charles had nightmares about the war ending before he could get into it. "Isn't that crazy? Oh, it's understandable, I guess, knowing men I mean, and Charles is almost a man, at least that's what he thinks –"

Of course it was understandable. Two days ago Morrell had been feeling much the same way himself. The urge to get back to sea was still present, but he recognized that in this very short time it had changed significantly. It was the motive that had changed: before, the motive had been his anxiety not to miss the last months of fighting – all right, be honest, the chance to distinguish himself as a commanding officer. He'd be getting a D.S.O. for the U-boat – it was an automatic award, now – but he wanted more than that. A better ship, perhaps even a commander's stripes and brass hat. You were on a ladder, the natural thing to do was climb. But the motive now was more than that, it was an impatience to get on with the job and finish it. Switch to a more permanent ladder, get to grips with this suddenly arisen, exciting concept of making a mark in a brand-new world.

A new kind of impatience, and he was restless with it. Problems had always annoyed him until he'd broken their backs. On this one, so far, he could see no hand-holds. He could lie here beside McLennan's gleaming, kidney-shaped pool, look out over a couple of acres of smoothly trimmed lawn, glance back over his shoulder at the wide, white house behind its spread of terrace: behind all that, there was just one thing. Money.

How you acquired it in such quantities – that was the clue he wanted. Not that there could be just a trick, some password which when you knew it, would give you the key to success: but just as there'd been a route for McLennan which McLennan had certainly found and followed – there had to be a Morrell route too. Perhaps an entirely different one, but some tenet would be basic, some system of thought, approach. One had heard plenty of stories of men who'd made it to the top through years of slaving, saving, scraping, but he couldn't imagine that Gilbert McLennan would ever have done that. He hadn't started rich, either: Morrell had asked Hank Smith, and Smith had told him emphatically, "Hell, no. Came up from nowhere, sudden."

Charles McLennan uncoiled himself, and stretched. His body was as tanned as the girl's.

"Care to swim, Commander?"

"Not yet. You go ahead."

"Toni?"

"Not this soon after lunch." Morrell looked down at her: the glasses were blank, reflecting sun. He'd thought she was asleep.

"That's all boloney." Charles walked towards the pool. He called over his shoulder, "Excuse to spend all afternoon just lazing!"

"Who needs excuses to do that?" She'd spoken quietly to

Morrell, not to the boy. She asked him, "You're sick and tired of talking about the war, aren't you?"

"A little. It's been going on a long time. The war, I mean. But if I was that age, I'd feel as Charles does. What brought you here from Australia?"

"My aunt invited me, for the duration. Dad liked the idea of having me out of the way. At that time the Japs didn't look like getting stopped."

"Your aunt's American?"

"Her husband is. Seymour Laing. Have you heard of him?"

"No. Should I?"

"You would have if you lived here. He's in politics. He's a friend of Gilbert's, too." She raised a slim, brown hand, pulled the sun-glasses off her eyes and looked at him: her eyes were green, their pupils small against the glare of sun. It occurred to him that while he'd thought she was asleep she'd probably noticed the interest he was taking in her body. She asked him seriously, "Do you like it here?"

"You mean this place – this house?"

"America."

"I'm fascinated by it. There's something – well, vibrant, sort of compelling –"

"Ever been to Australia?"

"No. Not yet."

"Australia'll be like this, twenty or thirty years' time. We're thrusters, too. England, now – all that tradition and stuff, well, it's okay for us 'Colonials' to gawp at, but it keeps you sort of looking backwards, don't you think?'

"Elizabeth McLennan told me you're just eighteen."

"That's right. . . . Changing the subject?"

"You do a lot of thinking, for eighteen."

"Patting me on the head, Commander?"

"No, I –" he smiled at her. "Sorry if I gave that impression. And my name's Nick, Toni."

"Okay, Nick." She sat up. "So what'll you do when the war's won?"

"I don't know. I've only just begun to think about it. In the last couple of days, really. Now we're into Europe, you can see the end of it – a few months, a year. . . . Before, you – well, I hadn't seen the time coming when one could think in terms of laying plans."

"There's still some way to go in the Pacific. You could be sent out there?"

"Could be, of course. Send you a postcard from Australia, shall I?"

"Australia, eh?" Gilbert McLennan had come bare-footed down the steps from the terrace. "I don't believe you mentioned –"

"I'm not going there, that I know of." Nick lay back, looking up at his host. "It's not likely. But I go where I'm sent, that's all." He added, "Until the shooting stops."

"Then what?" McLennan sat down on the other side of Toni, where his nephew had been lying. He looked fit, trim, a man of fifty who'd looked after himself. Morrell glanced at Toni.

"I was answering that question just before you came. The fact is, I don't know. I've only just started to think about it." He looked back at McLennan. "To begin with, I'll have to learn something about business." He shook his head. "Learn something, period."

"Man can drive a ship around, navigate, sink U-boats, he should be able to make a living. Eh, Toni?"

"Imagine so." She smiled. "Long as he's not too darned honest."

"You calling me a crook, Miss Russell?"

She laughed. "I wouldn't say you were a boy scout, either. No more than my uncle Seymour."

"Now *there's* a man who's going places." McLennan nodded. "Nick, you ever thought of coming over here to work?"

"Well –"

"You should think about it. Take it from me, there's plenty of room here for a man with guts and brains. We're going to need all that kind we can get. You think about it, now." He stood up. "You're a hell of a looker, Toni. You know that."

Toni's smile was forced, embarrassed. She hesitated, her glance flickering from McLennan to Morrell and back again. She said, "Your nephew has the same idea. At least he keeps *saying* –"

"What's my nephew got to do with it?" McLennan stared, frowning, towards the pool. He looked down at Toni. "That intended to choke me off?"

"Why, no, Gil! I only said –"

"Yeah." He grinned at Morrell. "What's that French thing? *Si jeunesse savait* – huh?"

Morrell finished it for him. "*Si vieillesse pouvait.*" He chuckled, and told his host, "Nothing personal."

"I thank you for that assurance." McLennan's eyes were back on Toni, on the long, tanned curve of her thighs. He growled, "Because I damn well *pouvait*, if anyone cares to doubt it."

Morrell thought, astonished, And a minute ago *I* was feeling like a dirty old man!

In the Greenwich Yacht Club, Morrell sat chatting with Elizabeth McLennan. Gil was dancing with Martha, who'd arrived late in the afternoon and joined them immediately in the pool. Charles McLennan was dancing with his girl, Toni. Elizabeth didn't dance. She had done, she told him, before she lost her health: she'd swum, too, and ski'd, ridden horses and played a lot of tennis. She used the phrase "lost my health" as one might talk about losing a watch, a loss in one single time and place. Morrell didn't like to ask for details.

Beyond the windows, lights danced on the water of Long Island Sound. Down there a couple strolled along a jetty, the man's white tuxedo sharp against the dark water beyond him. The girl would have been almost invisible except for the way what light there was caught and gleamed in her blonde hair. Music and young voices drifted across the terrace. Morrell thought, enviously, All the men are rich, and all the girls are pretty: my God, what a country! Even Elizabeth McLennan must have been pretty at one time. . . . Perhaps she *is* ill. When someone talked a lot about it, you tended to regard the whole thing as exaggerated, even a system of defence against a husband who gave her too little attention.

"– have an officer of the British navy here." Her smile was taut: you could imagine the skull inside its envelope of flesh. He hadn't heard what she'd said, only those last few words. She talked fast, and you had to concentrate to follow. He smiled, feeling sorry for her suddenly and not wanting her to know it.

"This is certainly a most delightful club."

"Oh, it's nice for the young ones. And Gilbert finds it useful for entertaining, when I'm not too – well, you know how it is, even with good servants there's always a mass of things one can only be sure about when you see to them yourself. And sometimes I'm not – don't you smoke, Commander?"

"Not just now, thank you." He told her, "But I love your house. Those wonderful, big rooms, so light and –"

"Well, yes, it's nice." She nodded. "We're pretty lucky, I guess. But our *real* country home is on Nantucket. Now that's the house I *love*. I often think I'd like to – well, settle there, put down roots, you know? But Gilbert doesn't feel about it quite like I do, and of course he has to be right here in New York, we'd barely see each other, no more than two, three times a year. Then we've the plantation, that's in Georgia. I don't – well, move around like I used to, these days I kind of stay put, as it were, but –" that brittle smile again: "– shame you're with us only such a short time, Commander, I know Gilbert would just love to have you visit us down there – well now, look, they're coming back already. Now you'll dance with Martha, won't you? Toni too, if that wayward nephew of ours just lets up on her long enough for – look, you enjoy yourself, now –"

"Hi." Martha sat down. McLennan slid into a chair beside his wife.

"Crowd tonight. Hardly room to dance."

"Hah." Martha nodded. She said to Elizabeth, "*That's* why he kept walking on my feet."

"Oh, Gilbert!" Elizabeth looked shocked. She told Morrell, "My husband used to dance so *well*. Of course, lately I haven't given him much practice – why, Martha, that's too –"

"I was joking. He still does, don't worry, he dances beautifully. Well, how's the Navy?"

"All set to give it a whirl, if you are–"

"Give *what* a whirl, for heaven's sake?" Martha giggled, glancing at McLennan. "You whirl yours, I'll shake mine. . . ." She noticed that neither of the McLennans looked amused. "Okay, Nick. Let's go before I make it worse."

Dancing, she murmured, "You know my room's one away from yours?"

"Yes, I know."

" 'm. Well, listen. I have my own bath and john, but in that room you don't. Right?" He nodded. She went on, "Right across from your door, that's the john you use. So when you – Nick, you want to, tonight?" He nodded again. "Well, you walk in there and flush it, then simply go to my door instead of yours. Going either way, that's what you do. Worst anyone can think is you have a weak bladder. All right, Nick?" She reached out suddenly, tapped Charles McLennan's shoulder: he turned, surprised, Toni smiling. Martha said, "Hi, kids."

"Evenin', grandma." Charles put his cheek back against Toni's. Martha asked Morrell, looking worried, "You think they could've heard?"

He shook his head, feeling like a satyr because he was wishing Martha was Toni, and Toni Martha.

Surfacing, gasping because he'd just swum two lengths of the pool under water, Morrell saw Gilbert McLennan and Toni coming down from the terrace. Toni, in her white swimsuit, looked like Miss America. McLennan had on a grey lightweight suit: beside the tanned, half-naked girl, he looked strangely formal, out of place.

Morrell grabbed the edge, and hauled himself up out of the pool. "Morning!"

McLennan waved. "Nick . . . you had any breakfast?"

"I certainly have, thanks." He watched Toni: she'd dropped her towel across the springboard and now she was poised to dive. She hadn't spoken, or even glanced at him.

"Hello, Toni."

"Hello." She dived: clean, fast, hardly any splash at all. She broke surface in a fluid, rhythmic crawl. McLennan glanced at Nick, nodded towards the girl in the water. "She's good, eh?"

"Certainly is." They watched her turn, jack-knifing and launching herself into another length with the speed and grace of a seal. Morrell said, "Australians are practically born in the water, aren't they?"

"Yeah." McLennan turned to face him. "Nick, I have a visitor coming to the house this morning. Due eleven-thirty, actually. Kind of a business matter, but we'll be through with that inside of half an hour, and – well, I'd like you to meet this fellow and I believe you'd find it interesting. Would you care to drop into the library around midday?"

"All right. Your library is –"

"Off the front hall, door on your left when you're coming in the house. Noon – okay?"

"Who is it I'll be meeting?"

"Names don't matter, Nick." He glanced down at the pool. Toni was still pounding up and down, making racing turns at each end. McLennan shook his head, and smiled. "God, that's the age to be. What a future these kids have in front of them!"

"I suppose so."

"You're – thirty, did you say?"

"Almost."

"I'm fifty. So there's twenty years before you're the age I'm at now. In that time you could do a lot for yourself, you know that? As I said yesterday, we're living in a land of opportunity and we're coming up to a great moment of opportunity too. You handle yourself right, by God you have it made!"

Morrell glanced around, his eyes lingering on the house. He asked his host, "You think in twenty years' time I could earn myself a place like this?"

"Sure, why not?" McLennan looked down at Toni. "Looks like she'll keep that up all morning. Maybe once she starts she can't stop." He told Morrell, "I mean it, though. The sky's the limit. Well, see you in the library, twelve o'clock."

Morrell watched the tall, well-tailored figure saunter up the steps to the terrace, cross it and disappear into the house. From those remarks about the future, and the guarded invitation to meet some anonymous and therefore mysterious business man, he was feeling a glow of excitement. Now, just at the moment when he'd been not exactly worrying about his future but restless, preoccupied with it, something was clearly being worked out for him. He didn't know why, or how, but there was this feeling of doors being opened, plans formed. . . .

He told himself, *Hold it!* A damn sight too easy to feel optimism, euphoria, in surroundings such as these. Pampered, surrounded with every luxury, lazing in the sunshine while a lovely brown-skinned girl races through clear blue water and a rich man spins dreams of golden days ahead. . . . He told himself, *Careful, now! Keep your feet on the ground, Morrell!*

He walked along the pool's edge to the deep end, selecting a spot not far from the corner so he could dive in without risk of impeding Toni's five-mile marathon. He dived, held the dive along the bottom of the pool, counting tiles: he wasn't a swimmer in Toni's class but he was proud of his breath-holding capacity. He made it to a corner of the shallow end, turned and swam still under water to the other corner before he surfaced. He looked round for Toni, but she wasn't in the pool. Gleaming wet, she was running up the steps towards the terrace, trailing that brilliant towel.

He wondered if he'd insulted her, or something, last night. He didn't think he had. No – they'd all been friendly, when they'd said goodnight. Morrell frowned: could it be she knew about him and Martha, disapproved? Well, how could she know – unless she'd seen him, maybe, going into Martha's room? But he'd been so careful: and even if she had, what in hell would it have to do with her?

"Ah, Nick." McLennan rose, smiling. "Come on in. Now this is going to surprise you, I know, but – well, I'll be glad to explain this whole situation –"

McLennan's visitor was getting to his feet out of an armchair facing him. He had his back to the door, and Morrell was halfway across the room before the man turned enough to show his face.

Morrell stopped in his tracks. He couldn't believe what he was seeing. McLennan chuckled.

"I said you'd be surprised."

"A little more than that." He felt like a dog with its hackles up. He'd spoken slowly, letting the words out as they came while his brain geared itself to cope with this. The man facing him was tall, fair-haired, blue-eyed: Morrell had last seen him on *Wildoak*'s bridge. He'd been wearing oilskins, then, over a blanket, and nothing on his feet.

The German bowed stiffly: a small inclination of the head. He had on a lounge-suit which didn't fit too well.

"Mr. von Mettendorf has been paroled for a couple of hours so we could have this chat. He's a guest in my house, Nick."

"I see."

"Well, sit down, gentlemen!"

Morrell hesitated. Then he moved across the room and chose a hard chair beside McLennan's desk. He didn't look at the German.

"Nick, you're wondering why. Maybe you're wondering how, too. Well, the *how* bit is easy. I happen to know the right people to ask when I need a favour, and I asked them and they said okay. Why? Well, that could take a lot longer, but I'll cut the corners. This is confidential, Nick, you'll appreciate that. Well, now. Mr. von Mettendorf's father operates companies which cover pretty well the territory of industry which I intend to be running in maybe a year, two years from now. Now we're going to win this war, and soon. There's no argument about that, even if my friend here has some reservations. Fact remains, when Germany surrenders she's going to be in a mess. She's going to need a lot of outside help and finance so she can get back on her feet and assume a new, non-totalitarian position along with the other nations of the free world. As far as the von Mettendorf business is concerned, I want them to count on my organization for the full measure of that assistance."

McLennan spread his hands. "That's what we've been chewing over, Nick, and when Mr. von Mettendorf gets back to his own country, whether it's this year or next, he'll know what to tell his father. It's that simple."

Morrell asked him, "Presumably you stand to get something out of it?"

"Sure I do. I get access to the European market – a real inside position, way ahead of my competitors. A solid market tie-up that'll operate both ways." McLennan raised a finger. "This is the shape of industry in the future, Nick. International co-operation, big markets open to us all, bigger production, lower costs, bigger sales, bigger profits. I'm going to show 'em how to do all that." He nodded towards the German. "With Mr. von Mettendorf's help, of course."

"Why are you telling me all this?"

"Why? How can you ask that, Nick? Hell, you set this up for me! You brought me a ship to mend, and a man to work with!" McLennan leant forward on his elbows. "I'm grateful, Nick. I won't forget it."

"Well, just a minute, now! All that's entirely fortuitous. And – I'm a guest in your house, so's he, but I'm a commissioned officer and dealing with the enemy is –"

"I don't believe you're dealing with anyone, Nick, are you?" McLennan spoke softly. "Nor am I, as it happens. Just talking, that's all. However, I understand how you feel, of course. Well, you don't know anything, I've told you nothing. Okay, Nick?"

"That's how I'd like it." Morrell nodded. Then he looked

over at von Mettendorf. "There's one thing I'd like to ask you. Off the record."

The German nodded. "Please."

"Why the hell did you bring your submarine up like that? Why didn't you stay deep?"

"Unfortunately I was not aware of your ship's existence. It was a most unpleasant surprise to discover the mistake so suddenly. You see, I believed the ship I had sunk was alone." He shrugged. "If my – you call it Asdic? – if the operator was not already dead I think I would have him shot."

"But why were you coming up, anyway?"

"To look for survivors of the ship I had sunk."

"I see." Morrell stood up, and crossed the room. He held out his hand. "Well, thanks for telling me. And good luck."

Von Mettendorf sprang up from his deep armchair, and took the hand Morrell was offering. "Thank you. But I think you are my luck, Commander. I should be dead."

CHAPTER FIVE

1945

Lieutenant-Commander Nicholas Morrell, D.S.O., D.S.C., R.N.R., sat in the corner of a first-class carriage and looked out at the grimy, blackened roofs and brickwork of row upon row of houses lining the railway approach to London. The closer the train came to the capital, the more frequently there were gaps – ruined, roofless houses, here and there cleared sites with wild spring flowers climbing over rubble. First there'd been the Blitz, then flying bombs: the first V.1's had hit London nearly a year ago, when Morrell had been in New York and *Wildoak* was still in the McLennan dock.

Hank Smith's men had done a good job, and Morrell's corvette had been afloat again with the new bow on her just nineteen days after docking. She'd helped bring a convoy into Liverpool on the night a bomb intended for Hitler had exploded without killing him. Since then, the men who'd been in the plot or near it had been hung up on meat hooks to die in slow agony while their writhings were recorded on film for the Führer's pleasure. Morrell thought, grimly watching the smoke-blackened gardens of south-east London, The bastard's had all the pleasure he'll ever have. . . .

Last week, on April 30, Hitler had poisoned his mistress and shot himself. Goebbels had poisoned all six of his children, then had his wife and himself shot by an SS guard.

Wildoak had made up for her holiday in New York by staying at sea on convoy and anti-submarine duties practically continuously ever since. During the last week she'd been in on the climax of the long, hard slog. All over the Atlantic and North Sea, U-boats had been surrendering, surfacing under white flags on orders from Admiral Doenitz, who'd masterminded their operations through all the grim, cold years of killing. The U-boats had emerged from the sea like splinters from a corpse they'd poisoned, and British sailors watched them, as they escorted them in squadrons to Scottish harbours, with the kind of fascinated loathing which comes to a man's eyes when he looks at cobras behind glass in a reptile house.

Morrell lit a cigarette. He'd left *Wildoak* secured alongside a jetty in the Chatham dockyard. She'd be going to the breakers, now. Her job was finished and she belonged already to the past.

From Victoria he took a taxi to the United Hunts Club in Upper Grosvenor Street, where he'd booked a room. When he'd unpacked his bag, he went down to the bar. The barman's face lit up when he walked in and slid on to a stool.

"Been a long time, Mr. Morrell!"

"How are you, Johnny?"

"Same as ever, sir. . . . What'll it be? Your usual?"

Morrell nodded. He hadn't been in this club for a couple of years, and he was interested to find out what his "usual" had been at the beginning of 1943. In that year he'd seen more ships sunk, more men drowned, than Nelson saw in the whole of his career. Tankers going up like torches: men coming over the side coated with oil, alight, screaming – he told himself, Forget it. It's history, now. He noticed that Johnny was making him a dry Martini, shaking it in his silver, one-drink-sized flask. Morrell restrained the impulse to tell him that in America, spiritual home of the dry Martini, they didn't shake them now but stirred them. Johnny had been doing it this way for years, and it would have upset him to be told his technique was out of date.

When he'd finished his drink, he went to the phone under the stairs to call Diana. She didn't answer. It was disappointing: he'd been looking forward to hearing the surprise in her voice. He'd been saving up for this moment when he'd call her. He thought, hanging up, If I'd rung before I had that drink I might have caught her. She may have walked out of the flat while I was in there drinking it. She's probably gone out for lunch.

He walked up into Grosvenor Square, out of its north-east corner to Berkeley Square and down Berkeley Street to Piccadilly. The trees were all out, fresh and green, and the air was rich with spring. This was undoubtedly the time of year to be in London. And the right year too: if you hadn't known the war was over you could have read it in people's faces. The Germans had surrendered formally, a day ago on Luneberg Heath. Morrell turned into Hatchetts, and went to the men's bar half-way down the stairs to the restaurant. He was hardly inside the door when he heard his name called.

Pat Pelly: Engineer Lieutenant-Commander, R.N.V.R. The last time Morrell had seen him he'd been on the base staff in Liverpool. They'd seen quite a bit of each other, on and off. Pelly had been engineer officer of a frigate in the same escort group as *Wildoak* before he'd got his half stripe and the shore job.

"Hello, Pat. I'll have a Bass. How's tricks?"

"Not so bad." Pelly had the light skin and freckles that went with ginger hair. "Bloody Admiralty – I want to get out, got this marvellous job lined up, and damn it, I was in on September 3rd 1939. They talk about first in, first out, but – oh, a Bass, please. And another half of bitter...." He looked at Morrell. "Of course, they can keep me in, too. I mean, it's not over, in the Far East. But in fact they want me here, ships into reserve and all that. But I've got this offer of a damn good job, right on the ground floor –"

"Doing what? Cheers."

"Cheers. It's a machine tool business." He shook his head. "No point going into details. You don't know a machine tool from a sailor's –"

"I do, as it happens. I met a chap in the States last year. A baron, loaded. He –"

"Yes? Well, this is a terrific opportunity and I want to grab it *now*. If I have to wait a year, they'll have –"

"Can't you fix it?"

"I've been trying. But those bloody chairborne warriors –"

"Know Tommy Moffat?"

"I don't think so."

"Hell of a good bloke. Used to be, anyway. He's in where these matters get decided. Appointments, I mean. I'm thinking of going to see him on Monday. Ring him, anyway. Why don't you come along?"

Pelly nodded. "Try anything once. Yes, I will, thanks.... Got anything going tonight, Nick?"

"Depends on Diana. She may be out of town. I've been trying her on the blower, but –" He shook his head. "No go, so far."

"Well, try her again, old mate. Join us anyway, eh? Dinner at the Jardin des Gourmets, then the Orchid Room. I've booked, they'll only have to make it eight instead of six. If Diana's not available, line up some other bint."

Diana wasn't in her flat during the afternoon. Morrell called three times without getting any answer. At about five he decided to give up trying, and instead rang Sue Gilmore at her mother's house in Kensington.

"Nick, if only I'd known! You see, I've promised to –"

"Oh, that's all right. Well, I expected you'd have a date. I just thought I'd try the prettiest one first. Well, okay, Sue, have fun, and don't do anything I wouldn't –"

"Nick, I could – I *think* I could get out of it. If you'd like me to, really." She laughed. "After all, I haven't seen you for such an age. What are you now – an admiral?"

"I'm expecting to achieve flag rank by Sunday week. Sue, can you really make it?"

"Yes. I'll wriggle out, somehow. If I don't ring you back in the next half-hour, it'll be all right. Where are you?"

"Hunts Club."

"Right. Will you fetch me here?"

"Yes, of course. Six-thirty all right? We can go somewhere for a drink before we meet the others. Well, this surpasses my wildest dreams, and believe me I've had some."

"Nick, are you bald and fat?"

"Like one of the Crazy Gang. You know the big one with the fur coat?"

"Flanagan?"

"That's what I look like. Want to change your mind?"

Morrell hung up. On the point of trying just once more to get Diana, he thought, No – what would I do if she was there? Ring Sue and tell her I just broke a leg?

He'd known Diana since 1940, when they'd met at a party and she was engaged to a bomber pilot. The bomber had been shot down over Germany eighteen months later. Diana had been stricken, stunned with grief. After a few months she'd joined the MTC as a driver, and by luck she'd been stationed near Liverpool, so in the two years he'd seen her quite often between convoy runs. He'd persuaded her, a year ago, to go away with him; he'd taken her to a hotel in Edinburgh – picking that as the most unlikely place he could think of for an illicit weekend – and they'd registered as man and wife. But she'd been so miserable, so obsessed by the guilt of betraying a dead man with whom she was still in love, that Morrell hadn't touched her. He'd thought, It has to fade out some time. When it does, I'll marry her. Perhaps when the war's over, she'll snap out of it.

He came out of the telephone-box with Diana's face clear in his mind. She was the loveliest creature he'd ever met. In a way, not unlike a slightly more mature version of that Australian girl, Toni Russell, whom he'd met at the McLennan house a year ago.

Pat Pelly was a bit plastered, which under the circumstances Morrell didn't find surprising. They'd wined well with their meal in Greek Street, and now that the whisky which Pat had stored in his Orchid Room locker was finished he'd gone on cheerfully and without hesitation to the Duty-Free gin which Morrell had brought along – two bottles of it, one in each pocket of his greatcoat.

Sue Gilmore and Pat's girl were out in the powder-room, and the other two couples were dancing. The cabaret was over: the room was dark, and packed. Pelly was still talking about the job he'd been offered.

"Bloody shame, Nick. If you were 'n engineer I could get you in too. Be like ol' times, eh? But you haven't even 'n engineering bent."

"I could develop one."

"Gotta have qual'f'cations. I say that right? Qualifications. S'absolutely 'ssential have quafcations."

"I think you better lay off the Gordon's, Pat."

"Rubbish. Night's yet young. But y'see, if I can get out an' take this *now,* future's 'normous. *Enormous.* Chance of lifetime, ol' Nick. Chance 'f a –"

"I know. You've been telling us."

"Cer'nly. Y'see, year's time, millions o' blokes out looking f' jobs. But 'f I c'n land this *now,* flyin' start, right 'n groun' floor, why, tremen'ous luck –"

"Here are the girls, Pat."

"Girls? Where?" Pelly stared round wildly, as if he hadn't seen a girl in months. Nick stood up, pushed the table back so Sue could get in beside him. Pelly staggered to his feet. 'C'mon, Sheila. Strip a light fantastic, eh?"

"What?"

"He wants you to dance with him." Nick told Pelly's girl, "Get a good grip, or he'll drop at your feet." He said to Sue, as the others merged jerkily into the dark mass of dancers, "It's amazing that a first-class engineer can behave so much like a second-class moron. He's pie-eyed."

"I noticed. He's clever, is he?"

"Brilliant. I imagine that's why they've offered him this job."

"Don't let's talk about *that* any more."

"My God, you're right. Let's talk about you. What'll you do when the War Office throws you out?"

"That's quite a long story, Nick. The fact is – well, I haven't had a chance to tell you about this, but – well, I'm not actually engaged, we thought there wasn't much point really, while the war was on. Mike's in Burma –"

"Sue, I'm delighted! You're going to marry him, are you?"

She nodded, beaming.

"You could have told me. Hell, we're practically cousins or something, why didn't you let me know? – Oh, God –"

"What's the matter?"

"Here we go again. Old eager beaver. . . ."

Pat Pelly leant across the table, swaying. "Nick! Nick, I gotta tell you –"

"I know. If they don't let you out of the bloody Navy right away you'll miss the greatest opportunity a man ever –"

"I'm talkin' about that girl of yours, you stupid bastard!"

"You'd better shut up and sit down." Nick stood up quickly, and moved around the table. Pelly was in worse shape than he'd thought.

"Diana. Over there –"

"Diana?"

"Over by th' door. Jus' saw her, Nick. With some Air Force feller. Go 'n see f'yself –"

Morrell told Sue, "Won't be a minute. If he's right, I just have to –"

"That's all right, Nick."

He pushed his way through the edges of the crowd overflowing from the dance floor, turned right towards the far end of the "L"-shaped room. There was a knot of people in his way, two parties simultaneously leaving their tables to go and dance: for the moment he couldn't pass, but beyond them, in the light from the door, he saw Diana. She was on the point of leaving: she'd turned to say something to the Air Force man who was following close behind her with a whisky bottle in one hand. A Group Captain with a clipped, grey moustache and several rows of medals. If she hadn't turned at that moment and in the glow of light, he wouldn't have seen her and he wouldn't have believed Pelly's story that she'd been in the club.

"Excuse me –"

"Hey, look out!"

"Sorry." He was past that lot: they muttered angrily behind him. Now a Paratroop major and a plump girl completely blocking the aisle between the tables. The man had his arm round the girl and he was whispering, apparently with urgency, in her ear.

"Excuse me. I'm in a –"

"Darling, he wants to get by."

"All right, all right." The major glowered. "In a hurry, aren't you?"

"Yes, I am." Morrell squeezed past him, half ran to the door leading to the foyer. More people there, shedding coats or putting them on, two Polish pilots arguing about membership while two obvious tarts teetered haughtily behind them. No sign of Diana or her escort. He shoved his way through, muttering excuses. Outside, the doorman had just slammed the door of a taxi and it was pulling away from the kerb, gathering speed. Another was drawing into its place: Morrell wrenched its door open before it had stopped, and flung himself in. He yelled at the driver, "Follow that cab in front!" He saw that the other had done a sharp U-turn: it was passing them now, going the other way, but he couldn't see its occupants. He pointed: "That one! Quick as you can!"

His driver, an elderly man with a quizzical expression, glanced back over his shoulder. "Cops an' robbers, guv, or love lies bleedin'?"

"For Christ's sake, get a move on!"

"Oright, guv –"

"He may be going to Portman Close."

Morrell pulled down one of the small seats so he could sit within speaking range of the driver and see over his shoulder at the road ahead. They shot westward down Brook Street, and at the junction with Duke Street the taxi which they were following turned right. The driver muttered, "Could be Portman Close, so far." He chuckled. "Not goin' to' shoot 'im are yer?" He took the corner with squeaking tyres. Morrell felt hopeful, suddenly, that Diana would be in that cab in front: at least it was heading towards her flat. At Oxford Street it barely paused, then shot straight over, still up Duke Street, and he felt sure of it.

"Don't worry. Someone I spotted just as they were leaving. You can wait and take me back to the Orchid Room, if you will."

" 'Soright with me, guv. Long as I got no blood on me carpet."

Left into Wigmore, right into Baker Street. It was Diana, all right, it had to be. He thought, She'll have that surprise, after all. He was smiling to himself as the leading taxi slowed and swung into Portman Close.

"Well done. Will you wait?"

"You're the boss."

"Thanks. Won't be long." He jumped out, slammed the door. Diana and her companion had disappeared into the building. Her flat was on the first floor: pausing in the hallway, he heard her laugh, then the click of a closing door. He hurried up the stairs: as he arrived on the landing, facing her white-painted door with the number 3 on it, he heard the man's voice on its other side.

"My God, Diana, how I've waited for this!"

"Darling, take it easy!" That low, gurgling laugh of hers. "Don't rip it to shreds. There's a perfectly good zip –"

Morrell went slowly, quietly down the stairs and out on to the pavement. The taxi driver leant out, jerked the rear door open. "All correct, guv?"

"Eh? Oh ... yes, I suppose so." He nodded. "Back to the Orchid Room, please."

"Not too good, was it?"

"Not – all that good." He climbed in, flopped into the seat and lit a cigarette. Diana, he thought. Diana, the lovelorn widow.... Well, people change. It's been some time, too. People are changing all the time. Hell, I'm no saint, why should I think I can judge Diana? He frowned at the glow of his cigarette as the taxi trundled down Wigmore Street. A new thought struck him: he wondered, suddenly, if at the crucial moment with the Group Captain panting white-legged in his airforce-blue socks, Diana might burst into tears, grind her knees together and wail for the dear departed. Imagining the baffled fury on that florid face with its pretentiously aggressive moustache, he began to laugh.

The driver, half turning his head, joined in. "That's it, guv! Plenty more fish in the sea, ain't there?"

In the Orchid Room, they were pleased to see him back. Pelly asked him, "Catch her, did you?"

"Sort of." He grinned. "Yeah. You could say that."

"Is she nice?" Sue smiled at him: he was pouring himself a stiff Gordon's. "Is it serious, Nick?"

"Hell, no. Just an old acquaintance. I doubt if I'll see her again." He drank half the gin, and told Pelly, "When they let *me* out, Pat, I'm going to the States."

"States? Wha' for?"

"To work, old mate. You know, earn a living?"

Tommy Moffat wasn't hopeful when Morrell telephoned him at the Admiralty. He said he'd look into the possibilities, and meet him for a drink later in the day: six o'clock, at the Cheshire Cheese.

Morrell was there on the stroke of six. Ten minutes later Moffat stumped in. He hooked his walking stick over the back of a chair before he let himself down into another, facing Morrell across a table on which two pints of beer stood ready. Morrell nodded at them. "That do you?"

"Fine." Moffat lifted his, and winked his only eye. He'd lost the other, and some shinbone, at St. Nazaire. "Cheers. First today."

"What's the score, Tommy?"

"You're in luck, if you can face it."

"Face what?"

"Well, I'll tell you." He set his pint down on the table. "Things are a bit hazy at the moment, but you haven't a hope of getting out in less than three or four months. Maybe six, even. You want to get to the States, you said?"

Morrell nodded.

"Yes. Well, it's no good asking to be demobbed there, because you joined up *here*. If you'd joined over there, you'd be in clover, because we'd have to send you back to where you started. As it is, that's out."

"I thought you said I was in luck."

"Yes, I did. Ever run across the *Charley Brown*?"

"Try to make sense, Tommy, will you?"

"The *Charles E. Brown*, so-called ocean-going tug. Euphemistically, I may say. Known affectionately – well, perhaps not that, exactly – known to those acquainted with her sterling qualities as the *Charley Brown*. She's in Dundee, at the moment. Extraordinarily enough, still floating."

"Good for her."

"Yes. It's a miracle. *Charley Brown* got here – don't ask me why or how – with the Lease Lend destroyers. Now she has to go back. If she stays here she'll not only sink, we'll have to pay for her – on paper, anyway. It's cheaper to send her back. Only thing is, one can't be sure she'll make it."

"I'm beginning to get the drift of this."

"You're a smart lad, Nick. Anyway, they're going to fix her up a bit. Plug the larger holes, that kind of thing. She ought to be ready to steam out to a watery grave in roughly three months' time. You could look after the reserve ships in Harwich until then, and when she's ready we'll appoint you to *Charley Brown* in command and off you go. If her screws'll turn, of course." He corrected himself. "I should say screw. She has but one."

"What kind of crew?"

"They'll be a scratch lot, I'm afraid."

"Sounds lovely."

"The advantage to you, though, is that by the time you get over there you'll be due for release. About then, anyway. Once you're there, you can apply for discharge on the spot. So at least you'll have had a free passage, which we couldn't give you otherwise. What d'you say?"

"I'll buy it."

"Thought you would.... Another pint?"

"Thanks. Don't move, I'll get it. Tommy, did a plumber called Pat Pelly get in touch with you?"

"Indeed he did. He'll have to apply officially for compassionate release to take up that job, whatever it is. I told him to write a letter to the Secretary."

"Think they'll let him go?"

"Who knows? Their Lordships move in a mysterious way."

"You can say *that* again.... This tug. Do I park it in New York?"

"Baltimore. That's her port of origin." Moffat grinned. "Damn it, Nick, I almost wish I'd be going with you!"

CHAPTER SIX

Toni

Toni Russell swung her English sports car into the driveway to the Laings' home in Westchester, New York. She'd come from Greenwich unusually slowly, taking a deliberate care which had matched the cautious progress of her thoughts. Noting the time and how long she'd taken since leaving the McLennan house, it occurred to her that a psychiatrist could make something pretty weird out of that. A dramatic event, a day which could be the biggest single turning-point in her life – surely most people would react dramatically? Drive fast, not slowly?

But as for getting the news home fast, she thought, it'll almost certainly be here ahead of me. Probably been here for a day or two. He hedged, when I asked him if he'd spoken to them. You can understand that, of course: admitting he'd felt it necessary to discuss the matter with them would have been putting emphasis on my juvenility, on that thirty-two-year gap. The ostrich complex: ignore it, it'll go away....

Seymour was home. She found him in the library with her aunt Helen, checking over invitations for a party they were giving. Seymour was running a little to fat: in his late forties, he had the look of a man who'd played a lot of sport and stopped suddenly in recent years. He was a lawyer, as well as a politician.

Toni asked her aunt, "Do you have Gil McLennan on that list?"

Helen Laing smiled, looking up at her niece. "I believe so. Why, yes, I'm sure we have." She glanced at Seymour, back at Toni. "Why do you ask, though?"

Toni had flopped into a chair. She crossed one knee over the other, and began to pull off her gloves. "As if you didn't know." She laughed. "All right, let's pretend you don't. Gil McLennan asked me to marry him."

"Well . . ." Seymour Laing removed his glasses and sat back from the table. "Why, Toni, that's – I guess that's quite an honour."

"Nonsense!" Helen crossed over quickly, stooped like a hen drinking to kiss Toni's cheek. "It's Gilbert would have the *honour*. If Toni decided she wanted even to give a *thought* to it, he'd be –"

"Gil's a fine man, Helen. A respected, successful man. Okay, so there's a certain disparity in their ages –"

"There's more than that, and you know it!"

"Now, Helen–"

Toni said, "She's right, isn't she?"

Laing frowned. "Did you give Gil an answer?"

"Yes, I did."

Their eyes froze on her face. She smiled. "I told him I'd think carefully about it and let him know in a couple of days."

"Very sensible, Toni." Helen Laing nodded approvingly. "It's no kind of decision to be rushed. Of course, Gilbert and Seymour are close friends, so Seymour may not be as impartial as a man could be otherwise. But their friendship shouldn't influence you, it's no reason for you to think –"

"You're right, it isn't." Toni looked at him. "You wouldn't argue with that, would you?"

"Certainly not." Laing shook his head. "It's a matter of what's best for you, Toni."

"A little more than that." She smiled. "I'm not pretending it doesn't concern Gil –"

"He's made his side of it clear enough by asking you to marry him. All you have to think about is whether you want to take him up on it or not. So leave Gil's problems to Gil. If he has any. He can look after himself, I guess. You think about *you*." He grinned at Toni. "You want to just think about this, or talk about it?"

"Talk. I've done some thinking."

"Maybe you'd rather talk alone with Helen." He glanced at his wife. "In which case, I'll –"

"No, don't go. I mean, I'd be glad if you could stay." Laing nodded. Toni explained, "I've worked it out from the angles I know, but there could be some I haven't looked at. So if I tell you the points I've thought about, then if there's more I should think of or –" she paused, looking at him intently: "Or maybe *know* about, then you could –"

Laing chuckled. "Never met a female with such an orderly mind. Gil should offer you a job, not –"

"But he *has*." Toni looked surprised. "Hasn't he?"

"Toni, *dear*! That's not a very pleasant way to look at it!"

"Oh, I don't know. And I'd say it's Gil's way." She asked Laing, "Wouldn't you?"

"Only in the sense that to *some* extent any man with – well, position, public life, business leadership as in his case – any man in this situation does have to consider –" He stopped, looking at his wife. "No, I retract that. It's the wife who sees the job in it, not the husband. Take Helen, now. I didn't marry her to have her doing any damn job. She does one all right, but that's quite another –"

"Seymour, you're rambling." Helen looked at Toni. "You go on, now."

"Thanks. Well, as I remember the way I was working it out on the way over here, there are six main issues to work on. I hope I'll remember them all. If I don't, I imagine you'll –"

"What is this? A filibuster?"

"All right. First and foremost, the difference in our ages. I'm nineteen, Gil's fifty-one. B minus A equals thirty-two. Big gap, sure. But the way I see it, it's the least of the problems. I have the kind of mind – well, I *like* men older than I am. I mean intellectually. I don't mean to make myself sound superior, not at all, I don't even *feel* superior. All I know is I get on a lot better with a man like Gil than I do with – say, his nephew Charles. I'll come back to Charles in a minute. Well, now: the other side of the age thing is the physical. That doesn't worry me either. Gil's attractive, fit, sophisticated, he's been around, and – well, frankly I guess he might have a lot to offer that a younger man wouldn't. Now I don't want to embarrass anyone, but you're both older than I am, I can't pretend to have any experience in this department –

not enough to count, anyway – and if it sounds to you like I might be off-beam I'd be grateful if you'd tell me."

Helen Laing hesitated. Then: "I should say the only thing that really matters is the way you feel about it."

"Right." Laing nodded. "That's the obvious criterion. Being sort of on my honour in this, however, I think that without disrespect to my friend Gil McLennan I have to confirm your view that he has – as you put it – been around. He's been around a long time, and to be perfectly frank I'd say he hasn't wasted the spare minutes when he's come across them."

Toni smiled at Helen, "See how they let each other down? You and I would never say a thing like that about a mutual friend."

"The hell you wouldn't!"

"Seymour –"

Toni said, "I'd better get on with this, anyway. The next thing is one which to a lot of people could seem – well, distasteful. I don't like it much myself. Elizabeth McLennan died less than four months ago. I remember it was the day after the second atom bomb on Japan."

"August tenth, she died." Seymour Laing nodded. "Yeah. Nagasaki was August ninth. That's –"

"Less than four months. That seems sort of quick, now, to –" Toni asked her aunt, "Well, doesn't it?"

"There's plenty of people would think so. I'd say it's more a thing for Gilbert to consider than for you, though."

Laing coughed. He said, "There's no getting away from it. A lot of people, I mean friends of ours and Gil's, would be – well, surprised. Shocked, maybe. But there's a little difference here for those of us who happen to be acquainted with *all* the facts. I guess you won't know this, Toni, but Elizabeth Laing was living on borrowed time. Wasn't long after she married Gil that her doctors told him she probably wouldn't live six months. Well, she hung on two years. Just –" he spread his hands – "dying. They kept it from her, you know that? Sure, she was sick, but she didn't ever know the whole of it. Imagine how it must have been for Gil?"

"You're implying he loved her?"

"Toni!"

"Now, Helen.... Well, sure, Toni. Would you have some reason to doubt it?"

"Let me come back to that in a minute. First that little

point about Gil's nephew, Charles. It's only worth talking about because it was Charles used to take me over to Gil's house. But I wasn't Charles's *girl*. Any more than I was anyone else's. Okay, we danced together, went on parties, you know, all that stuff, but we never – well, we never had anything in common, anything at all. Only reason I even mention him is when he hears about it he'll say, 'Hell, my girl, and she marries my uncle!' It's just how it sounds and how it could look to outsiders, that's all."

"So, as you say, it's not of the slightest importance. Well, that's – what, three of the six points covered? Go on, Toni."

"It gets worse as it goes on, Aunt Helen."

"You want me to leave the room?"

"You may feel like sending *me* out of it."

"I won't do that, Toni. Telling the truth's no crime. And right now you can only straighten this problem out if you're completely open and frank." She looked at her husband. "Seymour will be anxious to assure you, moreover, that however friendly he may be with Gil McLennan he wouldn't dream of repeating a word of this conversation we're –"

"You don't have to tell her that." Laing looked cross.

"No, you don't." Toni smiled. "It's nice to hear it, all the same. However, you're a lawyer, Seymour, and this subject coming up now seems – I don't know, *could* be – slanderous. It concerns the circumstances of Gil's marriage to Elizabeth."

"Would that have much to do with you and Gil now?"

"It could. Linking with the *next* matter on the agenda."

Helen was looking interested. "Let's hear them one at a time, shall we?"

Toni asked Laing, "You know the circumstances I'm referring to?"

He frowned. "Let's see, now. Gil meets Elizabeth, he falls in love with her, asks her to marry him, she says 'Okay, why not', they have a wedding party out at Greenwich and the two of us attend it along with a coupla hundred others. The McLennans take off for honeymoon in Barbados. All right?"

"So far as it goes. The story I heard takes a bit longer than that. It starts with Gil needing money."

"Now that's something Gil hasn't needed in quite a long time. Sure, he likes making it, but –"

"This is 1942 I'm talking about. Gil needed money to take

over that shipyard of his. He knew it was a chance in a million to make a lot fast, but he couldn't raise the cash."

Laing snorted. "He has estates, property he's had for years –"

"All mortgaged to pay for its own upkeep and make good business losses. He'd mortaged everything he owned. So when suddenly he has this terrific opportunity he can't afford to do anything about it. . . . Look, I'm just telling you what I heard."

"Heard from whom, Toni?"

She shook her head. "Let me just tell it, please? Well, at that time Gil wasn't married to anyone. Right?"

"Right. He was divorced in '41. Elizabeth was his third wife."

"Well, what he did was he telephoned a woman named Bee O'Hara. D'you know of her?"

"I'd say I do." He grinned at Helen. "Remember old Bee? The one with the diamonds all over? Oh hell, Toni, Bee could have been Gil's mother!"

"Far as I'm concerned she's just a name in this story. Gil phoned her and said, 'Bee, I have to find myself a lot of money in no more than fourteen days.' So Bee throws a party for all the very rich widows and divorcees within a hundred miles or more, Elizabeth is one of them, Gil works his charm and within two weeks there takes place the marriage at which you were both present. That's the story. Do you think it could be true, Aunt Helen?"

"I would have no way of telling." Helen Laing wasn't anxious to be drawn. "Might depend on who told it in the first place."

"Yeah. It might, too," Laing said. "It's an unlikely story, Toni. But if it were true – just supposing for a minute it could be – what would it have to do with you and Gil today? Or is it a slant on Gil's character you're looking for in this?"

"No, not just that. Well, look. If Gil had some idea that I had a great deal of money coming to me?"

"No." Laing stood up, walked to the window and back again. "No, you don't have to worry about that. Several reasons, all of them good. One, he has no way of knowing any such thing. Two, even if he needed money four years ago, I'm darned sure he doesn't now. Three, even if he knew about your money and wanted it – neither of which is to my mind a valid contention – he couldn't touch it, because the way your grandfather tied it up, the capital I mean, there is simply no way at it. And look here, now: if Gil knew the money existed, he'd have to know simultaneously that it was out of his reach. Out of *anyone's* reach." Laing stopped walking up and down. He muttered, staring at Toni. "This is a hell of a way for a man to have to discuss a friend of his. You know that?"

"I'm sorry –"

"There's no need to be." Helen spoke quietly. "You're entitled to whatever help and advice we can give you. This is a most important decision she has to make, Seymour, a thing to change her whole life. It's no good hiding –"

"What d'you think I'm hiding, for God's sake?"

"I didn't say you were. What I'm saying is, Toni has these problems, we must discuss them. The fact he's your friend doesn't alter her being my niece."

"Well, okay, we're discussing them. I just want Toni to know I don't believe this story about Gil and Elizabeth, that's all."

Toni nodded. "What you've explained about the money ties that one up, anyway."

"I'd still like to know where it came from."

"I know you would. The source isn't important, though. Really." Toni looked up at him. "There's one last point. We all know Gil has that huge apartment on Park Avenue. Why does he need to have one in Sutton Place too?"

"Sutton Place?" Helen looked vaguely surprised. "Right by the East River there? Are you *sure*, dear?"

"I'm sure, all right." Toni was watching Seymour Laing: at the mention of the address he'd whipped round and followed his tracks back to the window. He was still there, looking out.

Helen asked him, "Seymour, did you ever hear of any such apartment?"

"Yeah, I did." Turning, Laing avoided both the women's eyes. "Well, Toni, I imagine that if Gil were marrying you he'd get rid of that second apartment. I couldn't put it any better than that. And if you remember, I did mention earlier in this conversation that Gil had – well, in the vaguest terms, been around, and so on –"

The truth had dawned on Helen Laing: she looked shocked. "If I don't misunderstand what you've been saying, Seymour, I believe that as Toni's aunt and *in loco parentis*, if that's the mumbo jumbo for it, I should advise her quite strongly against accepting Gilbert McLennan's proposal. I'd go further: I'd say –"

"Helen, Helen ..." Her husband's hand made soothing motions. "I think we should make certain allowances. Here's an active man, still in the prime of life, married for years to a chronic invalid. I'd say he's been extremely discreet – that's proved, since you knew nothing about it. And as I said, Gil would naturally – well, change his ways."

"He would, would he? Toni, are you even so much as considering now that you might marry Gil McLennan?"

"I guess I am, Aunt Helen."

"Knowing all *this*?"

"None of it matters so long as it's deadwood that doesn't touch us now, anyway wouldn't in the future. I've been bringing up all the dirt about Gil because I wanted to know how much of it's true. Well, I guess it's mostly all true, but also – from what Seymour's said – that I wouldn't be – well, vulnerable to any of it if I married Gil. Only one thing I need to do is see he gives up that apartment – anyway, whoever he has residing in it at the moment."

Her aunt still looked unhappy. "You surprise me, Toni."

"Can't see why." Laing said, "None of the matters we've discussed makes for any impediment. On the other side of the scoresheet I imagine there's quite a bit that's attractive. Is there, Toni?"

Toni nodded, watching Helen. "Gil's handsome, he has great charm and – well, presence – he has a fine sense of humour and a first-class brain. He also happens to be one of the richest men in the country and to occupy a position of – oh, power, I guess. That attracts me a great deal, and you see, I believe I have something to offer a man in his position. Like we were saying, sort of taking a job: I'd want to be Gil McLennan's wife not just for the obvious reasons, but to be involved with him in all the things he's doing. I mean I believe I'd have something to contribute, something he's maybe been in need of for a long time."

"Sounds as if you've made up your mind to marry him." Helen didn't sound too enthusiastic.

"I haven't done that, actually. First – before I decide either way – I'll need to talk to him like I've talked to you. It wouldn't be any good getting into this without us both knowing exactly what we're aiming for, if you see what I mean –"

"I'll be damned." Laing finished lighting a cigar. "You're a remarkable girl, Toni. You don't have a mind like a girl's at all."

"Why, that's insulting!"

"The hell it is. Ninety-nine girls out of a hundred would either have said 'Yes' right away, or they'd be running round in tight circles like hens squawking with indecision. You sit down and work over the pros and cons like – well, like I might settle down to consider the different aspects of some political issue." He smiled at her through rising smoke. "I'm not criticizing, Toni, I'm admiring."

"You could be underestimating, too. Women, that is." Helen shrugged. "I'm not saying I'd go along with Toni's reasoning, but why you should imagine we're – well, squawking hens?"

"I was talking about young girls, not mature women."

Helen sniffed. "He thinks *that* lets him off the hook!"

Toni said, "I'll be twenty in a month. I *am* a grown woman. Anyway, I can't see what's so strange. Look, suppose you see an advertisement for some automobile, a new model. Glossy ad, says it has everything you'd ever want, all that stuff. Well, you don't just write in for one. You look it over, ask questions, think about it, don't you?"

Her aunt frowned. "I'd say that approach was a little *too* cool-brained to apply to marriage. A human relationship's more than a piece of hardware, surely."

Toni was still thinking about the car. It had occurred to her that if when you'd inspected it and asked all the pertinent questions you were still interested, you'd almost certainly give it a trial run.

One week later, after most of his staff had left for their homes, Gilbert McLennan walked out of his office in the Empire State, rode down to street level and headed up 5th Avenue on foot. After three blocks, on the corner of 37th, he stopped and hailed a cab. Climbing in, he glanced at his watch: he'd be out there thirty minutes earlier than he'd arranged with Toni, but that was exactly what he'd intended. Elaine had made a hell of a fuss about getting out of the apartment at such short notice, and he wanted to make certain she hadn't tried to sabotage him by planting traces of herself or of their association. The cleaners would have been in, of course, and there shouldn't be any cause to worry: but a thing like this you'd be nuts to leave to chance. Toni had to be convinced that he'd kept his word: and with something as important as this – well, you saw to it for yourself.

He told the driver, "Sutton Place."

Elaine had made him pay through the nose in return for vacating the place this quickly. She'd be able to live well for a year or more, on the amount she'd squeezed out of him. Not that she'd be likely to take a holiday: there was a law of diminishing returns, and her assets were the kind that didn't last for ever.

McLennan lit a cigar, leant back and watched the bright, Christmas-decorated windows crawl by. He thought, Hell, I'll be saving more than that in rent. . . .

It was exactly seven-thirty when Toni put her gloved finger on the bellpush of the Sutton Place apartment. Gilbert McLennan had the door open for her almost before she'd taken the finger off it.

"Come on in, Toni." He shut the door before he kissed her. "I never knew a girl this punctual. Are you always on time?"

"Usually." She thought, smiling up at him, He'll have checked the place out, but I'll still look around. A token inspection: but it's a matter of principle, and he'd expect it. And it's more than that, it's a symbolic act – his surrender of this kind of living, and my assertion of the right to make damn sure he does just that.

It's also an excuse to meet him alone in a place that isn't lousy with flunkeys. . . . She smiled at him, making it look like a fiancée's smile, but in fact genuinely amused, thinking of the surprise she'd planned for him. All they'd discussed for the rest of the evening was that he'd take her out to dine in some quiet, informal place where they could talk without being interrupted.

She moved from room to room, opening closets, drawers. It was a formality: even if the girl had left any of her stuff, it would have gone down the garbage chute in the last few minutes.

"Nice place, Gil."

"It's not bad."

"Bringing back memories?"

"Actually, no." He followed her into the bathroom. "I'm

thinking of the future, Toni, not the past. It excites me to think of it. We're going to be a great partnership."

"I hope so." Toni stopped with her hand on the catch of the linen closet, and looked at him over her shoulder. "I haven't said I'll marry you, Gil, not yet. Don't start assuming –"

He slid his hands around her waist. "I'm being darned patient, Toni. I'm no chicken, and I'm used to getting what I set out for. I'm doing all you've asked me –"

"Then take these, will you?" She began to hand out blankets, sheets and pillow-covers. Surprised, he put his hands up, forearms horizontal so she could pile the stuff on.

"*Now* what?"

Toni shut the closet doors. "Bedding."

"Oh, Lord, Toni – this stuff goes with the furnishings, I suppose. It's nothing to do with –"

"Will you help me make the bed, please?"

"Make the –"

"The bed, Gil. It's in here. Hadn't forgotten, had you?" She glanced back at him. "Don't you think we should know what we're getting, Gil?"

CHAPTER SEVEN

1946

Morrell had left himself plenty of time to get to the Empire State Building by 10.30, the hour fixed for his appointment with Gil McLennan. He got off the subway – which he'd boarded near Martha Scotland's apartment in the East Seventies – at 33rd Street, walked back a block to East 34th and turned up towards Fifth Avenue.

He was wearing an almost new suit of charcoal grey West of England flannel. He'd had it made at Gieves just before he'd left England, and the bill would be catching up with him any time now. He wore suede shoes, and under the suit a cream silk shirt. His tie showed the interweaving red-and-white stripes of the Royal Naval Reserve: another link with the past was his overcoat, a naval British Warm, civilianized by the removal of rank badges and substitution of flat, black buttons for rounded brass ones. A dark green trilby completed this first civilian outfit. He felt like a new boy reporting to school at the start of term.

Martha had assured him he looked wonderful: she'd said so from her bed, sipping black coffee which he'd made in her kitchenette. The pillow beside her still carried the imprint of his head, and she'd waved good-bye with one naked, rounded arm.

"Luck, Nick."

"Thanks."

"Remember not to give my love to Gil."

"I will. And I'll call you."

Martha wasn't seeing Gil or Toni. Morrell had learnt about the new McLennan marriage the same way most other people had – from the newspapers. He'd called Martha to ask her what she knew about it, and that was the first knowledge she had of his presence in New York. About a month ago. He'd still been in the Navy, then, living in accommodation the Navy paid for. Since then he'd found himself a room further out, about the cheapest he could find, to make his money last until he had some kind of job. As soon as he'd known the date on which he'd be free, he'd called the McLennan office, only to be told that Mr. Gilbert McLennan was out of town and would not be back for at least another three weeks. Was there anyone else he'd care to speak with?

"I don't think so, thank you. It's personal, really."

"May I have your name, Mr. –"

"Morrell. Nicholas Morrell. But I'll ring again in three weeks' time."

"We'll look forward to hearing from you, Mr. Morrell."

He'd called Martha, then gone round to see her, and that was when she'd told him that she was no longer a friend of Gil's. Naturally he'd asked her why.

"Because of Toni, that's why. That little bitch has him fitted with a ring in his nose and she's hanging on the string. I don't know what she has against me, unless it's because I came near to becoming Gil's wife at one time. All I do know is I'm off their guest list."

"When were you nearly McLennan's wife?"

"Before he married Elizabeth, that's when. It was just kind of understood, everybody knew it. Then one day, boom, he's married. Just like that. I'd never *heard* of Elizabeth! Well, it was all friendly, she and I got on fine once we were allowed to meet - but can you beat it, just like that and not a solitary word to me before they'd done it? But now I'll tell you what else his little Toni baby did. You know he had a girl in a swank apartment on the East River?"

"McLennan had?"

"Sure. Well, Elizabeth wasn't interested. Doesn't that stone you, Nick? What'd he marry her for – companionship? Like hell it was. Well, that's one *you* work out. But Gil's keeping this girl in an expensive apartment he's been renting for her all the time he's married to Elizabeth, and Toni's heard about it – who hasn't, for Christ's sake? So before she marries him she goes down there and rips it apart. Beat hell out of the girl and wrecked the apartment. And Gil goes right ahead and *marries* her – after *that*!"

He remembered Toni very clearly. How she'd taken an unexplained dislike to him, that Sunday at the McLennan house: but what Martha had just told him – hell, Toni wasn't any kind of virago! He remembered her as being very young, having a quick mind and a body he hadn't been able to keep his eyes off. Not him, and not McLennan either: that first day by the pool, Gil had openly, even aggressively, tried to cut out his own nephew. Well, he'd done it, evidently! That sudden play for Toni – Morrell hadn't suspected that it had been prompted by any real intention: he'd thought of it as an ageing bull's sudden arousal of jealousy, sensing eventual displacement and resenting it. He'd thought at the time that McLennan had let himself down by a rather pathetic display: he'd felt sorry for him, more than anything else. Now he realized that he'd been way off-beam, that Gil McLennan had wanted Toni and was a man accustomed to getting what he wanted.

Martha smiled. "Toni's going to find her chickens coming home to roost, soon as Gil gets sick of her. He's not a one-girl man, not for long." She asked him, "You a one-girl man, Nick?"

"Only thing I can afford to be right now is a no-girl man. Until I know where my bread and butter's coming from I'm a non-smoking, teetotal layabout. No, I mean it."

"With a cigarette in your left hand and a scotch in the other?"

"Special occasion. Handout." He grinned, and shook his head. "Don't worry. I'm not planning to sponge on you."

He'd only called her to find out what she knew about McLennan and Toni. She'd asked him to go along, and here he was. He put the glass down. "I'm dead serious, Martha. I can't afford the bright lights. When I've got myself organized, I'll get in touch."

He thought, You'd do better to stick to your Madison Avenue friends.... She'd told him that she was right on the inside, now, in the modelling world. She wasn't able to fill all the jobs she was offered.

"You can run to a bottle of scotch once a week, Nick. So bring it round here, and we'll – well, call me first, you have the number."

"Martha, it's nice of you, but –"

"I get it." Her eyes were hard. "You expect to be working for McLennans, Gil and Toni seem to think I'm poison, so –"

"That's ridiculous!"

"I don't think so. You could be right, too. You want to get on in that business, you better be careful how you choose your friends." She stood up. "Okay, Nick, so it's good-bye."

The idea hadn't occurred to him for a single moment. He hadn't wanted to get involved with her again, that was all. But after she'd accused him of wanting to avoid her for the sake of getting a job with McLennans, he felt he had to see her now and then, if only to prove her suspicions wrong. Sometimes he'd call her, a few times she called him. It had been her idea that they'd "celebrate" the night before his appointment with McLennan.

10.25.... The girl had taken his name and asked him to sit down: Mr. McLennan would be free to see him in just a few moments. Morrell tried to make himself relax in one of the shiny blue armchairs. The girl had gone: across the room an older woman pecked at an electric typewriter with scarlet-tipped fingers, while a ticker-tape machine chattered intermittently beside her. It was pleasantly warm: the girl had taken his hat and coat away to some hidden closet.

Morrell wondered what kind of job Gilbert McLennan might offer him. It felt quite different now, sitting here, waiting to discuss the details of employment. Up to this point his view of it had been conditioned by his memory of McLennan's remarks to him about opportunity, room for men with brains and guts. That was exactly what he'd said: Morrell could hear the words now, feel the same excitement they'd given him two years ago. But now when it came to the point of walking into the man's office, it didn't feel so easy.

"Here I am, lousy with brains and guts, what can I do for you and what'll you pay me for it?"

Well, he deals with ships, and I know about ships. Not just warships, either. He's an administrator, and I know a little about controlling men. Leading them. . . . Morrell wondered, Do civilian bosses lead as well as organize? If they don't, they should learn to. Damn it, perhaps I do have something to offer! Then he thought, Business acumen: do I have that? Optimism subsided as he gave himself the answer – *I don't know.* . . . But selling, now. I could sell, I'm sure I could. I get on with people, and it would mean moving around a bit instead of sitting behind a desk. Have to learn the background first, of course, but – hell, selling ships, I'd like that –

"Mr. Morrell?"

He looked up.

"I'm Mr. McLennan's secretary. Will you come this way, please?"

He followed her out of the room and down a corridor: offices on either side, but McLennan's room, evidently, was the one at the end. The girl went in without knocking, sliding her back round the edge of the door to give him room to walk in past her.

"Mr. Morrell, sir."

A long room, not very wide but with windows all down one side to make up for that. Sofas, chairs, a big, low table in between them: more like a lounge than an office. But all that was to his right, he saw it before he turned the other way and Gilbert McLennan rose to his feet behind a desk which looked about nine feet square. The secretary had gone out, and shut the door.

"Commander, this is a pleasure." McLennan came towards him with his hand out. "Good of you to look me up. Now come over here, sit down. Well, you're looking fine. I'll say that!"

"You too." Gilbert McLennan looked not a day older than he had two years ago. He might even have shed a year or two. Silver hair gleamed over a healthy tan in which his light-blue eyes were clear and smiling. "You've been on holiday?"

"On honeymoon!" McLennan chuckled. "Had ourselves quite a time. Jamaica. . . .Now sit down, please."

"Thank you. Congratulations on your marriage. I met Miss Russell – at your house, that week-end when you were kind enough to ask me out there."

"Why, sure, I remember." McLennan glanced at his watch. Morrell was thinking that he ought perhaps to have said something about being sorry to hear of Elizabeth's death. Difficult, when he'd got himself a new wife so quickly, to combine commiseration and congratulation. . . .

"I should tell you I'm not a commander, now." Morrell settled himself in the chair. "Actually I never was, I was a lieutenant-commander." McLennan hadn't sat down yet: he was facing Morrell, looking down at him with his back to the windows. Morrell commented, "Must have a wonderful view from there. Right over to your yard?"

"Sure. Come take a look."

Standing beside McLennan, Morrell looked out north-west over the length of 34th Street and all the other great sky-scraping buildings, dwarfed by this one. A liner hooted in the Hudson River: you knew it because you saw the steam-trail from the whistle. A French ship, by the looks of her, and old to be on this run now. McLennan jabbed a forefinger at the glass of the window, indicating the river's far bank, a couple of miles away.

"There's Todds. Move right, McLennans. Put up a couple of new buildings since you had your ship in there. Workshops, mostly. Built a new dock, too." He turned back into the room. "Business never stands still, we have to move with it. Well now, sit down, Morrell. That look you just had out of my window – you go upstairs a deck or two, that same peek'll cost you a dollar thirty." He chuckled. "Pay on your way out. . . . Now tell me, this just a social visit or is there something you'd like to discuss with me?"

"Not just a social visit." Morrell thought, noticing that McLennan had glanced at his watch again, He must know damn well why I'm here. Guess, anyway. . . He told him, "When I was here two years ago and enjoying your hospitality, you suggested more than once that I should think seriously of coming back here to earn a living when the fighting stopped. You stressed what opportunities there'd be, room for men like me, and so on."

"Sure." McLennan had sat down on one of the sofas. He was leaning well back with his long legs stuck out in front of him, his head tilted back and his eyes on Morrell's face. "I believe I do remember it."

"Well, that's it. I gave it a lot of thought, and here I am."

McLennan watched him a moment longer without speaking. Then he nodded. "Certainly hope it works out for you. It's not often these days a young man takes an older man's advice." He smiled. "I'm flattered. . . . You like to smoke?"

"No, thanks."

"You don't, eh . . .? Well, what are you aiming to do, now you got here?"

"I've come to ask you about that. I want a job."

"Here? In my organization?"

Morrell nodded. "In view of what you said, it seemed the obvious thing to do."

"Now you embarrass me a little. I'd have been speaking in general terms, Morrell, not specific. This is a hell of a big country and there's opportunity all over. What you've been thinking is 'this guy builds ships, I'm a Navy man, guess he could use me'. But you see –"

"No, you're wrong. Nothing like that at all. I knew perfectly well I'll have to start in and learn. I'm ready to do that: I want to. All I want is the chance, the opportunity."

"Yeah." McLennan looked sad, now. "You know how many guys want that same chance? Morrell, I could spend my entire working day, six days a week, talking to men who want just that. Look out the window again, you'll see your *Queen Mary* at Pier 90. How many thousand soldiers, sailors, airmen came back in her in just this one trip? They're all out looking for jobs. And out of those thousands there's maybe a hundred who have some skill, some training I could use. But I don't have room for *them*, not right now. American veterans, Morrell, and trained men, and I can't use 'em. See the spot I'm in when you tell me you want a job?"

"When you put it like that –"

"No other way to put it. But don't misunderstand me. What I told you that time, it's the truth. Just at this moment, however – well, you hit the worst time, that's about the fact of it. Oh, things'll settle, bound to. Six months, a year, maybe I'll be ready to expand some more, could need a man of just your kind. But right now –" McLennan checked himself. "How do you see yourself? What d'you think you could do, in a business like mine?"

"Selling. I think I'd be good at it."

"Yeah." He nodded. "Could be. But I couldn't offer you a selling job, not at this particular time."

"What *could* you offer me?"

"Frankly, nothing. I'm sorry, Morrell, that's how it is. Well, you could go over to the yard, see my personnel man. Could be he'd have an idea for you. Feller named –" McLennan closed his eyes, tapped his forehead – "Schultz. That's it, Ed Schultz. You could see him. Tell him I sent you along, if you like. Mind you, though, I don't interfere in those areas. I run this outfit from the top, the guy with the oilcan I leave to put the oil in, if you understand me."

McLennan stood up, smiling. "Now you keep in touch, Morrell. Be sure and do that, huh?"

The dock where *Wildoak* had been given a new bow had been lengthened by thirty feet since she'd lain in it. He could see where the old masonry left off and the new bit started. Further north and parallel to it was the new dock which McLennan had mentioned. There was a tanker in it now, a fleet auxiliary, about 15,000 tons. Men were working on her propeller-shaft glands from staging built under the counter on each side. There was lighting rigged over the side of the dock so work wouldn't have to stop at dusk.

Morrell found the Personnel Department situated at the end of one of the two new buildings. He asked a clerk, whom he met in the passage, where he could find Mr. Schultz.

"Through that door, first right."

"Thank you."

"My pleasure."

The notice on the door read *Manager of Personnel*, and under that, *Edgar Schultz*. Morrell knocked on it. Nobody answered, so he pushed it open and walked in. There were two girls in the room, both hammering away at typewriters. One of them looked Chinese. Morrell asked her, "Mr. Schultz here?"

"Sure." She nodded her dark head towards a sort of glass-walled cubicle in the corner. "That's Schultz."

"Thanks."

"My pleasure."

He could see Schultz inside the cubicle. A small, very dark man: he looked more Armenian than German, which was what Morrell had expected from the surname. He tapped on the door, and the little man looked up. "Yeah?"

He pushed the door open, and went in – not far, because there wasn't much space. "My name's Morrell. Mr. McLennan told me to come and see you."

"Siddown." Schultz initialled a card, slid it into a folder. "Do some'n for you?"

"I don't know. I'm looking for a job."

"Fitter, rigger, what?"

"I've no kind of training. Mr. McLennan simply said to see you, and you might have some idea –"

"I'm fulla ideas, he knows that. You English, or some'n?"

"British, yes."

"So what's wrong with a job in England?"

"It happens I'm in America. On Mr. McLennan's suggestion."

"He didn't give *me* no suggestions."

"No. He said it was up to you."

Schultz stared out past Morrell's head, watching the Chinese typist. He said slowly, without moving his small, brown eyes, "Yeah, that's how it is, I guess. What can you do?"

"I'm ready to learn any job that's going." Schultz didn't speak: he just smiled a little. Morrell asked him, "Well, is there any kind of job?"

"Not for a Limey, there ain't." The little man swung round, rested his hands on the desk in front of him. They were as hairy as a monkey's paws. "You Limeys, we win your goddam war for you, but that ain't enough. You come here an' want our friggin' jobs too. There's *Americans* wantin' jobs, ain't there?"

"I suppose there must be. Mr. McLennan –"

"McLennan passed the buck to me, okay, I got it, right here. No jobs for Limeys, not today and not tomorrow. McLennan soft-talks you, here we hand out truth. You got that, Limey?"

Morrell stood up. He thought, I could pick this little shit up in one hand and break him in two without straining any muscles. Why don't I?

"You say you won the war for us. Take any part in it yourself?"

Schultz blinked, and shook his head. "Spine trouble. Gotta weak back, born with it."

"Does it hurt much?"

"Some, now an' then. What's it to you?"

"I hope it starts hurting continuously pretty soon, that's all. Good-bye, Schultz."

He stepped out of the cubicle and slammed the door hard enough to break its glass. It didn't break, though. Halfway across the room to the outer door he heard the Chinese girl laugh: he glanced back at her, and she winked.

"So long, mister."

He nodded. He was too angry to try getting words out. He told himself, speaking and thinking from way outside there somewhere, Steady, now. One oddball doesn't make a country. One miserable little sod in a glass box getting his own back on the world.... Morrell shut the door behind him, leant against it for a moment, telling himself, Cool down. That little runt's not big enough to remember for more than two minutes. There'll be plenty of other jobs to try, and there's probably only one Edgar Schultz in the whole damn continent.

Well, that's McLennans. One "keep in touch", and one "off, Limey"....

He walked back past the other offices towards the door at the far end of the building. Just short of it, a passage led off to the right. He was thinking that while he was this side of the Hudson it couldn't do any harm if he walked down to Todds Yard to see if they had any vacancies there. He thought, I'll try it a different way, this time. I'll say I want to get into selling, and that since I know a lot about ships I thought they might have some kind of training scheme.... In which case, it'd be quicker to go back and out the other door. He stopped, thinking about it. At the end of that short passage to his right were double doors, and right across them in gold script were the words *Hank J. Smith, Vice President.* Below that, and bigger, GENERAL MANAGER.

Morrell's mind was working on the plan to go along and see Todds, and a part of it was still reeling from his recent interview with Schultz: it was a few seconds before the inscription on the double doors sank into his brain and registered. His feet carried him down the passage: he thought, *Hank Smith....* Why the hell didn't I think of him?

"*Sure* I recognized the name. Remembered that face, too! Truth is, I never forgot a customer in my life." Hank Smith's smile was wide and friendly, his handshake strong. "Even without the fancy uniform, Nick. What you doin' on this continent – shipwrecked?"

"Only in a manner of speaking, Hank. Hell of a long story, though. I don't want to –"

"For a customer, I got time."

"Haven't brought you a ship to mend, either."

"Okay, so no custom. I'll hear the story anyway. Care for a cigar?" Morrell shook his head. Smith stuffed the end of one into his mouth, and went right on talking. "How about this big yard we got now? You looked around any? New dock, new buildings –"

"You thought McLennan might sell out."

"That's right, I did. So did a lotta other guys. While he was happy laying plans to tool up fast and grab a lotta custom. Payin' off all right, too. Come on now, Nick, whatya doin' in my goddam country?"

"I'm looking for a job."

"Job, huh?" Smith nodded slowly, staring at Morrell along the length of his cigar as if it was a rocket launcher and he was deciding when to pull the trigger. "Left the Navy?"

Morrell nodded. "A few weeks ago. I fixed it to get my discharge over here so I wouldn't have to pay a fare. I brought a tug over – thing called the *Charles E. Brown*. Heard of her?"

"Can't say I have."

"I wish I hadn't, in some ways. She damn near drowned the lot of us half a dozen times. Anyway, I left her to sink in Baltimore, where she belongs, and that was the end of my seafaring days."

"Didn't want to stay in England?"

"Not that, exactly. When I was here in '44, McLennan asked me out to his house, remember that? Well, in the course of the week-end he lectured me more than once on the great opportunities there'd be for a man like me here in the United States once the war was over. He really drove the message in hard, Hank. So, to cut the rest of it short, I decided I'd come, and here I am, God help me."

"You seen him?"

"Yes, I've seen him."

"What's his offer?"

"Offer, hell. I had to kick my heels for three weeks until he came back from his honeymoon, and I only saw him today. He said he'd been speaking in general terms and there wasn't a bloody hope of a job."

Smith nodded. "For you, Nick, I'd say that's about the truth." He grinned. "Whadya say about the new Mrs. McLennan, huh?"

"I met her that week-end. She was eighteen then."

"Makes her twenty now. McLennan's fifty-two. Nice to be rich, eh?"

"I liked her, Hank."

"Oh, sure, I never met her, I still worship the ground she treads on. So, McLennan can't help. What next?"

"He told me to see the personnel man here at the yard. I just saw him. Schultz. What d'you employ that little rat for, Hank?"

"Schultz knows his job. He's a nut, but –" Smith shrugged his heavy shoulders – "world's full of nuts, I guess."

"I'd say he was a fourteen-carat bastard."

"You could be right. . . . No soap, eh?"

"Not a smell of it. So, I was thinking of going round to see them in Todds."

"No reason why you shouldn't. . . . What sorta work you after, Nick?"

"If I go along to Todds, I'd tell them I aimed to get into the selling side."

"And if I asked you?"

"Pretty much the same, except I want a job, period. I mean, any job, so I can afford to eat."

"I see. Well, Nick, if you're sure that's your attitude, and you wouldn't feel insulted –"

"I'm sure, and I wouldn't."

"Okay, you're hired. General Cleaner in No. 3 Machine Shop."

"Cleaner –"

"You don't want it?"

"Hell." Morrell looked down at the knife-edge creases in his new, London-tailored suit. He thought, I'll need to go shopping. Denims. . . . He looked up, found Hank Smith watching him, waiting for an answer.

He nodded. "Yes. I want it."

CHAPTER EIGHT

Monday morning: he'd punched his first time-clock.

One dollar an hour, eight dollars a day. By the time he'd paid for his room and food, there wouldn't be much change in his pockets by Sunday mornings. There'd be no more games with Martha. He'd told her so, the night after he got the job, and she hadn't taken it too well.

Morrell moved down the line of machines, using his broom to hook out the litter of fallen swarf – metal shavings – and pile it into heaps so he could scoop it up, holding the broom short-handled to cram it into the bin and then tipping the bin into his wheeled trash-cart. You went down one line and then back the other way along the other, and when the cart was full you pushed it out, dumped the stuff, came in for more. You had to be careful how you used the broom, not to get the head of it between a man's feet. He'd only done that once, and he was anxious to avoid it in the future.

The first thing he'd done after he'd seen Hank Smith was go to find a room. It had been out of the question to keep the one he had: it would have taken too much time and too much money to get to work and home again at night. He'd prospected around the streets of Hoboken, inland on the other side of the railway tracks which lined the yards and wharves, and found a house with a notice in its window indicating rooms to let. A little Italian woman, dressed from head to foot in black, had answered his ring, staring at him cautiously round the half-open door as if she thought he might be someone from the government or the Mafia. He'd been aware that his clothes weren't right for the district. Eventually she'd led him upstairs and shown him an empty room, and he'd taken it, paying a week's rent in advance. When he'd fixed it with the landlady, he crossed the river and travelled by subway to his old room. He packed his gear and took it to the house in Hoboken. Then he called Martha.

"Nick! Where are you?"

"Hoboken. I've just moved in here."

"What d'you mean, moved in?"

"Taken a room. Important job, you have to live on top of it."

"Gil hired you, then?"

"Gil certainly did not. Hell, it's a long story, Martha. I came over to the yard here, and saw Hank Smith. Remember him?"

"Sure. What kind of job is it, Nick?"

"Cleaner, in one of the –"

"Nick, I didn't get that. I thought you said –"

"Cleaner. Big job, Martha. I have my own broom – new one, a hell of a thing. Well, I don't just clean, I do other things too. 'Help out on the shop floor', that's what the foreman said. 'Hump stuff around'. His exact words. Well, you know, first rung of the ladder –"

"You're joking, of course."

"What makes you think that? I have to eat, so I need a job. This is what they gave me. Simple as that, me ol' darlin'. But look, now. I won't be able to see much of you. For one thing, I'm too far away, and for another I can't afford it. Anyway, Martha –"

"Nick, you don't want to see me. You've been talking to Gil McLennan, and that's how it is. Well, okay, Nick, that's *it* –"

"That's not it at all. McLennan doesn't even know I'm working for him. He offered me damn-all, very politely. Now don't be crazy, Martha –"

"*I'm* crazy!"

"You are if you believe that stuff about me not wanting to see you. You think McLennan cares who his cleaners consort with? The situation, Martha, is exactly as I've described, there's nothing else to it. Look, this phone's no good, let me come and see you tomorrow?"

"I'm out of town tomorrow."

"All right, then, Sunday."

"Sunday's okay, I guess."

"Good. I'll explain it all then. I'll have to get back here that evening –"

"Well, don't bother, Nick. Don't damn well bother. You already explained everything, why –"

"Martha, I could come on Saturday evening and stay over. What time will you be back in town?"

"I have a date, Saturday night. Let's just leave it, shall we?" He heard her laugh. "Go sweep up something, Nick!"

At lunch in the cafeteria Morrell found himself opposite a short, swarthy, very square-built man with grizzled hair and about the lightest grey eyes he'd ever seen. He recognized him as one of the machine operators from the No. 3 Shop. Earlier in the day, the first time he'd passed that machine, they'd exchanged nods, and Morrell remembered that he'd thought then the man looked like a rugger player. The face and eyes were intelligent enough, but physically he looked as solid as if his skin was packed with bone. He looked up as Morrell plunked down his plate – hamburger and French fries.

"New here, ain'tcha?"

Morrell nodded. "First day. Nick Morrell."

The other man leaned over to shake his hand. "Owen Pugh. So where y' from?" He hadn't stopped chewing.

"England."

"English, huh?"

"British."

"British ain't English?"

"English is British. So's Scottish, Welsh, Irish. I'm all four."

"Part Welsh, huh?"

"Like yourself."

"How'd ya know that? 'Cept I ain't only *part* Welsh –"

"Owen Pugh's about as Welsh as a name can get."

"Yeah." The pale eyes stared at him: Pugh had even stopped eating, and there was still food on his plate. "Yeah, guess that's right."

"Could 'a fooled *me*." A thin, yellow-looking man on his left spoke without looking up from a plate of what looked like noodles. "Always thought y' was American."

"Who's sayin' I ain't?"

"Thought you did."

"Ain't no damn Frog, that's for sure." Pugh told Morrell, "This here's Potts Destier. His old man was a Frog. Told me that himself. Di'ntya, Potts?"

The man nodded, his Adam's apple working as he chewed. Pugh laughed. "Jumping kind, must 'a been. Else he couldn't 'a got here. . . . Hey, Nick, you say you're part Welsh?"

"Yes. Small part.'

"Know what day's tomorrow?"

Morrell frowned at him. "First of March?"

"Right. And?'

"Tuesday."

"That all?"

"All I know of."

Pugh looked at Destier, jabbed his fork towards Morrell. "Says he's Welsh. How d'ya like that?" He turned back. "Listen, Nick. March first is Saint David's Day, ain't it? Patron saint for Wales?"

"Oh! Why yes, of course."

"Forgot, didya?"

"Suppose I must have."

"Yeah. Well, we don't forget it, never. Special dinner, even. You care to come along?"

"Come where?"

"My place, where else? Stayin' near here, Nick?"

"Couple of streets up."

"Married?"

He shook his head.

"Okay, then, tomorrow. Soon's we knock off. Okay?"

"Thanks, I'd like that."

Owen Pugh stood up, wiping his mouth on his hand. He grinned down at Destier, who was still shovelling in noodles. Then he winked at Morrell. "We don't have no Frogs along, not for a Welsh day. Give a Frog a glass o' meddyglyn, he don't know what to do with it. Right, Nick?"

Morrell nodded. He hoped he'd know, or guess right, when the time came. He'd been told that his great-grandmother had come from Wales, and he'd been into Cardiff once or twice, early in the war, but that was all he knew about it, and he'd certainly never heard of meddyglyn. Since apparently it came in a glass, it was a reasonable guess that one drank it.

Having met Destier at lunch, Morrell noticed him in the machine shop that afternoon. He wasn't a machine operator: his job was to feed the other operators with work. A raw casting arrived from the foundry into one end of the shop and passed through a number of machines before it emerged at the other end gleaming smooth, shaped and honed to its exact specifications. Destier handled the flow, moving a part that had been finished in one machine to its next treatment higher up the line. Getting more used to his job, the sweeping and dumping routine becoming more and more automatic as the hours went by, Morrell found himself taking a close interest in the work going on around him. These were parts for ships' engines, steam turbines so far as he could tell: blades, rotors and the halves of bearings. Watching the movements of the operators, he was surprised to see that their jobs were really quite simple. The machines did the work they were set to do, and they needed little more than to be fed and watched. Adjustments were minimal, and infrequent. It struck him that an hour's training on any of the machines would be as much as he'd need to handle it with confidence.

He thought, I'll ask Owen Pugh, when I know him better – after a bucket of Welsh whatd'youcallit, perhaps – if he'll show me how to work his. Then when I know I can do it, I could ask the foreman to give me a chance when there's a machine vacant, a man sick or something.

He stooped, jerked the bin up behind the pile of swarf, shoved at it from its other side with the broom-head. A better tool would speed this up, he thought: the bloody handle's all over the place. A short thing, a pusher with a handle, you'd drop the broom and use it now.... The machines' whining drone filled his ears: you could sing or whistle to yourself, and nobody would hear.... He told himself, thinking of the machine-operating and Owen Pugh, Well, that's a plan of action. It's limited, certainly, but a lot better than no plan at all.

He straightened, up-ended the bin into the cart. Owen Pugh grinned at him: the ex-Welshman was standing back from his machine, waiting for Destier to bring him the next job and move the one he'd finished. Morrell grinned back, shoving the cart up level with the next machine where swarf was falling, showering, curling, golden like a woman's hair. He jerked the bin off the cart, clunked it down, and out of the corner of his eye he saw Pugh, killing time, stroll to the food trolley where you could buy cokes, coffee, doughnuts. Morrell slid his broom in under the side of the machine, dragged out the heavy troth of metal. His back and arms ached from stooping, shoving, lifting: he thought, It won't do me any harm. He knew he'd been getting flabby, sitting around in New York with nothing to do but wait for McLennan and, now and then, entertain – or be entertained by – Martha Scotland.

He wondered why there should be this rift between her and the McLennans. If Toni was jealous of Martha's earlier connection with her husband, she wouldn't have cared a hoot that he, Morrell, was having an affair with Martha that week-end two years ago. She'd have been glad about it, wouldn't she? But it needn't have been that, anyway, that had made her angry with him. She may not even have been angry: just in a bad mood, perhaps, and showing it. And surely she couldn't have been jealous of Martha on Gil McLennan's account, at that time when Elizabeth McLennan was still alive?

Morrell hefted the loaded bin, tipped its contents into the cart. You didn't want to touch this stuff with your hands: it was like handling a heap of razor blades. He noticed that Pugh was back at work. Destier had fed him a new part, moved on with the one he'd finished to the machine it had to go to next. Not the next-door machine, which was the same as Pugh's and doing the same work, but one in the next bank up the line.

Destier: originally, in French, d'Estier? With that scrawny, yellow neck he had the look of a half-plucked chicken.... Pugh's machine came next. Morrell moved his cart up, and began to sweep. Pugh didn't acknowledge his arrival, or even notice it: he stood with his short, thick legs apart, his hands up like a wrestler's, hovering above the machine's controls.

When they stopped work that evening, Morrell found his way to the Joiners' Shop and made himself a wooden pusher, selecting timber from a heap of off-cuts lying in a corner. A section of inch-thick wood eighteen inches long by six across was the pushing surface, and he screwed a handle in the middle of one side. When he'd finished it he thanked the foreman joiner, carried the pusher back to No. 3 Machine Shop and left it in his cart for use next day.

CHAPTER NINE

The wooden pusher was about an inch too long. That much shorter, and it would fit inside the mouth of the bin: as it was, you couldn't drive the swarf right in. It was pretty good even now, a lot better than using the broom, and when he'd trimmed it he knew he'd have made himself a really useful tool. He thought, At lunchtime I'll go along and slice half an inch off each end. Then he realized he probably wouldn't have time for that: he'd had a summons to drop by Schultz's office, to complete some documentation for his Social Security.

The noise of the machines was boring jagged holes into the tissue of his brain. He had no idea how he'd managed to get back to his own lodgings last night – or this morning, whenever it was. All he knew was that he'd woken up on his bed, a few hours ago. Fully dressed, and feeling like some cadaver misguidedly disinterred. A filthy taste in the mouth and a shattering pain in the skull.... He'd thought, shaving with a kind of wild panache, I'm still quite drunk. When I get sober I'm going to feel much worse than I ever felt before. Nobody, not even a Welshman, should be so rash as to swallow several pints of a fifty per cent beer-gin mixture. Whatever genuine meddyglyn might be, it couldn't be that: if it had been, the Welsh would have died off centuries ago.

Hefting the bin, tipping it, he thought, I should have known better than to drink the filthy stuff. Alice Pugh warned me what was in it. But hell, if I'd refused, Pugh would certainly have taken it as an insult. Pugh offended as well as blind drunk would have been a bit too much to handle.... But I'm *still* drunk! He told himself, recognizing the sort of haze which hung betweeen his consciousness and the routine reality of the day, Better watch it, now. Man does stupid things, in this condition. He dropped the bin on top of the swarf in the cart, pushed it higher up the line of machines. Owen Pugh was at his, feet straddled, eyes on the job, hands hovering.... Morrell thought, He must be like an ox inside as well as out.

"Whatya got there, Morrell?"

"Eh?" He looked up from his knees-bent position, saw the foreman staring down. He straightened, with the wooden pusher in his hand. The foreman frowned at it.

"Wheredya get it?"

"Made it."

"The hellya did."

Morrell turned it over to show the handle. The foreman nodded, stared at him curiously before he walked on up the line, pausing to exchange a word here and there with chargehands on the separate banks of machines. Pugh was standing back, now, his job finished until Destier brought him the next half-processed part. The foreman spoke to Pugh as he passed him, and the Welshman laughed, raising one thick hand in an obscene gesture at the broad, retreating back. Destier, Morrell noticed, was still down at the far end. Several of the parts which Pugh needed to keep himself and his machine busy were ready for him lower down the line, but until Destier's routine progress brought him this far up the Welshman had nothing to do but wait. Morrell thought, It'd take him about ten seconds to fetch one for himself: but presumably they don't want men walking to and fro about the floor. It seemed crazy, though, that expensive machines and trained men should stand idle for something like a minute in every ten.

When the shift knocked off for lunch, he went for a word with Owen Pugh.

"Some party, Owen. Thanks a lot."

"Liked it, didya?" He was wiping the palms of his hands with a wad of cotton waste. "Alice don't wanna know me. Won't talk, nothin'. Always that way, March second." He grinned, suddenly. "Two, three days, she'll come around, sweet as sugar... .Hey, Nick, hear what that guy Pirelli said?"

"Pirelli?"

"Goddam foreman. Says why don't I get me some brains like the cleaner got. Meaning you. What's got inta him, Nick?"

"Search me –"

"Somin' t' eat?"

"I have to see Schultz first."

"Well, you frig Schultz for me, willya?"

"I'd like to."

"Ain't nobody round here wouldn't."

Before he went along to the personnel office, Morrell bought himself a coke off the trolley, and drank it thirstily. For the moment, then, he felt a little better. He was thinking that in spite of Pugh's suggestion, he'd take things easy with Schultz – if Schultz gave him half a chance to do that. At all events, he must keep his temper. But walking out of the machine shop and across the yard towards the office block, he remembered that deliberately aimed malice, and he felt his own aggressive instincts gathering strength with every pace he took. He told himself, I won't start anything, but if that bastard utters one word out of place, by Christ I'll –

Now hang on. . . . I'm still half cut. And I'm a cleaner, been here two and a half days. I'm not in any position to throw my weight around. He turned in the door and headed down the passage. He thought, Just let the little sod start something, that's all!

Morrell pushed open the door marked *Manager of Personnel*. Rather a grandiose title, he thought, for a runt like Edgar Schultz. The man was a clerk, no more than that. You'd imagine in a business the size of McLennans they'd have a real manager in the job. Presumably Hank Smith or someone else in the front office took the decisions while Schultz carried the title and did the routine clerking. Just possibly, he thought, Hank Smith's too kind a man to be a good executive.

Well, *I* should complain, about that.... He shoved the door open, and walked in. His eyes went straight to Schultz's glass booth, in the same way that a fighter stepping into the ring looks right away at his opponent. But the box was empty.

"Well, hi, there!"

The Chinese girl smiled at him from her desk across the room. Dark hair hung straight to her shoulders on either side of the oval, high-cheekboned face. He thought, Just as well this place is well heated. Otherwise she'd freeze, in that dress. It was orange, low-cut, skimpy: she showed a lot of leg as she slid out from behind the desk and came towards him. She walked like a bitch on heat.

He pulled his thoughts into line. "Schultz not here?"

She shook her head. "Only me. It's okay, though, you only gotta sign a coupla things. I'm Mandy."

"Pretty name."

"Ain't it, though."

He thought, feeling and surprised by his own immediate and strong reaction to her, I must be sex-starved. Or that damn drink's an aphrodisiac. He shoved one hand quickly into his pocket: he needed to. Mandy saw the movement, and let him see her seeing it. Her smile deepened as she looked up into his eyes. He said, "I like you better than I like Schultz."

"Some compliment.... You're a nice lookin' guy, Nick. Nicer in that fancy suit, though." She laughed, a tiny murmur in her throat. "Boy, you sure got Schultz burnt up."

"That why he's not here now? Didn't he want to see me?" He didn't give a hoot why Schultz wasn't there: he'd only spoken to force his thoughts away from the girl's close and vivid sexuality. It made no difference, though: he'd barely noticed her the first time, he hadn't given her a thought in the few days since then, but now *wham*, he felt like a stallion led out to his first mare of the season.

Mandy shrugged, moving her shoulders forward so that the dress loosened and he could see clear down the front of it to where her nipples were just hidden by the top edge of a flimsy looking bra. She murmured, watching his face with her soft, brown, meaningful eyes, "Maybe I kinda suggested I'd save him the trouble."

"Oh, you did?"

He brought his hands up and forward, rested his palms on the soft upper parts of her arms. She whispered, "Whatya doin', Nick?" He kept his hands loose on her arms, half open, stroking her. Then he pulled her closer, and stepped back, taking her with him until he felt his back against the door. She was looking up into his face, not smiling now, her lips open and her eyes a different brown, lighter and at the same time cloudy. He kissed her: in the first second of it her mouth came wide open, sucking not just at his tongue but his lips too. She moved against him, first cautiously, feeling him, then wriggling like a belly-dancer while they kissed. He felt her shudder suddenly in his arms: then she'd brought her hands up between them and she was pushing at his chest. He let her go.

"Better sign them papers, Nick."

"Mandy, you can't just –"

"Over here." She'd turned away and she was heading towards Schultz's box. Morrell followed her, wondering if in that half minute of wriggling she could possibly have got as far as a clitoral orgasm. If she had, she was the fastest comer he'd ever encountered.... Schultz's desk was cluttered with papers, files, worksheets. Mandy picked up a clip of documents which had been lying on top, and she turned, as he came inside the glass box, so that they were both beside the front of the desk with Schultz's chair between them.

"Sign there and there." She handed him the forms, and a ballpoint pen. He was angry: she'd led him on, and then stopped dead. He tried not to look at her as he bent over the desk and scratched his signature on the papers. She took them from him, then held up a card.

"So now you get this, Nick. Ain't you lucky?"

He put his hand out for it: she pulled hers away, whipping the card out of sight behind her back. Then in a swift series of movements she pushed the chair back out of the way and swung herself up to sit on the edge of the desk, facing him. Her legs weren't long enough to reach the floor. The edge of the desk flattened her thighs, which were well apart, with the hem of the dress pulled halfway up them.

"Want your card, Nick? I'm sittin' on it."

She pointed at her crutch. The card was under there, where she'd pointed. She laughed right into his face.

"You wannit, Nick, you better take it."

He grabbed her dress, pulled it up, clear up over her hips. She helped him, lifting herself on Schultz's desk so he could do it without tearing anything. She had no pants on, or stockings: she was there, all of her, ready and open to him, right under his eyes. He kissed her, and she half swallowed him again, her arms hugging him around his head while he jerked his fly open and felt himself spring free: then he was in her and she was clinging to him and he'd pushed down the top of her dress, too, her breasts were out in his hands, the dress like a brilliant cummerbund around her waist. Schultz's desk rocked against the glass-paned partition as he drove into her and under his mouth she breathed in short, hard bursts, breaths that were words, "Yeah, yeah, yeah, oh God, Nick, yeah –" Then he felt it coming, and exactly in the moment he knew he was going to, Mandy squawked, a cat-squawk right in the back of her throat and stifled by his mouth on her.

He straightened slowly, panting. Mandy said, "Okay, Nick, you get your card." Her face was damp, bruised-looking. She pushed back that enormous length of blue-black hair: raising her arms to push it all over behind her naked back, her breasts rose, their nipples pointing pinkly at Morrell's face. He jerked up his zip.

"Better get you covered up before your boss walks in." He began to help her, starting with the bra. She watched his hands: she wasn't doing much to help herself.

"Real sexy, Nick...."

He glanced up, and saw new excitement growing in her eyes. He shook his head, smiling. "Haven't you had enough?"

"Sure." She laughed. "You had'n rung the bell, you wou'na got that card.... Whereya livin', Nick?"

"Rooming house, just up the way."

"Maybe I'll visit, sometime."

"My landlady doesn't go for that."

"Meanin' you don't want me there?"

"Don't be crazy." He smiled at her reassuringly. He thought, Yes, meaning exactly that. I've *had* you, Mandy darling....

"Well, you c'n visit me, then. My folks don't care."

"Better here in the office. I'll drop in now and then."

"I can't always get ridda Schultz. Sheila's okay, she does what I tell 'er, but Schultz –"

"You'll manage it." He patted her damp, puffed cheek. "You're a very capable girl, Mandy. I'm sure you'll find a way."

Mandy slid off the desk, wriggled while she pulled her dress down, smoothing it over her hips. He glanced behind her at Schultz's desk: it was in a hell of a mess, and on the bare, polished wood of its front edge was a clear print of Mandy's naked bottom.

He led her out of the booth before she could see it and wipe it off. He hoped it wouldn't fade before the Manager of Personnel got back from eating lunch.

By the middle of the afternoon he wasn't half drunk any more, he was just half dead. This was the real hangover setting in. He worked on, morosely shovelling swarf into his cart and dumping it, dragging himself and the cart back for more. His head was splitting: at the noisier machines, the high-pitched ones where tools bit deep into spinning metal, he worked with frantic speed so as to get out of their immediate range in a minimum of time.

This must, he thought, be one of the most monotonous jobs a man could find. However fast or efficiently you cleared the stuff away, there was always more of it piling up when you got back. . . . He thought, suddenly, the idea hitting his dulled brain with such impact that he stopped dead with the bin full and heavy, poised at the edge of the cart. Why couldn't there be a travelling band, conveyor belt, running all along under the fronts of the machines and taking the muck away continuously, right out through the end wall to the dump?

No, you couldn't do it. The machine operators had to stand on something, and if you had a travelling floor they'd need to keep walking sideways just to stay level with their work. All right for Laurel and Hardy, but – he thought. What if they had platforms to stand on, built out somehow from under the machines' bases, with the conveyor moving under the platforms?

He realized he was still standing there with the loaded bin up at shoulder height. He tipped it into the cart, thinking, It's feasible. It really is. You'd still need cleaners, but it would be light work compared to this, and a hell of a lot less of it. One cleaner could look after the whole of each machine shop, and still have time to spare.... And what you'd do – by God, yes, he had it now! – you'd mount all the machines on fixed, raised ramps running the length of the shop, and the platforms for the men to stand on would be built out from the ramps, extensions of them. The conveyor belts would be the width from the edge of the ramps to the outer edge of the platforms. Say three feet, maybe a little more. That would take ninety per cent of the swarf away. The other ten per cent would still have to be hucked out by hand, but the saving in time and manpower, plus fewer people cluttering up the shop floor, would be tremendous.

"Okay, Morrell?"

Pirelli, the shop foreman. Morrell nodded, snapping awake, realizing he'd been standing there for several minutes.

"I just had an idea –"

"Congratulations."

"Thanks. Look, it's –"

"Ideas you get in your own time, feller." Pirelli spoke pleasantly, just a man doing his job. He pointed. "C'mon, now, shift it!"

Morrell thought, shovelling, I'll sketch it out, tonight. Talk to Owen Pugh about it, perhaps. No, not to Pugh. His answer would be "the hell with it, I get paid to run a machine, you get paid to sweep". Well, bully for Pugh, he's happy, he'll be happy all his life. Perhaps I could talk to Hank Smith about it. He thought, tipping again, pushing the cart along to the next bank, I might still be drunk, seeing things more simply than they are. So wait, work it out on paper. Let's not go off at half-cock.... Now between the banks, that central ramp of mine would be continued without any machine on it, and the platform over the belt would be continuous through the gap to make a bridge so men can still pass at those points from one alley to another.

If the swarf piled up too thickly, it might jam under the platforms on its way by.... No, why should it? The conveyor's moving continuously, there couldn't be any pile-ups. The stuff would be carried off all the time, the minute it hits the belt it's moving on and out.

He didn't feel ill any more, he felt excited. He thought, working faster now, This has been a hell of a day. A day to end all days....

Or start them?

He'd stepped back to let Potts Destier pass him when the second idea smacked him right between the eyes. It was so damned obvious that he wondered right away how on earth he'd missed thinking of it before. Except, he realized, that on its own it would have presented problems which, when you coupled this new idea with the first one, making each plan use the other – well, the problems virtually disappeared.

He thought, stooping to his work and tingling with excitement, I've got to get it all down on paper and in detail. Find the snags, then knock 'em out. It has to be a complete scheme to which there can be no real or practical objections, and it has to be presented so clearly that only an idiot can fail to get the message.

To start with I need a blueprint of this machine shop with the tools sited as they are now. That shouldn't be hard to get hold of. Then I'd better have an outside plan, too, the layout of the yard as a whole. And I'll need a lot of paper, pencils, and so on.

He had drawing instruments already, in his navigational kit, and a slide-rule.... Morrell decided he'd go shopping for the other items that same evening, and work every night, if necessary all night, until the job was done well enough to show Hank Smith or McLennan, anyone who'd let him talk to them. He thought it might take a week, even a month. It didn't matter how long it took so long as he got it right.

CHAPTER TEN

It took three days: that Wednesday night, and Thursday night, and he finished it just after four a.m. on Saturday morning. He had a sheaf of plans that covered every essential detail: they weren't blueprints, but they were clear enough for any intelligent layman to understand or for an engineer to use as a starting-point for the technical design. Morrell hadn't allowed himself more than six hours' sleep altogether since Wednesday, on which day he'd suffered from that monster hangover, but he was too well satisfied now with what he'd done to feel tired. He felt more like celebrating. He thought,

It's Saturday: I'll call Martha, and take her out tonight. Unless she has a date already.

He'd meant to leave her alone, and he'd also meant to leave his money in the bank until he really needed it. He thought now, The hell with that. By Monday night I won't be a lousy cleaner any more. . . .

That was how confident he felt. He knew what he had, in those plans: his passport into Management.

Half down the stairs to the hall where the telephone was, he stopped and asked himself if he wasn't counting his chickens before they'd hatched. There could be snags he didn't know about, some basic objection to the whole concept which might show up in the first couple of minutes' discussion and whip the carpet right out from under his feet. Well, there couldn't be. The plan was necessary, logical and practical. It would cost money, but it would save that much every week. It was right: he knew it.

He went on down the stairs, and dialled Martha's number.

"Hello?"

"Martha, it's Nick."

"Nick? God, what's the time?"

"Roughly four a.m., me ol' darlin'. Woke you, did I?"

"Hell, no. I was knitting a rug. Always do, about this time in the goddam –"

"Watch your language, and I'll explain –"

"You on a party, Nick?"

"I've been working. Thought if I rang now I'd be sure to catch you, otherwise you'd be out to get photographed or otherwise drooled over, and I'd–"

"I don't work Saturdays. Isn't it Saturday?"

"Yes, it is. Martha, do you have a date tonight?"

"That what you called for at this ridiculous –"

"Martha, I've been missing you –"

"So hold the line while I burst into tears –"

"– and I want to see you and I have something to celebrate. Are you free, or aren't you?"

"I have to go to some kind of cocktail party –"

"How about either telling them you can't make it, or saying you'll be there if Morrell can bring you? We could eat after . . . . Martha?"

"You're taking me out to dinner?"

"Why not?"

"Thought you had to save money –"

"Perhaps I've saved enough now. What time – six?"

"All right, six. Now I want to sleep. Good-bye."

She'd hung up. Morrell went up the stairs grinning to himself in the dark: he felt better than he had in months. America, he thought, I love you. And you too, Martha....

With Martha, he thought, it's always mirrors.... He was seeing her in one now, and himself beside her, both of them on bar stools. He noticed that his face was slightly flushed from all the whisky sours he'd sunk.

"You're mad, Nick. You should get your feet on the ground!'

He'd told her about his plans and what he expected they'd do for him: she'd been quite the opposite of impressed.

"*That's* what we're celebrating?"

"What's wrong with it?"

"You get some wild idea, none of them's seen it yet, that makes a celebration?"

"Well, thanks for the enthusiasm –"

"You've been there one week, pushing a broom, and you think they'll –"

"Let's drop it, shall we?" He thought, It makes no difference if I'd been there a week or a year. I could have just passed by and looked in the window for ten minutes. What counts is what's in those plans, not where they come from or after how long.

"Gil McLennan doesn't take lessons from cleaners, Nick. He has engineers, guys like Smith –"

The cocktail party had been all right, except that he'd met some people there whose faces were vaguely familiar and who knew him right away. Martha had been on the other side of the room, talking to about five men at once, and Morrell was beating his brains out to remember who these people were and when he could have met them. A middle-aged couple, obviously well-off: the woman's fingers were loaded with diamonds.

"You don't remember us, Commander?"

"Yes, I do. But I'm sorry, I can't remember where."

"Why, in Gil McLennan's apartment, maybe two years ago. You had your ship in his dock, you'd sunk a German submarine, and we met at this party he was giving. Now I'll tell you – yes, it was D-Day, d'you remember now?"

"Of course I do. Sorry to have been so stupid. You're Mr. and Mrs. – Anderson?"

"Hamilton, Commander, John and Louise Hamilton. Now tell me, are you still in the British navy?"

"Lord, no! I'm – well, I'm working at McLennans, actually."

"You don't say?" Mrs. Hamilton looked delighted to hear it. "Why, that's marvellous! So you joined Gil. . . . Now don't think I'm inquisitive, Commander, but – well, you're settling here permanently, are you? In New York, I mean?"

"As far as I know."

"And did you bring your wife and family over with you?"

"I'm not married, Mrs. Hamilton."

"Well, now." She smiled at her husband. "*Well.* John, we must have the Commander up to our place the very next time we're entertaining. Hillary's just mad about the Navy: she has this little yacht, you know, I guess she'd truly love to – oh, Hillary, she's our daughter – she'd be just – now tell me, Commander, should we call you at your apartment, or at Gil's office?"

"It's most kind of you. Well, over at the yard. You know, across the river?"

"You're at the Hoboken end of the organization?"

Morrell nodded at Hamilton. "That's right. I'm living over there, too."

"In *Hoboken*?"

"Yes."

Hamilton cleared his throat. "Just – uh – what is it you're doing in McLennans? Are you in charge of the –"

"I'm in charge of a broom, Mr. Hamilton."

"Sorry, I – I didn't quite catch –"

"I'm a cleaner. They pay me a dollar an hour to sweep out one of the machine shops over there."

"Now you're joking, of course."

"I'm not, I promise you. I sweep. Eight hours a day. Well, it's most kind of you, Mrs. Hamilton, I'd love to visit you and I can't imagine anything nicer than sailing with your daughter. Whereabouts is it you live?"

"John, I do believe we've clean forgotten the time." Mrs. Hamilton seemed to be nudging her husband with her elbow at the same time as holding her wrist up to show him her watch. An interesting motion, like an eccentric camshaft. "That dinner party, remember? Why, we have to *run*!"

"I guess we do, my dear." Hamilton nodded at Morrell. "So long – er – Commander. Nice to have bumped into you. Now if you'll excuse us, we have to find Betsy and make our good-byes. . . ."

CHAPTER ELEVEN

Black lettering on a white door: *Herschel Green, Plant Manager*. Morrell knocked once, opened it and went in. Green looked up from his desk.

"You Morrell?"

He nodded. The Plant Manager glanced at his watch, sighed, slid a file into the drawer of his desk. Morrell shut the door.

"Okay. Sit down, Morrell."

About my own age, Morrell thought. Hersche Green was thin, dark-haired and pale-skinned, fairly obviously Jewish. He looked at first glance too slight and sensitive, with those small bones and large brown eyes, to run a plant and a labour force like this one. When you looked more closely, though, you saw the strength in those eyes. It was inside him, looking out.

Morrell pulled a hard chair closer to the desk and sat down on it. Green said in his soft, quiet voice, "They tell me you want to talk with me about some proposal you have for revamping the machine shops. They also tell me you're a cleaner with eight days' time on the clock and no other industrial experience."

"They're right."

"Yeah." The Plant Manager smiled gently. "I'll be honest with you, Morrell. The General Manager was with me when the news broke, and it was his idea I should look into it. Without that I don't believe you'd be in here now."

Morrell nodded. "I can understand that. But I'll be honest with you too. If you'd refused to see me I'd have gone straight to Smith or McLennan."

"You think they'd be more approachable?"

"I've met them both before."

"Yeah, I know that. However, you weren't on the payroll then, were you? Well, okay, let's have it." He frowned. "Make it brief, and if I want more I'll ask for it."

"I've made some drawings. Will you look at them?" He had his half-dozen sketches between two sheets of board. "They're here."

"Sure, if it helps." Green cleared a space on his desk. Morrell selected the first plan: then he hesitated, shook his head.

"No. I'd like to tell you about it first."

"Do it any way you like."

"Well, as you say, I've been sweeping. It's a slow job, it takes quite a lot of manpower and the cleaners get in the way of the productive work. So the first thing I thought of was to have a floor-level conveyor belt continuously removing waste."

"Machinists stand on it?"

"No. You mount all the machines on ramps which run the length of the shop, and at each machine there's a platform extended from the ramp. The conveyor runs under those platforms. They have to extend just beyond the belt so there's room for end support."

"Not totally impossible, maybe –"

"No, it's quite practical. You'll see, when you look at the plans. The belts carry the swarf right out of the shop to other conveyors which feed it to the central dump by way of a chute. I've an alternative here in case you find it better to have the chute on the wharfside so the waste goes straight into barges."

Green was sitting well back in his chair, watching Morrell as he talked. He said slowly, "I'll look at your plans, but from what you've told me I doubt whether the construction work involved would pay off in my lifetime. Or yours, for that matter."

"I haven't finished yet."

"Go right ahead."

"Right from the start I noticed something else that seems to me crazy. Depending on what's going through in any day or shift, you've got machine parts going from, say, number one bank to number three, then three to four, four to seven, and so on. At regular and quite frequent intervals the machine operators have to stop and do nothing until the man who moves the parts brings the next one up. I'd estimate from my own observation that you have an average of ten per cent time-waste on both men and machines. That right?"

"In most cases it's a little more than that."

"Well, if we call it ten per cent, that's the same as having one machine in ten doing damn-all day in, day out. So you've got a great deal of money tied up in useless plant, and you're paying ten men to do the work of nine."

"You don't have to tell me. I know it."

"So the answer – my answer – is to feed the parts up on a conveyor belt too."

"It can't be done. We've thought about it, Morrell. We aren't all morons in these offices, even if you may have that kind of impression of us. I know, you could run a small plant and show perfectly good profits using just the tools we have standing idle at any given moment. That's quite a thought, and it's to your credit that it's worried you. But you can't apply a conveyor system to those shops. It's a nightmare we've given up thinking about. What we've done is the only thing possible in our particular situation: that's to say we've costed to allow for that overall average of something like eleven and a half per cent non-productive machine-hours."

Morrell waited, to be sure he'd finished. Green added, "If that's the brick wall you've been beating your head on, you take my advice and drop it before you go out of your mind. Now I don't want you to let this get you down. I appreciate your interest and your imaginative approach, and from here on we'll be keeping an eye on you. You've done yourself no harm at all trying to think this one out, I promise you that's a fact. It's not unlikely we'll move you, maybe in a month or two –"

"Forgive me interrupting you –"

"I don't mind. But surely I've answered most of –"

"I've hardly begun to tell you about this idea yet. The answer is so damn simple that probably you *wouldn't* have got to it. I did, because – well, I'm not an engineer, I came to it with a fresh mind and no knowledge of what may be more orthodox systems. What's more I've had my nose pretty well rubbing along in it –"

"Eight days, huh?"

"Six and a half working days. But I got the answer in two and a half. I spent three nights last week working on these plans."

"I see." Green still wasn't taking him seriously. "And in that time you've licked it?"

"Yes. Remember the first part, how I proposed putting the machines up on a central ramp?"

"Sure."

"Well, the ramp's a few inches higher now than it had to be for that original purpose. And it's hollow, of course – like a steel bridge. So the second conveyor belt runs *inside* it. D'you follow me?"

"So far."

"Access to the conveyor for feeding in machine parts is through traps in the top of it. Four lanes, four traps. You could have six, probably, but I've made it four in these plans for the sake of simplicity. Depending on which bank the part has to go to, it's put into the appropriate lane. You can make it foolproof by having the other traps locked at the point of loading when you set up the system for whatever routine you need. Then at the delivery points you have baffles, which of course are adjustable, to take the job out of the lane at the point you want it. It gets fed out of the side of the platform into a ready-rack. . . . I probably haven't explained it too well, but if you'll have a look at the plans now you'll see much more clearly what I'm trying to say."

"Hold on a minute, will you?" Green seemed to be staring straight at him, but he wasn't focusing. He was looking through him, beyond him, trying to visualize the set-up which Morrell had been trying to get across. "Wait while I think a minute?"

Morrell separated the various plans he'd drawn, put them into the order he wanted them looked at, and slid them on to the Plant Manager's desk. He wasn't surprised that he had the man's attention now. He knew he'd won, he'd known it last Saturday morning. It was only a matter of waiting until Green, Smith and McLennan knew it too.

He had a feeling, watching Green, that he'd already crossed the first hurdle. And this was the tough one. Once the Plant Manager was pushing the idea, the General Manager would have to listen: and the General Manager, who was also a vice president, would take it right to McLennan. It was difficult to see how McLennan could turn down a plan to increase the plant's productivity by more than ten per cent.

Herschel Green was shaking his head.

"Morrell, I have to be dreaming, but I'd say this is a scheme we have to examine very carefully indeed. . . ." He frowned suddenly. "How about swarf getting in the main conveyor system and choking it up?"

"To start with, it couldn't happen to any large extent because the conveyor's enclosed in the ramp. Where it does – well, when you look at those plans you'll see there's access to the belt for lubrication and cleaning through hatches on each side between each machine. That's where you get at it when you have to."

Green smiled. "You've thought it out, all right."

"Yes, I have."

"But you won't have thought of everything. We'll find a few problems you didn't think of at all, when we look into detail. You realize that, huh?"

"I suppose so. But that's what engineers are for, isn't it? If the plan's right in principle – which it is – let them iron out the snags."

"How about the strength of a hollow steel ramp and the weight of the machines?"

"That's worried me, too. But if when they work out the stresses it's a real problem, the answer is that instead of just one belt inside the ramp, you have two. Divided by a centre-line support. Or four, giving you three supports as well as the two outer ones."

Green nodded. "Yeah, that's good. And if we have to do that, while we were about it we could possibly increase the height of the ramp and have the separate belts on different levels. Two in the middle high up, the outside pair lower. . . ." His voice tailed off. It looked as if he'd gone back into his daydream.

Morrell said briskly, "Shall I leave the plans for you to look at?"

"You do that." Herschel Green sat up straighter, brought his eyes back to Morrell. He told him, "I'm not much give to swearing. But I'm prepared to say right now, *I'll be goddamned.*"

Morrell stood up. He wasn't surprised, but he was about as elated as a man can be. He was trying not to let that show in his face.

"You'll let me know?'

"Yes, I will. Sure. . . . Mind you, Morrell –" he glanced

down at the sheaf of drawings – "mind you, this is going to take a little while. First I have to study the project, then if it holds up I have to talk with Hank Smith about it, and all that'll – hell, quite a few days, anyway. Okay?"

"It's in your hands."

"I guess it is."

Morrell stopped with his hand on the door. "Thanks for seeing me so quickly."

That was Tuesday. Herschel Green's warning that there'd be no developments for "quite a few days" devolved in Morrell's thinking to a minimum of two days, a likely maximum of seven. But you couldn't be sure of that. He warned himself, If Hank Smith decides to talk to McLennan about it before he talks to me, I might have to wait a whole damn month before I get some word.

Please God, not that long! He knew every inch of the floor of No. 3 Machine Shop. Every awkward corner and worn crevice, machine supports where a broom-head stuck: he swept floors, now, in his dreams.

By the lunch hour on Friday he felt sure it was going to take a lot longer than he'd hoped. This was the week-end, now, he'd have no news to give Martha and she'd be full of gloomy warnings. . . .

He was on his way out of the cafeteria when a clerk from the front office came looking for him with a message. Mr. Smith wanted to see him in the General Manager's office at 2.30.

Herschel Green was with Hank Smith when Morrell got in there. Green was sitting in a deep armchair, smoking a cigarette, and Smith was prowling up and down like a caged animal. Not a bad cage at all: not sumptuous, like McLennan's over in Manhattan, but modern, light, big enough to throw a decent party in. Smith had a cigar in his mouth, and from the smell in the room you could tell he usually did. When Morrell walked in, the General Manager wheeled sharp left and flopped heavily into the chair behind his desk.

"Siddown, Morrell. Take your pick." He waved his cigar in the general direction of the vacant chairs. Morrell took the nearest, facing Smith and with his left shoulder towards the Plant Manager. Smith stared at him, exuding Havana smoke.

"Hello, Morrell.'

He returned Green's nod, then looked back at Smith. He felt it was time to break the silence. "Nice to see you."

"Yeah, ain't it." Smith stared at him down the cigar. Morrell thought, remembering the habit as one he'd noticed before, He *does* use it like some kind of weapon. Defensive, perhaps: a symbol of where he's got to and his anxiety to stay there. Smith muttered, "I thought you were my friend."

"Aren't I?"

"– and you do this to me." Smith glanced at Herschel Green. "You too. You coulda thrown it out. Think I don't have enough pains in the head already?"

Green chuckled politely. Morrell just watched, waiting for the act to finish and the action to start. Smith said, "You got hired to push a broom, not turn the joint on its ear. Sweepin' looks like work, so you sweat out a way to have the shop clean itself, huh?" He dropped his cigar stub into an ashtray big enough to have once been a spittoon. "Well, listen. Puttin' in machinery to pull the swarf out's one o' the craziest ideas a man ever had. You understand me? We should spend Christ knows how many thousand dollars tearin' the shops apart to do the job a buncha idiots with brooms can do? Take all the tools out, build a ramp, holes in the wall, chutes – Jesus, Nick, you'd 'a had to be blind drunk to think of it!"

"But –"

"Hold it." Smith frowned. "Called you Nick then, didn't I?"

"I believe you did."

"Okay. So let's all relax. Nick – Hersch. You know my name. In here, mind, not outside. . . . Like I said, Nick, waste removal don't need automation. But like loonies can get brainwaves, you get home with the second strike. This one rings *all* the bells. Right, Hersch?"

The Plant Manager nodded, his eyes on Morrell.

Smith went on, "Way we've had to pack the tools in, we couldn't find space for conveyors. This way –" he patted the drawings on the desk in front of him – "this way, we can do it. Won't look like you've drawn it, not when the engineers are finished, but it'll set 'em going." He stared at Morrell. "So what do I say – you're some kinda genius?"

"No –"

"Right, I don't. But it's like this, Nick. We see a guy on the shop floor who thinks to turn the power off when it ain't being used, we think 'Watch him – maybe he'll make a foreman'. We get a foreman – well, look, like Hersch tells me, coupla days back, this Pirelli in No. 3 comes up with how to give the cleaners some tool for pushin' up swarf faster 'n brooms'll do it. So Hersch says, 'Let's keep an eye on this bum Pirelli – uses his head now 'n then'. See what I mean?"

Morrell nodded slowly, thinking about Pirelli. Bum, he thought, is right.

"Now I hired you on account you wanted the job, but I knew damn well you ain't no cleaner. Only job I had for you, that's all. No experience we could use, that war stuff don't mean nothin' – so I'm doin' you a favour, Nick."

"I know. I appreciate it, too."

"Looks like maybe I was doin' McLennans a favour, though." Smith looked at Herschel Green, then back at Morrell. He said blandly, "That's all the congratulations you'll get, so make the most of it."

"Thanks."

"But like I said, you ain't a broom hand. Now Hersch here needs a *right* hand. . . . Hersch, you tell him?"

Green cleared his throat. "This scheme of yours will come into it, Nick, but you'll be mixed up in production problems generally. You won't always have your hands clean, but you'll be learning all the time and I imagine that's what you'd want. You'd be kind of a management trainee – all right, Hank?"

"Sure, you could call it that. What d'you say, Nick?"

"I say thanks, I'd like it very much."

"Well, fine."

"But if I could make a couple of points. All right, I'm grateful, and I'd like to work with Mr. – with Hersch. But two things: one, I'd certainly like to learn what goes on in Production, but I don't want to find I'm stuck there. That leads to the second point, which is that I believe my best use would be in selling. I'd like to think that eventually I could move in that direction."

Smith said, "What you make of it is up to you. What you've shown this far, which is two goddam weeks, I'd say you'll end up where you wanna get. Hersch?"

Green nodded. "I'm happy. Production and Sales should go hand in hand anyway."

"I imagine I'll get paid more?"

"Sure, we'll fix that." Smith glanced at the Plant Manager.

"Hersch, that's your baby. . . . Nick, Hersch is your boss as of now. Check in to him Monday morning. Right?"

"I'm very grateful to you both."

Green over-rode the thanks. "Hank, I'll take him along now, if I may, and run over the ground generally. That all right with you?"

"Sure." Smith put a new cigar in his mouth. "About this scheme of yours, Nick. You shouldn't get excited if we don't go through with it. When it's costed and detailed I have to take it to the board, get McLennan's okay. Maybe he'll say we can't spend all that dough right now, interrupt current production, that kinda –"

"But you wouldn't have to interrupt production. If the ramp and everything was prefabricated in sections – you could make the whole thing here, couldn't you? – and the shop prepared with holes bored for the mountings, everything like that ready, then you could do it in one night and be running again in the morning shift." He asked Smith, "Well, it's not impossible, surely?"

Smith lay back in his chair, watched the smoke of his new cigar drift up towards the ceiling.

"Hersch.'

"Yeah?"

"Oblige me, Hersch. Take him away, willya?"

III
Fifties

CHAPTER TWELVE

Toni

Half an hour more, and they'd be landing on Antigua. Toni McLennan turned from the window and glanced at her husband, who'd been silent since he'd breakfasted on several cups of strong black coffee. Gil was watching his waistline, these days, but in any case he never wanted to eat much when he was travelling. They'd dined in New York, and slept through most of the overnight flight down the eastern seaboard. Now from the 'plane's starboard windows you could see Dominica, San Juan, a haphazard sprinkling of smaller islands in a milky-blue morning sea.

She put a hand on her husband's arm. "Gil, I want to talk."

He smiled at her: his left hand came across and patted her hand where it rested on his other arm. "Nothing to stop you that I know of."

"Question."

"Let's have it."

"This man Baines. Our host. Does he have any connection with the company?"

"None whatsoever. Why?"

"Does he want something from us?"

"No, honey, Baines doesn't want a thing except the pleasure of having us along." McLennan shrugged. "How he gets his kicks, I guess. You know, admire his boat, little parties, right kind of people, all that?"

"Will his wife be on the yacht?"

"Wife, hell. He's a – well, its a couple of years since I saw Cam, but unless he's had an operation or something, no, he's not married and won't ever be."

Toni wrinkled her nose. McLennan told her, "There's no harm in him. Just neuter, I guess. That all the questions you have?"

"No, there's more.... Gil, I've been thinking. About the Trust."

She saw the flicker of hard interest in his eyes.

"I've been thinking that if I were going to persuade the other trustees to make such a big investment in McLennans, I'd need to give them some positive assurance – well, guarantee – about how the money would be used."

"It's your damn money."

"No, it isn't. It's the Trust's money. I have the income, and now I'm twenty-five I have a say in how the Trust's administered. That doesn't make it my money any more than it's theirs."

"You're right technically, I suppose, but –" McLennan lit a cigarette – "the Trust was formed for you, not them. They're appointed to help you run it, that's all. In any case, all they have to know is we have an expansion programme, we intend to diversify in certain directions – hell, Toni, this is *McLennans* we're talking about. Let 'em make their own enquiries if they want to."

"That's not quite the point, Gil."

"How? If it's not, what *is*?"

"I'd rather you didn't bawl in my ear."

"I'm sorry, Toni." He looked away from her, frowning. "I guess I don't like to think anyone in his right mind could doubt the profit, let alone safety, of investing in McLennan stock. Why, in the last five years I've –"

"I know all that, Gil. The fact remains this would be a colossal investment. The Trust would be putting quite a lot of its eggs in one basket."

"If they know a better damn basket, let them go –"

"Bankers like security, Gil, you know that. Two of them are bankers. They like to spread their risks."

"Sure, I know bankers. Hell, if I'd had to rely on those goddam creeps, McLennans 'd still be a little two-bit –"

"Nobody's suggesting there's anything wrong with McLennans, Gil. It's simply that if you want the Trust to lend you that much money, they're going to want to know how you're using it. What you need it for in the first place, and then how it's being used and administered from – well, in the company's day to day operations. Surely that's quite reasonable?"

"The hell it is." McLennan stubbed out his cigarette. "*I* run

McLennans, and I'm not selling out to any long-nosed banker. I can get what capital I need any time I want it – and you know how? By saying I want it, that's how. People have faith in me, Toni, they've seen what I've done already and they know I'll be doing a hell of a lot more next week, next year. Why, I could have a drink with half a dozen guys I know on Wall Street and just let it drop I could use a little capital, any figure you care to name, and by God I'd have 'em competing to lend it to me! I don't have to accept strings from some lousy banker. Only reason we've discussed this like we have is that it might 've been a two-way advantage. I'd get what I'm going to need pretty soon, without talking to outsiders, and your Trust would get stock in McLennans, which is like buying a roomful of solid gold mice all randy as hell. Reproduce 'emselves twelve times a year. All you need do with mice is leave 'em to it, and that's how it is with stock in my company." He glanced at his wife. "Toni, you're getting –what, five, six per cent? Hell, you'd treble your income. And the capital value of the investment – well, maybe I'm wasting my breath. Your trustees are like that, the hell with 'em. You don't need more income, they want to – what d'you call it, 'spread their risks'?" He chuckled briefly. "Let 'em go and spread shit, for all I care."

"I'll suggest that." Toni glanced up at the stewardess, smiled and nodded. She told her husband, "They want us to clinch our belts, Gil. Well, you could be right. What I was going to propose was that if they made this investment you'd invite them to have their own nominee on your board."

"In a million years, I'd agree to anything like that!" McLennan smiled as he pulled his seat-belt tight and locked it. "Take a banker on my board?" He chuckled softly to himself while Toni looked out of the window by her seat, watching green islands rush up out of blue Caribbean glitter. "Honey, I'd do that like I'd keep a rattler in my pants."

Toni was thinking, with her face close against the window, If I had a child, or children, I'd be worried stiff at every take-off and landing. It would be nice to have a reason to be scared, a reason to *need* to stay alive instead of just preferring that as the alternative to being dead.... She sat back from the window, glanced at the smile which still lingered on her husband's face. She thought, looking at him and keeping all the thought inside her, Why can't you give me a child? You give me everything else: why not a child? Why don't you try harder or see a doctor or *some* damn thing?

She'd been to her own doctor and to a gynaecologist, and every kind of check and test had proved her normal, capable of conceiving and of bearing children. It would have been easier, in a way, if they'd told her that she couldn't.

McLennan said, just as she braced herself for the shock of the wheels touching the runway, "There is one person I can think of whom I'd accept on the McLennan board to nurture your Trust's interests."

"There is?" She was watching the edge of the runway leaping out, and behind the plane the soaring tops of trees. "Who?"

"You, Toni."

The wheels touched, bounced once, thundered....

"No, Gil, that's not on. First I wouldn't enjoy it, second I don't know enough to fill the bill, third – well, if the Trust did invest in McLennans there'd be a condition that nobody should know it was my money."

"Why would you want that?" He looked puzzled.

"It's how I feel about it, that's all. Gil, is *this* the airport?"

"Yeah, that's Coolidge."

"But its no more than a hut!"

"Exactly what it is." McLennan was loosening his seat-belt. "In the war it was an enlisted men's recreation room. Wasn't any airfield here before that. We built it, not the British.... Well, let's – oh, I beg your pardon –"

Sliding sideways out of his seat, he'd almost hit a shaky, elderly man who was being led down the aisle by one of the stewardesses and herded from behind by a tall, copper-haired girl young enough to be his granddaughter. She looked as if she might be some kind of show-girl. Toni, assessing her with one glance and Gil's interest in her with another, imagined the red-head might earn her living in a Las Vegas floor show. In something like three bits of tinsel. But judging by the weight of diamonds on her fingers it would have to be a darned fat living.

"I'm extremely sorry. Clumsy of me." McLennan, standing in the edge of the aisle, was eye to eye with the girl. Toni couldn't see his face, but from the tone of voice she knew the brand of smile he'd be wearing.

"Please don't mention it." Heavy lashes fluttered, and she flicked a glance at Toni. Toni smiled. The girl slid past McLennan and weaved provocatively after the small, old man who'd now reached the exit with the stewardess still gripping his arm as if she was scared he'd fall. He had a walking-stick in his other hand, and he certainly looked frail. They heard the girl ask, as she closed up behind him, "Are you all right, darling?"

Toni smiled at her husband. "Love's young dream?"

McLennan, grinning, helped her out. "Guess he must lash his to a toothbrush."

"Gil, really." Toni frowned, reaching back to the seat to gather up her bits and pieces. She thought, I'm twenty-five, Gil's fifty-seven. That creature's younger than I am, and that husband of hers can't be much less than eighty. At least I'm not in it for the money.

Well, what *am* I in it for?

She told herself, Don't be silly. I married Gil because he's an attractive man, a powerful personality, a *man*. He offered me the kind of world I want, and I have it. So why ask silly questions?

In the airport building, if you could call it that, when they'd been cleared by Customs and had their passports checked they found themselves with the show-girl and the old man again. Their host, Cameron Baines, had sent two cars with West Indian chauffeurs: one was for them, and the second for this other couple.

"Mr. and Mrs. McLennan? And Mr. and Mrs. Baines?"

"Sure, I'm McLennan, but –"

He looked at the old fellow leaning on his stick, still puffing from the exertion of a slow walk across the hut. "Your name is Baines, is that right?"

The girl's lashes went up and down like fans. "Why yes, Mr. McLennan! I'm Ava Baines, and this is my husband Eustace." She put out a hand to Toni. "Mrs. McLennan? Why, we must be fellow guests!"

Toni touched her hand. McLennan asked the girl's husband, "You're related to Cameron Baines?"

"Cam's my son." The old boy looked cross. "Thought he'd be here, darn it –"

"Darling, I'm sure he must be busy on his boat!"

"– ought to be here. . . . You *Gilbert* McLennan?"

"That's right."

"Heard of you."

McLennan smiled. "I'm flattered."

"Don't know why you should be." He inclined his head a little towards Toni. "Mrs. McLennan, I'm delighted to make your acquaintance. However, I'd like very much to get wherever we're supposed to be going, if anyone happens to know –"

"This way, sir, please, Mr. Baines." One of the chauffeurs managed to drag his eyes from Ava Baines. "My car's right here."

"We're going to that damn boat?"

"No, Mr. Baines sir, to the Beach Hotel. Very comfortable –"

"Thank God for that. Well, let's go." He looked at Toni, and nodded. It was like an ancient tortoise considering a lettuce. "Mrs. McLennan –"

"See you later, honey.' Ava smiled at Toni, then at McLennan. She took her husband's arm and towed him to the car.

The other driver touched his straw hat. "This way, lady 'n gen'leman –"

"Give us five minutes, will you?' McLennan muttered to Toni, "Come in here and we'll have a drink. Let those two get in the hotel and out of our hair. Okay?"

Walking beside him into the Coolidge bar, Toni asked him if he didn't think it was a bit early in the day for drinking.

"Can't see why it should be. Well, have a coke, if you like. But if you take my advice you'll try a rum punch. The rum they have here is Barbadian – not heavy like that Jamaican stuff, and not as light as Cuban." He smiled at her. "Long, iced, maybe a little on the sweet side –"

"I surrender."

"Sensible girl, Toni." He stared at the barman. "You open for business?"

"Yes, sir!"

"Give us two rum punches with plenty of ice." He led Toni tc a chair. "Look, I wanted a word before we get all caught up with those goddam peasants. First, tell me why you wouldn't want it known you had money in my business?"

Toni thought, Because I wouldn't want people saying "Oh, so *that's* why he married her!" People like that bitch Martha Scotland, who *still* thinks she'll get Gil one day. And I don't want the others sorry for me, either, whispering to each other at cocktail parties "Poor little Toni. He's just using her like he used that weretched Elizabeth".... I don't want them thinking those things, and they wouldn't be true in any case. If I persuade the Trust to invest in McLennans it'll be because it's good business – good for both sides. It would be stupid not to do it, really. Gil's right, McLennans is a winner, it's going places.

She told him, "I have to meet your colleagues socially, don't I? Not just employees, but associates, customers and so on. Well, I want to meet them as your wife – not as your sleeping partner."

"Hey, that's good!" McLennan slapped the table. Then the barman leant over, put their drinks down. Tall, frosted.... McLennan handed him a bill. "Keep what's left."

"Thank you, sir!" McLennan ignored him, turned back to his wife.

"Toni, that makes sense, what you just said. I hadn't thought of it that way, but you're absolutely right."

"I can't see it matters, since you won't consider letting the Trust appoint a nominee."

"Is that their idea, or yours?"

"I suppose mine."

"So I have to conclude you wouldn't be happy to leave the whole thing in my hands. Is that correct?"

"Of course it isn't. I happen to know those trustees, that's all, what they'll be likely to accept and what they won't. To them I'm just a little girl, anyway a scatterbrained female. Anything I recommend has to be backed up about seven different ways before they'll look at it without smirking."

"Okay, I see that now. But I can't see any way I'd –" he looked up from his drink. "Toni, you've obviously given this quite a little thought. What kind of man d'you reckon they'd want to foist on me?"

"Left to themselves, they'd suggest a banker, as you said. No, I know, you wouldn't – but now, look. I did think of one particular individual whom I might be able to persuade them to accept."

"Who's that?"

"Seymour Laing. Being more or less a relation of mine, that would satisfy the trustees, probably, and since he's a friend of yours it seemed to me he might – well, it was just an idea."

"I'd say it could be a good one. You like that drink?"

"It's delicious, Gil."

"Yeah ... Seymour Laing, huh? Now that *is* a thought. He

could be a useful man to have. He's a fine lawyer, and politically he's – well, he's in the swim, all right –"

"I was thinking more because he's your personal friend."

"Don't want to get too much carried away with the friendship stuff, honey." McLennan smiled into his glass. "Business...." He shrugged. "Still, we should think about this a little longer. Right?"

Cameron Baines met them when the car got to the Beach Hotel. A tall man, narrow-shouldered, with eyes close together and crowding his large nose so effectively that Toni thought perhaps they resented having that proboscis separate them at all. He pressed her hand very lightly, then let it go.

"Not too rugged a journey, I hope, Mrs. McLennan?"

He had a way of pursing his lips together when he was waiting for the answer to a question.

"No, it was very pleasant, thank you." Toni glanced around at the foyer of the hotel. "Are we staying here?"

He nodded. "You expected to be taken straight aboard the yacht, of course. Yes, well, I had intended that, but then I thought perhaps after the flight you might all prefer a night here before we move to –' he smiled deprecatingly – "I trust no less comfortable, but perforce less spacious accommodation. To – is the word 'unwind'?"

Toni thought, Christ! A whole week or more, cooped up in a little boat with *this*.... She glanced at her husband, wondering how he could possibly have let her in for such an ordeal. And without a word of warning. Hell, if there'd been a word of warning, she wouldn't have been standing here in the beam of that almost unifocal smile.

"I believe you already met my father and his – er – wife. On the plane?"

"That's right, we did." McLennan smiled. "Striking woman." Baines quivered: McLennan added, "Unexpected pleasure to meet your father, Cam. He seems a – well, for his age –"

"He was a great character in his day. Unfortunately he's – h'm." Baines looked back at Toni. "I suppose in time we all – er –" he glanced down at his watch. "Goodness. Getting a little absent-minded myself, I'm afraid. I've arranged for pre-lunch cocktails on the terrace. If you'd care to inspect your room, and so on, then join us there when you're ready?"

Toni said, "That'll be lovely."

"Yes." Baines led them towards the lift, beckoning a porter as he went. "Let me tell you briefly what I have planned for our immediate future. Mrs. McLennan. This evening at six we have drinks aboard the yacht. From there we move on to a supper party to which we've been invited, at Mill Reef. Well, Gil knows all about Mill Reef, but it's a club, American membership exclusively, kind of an outpost of ours in this British island. Oh, there's a central guesthouse, and the members have bungalows they live in, that's the kind of place it is." He nodded. "The most *hospitable* place, I can tell you, on this island. So then we return here for the night, and tomorrow at about noon, if we all feel up to it, we'll sail for Martinique."

Toni couldn't say anything to Gil in the lift, since they had the porter with them. But as soon as they were alone in their room, she let him have it.

"Gil, how *could* you? I don't care if he's *fifty* times a millionaire, he's *weird*!"

"Yeah." McLennan stood looking at her, rubbing his silver head. He seemed as numbed as she was. "You're right. He's gotten worse."

"He's –"

"A whole lot worse. . . . Well, Martinique, he said. I'll have the office cable me there saying we have to fly home fast. You'll only need to stand it a couple of days, maybe three depending on how fast his damn boat moves –"

"Gil, I'm by no means certain I could stand three days of your friend Cam. When you throw in Cam's grouchy father and his tarty stepmother, it looks to me like the kind of holiday you'd reserve for war criminals."

He chuckled. "Three days isn't much, Toni. Be gone in a flash. Well, what an experience –" He saw the way she'd reacted to that line, and dropped it. "Look, I don't want to offend Cam. I've known him a long time, and –" McLennan opened a door. He said, "Shower and john. Well, that's something."

"And *what*, Gil?"

"Well, you know the situation. I'm going to need a very large new infusion of capital. Cam Baines is one guy I can get it from just like that." He snapped his fingers. "So naturally I wouldn't –"

"Is that why we're here, Gil?"

He dropped his jacket over the back of a chair, and began

to loosen his tie. "Not exactly. Maybe a little business along with the pleasure."

"Some pleasure!"

"I told you, he wasn't always like this."

"He is now, though. Gil, you won't need his money, will you, if my trustees agree to come in with the capital you want?"

He stood still, staring at her.

"You going to ask them?"

"I can't see why not, if you'll agree to Seymour Laing joining your board."

"You think your trustees'll buy it on those terms?"

"They'd find it difficult not to."

"Then you're right, I don't need a damn thing from Cam."

"Anyway, you couldn't work with a man like that."

"Oh, you're wrong, honey. I can work with anyone. I *run* the show, remember? Nobody has to like me, I don't have to like them. I *run* it. Any case, you're right, I don't need him. But I'm not going to offend him if I can help it, because one day I *might* need him. We'll go along as far as Martinique."

"If you called the office now –"

"No, he's got this place organized for all of us, they're on his side. Switchboard, porters, all of 'em. He could catch on, and I don't want that. Tomorrow, before we sail, I'll cable, and they can wire the boat or the consul in Martinique."

"Three whole days." Toni kicked off her shoes dejectedly. "The things we do for our husbands. . . ."

McLennan crossed the room, barefooted and with his shirt pulled out of his trousers. He said, "Just one *important* thing you have to do for me, baby."

"Be nice to Cam?" She began to laugh. The idea was so horrible it was funny.

"No." He put his hands on her shoulders, bent and kissed her eyes. He murmured, "Nothing like that. Just stick around. All the rest of my life, just stick around. That's all I ask."

She thought, half mesmerised by sunlight on the tiny silvery curls on the side of his neck, Yes, that's all. That and around a hundred million dollars.

She pulled his head down. "You're sweet to me, Gil."

Eustace Baines opted out of the evening's entertainments. He'd appeared for luncheon, and then retired to his room.

When the rest of the party assembled again just before six o'clock, Ava told them her husband had decided to spend the rest of the evening in bed so he'd have enough strength to enjoy the remainder of the trip.

Ava was wearing a silver sheath which left about half her body naked and fitted the rest like a coat of paint. Her stepson, her senior by at least twenty years, had closed his eyes convulsively at sight of her, just as if he'd suffered a sudden stab of toothache. But Toni noticed Gil bristling like a dog: if he'd pranced round Ava on his toes, growling, his interest in her wouldn't have been much plainer. Toni found herself not caring. Ava Baines presented no threat: she was so obviously what she was – a caricature, even, of her type – that you could laugh with her as much as at her, see her as a kind of joke played on the male sex. A highly effective joke, too: her own husband's reaction to the girl was a perfect illustration of the childish vulnerability of men. All Ava had needed to do was tart herself up with cosmetics and scent, arrange a little additional uplift on her well-filled bra, drop the neckline a bit, totally bare her back, and ensure that the dress clung to her bottom tightly enough to show and even exaggerate its every movement. A few small preparations such as these, and her instant-mix had the great Gilbert McLennan grinning and gibbering like something in a cage.

Toni thought, I could do it too, if I wanted to. My figure's as good as hers, maybe better. If I had the inclination plus the nerve to get myself up like that, I could have any normally sexed man acting like a randy schoolboy inside of thirty seconds. Gil included.

She caught Ava's eye, and smiled. Ava drifted towards her. Toni murmured, "At least the party's balanced. I mean, you and Cam –"

Ava whispered, "Guess I'd sooner play with your man, honey. If you don't mind, that is?"

"Within reason, I don't mind." Toni's smile was as sweet as Ava's. Gil, she knew, was watching them both over Cameron Baines's shoulder. "As long as you don't leave me with our horrific host."

Ave gurgled with amusement. "Now careful, honey! That's my *stepson*!"

They were drinking rum swizzles, a mixture Toni hadn't tried before. It tasted more of angostura than of rum, and its sharpness made her shudder. But you got used to it, she found, and accepted a second at about the time Ava had her third: then Baines came over with Gil and suggested it was time to move down to his yacht.

"Car's waiting, and my captain will have everything ready for us. At least, I sincerely hope we'll find that's so."

"Captain, eh?" Toni smiled at Ava. She asked Baines, "Does it have a large crew, this yacht?"

"Well, no, quite small actually. There's the captain, two deck-hands, and of course the cook. The cook is also the steward, pantryman and bartender." He smirked. "Well, he has only the five of us to look after.... Now, Mrs. McLennan?" He was offering her his arm, as if they were about to take the floor for a Mazurka, or something. "Shall we make a start?"

Behind her, Toni heard Ava's now familiar gurgle, and Gil's husky "My dear, please allow me?"

Toni thought, She'd allow him any damn thing he could think of. Funny thing is, though, I like her.... On Cameron Baines's arm, Toni swept in through the glass doors. She thought, hysterically, There should be a band in here, bursting out with *Here Comes the Bride*. This whole thing's ludicrous: there's no reason why we should be here, going through this crazy performance.

All we need now is to get seasick, on his awful boat.

Their car stopped on the wharfside right opposite a white-painted ship's stern. The yacht appeared to have her bow anchored out in the basin, her stern secured like this to the jetty. A plank gangway with a rope handrail connected ship to shore.

They all climbed out of the car. Ava murmured, "Not very big, is it?"

Baines frowned at her. "Seventy-eight feet overall. That may not be big, but – oh, here comes our captain."

A dark, strong-looking man in his middle thirties was coming across the gangway. At first glance, Toni thought there was something vaguely familiar about him: suddenly she realized that she knew him. Baines was saying, "Now I want to introduce Captain Morrell, who'll be looking after us. A fine seaman, I may say, even a *distinguished* seaman. Am I right, Morrell?"

Toni looked from Morrell to her husband. She couldn't understand it. She saw he didn't understand it either.

Morrell was completely relaxed. He grinned at McLennan, and saluted Toni. "Vacation job, that's all. Only heard this morning my boss was among the passengers." Toni saw Morrell's eyes linger on Ava Baines: she glanced at Ava, and knew at once that Gil was out of the running completely. He was shaking hands, now, with Morrell.

"Nick, this is about the goddamnedest surprise! I thought you were back there in Hoboken, building ships."

"Been selling some, lately."

"I know it, Nick, I know it and my board knows it and I can tell you you have not heard the last of that. In fact when we get a moment there's a couple of matters I'd like to chew over with you. Maybe later on we could –" McLennan caught Toni's look and registered its warning. "Hell, we've got seven, eight days –"

"I had no idea you were – er – connected –"

Cameron Baines looked as if now he did know it, he didn't much like it. McLennan glanced at him in a casual, friendly way.

"Nick here is one of the up-and-comers in my organization, Cam. He'll be up there where he's noticed before much longer. Right, Nick?"

"It's a nice thought." Morrell looked at Baines. "You have all my background in my letter of application and from the interview I had with your attorneys. I've worked in McLennans since 1946 – that's six years now. You'll find it all there if you look."

Baines looked embarrassed. "Your qualifications to sail this yacht were all that concerned me, Morrell –"

"Nick, you've met my wife, I think. Toni?"

"Certainly I have.' Toni felt herself almost flinch from the warmth in Morrell's eyes. Surprised by her own reaction, she forced herself to meet it squarely. He was saying, " – haven't had a chance to congratulate you on your marriage. So let me do that now." He glanced away, towards McLennan, and caught Ava's eye instead: Toni saw it happen. She said quickly, "You haven't met Ava Baines. She's *this* Mr. Baines's stepmother."

"Stepmother?"

Ava told him, "My husband is Eustace Baines, Cam's father.

He's not feeling so hot tonight, so he's staying home. In the hotel, that is." She turned to Cameron Baines. "Cam, we can take the Captain along with us to Reef Mill, whatever you call it, now can't we?"

"Mill Reef – well, Ava –"

"*Sure* we can." She looked into Morrell's face with eyes that moved a little, studying his features as she spoke. "Could you bear to act as my escort tonight, Captain?"

Morrell said, glancing at Baines, "Can't think of anything I'd like better. But I'm a paid hand. It's entirely up to –"

"That's all right, Morrell." Baines sounded peevish. "Mrs. McLennan, would you care to step aboard, now? Perhaps you'd like to see your stateroom, then we'll have a little drink. Gil? Now Ava, come along, we don't want to stand here on the –" He asked Morrell, "You have it all ready down there, I hope?"

Toni went ahead, over the planks and on to the yacht's stern. She heard Morrell answering Baines, telling him he'd find everything as he wanted it: the cook, he was saying, seemed to know his stuff all right. She was on the yacht, now, and their voices were a mumble on the jetty. Then Ava, stepping off the gangway, moved up beside her.

"All right, honey?"

Toni smiled at her. "Do I get mine back, now?"

'Sh!" Ava winked. Gil was coming over the planks, behind her. She whispered, her head close to Toni's and her hand on her arm, "The Captain's *just* my kind of man!"

Toni suddenly resented both the contact and the intimacy: she moved sideways so that Ava had to let go of her arm as she turned to look back at Gil. Her own reaction bewildered and annoyed her. Five minutes ago, when it had been Gil to whom Ava had been deploying her rather obvious charms, all she'd felt was a mild amusement, the tolerance one can have towards a wayward but intriguing child. Now, it was an effort to keep the smile on her face and the friendly tone in her voice. She murmured, "Well, good luck...."

CHAPTER THIRTEEN

When he woke up, he felt as if he'd run a dozen miles and then had fifteen minutes' sleep. The cook was shaking him by the shoulder.

"Better drink that while it's hot. More if y' wannit."

"Thanks." He looked at his watch. Eight-fifteen: he'd dropped Ava at the Beach Hotel all of four hours ago. He sat up, thinking, Hell! That message for Gil McLennan.... The cook was still standing there, staring at him. Morrell scowled. "Well?"

"Want breakfast?"

"I don't think so."

"Rough night, huh?"

"Wouldn't say that." He followed the direction of the cook's eyes. Ava's stockings, on the chart table. Christ, he thought, how careless can a man get? Of course, we couldn't put a light on.... He said, as if it didn't matter, "One of the – well, some woman changed in here, that's all."

"Yeah." The cook nodded. "They all do that. Specially when they have their own cabins for changin' in." He grinned. "Don't worry about it, Skipper. Amount I see, if I talked much I'd 'a gotten dead years back."

"You'll be dead in thirty seconds if you don't get out of here."

"Okay." The cook slopped over to the door. He was going to have to smarten himself up when the passengers moved in, and he was making the most of an easy life. "Some time I might ask you not to see somethin'. Like a drowned body, maybe. Who knows, could be Cameron Baines's." He scratched his belly. "What time they comin', Skipper?"

"Better be ready for 'em by eleven." He nearly added, "The McLennans won't be coming." He stopped himself in time, remembering he hadn't had the message yet. The cook shrugged, and shuffled out. Morrell leant up on one elbow, and began to sip his coffee. He thought, I hope that old man sleeps as heavily as she says he does. If he forgot to last night, I could have trouble coming.

After they'd seen their cabin and had a preliminary drink in the saloon, the McLennans had asked him to show them round the yacht. It was a yawl, actually, seventy-eight feet long with twin diesel auxiliaries. In the wheelhouse, where Morrell had his own bunk and locker, he'd shown them the radar, echo-sounder, ship-to-shore telephone and various other equipment, but he'd realized that Gil McLennan was less interested in the inspection than he was in the opportunity for a private chat.

"Nick, first thing I want to say is this. You got yourself into my organization and you've been doing a damn good job ever since. Don't imagine I haven't been aware of it, because I have. Soon as I heard you'd started with us, I said to Toni, 'That guy'll go places, now. He's got what it takes, and then some.' Didn't I say that, honey?"

"Yes, I remember."

"Sure. Well, Nick, you may have wondered how come we never had you up to visit with us at Greenwich?"

"No, I didn't. It never occurred to me."

"I guess it might have done, at that. I'll tell you, Nick. Toni and I talked about asking you more than once, and we wanted to have you out there, you can take my word for that. But you see, you've been working all this time for Hank Smith, and I have to be careful not to tread on his toes. Fellow like him – well, he gets sensitive. I couldn't invite you home without I have him along too. Now Hank Smith is a fine man, good manager, none better. I think the world of him, believe me. But to mix Hank Smith in with our kind of people – hell, Nick, you know what I'm talking about. Be like giving strawberries to a pig, wouldn't it?"

Morrell started. McLennan had slipped the phrase out as smoothly as if he'd been paying his General Manager a compliment.

"So that's the reason we've had no social contact, Nick. Well, you're smart, I guess if you did think about it at all you'd have known it was something like that, huh?"

"If I *had* thought about it."

"Yeah, well, it's nice of you to take it so pragmatically. You have your head screwed on, all right."

Toni had been fingering the wheel. She turned round, now.

"It was also to save you embarrassment, partly. I heard you

ran into the Hamiltons some place. When you were only –" she smiled – "sweeping? They appreciated it couldn't have been easy for you."

Morrell laughed. "It didn't worry me nearly as much as it did them. It was a cocktail party: I didn't even know my hosts. Martha Scotland took me along."

"Martha Scotland?" McLennan glanced up with what looked like keen interest in his eyes. Then he noticed the way Toni was watching him. He looked away. "See much of Martha, Nick?"

"No, not much. I run into her now and then." Morrell told Toni, "At that time she was one of the few people I knew in New York. I used to take her out fairly often."

"We haven't seen Martha in years, have we, honey?" McLennan looked up at his wife. "Don't even see her picture much, like we used to, in magazines and – you know, modelling stuff. Maybe she's not doing that so much."

"Last time I saw her she told me she was keeping busy mostly in television."

"That so? Well, that's where the money is.... Nick, what I said about us getting together, seems to me the time's coming when we can do something about that." He tapped his forehead. "I have an idea in here that I want to discuss with you. Not now – later, maybe, or tomorrow. Right now I want to ask you to do me a considerable favour."

"Anything at all."

McLennan pointed. "That telephone. Can you speak to New York from here?"

"Certainly."

"Fine. Nick, my secretary gets in the office around eight-fifteen in the morning. I want you to call her tomorrow at eight-thirty. Now we'll say I want you to check on a contract I'm worrying myself sick over. I'll fix it with Cam Baines to-night so you can make the call for me. What I really want out of it is for my secretary to tell you there's a real mess brewing and I should get back to New York just as quick as I can. Think you can fix it to go like that?"

"You want to duck out of this cruise?"

"Bet your sweet life we do. You'll fix it, huh?"

Morrell nodded. He was sorry. He'd been looking forward to seeing more of Toni.

"Come up to the hotel in the morning, then, soon as you've

made the call. We'll take breakfast together, and we can discuss this other thing without any need to hurry. That okay with you, Nick?"

Morrell nodded again. "Sorry you won't be with us. There'll be wonderful swimming on some of those beaches."

He was looking at Toni when he said it. She smiled. "Some other time, Nick."

"Yeah." McLennan stood up. "I'll buy one of these things myself. Build one, maybe. Then we can choose our friends, huh?" He frowned. "Nick, you shouldn't need to take vacation jobs when you're working for McLennans. Well, we'll talk about that in the morning. We'll talk about a lot of things. Right now, we better go back to the others."

The party at Mill Reef had been going full blast when Ava announced that it was time she went back to the hotel. Eustace, she explained, might not be sleeping too well, he sometimes didn't when he'd taken himself to bed real early. She didn't like to think of him all alone and restless while she was out enjoying herself. Besides, he wouldn't know where his pills were if he did wake up and needed to take another.

Cameron Baines looked first surprised, then approving. A number of people expressed regret. As the general murmur died away, Morrell said, "I should get back to the yacht, too. I'll drop you off at the hotel, if you like."

He'd driven out to Mill Reef on his own, following the others, since their car was crowded enough. He had a car which he'd hired, after some hard bargaining, for the duration of the yacht's stay.

Toni murmured to her husband, "Just hark at duty calling."

McLennan chuckled. But the look of approval had deepened on Baines's face. "That's a good idea, Morrell. And you'll have her ready to sail by noon?"

"Earlier, if you want to."

McLennan said, "I guess noon would be early enough for most of us. Eh, Toni?"

"I'd second that."

Ava kissed everyone goodnight.

"Well, Captain – I mean, Nick – if you really will be so kind –"

"It's no trouble at all, I promise you."

In the car, she mimicked him. "*No trouble at all*, huh?" Her hand stroked the back of his neck as he drove. "How d'you know I won't give you trouble, Nick?"

"If it's the sort of trouble I'm thinking of, I want it."

Her other hand moved into his lap. "Why, I believe you do...." She leant closer, kissed his ear: he jerked, swerving dangerously as her teeth suddenly nipped its lobe. Ava laughed, her breath warm on the side of his face.

"For God's sake! You want us to end up in the ditch?" Her voice murmured in his ear, "I've been waiting all night to be like this, just the two of us.... You knew that, didn't you, Nick?" She had the zip down now and her fingers were inside his trousers. "Didn't you know it, all the time?"

"I know, *I* have been.... Ava, what happens when we get to the hotel? Wouldn't it be better if we went to the yacht?"

"I don't think so, Nick. See, I go up and make sure the old bug's asleep. If he's not, I feed him a pill. I pick up my costume and a towel and you take me swimming. Not the hotel beach, mind –"

"We're going swimming?"

"Why not?"

"And you need a costume?"

"Little bikini. Just so's to get it wet.... Nick, put your arm up higher?"

She moved his nearside hand higher on the rim of the wheel. Then she squirmed away from him, sliding her hips over against the door: she ducked down, pushed her head under his arm. Her face was in his lap, now, and she was using both hands to open the front of his trousers wide.

He braked the car and stopped close into the side of the road against flowered, sweet-smelling bushes. Jasmine? Ava had turned her head, resting it in his lap, looking up at him, her face like a big white flower. She asked him, "Don't tell me we're out of gas?"

He lifted her back to her side of the car. Getting himself straight and zipping his trousers, he told her, "I can't drive when you're doing that."

She was in the hotel about five minutes, but it felt like ten. He sat waiting for her in the car, parked in the shadows of palms. Then he saw her coming out, the moon bright on her silver dress as she crossed the open space between the hotel and the lines of cars. She slid in beside him.

"Old coot's out cold. We could be doing it right there in the room and he wouldn't know a thing."

"I don't think I'd enjoy that, much."

"I could make you enjoy it any place, Nick."

"Yes."

"But I want to do it in the sand. What beach we going to?"

"St. James. Some way, but it's a good one. We should have it to ourselves."

"We'll need to, I guess."

He started the car, and set it moving. "Except that anyone else on it at this time of night will have the same reason to be there."

"Only not as much." She put her arm round his neck, stroked his cheek lightly with her fingers. "Nick, you won't be – hell, *gentle* will you? Please? You're strong, Nick, I want to *know* it. I'm sick of an old man's paws feeling round, all that creepy kinda fiddling like I'm some *object d'art* – know what I mean, Nick? I don't care if you hurt, I'd rather that than – Nick, you understand me?"

Morrell put down the empty coffee cup and lay back, thinking about Ava Baines. She'd been here on this bunk with him a little more than four hours ago. After the St. James beach, he'd brought her back here to clean up and get her clothes on: well, that had been the excuse for coming to the yacht. She'd argued that it wasn't necessary, that if anyone saw her going into the hotel or if her husband had woken before she got back it would be best if she looked as if she'd been swimming. He'd pointed out that she could use the swimming as an alibi anyway, she had a wet bikini and a towel to prove it, but if they were lucky and nobody knew she'd been out at all then she wouldn't even need to mention it. So why not wash the sand off?

All he'd wanted was to make the night last longer. He hadn't wanted to let her go.

He thought, If anyone saw us, anyone awake up there on the shore, they might have thought it was some kind of threshing shark, beached and frantic at the tide's edge. . . .

Eight-thirty. Morrell rolled off his bunk. Time to make that call, then go and find McLennan.

"More coffee?"

"Thanks."

"Sure you don't want more to eat?"

"Yes, I'm sure." He'd eaten a large breakfast, out here on the hotel terrace while Gil McLennan toyed with a couple of pieces of thin toast. For a big man, McLennan didn't seem to have much appetite.

Pouring black coffee, McLennan said, "I'd like to hear about that contract for the harbour-patrol craft. How did you land it, Nick?"

"The short answer is – by not tendering." Morrell spooned in sugar. "It was pretty obvious when we examined the specifications that if we met them in detail we couldn't be competitive. We weren't equipped to do it. So I had them draw up an alternative that suited *us*. It had to fill the bill they wanted – speed, range, draught, capacity, deadweight and weapon-load, all the essentials, but come out in a design we could handle with a minimum of re-tooling. When I'd got it and had a few more changes made, I took it down to Washington and talked. Well, I was lucky, I didn't have to start from scratch because one of the key men in that department was commanding a destroyer when I was in New York with *Wildoak*. You know, the ship you mended for me?"

"That was a piece of luck, all right."

"It didn't affect the decision. It gave me the access I needed, that's all, saved a lot of time and closed doors. As it turned out, they liked our design better than their own. And of course, our price couldn't have been beaten by anyone else. So –" Morrell shrugged – "Bingo. And we had the lot instead of just a share of the programme."

"Three years work, Smith reckons."

"On the face of it. But it could be done in two."

"Well, that's –" McLennan frowned. "They wouldn't pay in two, anyway. The deal was it's spread over three years, isn't that right? They have to keep it inside their estimates, Nick."

"Not on this one. The three-year stipulation was to match what they reckoned as minimum period for complete delivery. We deliver in two years, we get paid in two."

"Assuming you're right about that, how do we do it?"

"I've left some proposals on paper for Hank Smith to look over. I'm pretty sure it's viable."

"Okay, we'll go into it." McLennan shook his head. "Be fast work, Nick, if we can pull it off. And I'm not sure it's generally in our interests to rush it, when you take in other commitments already on hand."

"I hope when you see it you'll find those doubts vanishing. That contract seems to me something of an object lesson. Instead of tendering to precise specifications, if we produce designs to fit not just one contract but to cover a much wider range of requirements – with adaptations, of course, but I mean *basic* designs – we're moving from single or small orders to mass production. Save a year on the harbour patrol ships, we can use it on whatever we pull in next."

"As you see it, this is only a beginning? There'll be more?"

"I can't see it any other way."

"Well, we can discuss it when you're back at work." McLennan smiled, and lowered his voice. "Talking about fast work, Nick, how'd you make out with the beauteous Ava?"

"Make out?"

"Now, Nick –"

"I dropped her off here, after the party. Did it go on late, at Mill Reef?"

McLennan laughed. "Okay, so keep it to yourself. Hell, if I'd been in your shoes –"

"H'm?"

"Guess I'd keep it to myself too. All right, Nick. You had yourself a good time though, huh?"

"It was a good party up to the time I left."

"Yeah." McLennan stared at him, half smiling. "You know, Nick, I'll tell you something. You're my kind of guy. We can cover some ground together, you and me. You go with that?"

"Certainly."

"So to kick off with, as from the date of your return to New York you'll be appointed a vice president of McLennans."

"You mean that?"

"Sure I mean it. You declining?"

"Jesus, no!"

"Okay, then. Now a new subject. That yacht this crum Baines has. Reckon we'd find a market if we turned out a few like it?"

"No, I don't."

"Steel hulled?"

"No. It's a one-off project, nothing in it except headaches. For us, I mean. What I *have* been thinking about quite a lot is smaller stuff, the pleasure-craft market. Family cruisers."

McLennan slapped the table. "Nick, I knew I was right, I damn well knew it! Your mental tracks and mine have a remarkable tendency to converge."

"You mean this is what you were leading to?" McLennan nodded. Morrell said, "I've roughed out a few thoughts on it, during the past months. It's like this. The basis of it, I mean . . . we already have the two-car family as a sizeable hunk of our society. Now boats are coming into the same category. Soon it'll be the two-car and a boat family. Not sail, I don't think – they don't have time to drift around and enjoy it, they want to be able to press a button and go from A to B in the weekend or whatever time they have. Power – plenty of power, on safe, comfortable, well-furnished family cruisers. And no timber hulls now – fibre-glass. It's the biggest persuader of the lot – a man who sweats his guts out five days a week doesn't want the chore of scraping, varnishing, all that. He probably doesn't want the expense of it, either. He wants a boat just like he has a car – pack the kids in, and off he goes. . . . Now in *this* market, we could make a killing."

"You're talking sense, Nick." McLennan called a waiter. "Bring us another jug of coffee, will you?" He looked back at Morrell. "I've been thinking around it on much the same lines."

"You realize it's going to cost quite a pile of money to set the thing up?"

McLennan smiled. "Nick, that is a detail which needn't cost you a minute's sleep. If it was a headache at all, it'd be mine, not yours. As it happens, there's no headache in it. I don't want you quoting me on this, not even inside the company, but you can take my word for it that McLennans can put up the dough when it's needed without so much as a call to the goddam bank."

"That's good to know."

"Sure. Now, Nick, I tell you what your programme's going to be. First, like I said, you become a vice president of my company. Second, I'm taking you away from Hank Smith. Oh – salary. . . . Well, you come and talk to me when we're back on the job, and we'll fix that up between us. That's no kind of worry, none at all –"

"It worries *me*."

McLennan frowned. "I said, we'll fix it. Okay?"

"Okay. Thank you."

"I want you to move into the Manhattan office. You'll have six months to get out a complete survey of the pleasure-craft project. Think of it as a separate division of McLennans. I want market research, designs, cost of plant and labour, selling – all broken down to detail. Yeah – and a budget to cover the first three years' trading. Think you can do that?"

"Of course I can. Would you aim to run it from the yard at Hoboken, or set it up on a new site?"

"Nick, how in hell do I know the answer to that? Until I see your report, how do I know any damn thing about it? You have to give *me* the answers!"

"Right. But one question, off the record?"

"What record are you talking about?"

"It's personal. Why are you giving me this job?"

"Why?" McLennan snorted. "That's a damn fool question, but I'll give it a better answer than it – yeah? You want something?" The hall porter had come over to their table: he was standing beside McLennan, waiting for a break in the conversation.

"Your reservations to New York, Mr. McLennan. You and Mrs. McLennan are booked out on the midday flight."

"Great. Thanks." He turned back to Morrell. "Give you the answer to your question. Nick, this is what most of business is. Picking the right guy, putting him in the right job and then handling him so he uses himself to his own best advantage. Business is people, Nick. You remember that, you won't go far wrong. . . ." McLennan glanced round, stretching. "Now I have to take the glad news to Toni, and break it like it was all deep sorrow to Cam Baines." Standing, he held his hand out. "Thanks for what you've done for us, Nick."

"Thanks for the breakfast. And everything else too."

"Thank yourself, not me."

Morrell sat down, and pulled the coffee jug towards him. It was a big one, and McLennan had left him nearly all of it.

He leant back, enjoying the cool of this new Antiguan day while he began to collect his thoughts. He had a lot to think about, and all of it was pleasant. Sudden, too: like putting in your last coin, and *clunk,* three lemons in a row, jackpot. . . .

It struck him that however well things went from now on, however high he climbed, there wouldn't be many mornings quite as good as this.

CHAPTER FOURTEEN

He had the same view that McLennan had, only from one floor lower in the building. He enjoyed it: it was more than a view, it was a slice of his own history. Over there across the Hudson he could see where he'd brought *Wildoak* in and docked her with her damaged bow. He could half close his eyes and see her, like a ghost ship, creeping up the river. Ten years ago. He thought, I'd been at sea fighting a war for five years then, and I reckoned I knew what it was all about. I was a babe in arms, I hadn't *started* learning! And that yard, those buildings behind the cranes: he could see himself walking in there in his shiny shoes and smooth grey flannel suit, looking for a starting point but even more than that wanting just a job, something that would pay for a bed and a reasonably full belly. Only eight years ago. I'm the same man that walked in there, and I'm in the hundred-thousand a year class.

But that's nonsense. I'm not the same man at all. How in hell *could* I be?

He'd been a vice president of McLennans now for about three years. The boatyard he'd set up, higher up the river, was a thriving section of the business. He'd planned it, set it up and brought its products to the market. To start with he'd given McLennan more than just the plans, figures and budgets he'd been asked for: in the same folio he'd presented a draft contract already agreed in principle with General Motors for the supply of engines, spares and servicing. The contract was based on quantity, planned output: it assumed the marketing success forecast in the plans. The terms were excellent, but only on that mass-production basis. If the pleasure-craft project had flopped or even fallen short of expectations, McLennans would have been committed to accepting delivery of a stream of expensive hardware they'd have no use for: that, or facing enormous cancellation fees. It had been a calculated risk: nobody had needed to spell out to Morrell the alternative to complete success.

McLennan, he remembered, had told him in one of their conversations during that strange interlude in Antigua, "Business is people". Morrell thought, turning away from the window as his secretary came into the room, It's not: it's people plus risk. You took your hunch on people, and you had to trust your own acumen to evaluate the risk. Then you went in, right up to your neck. In this case he'd gone in and come out with all the plums. Too many plums, apparently, to suit Gil McLennan. That was what this morning's meeting was going to be about.

His secretary had put a file on his desk. He asked her, "That the stuff for the meeting, Priscilla?"

She nodded. "It's all there. All you asked for, anyway. And I put in copies of your reports from London."

"Oh, you have?"

He couldn't think why he should need those. They contained, when you boiled them down, one simple message: success. He had all the figures in his head, and what they added to was the fact that at the London Boat Show the McLennan pleasure-craft division had repeated the success it had achieved in the New York Boat Show last year. Bigger orders than any other exhibitor in the same categories. And free publicity by the column-yard.

Like falling off a log.... But of course it wasn't. To get these results he'd worked like a slave every day and quite a lot of nights and week-ends for three damn years. There'd been construction difficulties, labour trouble, design snags and a near breakdown of the General Motors contract when Gil McLennan had taken it on himself to try re-opening negotiations in order to get more favourable terms. General Motors' reaction had been first incredulity, then anger: there'd been a weekend when it had looked as if they might pull out altogether. Morrell wouldn't have blamed them if they had: McLennan, by proposing a revision of the terms, had given them the "out" if they'd wanted to take advantage of it. As it was, Morrell spent the weekend practically on his knees to the motor giants and using language to McLennan which under other circumstances would have been enough to get a man fired. By the Tuesday it was all patched up.

If the G.M. agreement had fallen through, it would have cost McLennans a packet. They could never have had such terms again from any other supplier, the costings on the boats and the servicing guarantees would have gone to hell, the whole basis of the operation would have been threatened. Morrell had made an issue of it at a special directors' meeting.

Seymour Laing was on the board by then, representing some financial Trust which had put huge reserves into the company. Laing had backed Morrell, who was asking for the board's formal recognition that he himself was in sole charge of the new division and that there'd be no further interference from the President or anyone else without full prior discussion. Morrell had made it plain that without complete acceptance of this, he'd resign. He'd meant it, too: better to get out than stay in and fail.

McLennan hadn't taken it lying down. If it hadn't been for Laing, the whole project might have blown itself to pieces there and then. But Laing carried power, stockholding power. As an experienced politician he knew how to combine the actuality of power with shrewdness and personal tact. The resolution had been accepted not as an indictment of McLennan's blunder but as a statement of policy for the future of the pleasure-craft division. When at the closure of the meeting Morrell had shaken McLennan's hand – McLennan smiling, murmuring, "No hard feelings, Nick. We're alike, you and I. Now get in there and win, huh?" – Morrell had seen in the hard, cold eyes above that would-be disarming smile a message as clear as if it had been painted on the wall in letters a foot high: *You slip up once, I'll cut your goddam throat*.

There'd been no slip-up. The new division was doing better than even he'd hoped it would. It had made such impact that there had been comment in financial and industrial columns, he'd had his photograph in the *New York Times, Washington Post, Los Angeles Herald Tribune* and *Sun,* the *Baltimore Herald* and a lot of other papers too. In London the *Sunday Times* had run a half-page article on him and his career: the *Financial Times,* after the Boat Show closed, gave him a short but flattering build-up, the *Economist* had drawn attention to the achievements of an Englishman in the American business world, and the *Daily Mirror* had hung an article about the brain-drain on him personally as one of Britain's major losses to the dollar lure. Morrell had received a vulgar, Brighton-type postcard from Pat Pelly with the *Financial Times* paragraph pasted to the correspondence space and the words *All lies!* scribbled underneath.

Nobody could say he'd slipped up.

But Gil McLennan was expecting, this morning, to cut him down to size.

Morrell moved over to his desk. He told Priscilla, "Soon as this bloody meeting's over, we'll get some of those letters out of the way."

She looked worried. "Are we expecting trouble?"

"Hell, no." He grinned at her as he sat down. "A little shouting to and fro, maybe. Fortunately I'm in good voice." He glanced at the time. Ten o'clock: that made it three p.m. in Hamburg. Karl would be back from lunch, by now. "Priscilla, get Karl von Mettendorf on the line. Make it person to person."

Waiting for the call to come through, Morrell began looking through the correspondence which Priscilla had sorted for his attention. After a minute or two, he realized he wasn't concentrating: his mind was on this meeting. He threw the sheaf of letters back into the tray, sat back to consider the immediate and more personal problem.

Seymour Laing had tipped him off. He'd asked Morrell to lunch with him at his club, a couple of days ago. They'd been winding up the meal with cheese when Laing had said casually, "Gil reckons you're being paid too much. He'll be airing his views on it when we meet Wednesday morning."

Morrell sat with a biscuit in one hand and a knife in the other. He stared at Laing.

"Well, he can stuff that. He agreed the basis of my remuneration and that's all there is to it."

"Naturally that would be your first reaction, Nick. But the fact is that you'll soon be drawing more than he's getting himself. It's his business, he's president, and it worries him. Wouldn't it you, in his shoes?"

"Let him pay himself more. It's how we agreed it, he can't squeal now."

"Frankly, Nick, I don't think this is one to meet head-on, not as simply as that. We all know what you've achieved and what the company owes you. *I* don't think you're being overpaid, don't imagine that for a minute. But Gil has something on his side too. Apart from the comparison with him, you're getting twice the salary Hank Smith has, and he's been in the company thirty years, a vice president for twelve. Gil could get plenty of support if he needed to, and it'd be bad for all of us. Now wait a minute, Nick. I want to ask you this: could you take on a bigger load than you have right now?"

"You don't imagine I'd be happy to spend the rest of my life building motorboats, do you?"

Laing grinned. "Lot of men I know would be more than satisfied with what you have already. *Most* men would. You've broken through, but it's still a full-sized job to run your end of the business. You could be content to rest on your laurels."

"I could be – if I was a different sort of man. Don't misunderstand me, Seymour, I'm not trying to say I'm something special. It's just that I don't believe there are so many very special people knocking around. I'm ready to back my own horses, and you can't back a horse if it doesn't get a chance to run."

"Well, I'd put my money down."

"If that means what it sounds like – thanks."

"Nothing personal, Nick. I'm in this business to protect the Trust investment. Which means I take whatever line looks best for the McLennan long-term prospects. If you began to look like a bad bet –" He shrugged. "Well, that doesn't appear likely enough to warrant any expansion of the hypothesis."

"Except that at any time a political situation could arise within the company which might change your mind."

"It could. We're realists, Nick, we have to be. A ball doesn't always bounce straight. Thrower puts a bend on it." He paused. "Nick, what you were saying a minute ago adds up to the fact you want more on your plate than's there already. Right?"

"You could say that. No *immediate* hurry, but –"

"What do you have in mind?"

"In two words – Gil's job."

Laing showed no surprise at all. "Which, of course, Gil knows damn well. That's why he'd like to trim you now. Don't underestimate him, Nick. The boys over there don't call him the Silver Fox for nothing."

Morrell grinned. "Where'd you get hold of that?"

"I keep my ears open. Nick, don't under-rate Gil's value to the company, either."

"I don't. But I'm not expecting kicks in the teeth for prizes either. I don't have to, Seymour. I've had five or six approaches in the last four months. I could walk out tomorrow and –"

"Let's avoid that kind of talk, too. It isn't necessary, it isn't good for the company and it isn't even good for you. There's a saying, 'winners don't quit, quitters don't win'. Old as the hills, but it's true."

"Hell, I don't *want* –"

"Of course you don't. ... I'll tell you what *I* want, Nick. When we sit down at that table on Wednesday, play it cool. Don't say more than you have to. Okay?"

*

Gil McLennan sat back from the table. He said, "I guess that concludes the routine business, unless either of you has anything further that calls for discussion?"

"Yes, there's one thing. Two, in fact." Laing and McLennan looked at Morrell. "As you know, I spent a few days with Karl von Mettendorf in Germany after my London visit. As I mentioned in my report, he was optimistic over sales of the pleasure-craft in Europe generally. Well, I had him on the telephone an hour ago. He confirms all that, but now he wants a free hand right through the Common Market countries. I'm inclined, myself, to let him have it." Morrell looked at McLennan. "The link-up you organized with von Mettendorfs is working very well, even better now Karl has taken over from his father. Although we could possibly do better profit-wise if we sold direct to European outlets, it seems to me it might be in the overall interests of the McLennan organization to tie this one in too."

McLennan looked bored. "The pleasure-craft operation's all yours, Nick. How you paddle your canoes is your own damn business, so long as it pays off." He smiled at Laing. "I seem to remember this very issue was the subject of somewhat acrimonious discussion in this room a year or two back?"

"Well, I'll explain why I'm bringing the matter to your attention." Morrell spoke evenly, ignoring the reference to that row which evidently still rankled in the President's mind. "It's not the simple question of how we market boats in Europe. You're right, I wouldn't need to ask you about that. It's whether I have your approval of using von Mettendorf as agent. McLennans and von Mettendorfs being associated companies now, I can't act just as I like any more than I could take a decision affecting this organization as a whole. I'd be stepping outside my limits – something which I believe would be –" he glanced at McLennan – "shall I say, contrary to the promotion of the joy and harmony which pervade our present relationships."

"You can lay off the heavy sarcasm, Nick."

"I was trying to strike a humorous note. Sorry."

"Even between people speaking the same language, humour can on occasion blow right back in the user's face."

McLennan was certainly on edge this morning: Morrell wondered if something had happened to upset him. He said, "Gil, all I want is your authority to appoint von Mettendorfs as sole agents on the Continent of Europe for our powerboats. Can I take it you're agreeable?"

"Sure. If Karl wants it, let him have it. Anything more?"

"Yes. He – Karl, that is – asked me to raise with you an idea he has in a much wider field. I'm talking now about the organization as a whole, not just the pleasure-craft division. He believes we should give serious thought to establishing a permanent connection in Britain, just as we have with him in Germany. His own interest in it isn't hard to see – he'd be part of a three-way link-up, and it would broaden his own market. He's suggesting we might take over an established British shipyard."

"Does he have a particular yard in mind?"

"No, it's simply a proposed course of action in general terms."

McLennan glanced at Laing. "The Krauts are telling us how we should run our business, now. I thought *we* won the goddam war!"

Morrell said, "He's seen how our methods are paying off here, and he believes if we applied them there we could pull in a lot of business. The British yards are *losing* business, particularly to Japan, and what the Japanese are doing isn't so different from our own pattern in the McLennan yard. If we're interested, he suggests two things: one, he'd be happy to come over and discuss it, and two, Mettendorfs would take a stake in it if we went ahead. That's the extent of what he asked me to convey to you."

"If he feels strongly enough to want to come in with us, I guess we could do worse than think about it." McLennan said, with his eyes on Laing, "Be spreading our money kind of thin. I'd want to know a hell of a lot more about what returns and advantages we'd derive. We have Union troubles here, but my God, the British.... Nick, tell him we'll think about it and maybe have him over here some time. Right now we have all we need to bite on. Eh, Seymour?"

Laing suggested, "Von Mettendorf might like to give us his thinking on paper, elaborated somewhat, as a preliminary to fuller discussion?"

"I'll ask him to do that." Morrell eased back in his chair. "Well, *I've* no more for this meeting."

"There's more, though." Laing cleared his throat. "As it happens we do have a matter of considerable importance to discuss. Primarily, Nick, important to you."

"Me?" Morrell managed to look surprised as well as unworried. He glanced enquiringly at McLennan.

"Seymour will do the talking, Nick." McLennan's tone gave nothing away. "We've been chewing this over before you got in here. If I seem a little short-tempered it's on account I've been sitting in this damn chair so long my arse is paining me." He nodded to Laing. "Go ahead, will you?"

"All right –"

"Excuse me." McLennan rose slowly to his feet. He groaned, rubbing his behind. "Guess I might as well make it easier for myself." He strolled towards the window. "Go on now, I'm listening."

"Nick, I'll start by going over some of our thinking. As you know –" he smiled – "well, who should know better? – one way and another you're getting a hell of a big salary, and the direction we're moving it can't help getting bigger. When Gil asked you to take on the pleasure-craft project, you insisted, and he agreed, that you'd take no salary from that end of the business, only a share of its profits before tax. A darned big share, I might add. That seemed fair enough, particularly as it might not have shown any profits at all, at least for the first few years. You had your salary, as you still have, as a vice president of McLennan's, so from your point of view if you made any more out of the new project that'd be all jam on the bread and butter. Okay, from the company's angle it meant a lower overhead on the new baby, so from Gil's way of seeing the proposition there wasn't much argument against remunerating you on that basis. The way it's turned out, however, is quite another matter. Here's where I come in, Nick, since finance is what I'm here to help Gil with.... The way it is now, you're taking out a real sackful of dollars and pretty soon it might be two sacks and a bucket. Okay so far?"

Morrell smiled. "Entirely satisfactory."

"For you it must be. And you've earned it. We all know that. The pleasure-craft business is your baby, you've done it on your own and nobody's disputing that. You're getting this big cut out of it, but even at the price it's darned good business for McLennans. On the McLennans side, meanwhile, you've surely justified a vice president's salary too. Your idea for speeding up production has paid off several times over, you brought in that first miliary contract and it hasn't ended there either. You've done this company a hell of a lot of good, and Gil's come to rely on you like nobody he's ever had to work with him before. That's right, Gil?"

McLennan, with his face at the window, grunted an affirmative.

"However. As I said, I'm here to watch the pennies. I'll come clean with you, Nick. I've been thinking on the line that you should be prepared to rationalize your salary structure."

"Because I've made a success of the pleasure-craft?"

"Now wait, Nick –"

"Suppose it hadn't come off this well. Suppose there'd been no profits showing yet. If I'd said to you, 'Look, I'm not getting as much as I'd thought I'd get, I'd like you to increase my flat salary' – would you have considered that reasonable? No, damn it, *you* wait! It's the same thing, only in reverse. It's gone well, so you say I should take less. If it had gone badly you wouldn't have paid me a penny more than the original agreement. So what you're saying now is 'You don't make it, too bad. Make it, we'll run out on the agreement.' Well, let me put it like this: we have an agreement, bilateral, and I expect you to stand by it."

"You wouldn't be prepared to discuss – well, even stabilizing your cut of the pleasure-craft profits at something like the present level?"

"I can't see the slightest reason why I should." He checked. Laing had winked, and nodded emphatically. "Well, all right, I'll *discuss* it."

"Thanks, Nick. I appreciate that, and I'm sure Gil does too. But in fact, I haven't asked you to take a cut. All I said was that I'd been thinking on the line that maybe we should consider some adjustment. Never said I was proposing it. It was my feeling that such a course might not be too unreasonable. However, this is what Gil and I have been discussing earlier this morning. I gave him this thought as I've just described it to you, and he came up with a counter-proposal."

"He did, eh?" Morrell threw a glance at McLennan's back.

Laing nodded. "Gil's proposal does not contain any reference to changing the basis of your remuneration."

Morrell grinned. "I knew I had a friend somewhere."

"Maybe you have more friends than you're aware of, Nick. What Gil suggests is that instead of paying you less, we allow you to justify the amount you're drawing by increasing your executive responsibilities. How does that strike you?"

"If you'll spell it out, I'll tell you."

"Okay. The proposal is that you take some weight off Gil's shoulders. That you become, as of now, executive vice president of McLennans. You retain control of the new division, but you also take over full responsibility for all McLennan production and marketing. In effect, chief executive. We'll call you that, if you like."

"You can call me a horse's arse, so long as –"

"Hold it there!" Gil McLennan had turned to face Morrell. He was pointing with a rigid forefinger. "Nick, you're a horse's arse!"

CHAPTER FIFTEEN

Morrell looked round at his guests.... Well, they all had drinks in their hands, they were all talking or shouting at each other, nobody had passed out yet or burst into tears. Presumably the party was a success.

It was the first he'd given in this new Park Avenue apartment. Its purpose, ostensibly, was to welcome Karl von Mettendorf, who was on a visit to New York. He'd come at McLennan's invitation, to discuss the British project. He was planning to be here a week.

While Morrell had been getting the pleasure-craft division into gear, he'd been too busy to be bothered with moving to a new apartment. His rocketing income had suggested that more suitable accommodation might be found, at least something better than the adequate but dingy place he'd rented since he first moved over from Hoboken, but he'd not had time to think about it. Besides, he'd been away a lot. Then when the new business had begun to settle down and he was getting at any rate some week-ends to himself, he'd looked around at the scruffy walls as if he hadn't seen them before, and realized it was time to make a move. Before he'd done anything about it he'd been appointed chief executive of the whole company, so once again he was running flat out to keep ahead of the game.... That was a year ago. Now he had the job tightly in his hands, he'd completed a re-organization and general streamlining of departments and jobs, and there was time to breathe again. He'd asked his secretary, Priscilla, to scout around for somewhere he could live and entertain, and she'd come up with this. It belonged to some well-heeled socialite who'd gone to spend a few years in Paris. He was a young fellow, and he'd modelled the apartment on the one Sinatra had in the film *The Tender Trap*. Big, very modern, and with a bar made mostly out of black glass which lined one corner of the enormous living area. It wasn't much as a place to live in, but it was fine for entertaining. Like now.... Von Mettendorf, he noticed, was talking to three girls at once, and all of them were pretty. Hank Smith, who said he never went to parties nowadays but had consented to drop into this one for just five minutes a little more than an hour and four highballs ago, put his empty glass down on the bar and wiped his lips on the back of his hand.

"Nick, I better leavya. My ol' woman –"

"She won't mind if you're a bit late, Hank. You never come out – so now you're here, let your hair down."

"Ain't enough left for that. Been fallin' out on account of your darn harassment. Christ, we useta have a nice, quiet life, over 'n the yard." He pointed his cigar at Morrell's face. "Next time some goddam Limey busts in wantin' a job, I'll throw him clean out the window." His eyes wandered in von Mettendorf's direction. "Where'd all the broads come from, Nick?"

"Here and there." He changed the subject. "Hank, I'm glad we're still friends. A lot of men in your position would have hated my guts for moving up like I have done."

Smith shrugged. "I should worry.... Hell, I told you once, where you wanted to get, you'd most likely get. Remember that, when I told you?"

Morrell nodded.

"So who's surprised? No skin off *my* arse."

The buzzer went. Morrell murmured, leaving Smith, "Excuse me, Hank." He knew who this would be. Well, he hoped he knew. Gil had been unsure whether he and Toni would be able to make it: there'd been some other party, an official reception of some kind which they'd been obliged to attend, and Gil had said they'd come on from there if they could get away early enough to make it. Morrell told himself, This *must* be her – them. . . . He opened the door: Gil McLennan was alone.

"Well – Gil. Come in."

"Toni sends her apologies, Nick. She had a lousy headache, didn't want to go out at all tonight. I dropped her home at the apartment. Say, this is nice!"

He stood just inside the room, using his above-average height to see around it over people's heads. To see, Morrell thought, and to be seen. Letting people see him and come to him, instead of the other way about. . . . Hank Smith was ploughing doggedly towards them from one end, and Karl von Mettendorf approached more slowly, tailed by girls, from the far corner. Karl, who like Morrell had recently entered his forties, was obviously attractive to women. His height – about the same as McLennan – his yellow-blond head, and that aristocratic charm of his. . . . Morrell wondered if the girls were aware that Karl had a wife and four children back in Hamburg. Well, why should they care? This was New York, not Hamburg.

"Hank! Nice to see you, boy!" McLennan, grasping Smith's arm, turned to Morrell. "How'd you get him out this far? He won't come to *ordinary* folk's invitations –"

"Happened to be this way." Smith asked him, "No wife tonight?"

"She has a sore head, unfortunately. Thanks, Nick. Don't even have to name it now, huh?" McLennan took his drink, and sipped it. "Why, Karl! Good to see you again, boy!"

Watching them, Morrell remembered Karl von Mettendorf as he'd first set eyes on him. Bare-footed, wrapped in a blanket, still shocked with the trauma of destruction and near drowning: trying, with that absurd protest against his men being made to work, to cling to the authority-by-right, the arrogance which had been a part of him. *Had been?* Yes, that was right. Karl was a man of the world, now, a realist. The new Karl von Mettendorf – a power in the world of international business and a strong ally of McLennans – was comfortably at home in these entirely unmilitary surroundings.

Glancing away from McLennan, Karl saw Morrell watching him. He smiled, and nodded affably, a hint of amusement in his eyes, and Morrell realized he must have guessed what his thoughts had been about. He must think of it now and then himself: I would, in his place. If he'd been a little more cautious, if he'd searched properly and seen us through his periscope before he gave the order to surface to look for *Dunnock*'s survivors, I wouldn't be here now.

I wouldn't have met Toni, either.

He wondered if she really had a headache, or if she'd ducked out of coming. She must know, he thought, how I feel about her. Women sense emotional response, and since I'm not good at disguising my feelings she wouldn't have needed particularly sensitive antennae.... When he thought about Toni, he felt a kind of tightening in his stomach.

He joined McLennan, Smith and Mettendorf. He told Gil, "Karl wants a new line from the pleasure-craft plant. A fast two-seater skiboat. Thirty knots and small enough for a car roof. We might think about that, eh?"

McLennan nodded. "Sure. Anything, if there's a market for it. Talk about it tomorrow, Karl, if you like. You staying here, with Nick?"

"No. I am at the Waldorf Astoria. Your office booked me a very attractive suite."

"Good. Quite a few attractions right here, too." He glanced around. "Put Nick Morrell down any damn place you can think of, they're swarming round like flies.... Karl, come out to my place this week-end? Nick, how about you too? Bring him with you lunchtime Saturday, stay over Sunday night?"

"I think so.... Yeah, thanks, I'd like that."

"Fine." McLennan became aware of Hank Smith trying to look as if he wasn't within earshot. Morrell saw indecision and annoyance in his president's expression: then McLennan said, without enthusiasm, "Hank. How are you fixed on Saturday? Bring your wife out for lunch? I'd ask you to stay, but with this pair and a couple more we asked already I guess we'd be short on beds. Could you and your wife make lunch?"

"Nice of you, Gil." Smith glanced at Morrell. "We can't, though. I was telling Nick, Saturday we have to choose between a funeral and a wedding."

"Well, that's a shame." McLennan looked enormously relieved. He chuckled. "Take the funeral. That guy's out of his misery, the other one's just starting it. Nick, isn't it about time *you* got married?"

Morrell drifted away to check on the wellbeing of his other guests. The next time he was near McLennan, Gil asked him quietly, "See Martha lately? Martha Scotland?"

"Not in two years."

"Oh . . . she left town, or something? Hell, don't tell me she got married?"

"May have done. Last I heard, she was on the coast, working in some TV serial. *Peyton Place*, maybe, I don't remember."

"Is that so?" McLennan shrugged. "Well, I'd wondered, knowing you used to be – well, Martha's doing okay, is she?"

Morrell didn't have the slightest idea how Martha was doing. He didn't bother to remind McLennan that this was the third or fourth time he'd asked about her. In the last year the only times Morrell had heard the name of Martha Scotland had been the occasions of McLennan's enquiries.

At the Greenwich Yacht Club, Morrell watched Toni McLennan talking with Karl von Mettendorf and Seymour Laing. Gil was dancing with Helen Laing, Toni's aunt. They'd dined, there was brandy on the table, and Laing and the German had cigars. Karl was saying to Toni, "I think Gil must come to visit us in Germany soon. When he does, I hope we will have the pleasure to welcome you also?"

"Thank you, I'd love that." Toni added, "As it happens, I'm going on a trip in about two weeks' time. To Australia, looking up old friends and relatives."

She glanced at Seymour Laing, who nodded: he knew about this trip, apparently. He and Toni seemed pretty close. A few months ago, Morrell had come across them lunching together in a restaurant which he'd carefully selected as a place in which he'd be unlikely to run across anyone he knew. His was a business lunch, and neither he nor his guest had wanted to be seen in each other's company. It didn't matter that Toni or Laing saw them, since it was McLennan business anyway, but it surprised him that the two of them should have chosen that small, out-of-the-way place to eat in. Well, all right, Seymour was Toni's uncle by marriage, maybe they had family things to discuss – but why do it hiding in a corner?

Cigar smoke trickled from von Mettendorf's mouth. "Will it be a long visit, to Australia?"

"I'll be away a month or so, I guess," Toni smiled. "Silly to go that far and rush straight home. It's a big country and I have friends all over."

"I believe you."

Morrell had spoken without thinking: now Laing was staring at him interestedly, and Karl, after throwing him a quick glance, was smiling at Toni. "Yes. I would guess that wherever this one goes she must have friends."

"Right." Laing nodded affably. "You don't often get beauty and brains in one package – eh, Nick?"

"You don't? Well, I don't want to sound conceited, but –"

They all laughed with him. Then McLennan towered up, bringing Helen back to the table. A minute later they were all busy in some new conversation, and McLennan was leaning back in his chair while a club steward held a light to his cigar: Morrell glanced up at Toni, and she was watching him. An intense, close look, as if she was trying to read his thoughts, contact his mind with hers. When he caught her at it, she held his eyes steadily for a moment before she looked away, joining in the talk. Morrell glanced round the other faces: nobody seemed to have noticed.

"Toni, would you like to dance?"

"Well, Nick –"

"Come on. Let's get out of these fumes."

"Maybe that's a good idea."

McLennan confided to the Laings, "Nick's on a health kick, evidently. Fresh air and exercise –"

"Toni." The band was telling Tom Dooley to hang his head down.

"Huh?"

"You know I'm in love with you?"

"Don't talk such nonsense."

"It's true. I've never felt like this about anyone in my whole damn life. Toni. I shouldn't be saying this, I know, but –"

"You're right, you shouldn't. So stop it, else I want to sit down."

"Are you in love with Gil?"

"That's an impertinent question."

"I'd still like the answer to it."

"You'd *like*. Nick, I have a feeling you get what *you'd* like too easily and too often. That won't happen in this area, so lay off, will you?"

"Toni –"

"I'm not Martha Scotland, Nick. I'm not Ava Baines, either, or any of a dozen other women you've – been around with. I'm –"

"You're Toni McLennan. I know. But it's possible I fell in love with you when you were still Toni Russell. That weekend I spent out there –'

"With Martha Scotland."

"Gil invited Martha. I didn't.'

"Nick, I was young then, but I wasn't blind."

"You were beautiful, but not a patch on how you are now. . . . Well, okay, but that's nothing to do with *now*."

"I think it has. You have the nerve to say now that you – what, *fell in love*? With me, that weekend? Nick, give me credit for just a *little* sense!"

"I know you have a great deal of sense. Toni, believe me, I'm crazy about you –"

"You're crazy, all right. Let's sit down."

"No, not yet. Please? Toni –"

"You're probably crazy about women generally. Comes to the same thing as being crazy about Nick Morrell. You should watch that, Nick."

"You're saying it *sober*, now!"

"I was sober last night."

"More reason to be ashamed of yourself."

He nodded. They were walking in the McLennan garden.

"I've plenty to be ashamed of, I admit that. As it happens I'm not ashamed of any of it, though. None of them ever meant anything to me, and I never let them get any impression they did."

"Just casual."

"I've done nobody any harm, Toni. If you want to set rigid standards, *thou shalt not* this, that and the other, all right, it's sin and immorality, all that. Okay, perhaps I make it easy for myself, but the way I see it is if I don't damage anyone, persuade anyone to do anything they didn't want to do anyway, I'm not inflicting pain, am I?"

"If those are your simple standards –"

"I'm a man, Toni, I *act* like a –"

"Like a yahoo.... Being a man excuses just about everything, huh? You're a big man with a thick hairy chest and you need a woman in your bed. First come, first served. It may be difficult for you to see this, Nick, but the fact you're turning your attention on me now isn't flattering, it's downright insulting. You have the nerve to come to me after all those cheap little –"

"Toni, you've got it wrong. Believe me, you've –"

"Why on earth should I believe you? The way you've racketed around is common knowledge!"

"I'm not talking about that. As it happens, I haven't had much time for 'racketing around', in the last few years. Anyway, what I'm saying is that I'm not – hell, *approaching* you in that way at all. I'm not trying to lay you, Toni. I just –"

"Don't tell me. You want a pure exchange of spiritual affection. Oh, that's you, Nick, that's the *real* you!"

"I'm in love with you, Toni. Sure, I'd like to go to bed with you. But that's only one part of it. I'm *in love* – you understand what I'm saying? I've never felt this way about anyone, ever. It's a bigger, stronger feeling than I knew could happen in a personal relationship. I don't even *understand* it. It's got so much that I had to tell you about it."

"Well, you shouldn't have, and you know it. You should have had the decency to keep it to yourself. Not decency, even – common sense. Nick, I'm Gil's wife – remember?"

"Only too well. If you weren't you'd be my wife, by now."

"I was right. You are the most conceited –"

"No. Well, yes. Maybe I am. What I'm saying is – if you weren't Gil's wife, I'd be on my knees to you, Toni, begging you to marry me. I wouldn't give you a moment's peace until you said you'd do that. I'd do *anything* –"

"Nick, hold it now. Let's look at this from another angle. Now don't get angry, don't let that bloated ego swell up and blind you.... Look at it this way. As a theory, if you like – see if there may not be something in it. You came into Gil's firm at the bottom, after he'd seen you and thought you wouldn't fit. Well, he told me, never mind that. But you got in. You're a very capable, potent sort of character, and you set your aim as high as you could – at the top. So now you're there. You've got half of what was Gil's job, even. There's no higher you can go."

"The hell there isn't."

"How?"

"Gil is chairman and president. He's not getting any younger, so before too long he'll want to take things easier even than he has it now. So he could step up to be the summit man, the figurehead – I mean chairman, period. Someone's got to be president, haven't they?"

Toni laughed. "Thanks for the warning."

"Warning, hell. Think Gil doesn't realize I'm still looking up? It'll happen when *he* wants it, not when I do. But a man can't stand still, Toni."

"You're certainly – open." She glanced at him sideways. "Maybe *too* open, Nick. You should be a little careful, don't you think?"

"No, I don't. It's the way I am. I can't change it, even if I wanted to. I'd make a lousy politician."

"That's true." She nodded. "Well, what I was saying. There you are pretty well on top, for the moment anyway there's no higher you can climb. But you're the kind of man who needs targets, battles, things to go out and win. Aren't you?"

"You could be right."

"So you look around, and think, 'I've got Gil's job, now I'll have a shot at his wife'. How's that for the *real* motivation, Nick?"

"You aren't seriously postulating this, are you?"

"Why not? Isn't it in character?"

"No, of course it's not." He stopped, and put a hand on her arm. They were getting close to the house, now. "Toni, what I've been telling you, I've told you because I had to. Just *had* to, you understand? Not to persuade you into anything, but just to have you know it. And if you ever –"

"Okay, Nick. *If I ever*. Leave it at that, shall we?"

"If that's what you want."

"Yes, it is. And now we forget it. *I'm* going to forget it, Nick. Completely. You've been telling me about – oh, ships, that kind of thing. Not –"

"Not about how I love you."

"No." She turned abruptly, and set off towards the house, walking quickly. Morrell had to hurry to catch up with her. When they got inside, Toni ran straight upstairs: she called without looking back at him, "Thanks for the promenade, Nick!"

McLennan came through into the hall. He glanced up after his wife, then stared at Morrell.

"Taking this fresh air thing kinda seriously, aren't you?"

Karl von Mettendorf pointed to the file which rested on the arm of Gil McLennan's chair. They were in McLennan's office, the three of them, discussing Karl's ideas for a British link.

"Everything we were able to gather without actually making contact with the company is in those papers. The information is of course not complete, but so far as it goes I can assure you it is accurate."

McLennan nodded. "I read through it yesterday. Nick, you've not seen it, have you?" He passed the file over: Morrell reached for it. McLennan said, "Let's hear how you see the Ridgeway setup, Karl."

"Certainly. . . . Well, they have three separate yards, all of which have lost money every year since normal conditions were restored in 1946. That is ten years losing money. Five, six years ago the British government began to subsidize Ridgeway – not only them, because the whole industry was losing ground, only a few exceptions –"

"You mean losing orders."

"That is so. To ourselves, to the Scandinavians, most of all to Japan. So the British government has been – ah – subsidizing to a considerable extent. In the process of doing so they have acquired a large proportion of the Ridgeway equity – in fact they are now the controlling stockholders. They appointed – I think four years ago already – their own choice of chairman, a man named Sir Charles Briscoe. Briscoe was until then a civil servant. That is to say, a state employee." Von Mettendorf shrugged. "I suppose he is still a state employee. One thing is clear: he knows nothing about this business. I believe there cannot be any others on his board who can know much either. Ridgeway is still losing money. This is an embarrassment to the government, who are now responsible for the company direction and results. I am advised they would be very pleased indeed to reduce their investment, to recover a proportion of the money which they have so far put in for their man Briscoe to lose, and at the same time, to –" Mettendorf frowned – "I cannot recall the exact word. They would prefer not to be responsible for this company's operation. You see?"

"So it's a buyer's market.'

"It should be. Who likes losing money? Taxpayers' money, a great deal of it, over these years, and still they cannot make it pay."

"You reckon we could?"

"Why not?"

"Then what's wrong with them that they can't?"

"They don't know the business. They will not accept the necessity for change, new ideas. They don't *have* any new ideas. They employ a great number of men to do very little, instead of fewer men to do more for greater reward. They pay bad men too much, good men too little. A great deal of their plant is out of date. How can they compete with yards employing the latest technology when their tools were old-fashioned before the war began? They antagonize the unions on matters of little consequence, thus creating stoppages and ill-will, but cheerfully allow them to pursue practices which seriously reduce productivity. I mean they are weak where they should be strong, and vice versa."

"Okay, Karl, take a breath. What you're saying is, this outfit Ridgeway is run by a bunch of halfwits."

Von Mettendorf inclined his head. "That interpretation might be justified."

"Can't the British government see that for itself?"

"Apparently they cannot. Perhaps governments are not suited to management of business."

"This man – what d'you call him – Briscoe? Is he wet, too?"

Von Mettendorf smiled. "I have not had the pleasure of making his acquaintance. Judging by the figures, however, and the complacency of his last annual report, I do not believe *I* would offer him employment."

"So if we did go into this, and they let us in, the first essential is full operational control."

"But naturally."

McLennan looked over at Morrell, who'd been listening while he glanced through the documentary evidence.

"What d'you think, Nick?"

"From what Karl says and what I see here, they must all be dead from the neck up."

"Well, now!" McLennan chuckled. "That's a Limey on the subject of his own compatriots!"

"I wouldn't say we British had a monopoly on stupidity. It's not so long since your own plant was quite cheerfully throwing away a big percentage of its productivity."

"Okay, Nick, okay." McLennan winked at Karl. "Have to be careful what you say to this guy. Specially since he became chief executive. Well, Nick, how'd you like to go over there and see if they want to talk?"

"Why me, for Christ's sake?"

"You're the only Britisher on the payroll. You talk the goddam language, don't you?"

"Why not write? You, I mean. To Briscoe."

"Sure, I will. Couple of days before you leave. I'll write saying my chief executive, Mr. Nicholas Morrell, will be calling on him shortly to discuss matters of mutual interest. Aim it so you bust in on him same day he gets the letter. When'll you leave?"

"Not for a month. We have those Pentagon contracts –"

"Don't you think I could handle them?"

"Sure you could, Gil. But it's a thing I started, and I want to see it through. And there's no hurry for this British visit. I could go to England a month from now – if we're sure we want to go ahead on it at all –"

"You'll be looking at it, Nick, that's all. Find out what sort of deal we could get, if any."

"And if it's no deal?"

"See what else there is. . . . Karl, one thing. I understand your company would like to participate in any deal we make in England, is that right?"

"Yes. Provided the business is controlled and operated by McLennans, we would like a stake in it. I think you would not expect me to be more definite than this before there is a firm proposition, all the figures –"

"Of course not. Nobody knows what he's doing until Nick gets over there and back." McLennan stared at Morrell. "I guess we have to wait on his convenience, huh?"

Morrell nodded. "I said, I'll go in a month. Gil, shall we ask Karl to tell us about this new line he wants? The skiboat?"

"Sure. Go ahead, Karl."

"He has another idea, too. I think we should listen to this one very carefully, Gil. A new compact radar they're making in Germany. We might get it cheap enough, on a long run, to install it as standard equipment in the cruisers. Karl, will you talk about that first?"

CHAPTER SIXTEEN

It was fifteen months since his last visit to London. January, last year, for the Boat Show. This year he'd sent a team but he hadn't been able to spare the time himself. As head of the pleasure-craft division he'd have needed to, but as chief executive of McLennans there'd been a host of wider issues that tied him to the States.

Now it was April, which was a great deal better than January as a month in which to visit Britain's capital. The trees were coming out, pale green not yet darkened into summer foliage: the breeze was cool, but it carried the scents of spring.

He was staying, as he always did, at the United Hunts Club. He'd have gone there anyway, out of nostalgia and for old times' sake, and because Johnny still worked the bar, but another reason on this trip was that he'd brought Will Selby and Harvey Stone with him. They were both McLennan accountants, and he'd need them to get down to the nuts and bolts of Ridgeway's financial setup. But he didn't want to be cooped up in the same hotel with them, and his membership of the Hunts Club had come in useful. The accountants were at the Washington in Curzon Street, a stone's throw from the new Ridgeway building.

Morrell stopped, now, looking up at its fifteen floors of glass and concrete. A fine headquarters, he thought, for a big, loss-making group of companies.... With an eye on the traffic, he crossed the road, went up the steps in front of the wide, glass doors. A man in uniform held one of them back for him.

"Morning, sir. Help you?"

"I've an appointment to see Sir Charles Briscoe. My name's Morrell."

"Right, sir!" The doorman's face had changed at the mention of Briscoe's name. He was probably, Morrell thought, an ex-soldier: his reaction had been that of a soldier suddenly aware that the geezer in mufti was a general. He spoke authoritatively to the girl behind the reception desk. "Mr. Morrell to see Sir Charles Briscoe." He turned back. "Take a seat, sir? While you're waiting?"

"Thanks."

Steel-framed leather chairs and sofas, airport-style, lined one end of the foyer. On a table amongst them was a pile of today's newspapers. The doorman stood with his hands behind his back, swaying to and fro, his feet spread in the at-ease position. As he swayed, only one heel rose: Morrell realized, looking at the shape of the trouser leg, that the right leg was artificial. He asked him, "You an army man?"

"Regimental sar'nt major, sir. Airborne Division." His head jerked round as the girl put down her telephone, stood up and came over to speak to Morrell.

"Sir Charles's personal assistant is coming down, Mr. Morrell. Won't keep you a moment."

Morrell stood up. "Tell me which floor. I don't need a chaperone."

"But Mrs. Grierson will be –"

"This lift?"

"Well, yes, but –"

"Which floor?"

"Fifteen – the top. But Mrs. –"

He had his hand out to jab the call button when a light came on above it and the doors slid open. A big, grey-haired woman who must have tipped the scales at nothing less than two hundred pounds moved out of it towards him. Like, he thought, a battleship coming out of dock.... He heard the receptionist saying behind him, "Mrs. Grierson, this is –"

"Morrell."

The woman stepped aside. He wondered how she could have done it so neatly without the aid of tugs. He certainly couldn't have got inside the lift while she was between its doors.

"I was coming to find you, Mr. Morrell."

Reproof, that was. He thought, Roedean. Or Cheltenham. Graduated in weight-lifting and the discus. She'd make a splendid attendant in an asylum where the patients were violent. Maybe she has her uses here, too?

"A great pleasure, Mr. Morrell."

Sir Charles Briscoe placed the tips of his fingers together and smiled at Morrell across his desk. They were long, pale fingers, and he had a long, pale face. Pale eyes, too, almost colourless, and a small, nervous mouth. He wore a stiff white collar above a blue shirt with white stripes, and the shirt's cuffs protruded far enough from the sleeves of his dark suit to reveal cufflinks sufficiently ornate to be classifiable as costume jewellery.

Morrell pushed his hands into his pockets, and leaned back.

"I guess you know what I'm here about. You swapped a couple of letters with Gilbert McLennan. So we both know where we're starting."

"Indeed, yes." Sir Charles smiled. "In broad terms, that is. ... Mr. Morrell, forgive a personal question, but – I was given to understand you were an Englishman?"

"I am. But I've been in the States since the end of the war. I still sound like an Englishman over there, but maybe to you it's not so obvious. Frankly, I don't care if I sound Chinese."

"I assure you, no criticism was implied –"

"I know that. Now, about your company, Sir Charles. The exchange of letters has established two things: one, that you'd be interested in principle in selling out –"

"Shall we say, rather, in some form of merger?"

"How you describe it, that's your business. If we buy, you have to be selling. You want to call it merging – well, I'll stick to plain English, if you don't mind. The second thing established is that we, also in principle, might be interested in buying. You do understand, I'm sure, that if we went ahead on this we'd be interested in nothing less than control of the company, to apply our own methods to its operation. And you're aware, too, that Ridgeway performance over the last dozen years makes extremely depressing reading. If we came in here, we'd make a lot of fundamental changes. In six months, you'd hardly recognize your own organization. We wouldn't put a penny into it, though, without that administrative control, because if we wanted to throw money down the drain there are plenty of easier ways of doing it."

Briscoe looked pained. "Mr. Morrell.... I appreciate, of course, your – directness. But I wonder if you – whether at this early stage you have sufficient knowledge of my company's affairs to speak so – as it appears, scathingly. Ridgeway has indeed been passing through a period of great difficulty. Manifold difficulties, Mr. Morrell. I think I can say that under the circumstances with which we have been faced, we've done a – well, not a bad job. You refer to our past results: it might interest you to know that at the end of this current year we shall have broken even. This year, there'll be *no* loss –"

"No profit, either. To break even, with the size of the capital investment you're sitting on here, doesn't seem to me any cause for wild celebration. Frankly, the situation of this company is terrible. It's deplorable."

"This year's results, compared to recent years –"

"How about *next* year's?"

"I beg your pardon?"

"What's your forecast for next year?"

"Oh. Well, the present upward trend, which as I've mentioned will be reflected happily in the current year's trading results, may be expected – barring unforeseen circumstances, of course – one may expect to see a small profit. . . ." Briscoe suddenly noticed Morrell's expression. "Morrell, to forecast specific results at this particular moment is hardly –"

"How many years of small net profits would it take to recoup eleven years of damn great losses?"

Briscoe stared at him like a person looking at a drunken bridegroom.

"We're turning the corner, Morrell."

"Yeah. Sir Charles, unplatable as it may be, I have to impress upon you that McLennans see this company as a recurrent loss-maker which would need complete overhaul and reorganization if it's to realize whatever potential it may have. Maybe it hasn't any potential now, I don't know. That's what I'm here to find out. But the purchase price of a controlling interest would be only the start of the investment, the tip of the iceberg. What we'd have to look at is the total cost of buying and reorganizing: that's the real cost to us, because we're only interested in the machine if it can be made to work. The cost of a takeover, as we'd look at it, is the price of the equity plus what it'll take to transform the company into a profit-maker. So you'll understand that if we came in at all it would have to be at a very realistic valuation."

"I see." Briscoe frowned at his fingers. "Of course, past performance is one thing, present and future performance quite another. A *trend* in the performance chart must be regarded as significant. As I've told you, we have an up-turn now –"

"What you mean is you won't be losing so much money this year as you did last year and the year before that, and so on back almost as far as living memory. Sir Charles, I'm a crude man, let me put it like this: anything short of good, solid profits is about as interesting to me as a turd in a bathtub. Now if we did come in, and it would have to be at a *very* realistic price, you must realize here and now that we'd install our own management, tear the place to pieces and then stick it together again in quite a different shape. We'd have a free hand to do whatever we damn well needed to get this concern looking something like a commercial enterprise instead of a benevolent trust.''

"Now, really –"

"I'm not exaggerating, and you know it. This business has survived on large annual injections of taxpayers' money to make good the gross inefficiency of its management. Now you know that's true, and there's figures to prove it."

"This would appear to be an indictment of me personally –"

"I don't know who's to blame. I don't care. What I'm saying is that if we take over, *we'll* run it."

"My managing director, Norman Wilmott, is an extremely capable executive, Mr. Morrell. I should have thought even McLennans would be glad of his continuance here –"

"You'd have thought wrong. McLennans would appoint a man of their own choice. From what I've said already, that's fairly obvious, isn't it?"

"Would you like to meet Wilmott?"

"Sure. But first let's have this straight between us. I've told you how we'd approach it. If you couldn't accept that approach, or wouldn't want to, okay, let's stop right here. On the other hand, if you'll go along with it, I'd like to start looking into your company's affairs much more closely than I have been able to so far. Well, do we drop the whole thing, or carry on?"

Briscoe smiled warily. "I see no reason why we should not proceed a stage or two further."

"Okay, then." Morrell smothered his surprise. He was certain that everything he'd said had been received by the Ridgeway chairman with extreme distaste. The fact he wasn't calling off the negotiations seemed like a good indication that the government, who in fact were his masters, wanted McLennans to dig them out of the hole. If that was so, Karl von Mettendorf was right, and a deal on favourable terms might not be too difficult to arrange.

"Sir Charles, most of the Ridgeway equity is in government

hands. So if we did want to go ahead after we've carried out certain investigations, we'd have to talk to the government, I imagine, more than to you."

Briscoe nodded. "That is correct. Although, in fact, my own position is somewhat equivocal. I was appointed to this company by the Minister, and in relation to Ridgeway affairs I think I can say I am his chief adviser." He smirked. "Confidant, you might say. I have a great respect for Mr. Hooper –"

"That's the Minister?"

"Yes, Elliot Hooper. When you're ready to talk to him –"

"It's quite possible I may not get as far as wanting to do that."

"Quite so. But if you do decide that you should meet him, I can easily arrange it for you. He is in fact a most approachable person, but as a Minister of the Crown he naturally has many preoccupations –'

"Yeah. Sir Charles, I have two McLennan accountants over with me, and I'd like to turn them loose in here."

"In *here*?"

Morrell smiled. "Wherever the books are kept. I suppose I can fix that with this man Wilmott?"

"Certainly."

"While they're getting the financial picture, I'd like to look around your three shipyards. Perhaps you'd have instructions passed to the yard managers to let me see what I want to see? And I'd like the names of the top men so I know who I'm talking to."

"By all means. We'll provide you with a car and a chauffeur, if you would like that. You'll need hotel reservations, too, and I'll ask Mrs. Grierson if she'll attend to that."

"It's very kind of you, Sir Charles, but I'd sooner look after myself. I don't want to be tied to an itinerary."

"Oh, but you wouldn't! Well, take one of the company cars in any case. That's the least we can –"

"Thanks, but I'd rather not. If you'd just tell them I'm coming, that's all I want. No red carpets, just unrestricted access and any information I may ask for on the spot. I suggest you let it be known that I'm a potential investor in a smallish way?"

"I think we'll let them guess. Say you're making a survey at my request. Wouldn't that be better?"

"All right. Now I'd like to meet Wilmott – unless there's anything else you'd like to talk about first?"

Briscoe flicked a switch on his intercom.

"Yes, Sir Charles?"

"Norman, I have Mr. Nicholas Morrell with me. Can you spare us a few minutes?"

"Of course."

Switching off the box, Sir Charles murmured, "Wilmott came to us from the motor industry, where he had a considerable reputation. It would do us no good to lose him at this stage, Morrell."

"I don't agree with you."

"But you haven't even met him yet!"

"I've seen a resumé of your company results. That's all I need."

"I did mention, I believe, that the situation is improving. Wilmott must have most of the credit for that."

"He's welcome to it. And the motor industry's welcome to him." Morrell stood up. "What this company needs isn't a pleasant little change for the better. It needs dynamite in the basement. If we take over, that's what it'll get."

"I picked Norman Wilmott myself, Morrell –"

And you have what you call an upturn, so if he stays on and we jack the whole thing up to where it ought to be, you can take credit for hiring the man who did it....

"– contract has several years to run. So if you –"

"We'd have to pay him off. Another item on the cost of takeover, that's all."

"I see. I take it you'll tell him this yourself?"

"Do I impress you as a man who'd be scared to lay it on the line?"

"No." Briscoe smiled thinly. With those lips, Morrell thought, and that tiny mouth, he couldn't do it any other way. "No. I wouldn't say that either sensitivity or reticence were your more noticeable attributes."

"Thanks." He turned, as the door opened and Ridgeway's managing director walked in. Norman Wilmott was about fifty, slim, grey-haired. He looked alert, and fit. Morrell put out his hand.

"Norman, this is Nicholas Morrell. You know why he's here."

"I believe I do." They shook hands. Wilmott, unlike his chairman, had something like a handshake. He asked Morrell, "You want to take us over, isn't that it?"

"I've come to find out if my company might do that."

"You mean, if we're worth having?"

"And if the price makes sense."

"Of course. Well, anything I can help with, just ask for it."

"Thanks. You may come to regret that offer by the time I'm through." Morrell glanced at Briscoe. "May we sit down a minute?"

"Of course, my dear fellow!"

"Thank you. I'd like to say this to Mr. Wilmott in your presence, Sir Charles. So we'll all know where we stand. . . . Mr. Wilmott, I don't know, I simply don't know at all at this stage, whether we'll want to buy control of this company or, if we do want to, whether we'll be able to make a deal that suits both sides. But one thing's certain: if we do, it's *control* we'll be buying. That means we'll appoint a chief executive whom we'd select ourselves. Very likely an American – maybe not, that's for my board to decide. You see, we have our own way of doing things, we do them a little differently from you, but that's how we'd want them done. So we'd need to have our own man in the hot seat."

"I see."

"It's not a personal matter. Please understand that. Sir Charles has been telling me he's convinced it'd be a mistake to let you go. It happens this is the way we operate, that's all."

"Yes, I understand. It'll cost you a packet, though."

"Your service contract? Sure, that's okay."

"In that case, I'm not worried. Not in the least. I'd go back to making cars – they're a damn sight easier to sell than ships, I can tell you!"

"Well, I'm relieved you take it that way."

"Why not? There's at least one job I could walk into tomorrow."

"Only thing surprises me is that you've started to pull this company into shape, Sir Charles tells me, and I'd have thought from that point on you'd want to see it through."

Wilmott smiled. "Satisfaction of the job well done? Kudos?"

Morrell nodded. "All that stuff."

"Well, it's there, certainly. I'd regret leaving, in a way. But –" he shook his head. "I'm not worried about it, Morrell. So don't you be."

"Okay, I won't. But I wonder, now – would you be free for lunch today? I guess you probably do have an engagement, but if you could – you see, I have two of our McLennan accountants at the Washington, just round the corner here, and I'm due to meet them for lunch. If you could make it as well, we might save a lot of time by getting acquainted right away. And I do need to talk to you myself. Could this be possible?"

"Yes, I think so." Wilmott was cheerfully relaxed. He certainly didn't look or behave like a man who'd just been told his job might fold under him. Morrell thought, That must be a wow of a contract he's sitting on. . . .

"Well, fine. Thanks, I'm more than grateful. How about your company secretary? Would you think he'd – well, it's up to you, of course –"

"Good idea. Alan Garwood. If he's free, I'll bring him along. Twelve forty-five all right?"

Morrell nodded. "In the bar. Well, that's a good start."

"Gentlemen. One small matter." They both looked at Sir Charles. "The word 'takeover'. I dislike it, and I believe its use at this juncture would be – er – unfortunate. The entire negotiation must, as I'm sure you're both aware, be treated as extremely confidential, but I suggest it would be to the general advantage if those of us who have to know about it should regard these tentative proposals as – er – overtures possibly leading to some form of merger. Merger, as opposed to take-over. Do you follow me?"

Wilmott nodded. Morrell said, without execessive interest, "We can make that the formula, if you like. For the time being."

"Quite." Briscoe eyed Morrell coldly. "It's not impossible, you see, that bandying this expression 'takeover' about could lead to – er – political considerations arising which might – well, which *could* make progress difficult at another level. I'm sure that on reflection you will see my reasoning."

Morrell put his hands in his pockets. "You tell us the words, Sir Charles, we'll use 'em." He nodded to Wilmott. "See you later, then."

A day was all he needed for his inspection of the Ridgeway yard at Hamble. He'd completed his notes on that area of the operation by the time his train pulled into London. This was the day after he'd lunched with Wilmott and the accountants. He telephoned Selby that evening from the Hunts Club, and Selby told him they were making progress and getting reasonably good co-operation. The story they were putting out in the Ridgeway building was that they were management consultants making a preliminary survey to establish whether there might be a full-scale job to do on the Ridgeway group's accounting systems. They'd decided this was to be the cover all through the present enquiries.

Next morning Morrell flew from Heathrow to Glasgow, hired a car and drove himself down to Gourock. Both the other Ridgeway yards were on the Clyde and within striking distance: he booked himself into the Bay Hotel. Just at the sight of it, memories flooded back. Wartime memories: small, grey ships anchored at the Tail o' the Bank, filthy weather, convoy orders, conferences, the journeys in small ships' boats through rough water and horizontal sleet to attend parties in the bar of this hotel. . . .

He spent two days in one yard and three in the other. Things were entirely different, here: it was another world from Hamble. The only close similarity was the yard managers' tones of frustration when they talked about Ridgeway administration and red-tape controls. Morrell flew back to London with two more thick files of notes, and firm conclusions in his mind.

He rang the Ridgeway office, and got Selby. Sure, they were just about through. This last day and a half, they'd been only filling-in with detail. Now Morrell was back from Scotland, they could wind it up and fly home tomorrow, if that suited him.

"Fine, Will. Now here's what you do. Get on to Pan Am, book us for tomorrow. I'll meet you this evening at the Washington. What time, six?"

"Could you make that seven?"

"Okay, in the bar at seven. Now look. I don't want to have to talk to Briscoe or Wilmott if I can help it. So you see them yourself, tell them I called from Glasgow, I'm flying down tonight or tomorrow and leaving right away for New York. I've asked you to say good-bye and thanks for all their help, etcetera, and we'll be in touch soon as we've done our homework. Okay?"

Selby chuckled. "I'm not much of a liar, Nick, but I'll do it. . . . You know, this is a crazy place."

"London?"

"Oh, sure. But I meant Ridgeway. Wilmott's okay, but –"

"Save it, Will. Seven o'clock."

He'd killed an hour or so shopping, but mostly window-shopping, in Bond Street and Piccadilly. Then he'd strolled up the Burlington Arcade and window-shopped some more in the jewellers' boutiques. At one of them, on impulse, he went inside and bought a pair of Victorian ruby ear-rings. They'd look wonderful, against her slim, tanned neck, brushed by the soft fall of dark hair. He thought, watching the man wrap the little box, *I'm buying jewellery for the boss's wife, I should have my bumps read....*

He hadn't been aware that he was looking for something to bring Toni. He'd been goofing, that was all, killing time, and he'd spotted the earrings and liked them. Next moment he'd been in the shop putting down a ridiculously small amount of money, and only at that point had he admitted or acknowledged to himself that it was for Toni that he'd bought them. He'd done the whole thing like a man in a dream.

Half an hour later, when he saw her, he was as stunned as if he'd been hit over the head with an axe.

CHAPTER SEVENTEEN

"Nick? I can't *believe* it!"

He stood in front of her, speechless with surprise. Wanting to throw his arms round her and hug her, he only held both her hands in his, stared bemusedly into those green eyes with the brownish-golden haloes circling the pupils.

"Toni...." He said slowly, gripping her hands to make sure she was solid and not a figment of his imagination, "I don't understand how this can be for real –"

It was six-thirty, in the foyer of the Washington Hotel. He'd been intending to wait in the bar until the two accountants showed up, and as he'd crossed the foyer he'd met her face to face. In a mink coat and matching hat and with a porter piling her luggage by the desk.

"Is Gil with you?"

"No, I'm alone." She smiled. "Supposed to be in Sydney, Australia."

"So you are." He'd driven to the airport to see her leave:

the Laings had taken her out there, because Gil had been away in California chasing some scheme he'd dreamt up and wouldn't talk about. That was the last time he'd seen Toni, going up the steps into the plane that would take her to Australia. The Laings had seemed surprised as well as pleased to see him there.

His mind was beginning to work again. "Listen, Toni. This isn't a good place for you to stay. Selby and Stone, Gil's accountants, are living here until tomorrow. They'll be walking in that door no later than seven, maybe sooner. You and I know this is accidental, but how would it look to them?"

"They want to make something of it, let them." She looked annoyed. "I decided I'd go home through London to buy some clothes, that's all. This hotel's central, lots of Americans stay here. I'd no idea *you'd* be –"

"Of course you hadn't. But how would Gil see it – you and me meeting here?"

"You want me to hide? Make it look *really* surreptitious?"

"I think it'd be a darned good idea if you went to another hotel. Caesar's wife – you know? Look, the May Fair's just down the road and there's half a dozen taxis right outside this place. Toni, I'd like to take you to dinner tonight, and I can't if you stay here. They really would imagine we had it planned."

"Any such thought would be *purely* imaginative, Nick. The fact we're in London doesn't change what I told you before. You've got to know that. We could be in Timbuctoo, I still wouldn't –"

"All right, Toni, I know. I won't even *try* –"

"Like a leopard changes its spots?" She laughed. "Okay, I'll go to the May Fair. If that's full, the Hyde Park, maybe. Where are you staying – here?"

"United Hunts Club."

"If I don't stop at the May Fair, I'll call you. What time dinner?"

"I'll pick you up at eight-thirty. Okay?"

In the bar, sipping a scotch and water while he waited for the accountants to show up, he couldn't believe it had happened.

"Oh, you're awake, all right!"

They were dining in the Caprice: Mario had professed to remember him, and given them a table against the wall, a banquette table. Toni looked marvellous. He'd found her at the May Fair, and taken her back to the Hunts Club for a drink before they went on to eat. He'd wanted her to see one of his oldest stamping-grounds. He'd offered to take her up and show her the suite he had, but she'd declined, adding that if he'd done any etchings lately she didn't want to see them either.

She told him now, "But you mustn't imagine I had the slightest notion I might meet you here in London. I'll admit I did think of you, once or twice –"

"I'm glad."

"– in connection with this English move Gil's been telling me about. But I thought you'd have done whatever it was you had to do, and gone back to New York by this time. Is it going to add up, do you think?"

"Looks like it might. Be a hell of a job for somebody, though."

"To put them in shape, you mean?"

"Yeah. Toni, let's not talk shop. . . . Oh, look. I found this." He put the little package on the table. "I saw it in a window this afternoon, and – well, I thought it might look nice on you. Go on, open it."

"Now, Nick –"

She hadn't touched the package.

"Believe it or not, I got it about half an hour before I ran into you. Had it in my pocket then. . . . Hell, people bring little presents home from trips abroad, you know? It's only a trinket, anyway."

He watched her hands, her tanned, supple fingers working at the paper with neat, feminine economy. She got one end open, and slid out the little box. Then she pressed the catch, gingerly, as if she was thinking this might be some practical joke: the lid went up, and she was looking at the ear-rings.

"They're lovely, Nick. But –"

"But nothing. I told you, it was just a few shillings. Toni, you're not –"

She'd turned away from him, grabbing for her bag and fumbling in it, pulling out a handkerchief. He touched her arm. "Toni, darling –"

He saw Mario looking at them across the room with eyes which must have witnessed a thousand human dramas, or the signs of them, their momentary surfacings. Mario smiled at Morrell before he looked away. Toni said, composed, clicking her bag shut, "Nick, you should not have bought me these. You know damn well you shouldn't."

"Then I apologize."

"Don't do that either. I love them, and it was sweet of you –"

"It wasn't premeditated or purposeful. I just saw them, and the next thing I knew I'd bought them."

"You walk around in London thinking about *me*?"

"You don't have to ask that, Toni. I've told you how I feel about you."

"Like you think about that Martha creature?"

"I don't feel a thing for Martha. Not a damn thing. I don't feel anything for anyone except you."

"Gil's with Martha now."

"Gil's *what*?"

"That's why he went to California. To see her. I don't know he's with her now, but with me away I don't imagine he's pruning roses. I was *there* when he went off on that phoney trip. He wrote to her before he went, and she phoned him. I heard him talking to her."

"He must be wrong in the head. When he's got you –"

"We get on very well, Gil and I. But he's always had this thing for her. When he was married to Elizabeth, that's why he took every excuse to ask her out to their house. Our house. Like that week-end you came there, in the war. Elizabeth knew all about it, poor thing."

"But he threw Martha at *me*."

"You'd think that, but he didn't. He used you as the excuse to invite her, that's all. Martha had it in for him because he married Elizabeth instead of her. She threw *herself* at you – well, at anyone who was around, practically – to get her own back on Gil. She made sure he knew about it. They used to have terrible rows when they were alone. He had another woman, too, in an apartment he rented for her, but it was Martha he was mad about. I only agreed to marry him on condition he never saw her and I didn't even have to know her. I don't know why I'm telling you all this."

"I'm glad you have. Toni, I'm awfully sorry. Why did you marry that bastard, anyway?"

"Forget it, Nick, please? I don't know why I should have got all emotional like this. I wish I hadn't. Will you forget I told you, please?"

"Why not divorce Gil?"

"Because I don't want to."

"But if he's chasing that little bitch –"

"Two wrongs don't make a right, Nick. I'm married. For better or for worse – you know?"

"Divorce him, and marry me. Toni, will you?"

"That'd be just dandy for McLennans, wouldn't it?"

"*The hell* with McLennans! I *love* you, Toni –"

"And I happen to be Gil McLennan's wife. Now that has to end this particular conversation. I mean it, Nick. Talk about something else, or take me back to my hotel."

He stared at her. "Toni, I don't care how long I have to wait."

"It would be for ever if you did. I warned you, didn't I?"

"You're really thinking of McLennans? Effect on the company?"

"Partly."

"You aren't married to a company, Toni. We're human beings, flesh and blood –"

She looked away. "You'd better take me home, Nick. Will you, please?"

"I'd rather take you dancing first."

"You believe me now, don't you?"

"I don't know, Nick. Anyhow, what's the difference, whether I do or don't?"

"It makes a lot of difference to me. If I could think of a way to convince you –"

"I'd rather you didn't." The candle on their table had burnt low, but the nightclub was still crowded. The band was playing *The Lady is a Tramp*. Toni said, "It would be a lot easier to think of you in your former guise. A randy Limey on the make. A dash of Scottish for persistence, a little Irish for the blarney. I don't know where the English part comes in. Maybe that's what cools the mixture, saves you from being an out-and-out rapist."

"You could be right. You'll admit I don't *dance* like a rapist."

"Only because I hold you off."

"I've been as good as gold. Everyone on that floor's practically – well, it's not because you 'hold me off'. It's because you made it plain you don't want to. I swear to you, Toni, I love you and I wouldn't do a thing you didn't want me to."

"God, how dull!"

"Now that's called being a tease. You can't have it both ways."

"You're right. Crazy, isn't it? I don't intend to give way even half an inch, but I want to think you'd try."

He looked at her. "If I was to try, Toni, really try without thinking about what you wanted or didn't want, it's just possible I might win. And I'd be sorry if I did, because then you'd be *sure* I was what you thought I was. Well, I *am* a randy Limey on the make, I admit it. But I love you, too. Remember that night at Greenwich, the week-end I first met you? I was dancing with Martha and I looked at you dancing with young McLennan, Gil's nephew – hey, did they ever find out what happened to him?"

"Nothing beyond he was reported missing, believed killed. In the Philippines. Gil never had much time for him, I think because he always disliked his sister, Charles's mother."

"That's our Gil.... Well, I had Martha and Charles had you, and I remember you dancing close to us – Martha was scared you might have overheard something she'd just said – and I thought, God, if we could only be the other way around, that Russell girl's a *wow*...."

Toni laughed. "Now there's the blarney –"

"It is not. It's true. And I felt guilty about thinking it because you were just a kid. You were too – and I was twenty-nine. It seemed such a hell of a gap between us. Then you up and marry *Gil*, for God's sake!"

"Don't let's go back to that. Nick, you never mention any family of your own. Don't you have one?"

"No, I don't. I did have a mother and a father, like most people do, but they're both dead and I was their only child. I don't think I have any uncles or aunts, anything like that. If I did, I never heard of them. My mother died when I was about four. She had tuberculosis. My father was a parson, son of a younger son, never had two pennies to rub together. If he had, I suppose they might have saved my mother's life. I don't know. In those days you needed to be rich if you wanted to be ill."

"Nick, that's awful!"

"A lot of people had it worse. I got dragged up, somehow, and I went to a merchant navy training school, the *Worcester*. I was all right then. My father died in 1941, in London. He'd retired, but he took on a temporary job, standing in for some curate who'd joined the Army. A parish on the edge of London. They told me he died of starvation. I wasn't there."

She looked horrified. "Surely that can't be possible –"

"It's more than possible. Wartime rations weren't too bad for families who could lump it all together. But an old man on his own, living in one room with a gas-ring and getting those little bits of food, too damn poor to afford anything outside the ration – well, he was seventy, a little skinny fellow even before it started.... I've never talked to anyone about this, Toni."

"I don't think I've ever heard anything so sad in my life."

"One thing it did for me, all that. It gave me a feeling about money. When I think of not having any, I think of that old man dying by himself.... Toni, you got me on to this, and the evening's beginning to feel like some kind of wake. Let's snap out of it, now?"

"We could dance?"

He pushed the table back. "Your way or my way?"

"Let's see how it goes –"

They were playing *I've Got You Under My Skin*. Morrell murmured into Toni's ear, "The vocalist must have a Sinatra recording of this. He's trying to do it the same way."

"I like it." Her hair brushed his face, and he loved the feel of it. She wasn't holding him off, but he wasn't taking advantage of that either. She told him, "It's one of my favourites. So's Frankie, if it comes to that."

"He came from Hoboken, did you know that?"

"No, I didn't."

"My Alma Mater."

"Poor Nick!"

"Poor nothing. I liked the place. It taught me things."

The man sang, "– *said to myself, this affair never will go so well* –" and Morrell wondered if the words rang the same bells in her that they rang in him. He whispered, "Toni, I've had an idea."

"Gil always said you were the best ideas man in the business.'

"Gil can go to hell. Forget him, will you? Just for tonight?"

"Okay. What's this idea?"

I'd sacrifice anything, come what might –

"A way I could prove to you conclusively that I love you."

"Oh, stop it, will you?"

"That I'm not – what you said – 'on the make', so far as you're concerned.'"

"I believe you. You don't have to prove–"

"But I *want* to. Toni, darling –"

"Don't talk like that –"

"Will you give me the chance to prove it?"

"What'd be the point? It can't lead anywhere."

"It'd lead to you knowing what I want you to know. If you just know it and I know you know, that's – well, I could live with that."

– really a part of me –

"It's true. You – like a part of me. That's absolutely how it is."

"You'll only be hurting yourself, if it is true. Hurting me too if I knew it was. So –"

– don't you know, you fool, you never can win?

"This idea. If I had you all to myself for a couple of days, miles from anywhere, and I didn't touch you, even *try* to touch you – wouldn't that prove something?"

"I don't know. It's impossible anyway –"

"No, it isn't impossible. Nobody knows you've left Australia. You said that, didn't you?"

"Yes. But –"

"Listen. I could send those two guys back on their own. Maybe I want to take another look at the Clyde yards. An off-the-record look, without Ridgeway knowing I'm going back up there. That'd make sense. I'd go up to Scotland, but not there. A place I know called Arrochar. I was there once in the war. It's at the top of Loch Long, and there's a hotel. Very quiet, most peaceful place you ever saw. Just across the way from Loch Lomond. We'd just walk, and –"

"Nick, you must be crazy."

– tried so, not to give in –

"Hear what he said?"

She didn't answer.

"Toni, darling, I'm not asking you to *give in*. That's the whole point. This place is in the wilds, we wouldn't see a soul we could possibly know. We'd book separately, travel there separately, we could have rooms on different floors and opposite ends of the hotel, if you like. You could lock your door and put all the furniture against it –"

"Wear a chastity belt?"

"Full armour, if you like."

"It'd be *mad*. You know that? I don't know why I'm even letting you talk to me about it."

"Let's sit down and talk about it some more. Toni, it'd be like – oh, out of this world. Three days in Shangri-La."

"I thought you said *two* days."

"Long way to go for just two days. The one chance we'll ever have. Four or five –"

"No, Nick. I can't. It's out of the –"

"All right, I give in. Three days. Even two. We could book for two, and if you found you liked it we could –"

"Two."

"Toni – did I hear you say . . .?"

She'd stopped dancing. She was standing quite still, and she had her eyes shut. She said, so quietly that he only just caught the words above the last notes of the song, "Two days, Nick."

CHAPTER EIGHTEEN

It was July, and McLennans had bought control of Ridgeway. After two weeks in London negotiating with the company and with the government, Gil McLennan had telephoned asking Seymour Laing to join him in the British capital. Three days later he'd phoned New York again and told Morrell the deal was clinched: he and Laing were flying on to Hamburg together to finalize with von Mettendorf an off-loading to the German firm of part of the equity in the new joint company, McLennan Ridgeway Limited. Now Karl von Mettendorf had flown with them to New York. It was a Saturday, and Morrell had been invited out to Gil's house at Greenwich to hear about the deal and discuss working arrangements.

From the way Gil McLennan had phrased it on the telephone, and from a remark Seymour Laing had made in another call, Morrell thought he knew what they were going to ask him. He drove out to Greenwich with blank refusal framed clearly in his mind.

The last time he'd seen Toni alone had been at Arrochar. He'd met her once, with Gil, soon after her return to New York. He'd got back a week before her: she told him, in Gil's presence, that she'd travelled home the long way round and stopped off in London for a couple of days to buy some clothes. He'd shaken her hand, asked polite questions about her Australian visit: her left arm had been hooked inside Gil's, and he'd thought the two of them seemed closer than they had in years. He'd been trying, ever since, not to think too much about that.

While Gil had been away in England and Germany, Toni had stayed at their Nantucket home. He'd wanted badly to fly out there and see her: but he'd promised, when they'd said good-bye at Arrochar, that he wouldn't do anything of that kind. In any case he'd had his days full, particularly with Gil away. Running McLennans single-handed was a full-time job.

But driving out to Greenwich on that summer morning he wasn't thinking much about the Ridgeway deal, except that he'd turn down flat the proposition which he guessed Gil and Laing were going to make him. He was thinking mostly about Toni.

They were on the terrace, the five of them – Gil, Toni, Seymour Laing, von Mettendorf and Morrell. They'd had lunch, and later on they were going to swim, except for Laing, who said he'd given up violent exercise twenty years ago. The temperature was well up in the eighties and from where Morrell was sitting the blue gleam of the pool had a draw like a magnet's. So had the sight of Toni, in shorts and a loose, striped shirt. She wore sunglasses, and it frustrated him that he couldn't see her eyes.

McLennan lit a cigar.

"Nick, that's the deal. We've signed to buy sixty-two and a half per cent of the Ridgeway equity. Out of that, Karl here is taking twelve and a half. Leaves us with fifty per cent. But we're in partnership with Mettendorfs, so in fact we carry control with our sixty-two and a half. The other thirty-seven and a half stays with the Ridgeway people, private shareholders and the British government. Of course, if Karl wanted to double-cross us, vote with the opposition, we'd be in deadlock. But I guess –" he stared at von Mettendorf – "I guess we don't have to worry about *that* happening. Eh, Karl?"

"I think so too. That you don't have to worry."

Morrell frowned into the sun. "Why take that risk?"

"Hell, Nick, you don't imagine –"

"It's fine to trust Karl. I would too. But suppose his board swamped him? Suppose someone took *him* over?"

Von Mettendorf shrugged. "Nick, the possibility is – remote."

"I still don't like it. It's control on a knife-edge. There's a hundred ways he could lose control of his own company, you know that as well as I do. Seems to me you haven't got the deal you set out to get."

"I don't much like your attitude, Nick." McLennan's expression made that obvious. "We had one hell of a tussle, over there, and in my view the deal's a good one. The only point I had to give way on is that Briscoe – Sir Charles, whatever you call him, but he looks like a goddam nancy to me – he stays chairman with half a dozen goofs on the board. Their government wouldn't budge on that. Well, so long as we have control, I guess Briscoe can't do much harm."

"He can't? You think he's done them any good, the last three, four years, however long he's been roosting there? That fellow Wilmott's all right, we could use him, but he told me – well, as good as told me – Briscoe and the others wrapped him up so tight he couldn't do half what needed doing."

"Yeah? That's interesting –"

"It was in my report, and we discussed it."

"Sure, I remember now. But I'd say, from what I saw myself, maybe he has done a little good, here and there. And now *we* have the say in what goes and what doesn't."

"I'd suggest it would be a whole lot better if Karl's company took ten per cent instead of twelve and a half. Then you'd *know* you had control."

"God damn it, Nick, I didn't ask you out here to fight!"

"I see. Well, if you don't want to know what I think about it, I might as well get back to town. I don't think you've got a deal this way, I'd call if half a deal. You'll be in the pocket of anyone who gets his hands on that German stock." Morrell looked at von Mettendorf. "Karl, would you accept ten instead of twelve and a half?"

"If McLennans preferred that, yes. But –"

"Yeah." McLennan nodded. "*But*. Nick, Karl's allocation brings our commitment down to a sum we can afford to pay. To give out more than that right now would be –" he glanced at Laing – "well, this way's more comfortable."

"I see." Morrell said, "If it leaves us so strapped, how about the cost of re-organizing the new company? Makes me wonder if we can afford this deal at all."

Laing sat forward. "Nick, maintaining adequate reserves has been a primary consideration. It's to be sure we have the funds we'll need for reconstruction that we've been thinking this way."

"Who else will be providing working capital? The British?"

Laing shook his head.

"You, Karl?"

"It hasn't been suggested."

"So maybe we're going to need a bank loan in England before we even start. Or halfway through. Against the security of our stockholding, which is already minimal to the requirements for control. Right?"

McLennan said tersely, "Sir Charles assured me there'd be no difficulty in that direction. He's not my kind of man or yours, but he'll be useful to us, Nick."

"Puts a lot of power in his hands, doesn't it?"

"Only so far as we allow him to exercise it. We control the company, we control *him*. Nick, stop seeing ghosts!"

"Briscoe's spooky, all right. . . . Well, maybe I'm looking too much on the dark side. Finance is your business, anyway, not mine. My job's to run your organization here, and that's all I want." He glanced over at McLennan. "If you're happy with it as you've described it – well, it won't be my headache. So if it'll make you happy, I'll shut up. Karl, feel like swimming, now?"

"Nick, just a moment."

Morrell looked at Seymour Laing. He thought, Here it comes. Wait till you see the whites of their eyes. . . .

"Nick, there's a certain amount of sense in what you've been saying. The fact is, we could have bought some smaller outfit lock, stock and barrel. But that wouldn't have been what we needed. Ridgeway's right for us. It has – well, you saw for yourself, and you've seen the figures – it has the potential for real big development. To me, and I dare say to you too when you think about it, that makes it a very exciting proposition. As far as finance is concerned, we aren't as strapped as all that. We could hang on to all the sixty-two and a half per cent. But I'm personally satisfied, as Gil is too, that we're equally safe with a quota of that in Karl's hands. So why shouldn't we save the money? Means we get control at a bargain price, doesn't it? Working capital, that's another point you raised – well, that's okay too. The reserves are more than adequate, and if Briscoe did want to make a nuisance of himself, and why the hell he should I'm damned if I know, I guess we *could* get rid of him. So maybe we haven't been quite as stupid, Nick as it's looked to you at first sight."

Morrell nodded. "Let's hope you're right."

Laing continued, "What we do need over there, however, is a chief executive big enough to stand on his own feet and keep Briscoe and his friends in line at the same time as he gets on with the job. A real man-sized job it's going to be, too. So this guy has to be right off the top of the pack. He has to know the business, and he has to be able to work in with us and with von Mettendorfs. He has to be a trouble-shooter: he'll need the strength of Joe Louis and the fighting spirit of a tiger. He'll need to handle people as well as money and plant. There's a phrase I heard or read someplace not long ago, describing the pattern for executive responsibility: the guy has to be 'ruthless in the intent, humanitarian in the execution'. So anyway, this guy we need has to be about a hundred men rolled into one. . . . You know anyone to fit all that, Nick?"

"Sounds like a cross between Leonardo da Vinci and Sir Winston Churchill.'

"I'm serious, Nick –"

"No. I don't know anyone like that."

"No? Well, I do." Laing nodded, smiling. "I do, Nick. I'm looking at him right now."

"*Me?*"

"As you well know." Laing nodded. "You."

"Well, Seymour, it's kind of you, I'm sure, but all that flattery was a waste of breath. Save it for Congress. I'm not susceptible."

"You're an offensive bastard sometimes, but you're the one man for this job."

"You're so damn wrong, Seymour. I chose to *leave* England, remember? I should say I was the last man you'd expect to send over."

"You could do it, Nick."

"Sure I could. And that's a clear indication there must be at least a hundred other men who could do it, too. That fellow they had in the job already – Norman Wilmott. You could get him over here and educate him –"

"Not in a million years." McLennan scowled. "He'd be right back under Briscoe's thumb. *You* wouldn't be, though."

"Damn right I wouldn't. I wouldn't touch it with the longest pole you ever saw, Gil. I wouldn't consider it for ten seconds."

"Now listen, Nick –"

"No, Seymour, *you* listen. I've made myself something here. I'm not saying I've made McLennans, don't imagine that, but it's a fact I've made quite a lot of what's in McLennans now. I enjoy running my part of it. I like the job, the country and the money. I have friends here, it's my home. It's more my home than England could ever be again – this place has formed me, I'm the man I am – whether that's good or bad – because this is where I've been, the air I've been breathing." He looked up at McLennan. "I belong here, and I'm staying. Wait, Gil, I've not quite finished. If you want to make it tough for me, you can buy out my contract. I'd rather leave McLennans than go over to run McLennan Ridgeway."

"There's no question of coercion, Nick. We're *asking* –"

"Yeah, that's right. But think about it, Nick." McLennan's tone was almost pleading. "Give it a little thought."

"I've given it plenty. I had some idea you might come up with this, and I've done all the thinking it needs. The answer's no, Gil."

"You could name your own price –"

Laing stirred restlessly. He looked deeply troubled. "Nick, this is Friday. I'll be coming into the office to see Gil on Monday, about noon. How about us deciding now that you'll think about it a little more over the week-end, and give us your final answer then? I go along with what Gil just said – you can write your own salary in the contract. Anything you want."

"I have everything I want right here." He thought, *Except one thing. One thing I can't even ask for. Would Gil give her to me, if I made that the condition for going to London?* "Except I'd like to swim now.... You mind if I swim, Gil?"

"Why should I mind? I'll join you. Karl, swimming? Toni?"

He might even agree, at that. He's a ruthless bastard....

Toni was the first to join him in the pool. He was sitting on its edge, and she dropped down beside him.

"Hello, Nick."

He smiled at her. "My God, you're lovely."

"Nick, I think you ought to go to England."

"You want to ship me out too, do you?"

"In a way, that's what I want."

"Why? I'm keeping my part of the bargain, aren't I? I haven't even telephoned."

"I know."

"Don't think it's been easy –"

"Nick, I have to talk to you. Sunday, at your apartment?'

"Make it *all* Sunday."

"About an hour, Nick. Say eleven o'clock?"

"Morning or night?"

"Eleven a.m., Nick. I'll have to say I'm visiting Helen, or – now Gil's coming. Sunday at eleven, okay?"

Toni launched herself into the water, breaking straight into that smooth, rhythmic crawl which he remembered watching before, here in this very pool more than a dozen years ago. At this moment, although the picture in his memory was almost as clear as the one before his eyes, the lapse of time felt much greater than it was: it was more like looking back over a whole lifetime, right into some form of childhood, a period before the realities of life had taken over.

"Toni, darling!"

She came in quickly: he shut the apartment door and locked it.

"You should be more careful, Nick. Yelling 'darling' at me down the hallway. Suppose Gil had been with me?"

He put his hands on her shoulders. "Am I allowed to kiss you?"

"No, you are not. We have an agreement – remember?"

"I dislike that agreement. I've more than half a mind to – Toni, would you like a drink?"

"Do you have a coke, something like that?"

"Sure." He told her from the bar, "I'd welcome a real bust-up, Toni. We know how we feel about each other, for God's sake let's stop hiding. I want to go and see Gil and tell him how it adds up. If you'd come too, I'd even take that job in England. Or I'd leave McLennans and stay here. The only thing I want in the whole damn world is you."

"Stop it, Nick. We've had all that."

"Why you should feel any obligation to stay with Gil, when he –"

"Things are much better now. I've no intention at all of breaking up my marriage. Nick, whatever there was between us, it's over and it's best forgotten. As we agreed it would be."

"You forced that agreement out of me. Emotional blackmail –"

"Stop loving me, Nick. Just *stop*."

He put the glass down beside her. "That's a lunatic thing to say. I should just – what, switch off?"

"For your own sake." Her eyes were steady, cool. "I'm in full control of my emotions now. You get a grip on yours. It's over, Nick. I'm Gil's wife, and I *stay* Gil's wife. Quite apart from the fact we agreed it would be this way, things are – I told you, different now. Between me and Gil, I mean."

"So these are my marching orders?"

"Don't make it more difficult than it is. I told you, I've got control of how I feel. It's true, I have. Don't take that away from me, Nick. Please don't try. I'd just run straight out the door."

"I can't understand why it has to be like this. Why you want it. I love you, you told me you –"

"It has to be like this because I'm Gil McLennan's wife. That's why. When I married him I promised things, and I want to keep my promises. At least those I haven't already broken."

"But *he* doesn't –"

"That's over, now. Things are a lot different. . . . Nick, for my sake, won't you take that job in England?"

"Not even for what you call your sake. I think one day you'll –"

"There's no future to look to, Nick, not for you and me. Don't think that if you wait around anything's going to change. I promise you it isn't. It'd be so much easier if you'd go."

"I'm sorry, Toni."

"For *both* our sakes!"

The eyes not quite so cool, now. The green warmer, and the gold alive. But he'd seen them on a Scottish hillside, the day they'd climbed the Cobbler....

More a walk, really, than a climb. From the top, the view was wonderful: Loch Long at their feet, Loch Goil to the south-west, eastward to Loch Lomond. Then Toni had started down, running, running faster and faster, her legs running away with her and her dark hair flying in the wind. Morrell pounding down behind her, hearing her laugh as she ran: she'd tripped on a loose rock, and went flying. She lay still, face-down in the heather: he thought she'd broken something, or concussed herself. He flung himself down beside her and she rolled over, laughing up into his face. He kissed her. It was the first time he'd ever done it: there'd been no other women, ever. But it was the first time he'd so much as touched Toni: they'd been at Arrochar three days, and this was the fourth, the last one, but right at the beginning he'd sworn he'd behave like a saint to prove he wasn't on the make.

He'd never known a kiss last so long. When it ended, neither of them spoke: they were examining each other's faces, still breathless from the run downhill, panting, both of them surprised, overtaken by something they hadn't done themselves but which had happened to them. Toni's lips moved: he watched them closely, thinking, I'm going to kiss her again, now. I can't *not* kiss her again. This time I won't stop at all. It'll go on for ever, the longest kiss in human history....

"Nick, I'll come to your room tonight."

"Why wait for tonight?"

"You mean – *Now*? Out here?"

That wasn't what he'd meant, but he nodded.

"No. I want – comfort. A locked door. Not –" Her hand brushed the heather beside her face.

"Come back to the hotel now. We'll lock the door. Toni?"

He remembered that door closing, the cream-painted wood in front of his face like a shutter on the world, on everything that had gone before. The squeak of the old-fashioned lock as he turned the key: Toni's arms sliding round him from behind as she pressed herself against him. She'd kicked off her shoes, and crept up on him, taking him by surprise while he'd been moving with deliberate slowness, drawing out the moment, thinking, *Now, this is what I've dreamed about, it's happening.*

Her fingers were loosening his tie: he felt them soft and light against his throat. He took hold of them and kissed them before he turned around inside the circle of her arms and kissed her mouth. While they kissed, he found the zip on the back of her dress and ran it down, unhooked the catch of her bra in the soft, warm space between her shoulder-blades: still kissing, he moved back a little so he could push the dress off her shoulders. Then the straps of the slip. She didn't take her mouth from his, but she let go of him, wriggled as she pulled dress and slip up over the swell of her hips. Her breasts were in his hands and he was drowning in the sweetness of her mouth. Then not kissing: she'd tilted her head foward, taking her lips away from his as she looked down: her hands were up between the two of them, wrenching his shirt open button by button until they got down to his belt and they were working on that. His own hands rested on her naked waist, stroked her hips, moved round and met behind her in the sweet smooth hollow of her back then up again brushing the insides of her arms and to her breasts again, his finger-tips playing lightly around the nipples. Her hands jerked suddenly, opening his trousers, reaching down for him, folding, soft and loving, drawing, almost unbearably, exciting. He murmured in her ear, "I can't believe this is –"

"What?"

"For real."

"This is too damn *big* to be real."

"You think it's a dummy?"

"Better not be!"

She was sinking down, sliding down inside his arms to kneel in front of him. He caught her quickly, stopped her, thinking, I couldn't stand that. Not now: not *this* time. She glanced up into his face: she was flushed, and he saw with surprise that her eyes had changed, the green all splintered into the gold. "Nick, I *want* to."

"*I* want us on that bed." He picked her up, holding her high in his arms and bending his head so he could reach her nipples with his mouth. He told her, carrying her to the bed, "I've been wanting this since nineteen forty-four. That's a hell of a long time to wait."

*

"Will you go to England?"

He shook his head, without looking up from the Collins he was mixing. He'd given her a coke.

"There's a reason you have to go."

"Have to?"

"Yes. For my sake. I'd hoped I wouldn't have to tell you. Not as soon as this. If you'd agreed to go, I'd have – well, waited. Nick, I – I'm pregnant."

He crossed the room quickly, and grabbed her hands. "You're saying that –"

"What I say. I'm pregnant. It's going to be Gil's child, Nick. It has to be. Well, you can see that for yourself, *obviously* it has to be. I'm – three months pregnant."

"Three months ago was Arrochar."

"Yes. But this is Gil's child. I made sure of that. My first night back here: he knows, you see? Not about you – I mean that it's *his*. We hadn't been – you know, so good together, Gil and I . . . That's why he – that Martha business, you know? Gil's sixty-four, he's lived it up all his life, he needs – well, things I wouldn't – didn't much care for." She smiled. "I'm a straight girl, Nick. Remember? No – kinks. But I play games now, to – well, get him going. He needs that. You know, Martha's games? I've – you see, this way I have Martha licked. And I have a contented husband who next January will be a father. Nick, don't try to make any fuss about this, because I won't stand for it. All you'd do is hurt us both. We've done this, now, we have to live with it. The way I've just told you – Gil's child. But you must see I couldn't stand to have you walking around, have to see you, pretend there wasn't – I couldn't face the idea of seeing you, and if you stayed here I'd have to. Do you understand now what I've come to tell you? Why you just *have* to accept the London job?"

"It seems to me a damn good reason to stay right here?"

"Nick, *No*!"

"You want me to leave you here to have our child and call it Gil's. I understand that much. I have to get out of the way – *your* way – so you can –"

He felt drained. Bloodless. Toni bent forward suddenly: he couldn't see her face. He was still holding both her hands. She said, "I'm going to love our child. Like no child's been loved before. Don't you worry about that, Nick. This infant's going to be my life. It's because I love it that I can't subject it to – to–"

"To knowing its real father?"

"Yes, exactly that. Nick, be *sensible*!"

"Don't you think *you're* being a little selfish?"

"Selfish? No."

"I'm this child's father. And I'm in love with you. You take this – this unilateral decision – as if whatever I feel about you, I mean about us, doesn't count for anything!"

"Of *course* it counts!" Toni looked as if she was going to cry. "Of *course* I – I know it, how you must feel, it *does* count –'

"But not enough. Not as much as the master plan, huh? You have it all worked out, all cool, calm and deliberate, and there's no place for me in this solution you've come to, so that's *it* – the hell with me or any of the things we've felt together and talked about and I believed –"

"No." Her eyes were tight shut against the anger in his face and voice. "No. Please –"

"What do'you mean, *please*? You aren't *asking* me, you're *telling* me! You don't need to say 'please', do you? What you're saying is 'here's what I've decided and that's how it's going to be, and if that bum Morrell doesn't like it he can damn well lump it!' Goddam it, Toni, don't you remember I *love* you? Don't you remember *anything*?"

"Everything."

"But still the hell with it, all that –"

"You're yelling."

"So I'm yelling. Oh dear, dear. Allow me to apologize." He nodded. "I should stand respectfully to attention, and tell you 'sure, whatever you say, Mrs. McLennan' – stiff upper lip, shake hands on it and never a word to Carruthers – that what you were counting on? Good old Limey Morrell, take it on the chin, colours flying? Toni, you must have forgotten a thing or two. Like I'm flesh and blood – you cut me, I bleed. When I look at you, I burn inside. I *feel* ... *you* felt, too, at Arrochar –"

"That was –" She hesitated, not looking at him.

"Make-believe?'

"No. No, at the time, I – we –"

"But you don't feel anything now? Is that it?" He watched her closely. "There's a question you have to answer. Do you love me?"

"Nick, I'm *married*."

"You were married when we were at Arrochar, too." He moved closer to her again, but he didn't touch her. "Answer the question."

"You're being unfair to both of us –"

"Do you love me, Toni?"

She stared at him: then she shook her head. She whispered, "No. I'm sorry, Nick. I'm terribly sorry –"

The room spun. It was a strange room, suddenly, and he was a stranger in it. He couldn't look at Toni, now. He moved away from her, across the room until the bar stopped him: he leant across it, his elbows resting on its glass surface and his fists clenched in front of his face. In the silence, he heard music from the radio in the next apartment.

Five minutes after twelve on Monday morning, Gil McLennan poked his head round Morrell's office door. Morrell was fully awake to the fact of Laing being due in at midday, but he'd decided he'd leave it to them to contact him. He knew what he was going to do, all right – but they were going to have to persuade him to do it.

"You busy, Nick?"

He looked up. "Yeah.... Oh, hello, Gil. Come in and sit down, won't you?"

"I have Seymour upstairs, and we're just about to have a little drink. Why don't you come and help us out?"

"Well, now." Morrell stood up. "Since it's Monday –"

"That's my boy!" McLennan nodded genially. Morrell thought, He's a charming old bastard, when he wants something badly enough. Gil said, "You're right, too. Mondays take more killing than any day there is. Let's go."

Priscilla was at her desk, rattling out letters. Morrell winked at her as he followed McLennan to the outer door.

In McLennan's room, one floor up, he shook hands with Seymour Laing. McLennan opened his bar cabinet and mixed three highballs. Morrell sat back, nursing his drink and waiting for the action to start. Ever since Toni's Sunday visit to his apartment, he'd had this strange feeling – as if he'd been given a year to live, and had to make sure of turning it into the best year he'd ever had. If they were so anxious for him to run the British company, they were going to have to pay for it. At least he'd be miserable in comfort.

McLennan sat down. "Nick, have you thought any more about the London job?"

He nodded. "Matter of fact, I have." They both looked at him sharply: there was a gleam of hope in McLennan's face. Morrell said, "If anything, I dislike the idea more strongly than I did before I started thinking. I don't want it, Gil."

"Has it occurred to you, Nick, that it might not be half so bad as you imagine? You'd have a very large concern there, one of the biggest in the country. It's in poor shape now, but you could have it looking entirely different inside six, twelve months. You'd have made yourself a reputation, Nick, and knowing you as I think I do I guess you'd have fun doing it."

"You think working with Briscoe could be fun?"

"He's a figurehead, Nick, a goddam cypher. You'd walk over him and round him. The power would be in your hands, not his, because we control the company and you're our man. You'd have a free hand to do whatever you thought was necessary, and we'd back you all the way along. It's a chance in a million, I'd say."

Morrell smiled at him. "Well, since I'm your friend, Gil, I'm prepared to stand down in your favour."

"Yeah. I'll have a good laugh at that later. Right now I'm in earnest, Nick. We – Seymour and I – we've looked at this from just about every goddam angle there is. And – I'll level with you, Nick – every single time we take a fresh look at it, the answer comes up Nick Morrell. I'm not flattering you, now, believe me, I'm simply talking facts. We need the best man we have, in that job, and the best man we have is you. I'm talking plain facts, nothing else. Nick, I'm *asking* you to take this job for us. I don't know that I've asked a favour of you before, anything important. But this is more than just important, it's vital to us, vital's the only word for it. Nick, now look at me. This is Gil McLennan asking you. Maybe I've done you a little good in the time we've been acquainted – I don't know about that. I'm saying to you now, do this for me, Nick, and I'll be in your debt so long as I live."

Seymour Laing stepped in, now.

"Gil's right, Nick. Maybe there are certain reasons you don't want to make the move. Okay, you told us, we understand how you feel. But you work for McLennans, Nick. You've done plenty for the company, but the company hasn't been all that tough on you, I guess. You could try thinking in terms of – oh, I don't want to sound old-fashioned, but – loyalty? Even friendship – for me and Gil and Hank Smith and all the rest of us?"

Morrell got up out of his chair and walked over to the window. He stood looking out across the deep chasms of the streets, thinking, *They aren't doing at all badly. Even if I hadn't been intending all along to take the job, they might have swayed me with those last speeches. Okay, so I can afford to let up a little now.*

He turned round, and faced McLennan.

"If I take this job – which I still don't want to do – it'd be on my terms without argument. You did say that, didn't you?"

"Short of my head on a platter, you name it."

Seymour Laing put in, "If you did take it, it wouldn't have to be for ever. Maybe three, five years – unless by that time you wanted to stay there, a few years is all it needs to get the wheels turning.... Gil, we'd be happy on that basis, wouldn't we?"

"I'd say a minimum of five years."

Morrell sat down again. "I'll tell you what my terms would be. From McLennan Ridgeway Limited I'd want a basic salary of twenty-five thousand pounds a year. I'd also want an apartment – a flat – of my own choosing. Probably Eaton Square, Sloane Square.... I'd also want a Rolls-Royce and a personal chauffeur. Okay so far?"

Both men nodded. McLennan muttered, "Careful you don't stint yourself."

"I'll be careful...." Morrell sipped whisky. "I'd expect to remain a vice president of McLennans and to be paid accordingly in dollars. To start with, all you'd do in fact would be you'd take the dollars out of one pocket and put them in another. I'll explain that. This dollar salary would be used, to start with, to pay off the balance on my personal acquisition of five per cent of the McLennan Ridgeway stock. Yeah, that's right Gil, you heard me.... Now the fact you'll be allowing me to buy five per cent of the British company's equity from you means you'll have to look again at the way it's going to be held. As I said on Friday, I'm not happy with your proposals as they stand."

Seymour Laing said, "Perhaps you'd spell out your own proposals, Nick."

"Certainly. You sell ten per cent, not twelve and a half, to von Mettendorfs. And you sell five per cent to me. That leaves you with forty-seven and a half. So with either my stock or von Mettendorfs' on your side you have the control you need. Whereas Mettendorfs' stock could line up with the British, and they'd still be a minority. This way, you're safe, so your chief executive will be safe too. What's more, you get not only a better guarantee of control, but you get it a little cheaper."

McLennan, rubbing his nose, was looking at Laing. "I don't see any unsurmountable difficulty ahead of us in this, Seymour."

"No, I don't think there is. If von Mettendorfs will accept the reduction."

"Karl said he would, on Friday. I asked him. You were there, Seymour."

"Oh? Well, I should say you have yourself a deal, Nick."

McLennan growled, heaving himself up out of his chair, "Even if some people *might* call it blackmail."

IV
Sixties

CHAPTER NINETEEN

It was raining: a grey day in tone with the grey interview he'd just had with Pat Pelly. Their half-hour conversation had left in his mouth a taste of defeat, frustration, anger: in a sense that was good, because he'd be in the right mood now to handle the assortment of pasty-faced jerks who comprised the board of directors of McLennan Ridgeway Ltd. Well, they didn't all answer to that description: Admiral Vaughan wasn't pasty-faced, nor was Hunstanly or Valor. Chris Valor wasn't even a jerk. For the rest of them – excluding, of course, Gil McLennan and Seymour Laing, who were in New York, leaving their voting power in his own hands – it would be close enough for anything short of a police description.

Morrell looked up from his desk, across this penthouse office at the rain-streaked windows which led to his private balcony. He liked the view from there: not as dramatic as the bird's eye view of Manhattan and the Hudson which had been his outlook from the Empire State up to three years ago, but in its own way pretty good. London, from this angle, had the quality of an old print on which modern buildings and roads had been superimposed: you could see what the capital used to look like, and you could see what it was becoming.

He frowned, glancing at his watch, then jabbed a button on his intercom. Priscilla's voice asked, "Yes?"

"Isn't that call through to Grant, yet?"

"Sorry, but they're having trouble with it. Lines clogged up. But there's a call coming through this minute from Washington – I've been holding –"

"I want Greenock, not bloody Washington –" He checked, realizing suddenly what this call might be. He hadn't expected to hear either way until next week. "Who is it?"

"I think it's Mr. Swarthout's office."

"Oh, *is* it." He flicked the switch up, and his eyes were already on the other telephone, waiting for it to ring. He told himself, Early news is likely to mean bad news. Well, let's get it over with. But Swarthout was calling damned early in the morning, by Washington time: over there, they hadn't had breakfast yet. If the news was good – against which, he told himself, preparing himself for the worst, the odds must be a hundred to one – the timing of the call was just about perfect. The phone rang, and he grabbed it. Priscilla said, "It *is* Mr. Swarthout. You're through."

"Is that Mr. Nicholas Morrell?"

"Speaking."

"Hold the line, please." A click. The girl in Washington said, "I have Mr. Nicholas Morrell on this line. Mr. Swarthout."

"Fine. . . . Nick, you there?"

"I'm here all right. What's the news, Ed?"

"You won't believe it."

"Ed, I have a directors' meeting which should have started ten minutes ago. Let's hear the worst."

"You won't make 'em cry with this, boy. Ready for a shock?"

"I live in a permanent state of shock."

"Don't we all. You got it, though, Nick. The sub-committee stayed up all night and there's blood and guts all over the goddam floor, but like I said, you got it. I guess you better haul your arse over here, Nick boy."

"Well, my God. . . . Ed, did I ever tell you I love you?"

"Wouldn't have thought you were like that, Nick –"

"I caught it from my chairman. Ed, may I call you back in two, three hours? For some detail?"

"Make it four p.m. your time. I'll be here waiting."

"Right. Ed, thanks a lot. Christ, I *mean* that!"

"You did it, boy, I didn't. When can you be here?"

"I'll try for Monday. How would that suit you?"

"Sooner the better. You fix it before you call me back, huh? Nick, there'll be a release here at noon today. So if you hold the news at your end until after we've talked this afternoon, we'll be in step. Okay?"

"It's that firm, is it?"

"I don't get you" –

"It's that definite, is it? For a news release?"

"What d'you think I'm calling you for, before I've ever gone to bed?"

"Well, thanks. Sleep well. Sweet dreams, too –"

"Yeah. Well, four o'clock your time. And *Goodnight*."

Morrell slammed the phone down. On the intercom, he asked Priscilla "What in hell's the matter with that call we booked almost a bloody hour ago?"

His secretary's voice was cool. "I have Mr. Grant on the line now. Shall I put him through?"

The other phone tinkled as she asked the question. He muttered, "All right, Priscilla. Sorry." He picked up the other one.

"Grant?"

"Yes, Mr. Morrell."

"Bill, I want you to take over Mr. Pelly's duties. As of this moment. Mr. Pelly is leaving us – for health reasons. We'll call you Manager of Production, for the time being – make a good job of it and we'll see where we go from there. This is a temporary move, Bill, you understand?"

"Sure, Mr. Morrell –"

"Pelly knows I'm calling you. He's on his way back now. When he's cleared his desk, you move in. I want everything to go right ahead and no toes trodden on – except those that *need* treading on – all right?"

"Fine. And thank you –"

"I'll be up there tomorrow or the day after. We'll fix the details then. Now listen, Bill. I've just heard from Washington: we've landed that minesweeper contract. You're going to be a very busy man indeed."

"Why, that's *grand*!"

"It'll mean shifting some jobs from Number Two to Number One. We'll go into that when I see you. Meanwhile keep it under your hat. We'll be announcing it this evening and I don't want the Press coming out ahead of the gun. Well, that's all, Bill. Good-bye."

He dropped the phone, and buzzed for Priscilla. He thought, Grant will feel dizzy for about three minutes, then he'll start moving heaven and earth. Well, he's a damn good man, and they all like him up there. It's an ill wind . . . Priscilla came in, looking anxious.

"There've been two messages from the boardroom. They're all in there, waiting for you."

"Let 'em wait. They've more time to spare than I have. Priscilla, I want you to draft a statement for internal circulation that Mr. Patrick Pelly has resigned from the company for reasons of ill-health and that his duties are being taken over as of today's date by Mr. William Grant as Manager of Production." He glanced at her, watched her pencil flying to and fro across the notebook. When it paused, he began again. "Then have Braithwaite come up here, tell him we've won the American minesweeper contract. I want him to prepare a draft Press release – you've got all the details on file. But it's not to leave this office, and not a word to anyone. We'll let it out later this evening, but I'll check it over as soon as I'm clear of the bloody meeting. All right?"

"Right." She shut her book, and smiled at him. "Congratulations. It's terrific, isn't it?"

"Well, the timing's good. It'll make those creeps sit up a bit."

"It'll make *everyone* sit up."

He thought as he pushed his chair back, Gil McLennan won't like it much. Pinching a U.S. Government contract from right under his foxy nose. He'd have given his eye-teeth to get this one for the Hoboken yard.... Well, Gil should get closer to the ball. He'll be screaming mad, but he has only himself to blame.

At the boardroom table, two chairs were empty – his, at the bottom of the table, and Pelly's beside him. Morrell made a point of sitting down at that end. Briscoe had spent the first year trying to persuade him to sit on his right, a position which he believed was fitting for the company's chief executive. Morrell preferred to be on his own, facing them all – particularly facing Briscoe – as adversaries. At the same time he was able without much real effort to make his end of the table seem more like its head: he made the old men look at him instead of at their chairman. Morrell's sole object in this was to annoy Sir Charles: he'd been doing it for three years, now, and the endeavour succeeded every time.

"Nice of you to join us, Morrell."

The chairman affected what he imagined was a cutting tone. His pale eyes slid around the other faces as Morrell sat down. "This meeting should have started ten minutes ago."

Morrell nodded. "So let's start it now."

"One might have thought a word of apology –"

"One might have had one, too. Since you chose to open

with snide remarks the minute I got in the door, one has none to offer. However, I do wish to make a statement to the board before we get on with the other business. That all right with you?"

They all looked at him. On Briscoe's right, Sir Paul Wyllie, who was deputy chairman and, like Briscoe, a government appointee. Sir Paul had been a government scientific adviser until his retirement a few years ago, but since the formation of the new company and Morrell's appointment as its chief executive – a little more, actually, than three years – he'd offered no advice of any kind. The only times Sir Paul had opened his mouth were the occasions when he'd expressed agreement with Sir Charles. He was a thin man, almost entirely bald, and his eyes seemed more like a ferret's every time Morrell looked at him.

On Wyllie's other side, Mathew Scott-Ridgeway stroked the toothbrush moustache which adorned his round, white face. He was a relic of the old Ridgeway family control. An accountant, he was also one of the larger private shareholders. His cousin, Arnold Markwick, sat beside him. Markwick, white-haired and blue-jowled, was supposed to carry responsibility for Personnel, and his resentment of Morrell's personal control of all the more important staff matters had made him a staunch ally of the chairman. Next to him, and the last on this side of the table, was Admiral Vaughan. In full, Engineer Rear Admiral Sir Hartley Vaughan, C.B., R.N. (Rtd). Opposite the Admiral, and on Morrell's right now, sat Christopher Valor. Valor, a well-known and extremely successful Queen's Counsel, was still in his early fifties, which made him – apart from Morrell, who was still two years short of fifty – the youngest member of the board. Then came Thomas Johnson-Hughes, M.B.E., a retired naval architect who'd been appointed by Briscoe on the grounds that his wide technical knowledge would be an asset to the board, but whose theories were based on pre-war circumstances and requirements.

Admiral Vaughan had a face like a horse: an old one, out to grass and musing over greater days: Hughes had the horse look too, but mainly on account of his teeth, large and protrusive, dark yellow streaked with black. He never spoke, these days, but his teeth showed even in repose.

Farther up on that side of the table reclined Sir David Law, a tiny, silver-haired racehorse owner who'd been knighted after a term of duty as a governor of the BBC. Sir David spoke frequently and at length on the subjects of broadcasting and horses, but Morrell had never heard him express an opinion directly affecting the conduct of the company or the industry – unless nodding at the chairman could be taken as the expression of opinion. Finally, between Law and Briscoe, the benign and portly figure of Lord Hunstanly, whose retirement from the banking world had passed almost unnoticed a dozen years ago. Hunstanly, a large man with a florid complexion and brown hands as knotted as a gardener's, invariably agreed with everyone irrespective of the view they might be expressing at the time.

Morrell looked round the faces, thinking that perhaps it was better to have them against him than with him: either way, if he took the slightest notice of their views, they'd represent a heavy drag on the company's progress and prosperity. It was easier, really, to have them hate him, as most of them did. This way, he didn't need to pretend to listen to their advice.

They were waiting for the statement he'd told Briscoe he wished to make. From the light in one or two pairs of normally dull eyes, he guessed they might be hoping he was about to offer his resignation.

Sir Charles Briscoe sighed. "Very well. Although it is customary for 'any other business' to follow the agenda rather than precede it."

"Well, let's dispense with custom. I wish only to inform the board that McLennan Ridgeway's tender has won that contract to build a new class of minesweeper for the Americans. We've won this over the heads of a dozen American companies, and it'll be a good four years' work, at least, for Number Two yard."

Lord Hunstanly stared at him down the table. "What do the Americans want minesweepers for?"

Briscoe coughed. "This is excellent news, of course. Most – er – encouraging. Very good indeed."

Whyllie nodded. "Excellent. Excellent."

Admiral Vaughan muttered, "A fine fillip to morale, gentlemen. What we needed. Not only ourselves – the whole country –'

"I think –" Sir David Law addressed the chairman. "I suggest we should lose no time in releasing this news over television, radio, to the newspapers, etcetera."

Morrell nodded. "A Press release is being prepared. The news can be given this evening, though, not before, and I'll see to that. We'll put it out at the same time as it's released in Washington. And I'll be flying over this week-end."

"Indeed?" Briscoe looked down the table. "Are we to understand that the award of the contract is yet to be confirmed?"

"We've won the contract. There's nothing else for anyone to understand."

Chris Valor leant forward. "I think congratulations would be in order. Sir Charles, I move that this board expresses its appreciation of a brilliant *coup* by its chief executive."

"I second that." Lord Hunstanly smiled amiably at Briscoe. He said it again, to make sure. "I second that." Briscoe nodded without any sign of pleasure, and Garwood, the company secretary, scribbled on his memo pad. Garwood had been company secretary under the old administration, and Morrell had kept him on.

Sir Charles raised a pale hand to his lips, and coughed. He said, "However. This is perhaps an appropriate moment for me to raise a matter which is, I believe, overdue for discussion. We have before us an example of just the kind of situation – this –" he frowned – "in political circles I believe it has come to be known as a 'personality cult'. We are a *company*, gentlemen, not an individual. We are McLennan Ridgeway Ltd., we are *not* Nicholas Morrell Ltd."

"Hear, hear!" Lord Hunstanly smiled genially at Morrell.

Briscoe continued, "We are all aware of the quality of the services rendered to the company by Morrell. The expertise, the – er – energy and know-how, and so on. But one cannot overlook a tendency for all our achievements to become *personalized*.... I'm not saying, Morrell, that it's – er – deliberate, that you achieve this effect – er – consciously. The fact remains that every time the Press reports some item of news concerning this company, it reads as though McLennan Ridgeway were some kind of dictatorship."

Scott-Ridgeway chuckled. "Isn't it?"

"No, it is not." Sir Charles scowled peevishly. "Our achievements are the result of teamwork, joint effort. Morrell will agree with me, I hope?"

Morrell stared at him, waiting for the rest. It was best to have the targets in full view before you started shooting. Briscoe glanced round the faces. "I think we should beware of this tendency, gentlemen. I think we should, as a board, minute our – er suggestion to Morrell that he should in future take care that it is our company's – er – image which is enhanced and not so much, or so often, his – er – own."

"Absolutely." Hunstanly nodded happily. "Thinking the same thing myself, exactly, only the other day."

Admiral Vaughan's eyes glittered as he looked at Morrell. "Team spirit, Morrell. That's the thing. *That*'s what pushes morale up and wins the battles. Makes for a happy ship –"

Morrell leant forward. "Sir Charles. Would you like to make the announcement about the minesweeper contract?"

Briscoe nodded. "As chairman, I believe that might be entirely appropriate."

Sir David Law glanced up from the doodle he'd been making. "When I was at the BBC –"

Morrell cut him off. "You'll be prepared, Sir Charles, to answer the journalists' questions? How we tendered, why and how we succeeded? The techniques employed, where the costs are cut, the areas where we're scoring over our competitors? How we'll fit this in when we already have orders in hand only just short of ninety million?"

Valor laughed. Sir Charles glanced at him coldly before he answered Morrell's question.

"As chief executive, Morrell, you will naturally supply me with the information they are likely to require. You are, as it were, my right hand –"

"The *hell* I am!' Morrell had shouted: everyone else had jumped. "I'm as much your right hand as you're my left foot! I'm the man who's running this company. I'll sit down at this table with you and tell you what's happening, what I'm doing, and I'll go through the motions, but I'm *damned* if I'll be called your right hand!"

Scott-Ridgeway murmured, speaking softly but clearly audible in the dead silence as Morrell paused for breath, "Surely, Morrell, the board of directors of a company as large as this has *some* small function to perform. As a policy-making committee, if you'd like to put it that way –"

"Put it where you like." Morrell shrugged. "Make all the

policies you like. I'll still be getting on with what has to be done."

A pink flush had spread upwards over the chairman's pallid face. "Now there we have it. My second point, devolving from the tendency to – er – personalize. . . . I was intending to move on to this, and now you've admitted it – even proclaimed it –"

"What is *It*?"

"If I may be permitted to continue –'

"It would help if we knew the subject of the dissertation."

"The subject, Morrell, is your refusal to take cognisance of the recommendations of this board. To ride roughshod over perfectly reasonable proposals put forward by directors of the company. That, Morrell, is the matter to which I am now directing the board's attention."

"You want me to ask the board for instructions, for permission to perform my day to day function as chief executive, is that it?"

"No, not exactly –"

Hunstanly grumbled, "Don't see why he shouldn't."

"Morrell." Briscoe was still pink. "I simply draw your attention – as indeed several of our colleagues at this table have suggested I should do – to an element of discourtesy in your attitude to other members of the board. A tendency to pursue your own – er – devices often in direct contravention of views and resolutions expressed in this room."

"You're entirely wrong." Morrell glanced around the table, but only Valor met his eyes. "When I hear any view which could be of any benefit to the company's operations, I take very careful note of it indeed. But regrettably, such occasions are few and far between. In fact, it's high time I had some *help* from this board. One might hope for objectivity and an element of common sense." He pointed at the chairman. "All you're doing, Sir Charles, is raising petty objections and doing your weak damnedest to make my job more difficult than it need be. You're green with jealousy over what I've done for the company already – you'd like to take the credit for it, though, without ever having lifted a bloody finger, and that's what's behind this blather about personalizing the company's success. I agree, it's *not* a one-man band. There *is* a team, a damn fine one, too. The other members of it aren't in this room, though. A few of them are in this building, but most of them are in the yards, running the yards and building the ships. I picked the team, Sir Charles, and I'm leading it, and by God we're on the move!"

Morrell sat back. "Have you any other points you wish to make, Sir Charles?"

"Yes." Sir Charles's voice was so thin Morrell could barely hear it. "Yes, indeed. First I wish to draw the board's attention to the extreme discourtesy of our chief executive's – er – outburst." He glanced to his right. "Ridgeway?"

"Yes." Scott-Ridgeway's fingers were busy at his grey moustache. "I propose a resolution supporting the chairman's complaints of Morrell's behaviour, and deploring this latest example of that same offensive – *extremely offensive* – attitude."

Sir David Law said quickly, before anyone else could steal the thunder, "Seconded! Well, my word, if anyone at the BBC had used such –"

"Sir Charles." Morrell said, "With this new contract, and other quite urgent matters, I've a great deal to do. Shall we get on to whatever's next?"

Briscoe glanced at Garwood. "You have a note of that resolution?"

"Yes, Sir Charles." Garwood glanced fleetingly, apologetically, at Morrell.

Briscoe cleared his throat. The flush had subsided, now, and when he spoke his voice was almost back to normal.

"The next matter is of a domestic and extremely – er – delicate nature. It concerns our company's Director of Production."

The Admiral looked up. "You mean Pelly?"

"I do mean Pelly, yes. As you all know – or if you don't, I tell you now – Mr. Patrick Pelly was appointed on Morrell's personal initiative. Morrell assured me, I remember, that Pelly was in all respects qualified and suitable. I must confess I had my doubts about the man from a very early stage in our acquaintance, But since none of us except Morrell has met him more than three or four times – he's hardly bothered to attend a board meeting –"

"That isn't true." Morrell interrupted. "He's attended three meetings, when they've coincided with his days in London. And both the AGMs since he's been a director. I've insisted he should spend most of his time up there where the work's done, in the yards."

"Be that as it may." Morrell could tell from the chairman's bland manner that he thought he was closing in smoothly for a kill. "Be that as it may, the facts which have *now* come to light are extremely – er – disquieting. To put it briefly, Mr. – er – Pelly is an alcoholic. The facts which have come to my notice indicate beyond question that over the last –"

"Wait a minute." Briscoe frowned at Morrell's new interruption. "There's no need to go on –"

"There is every need, Morrell. Here is a man appointed by you, an executive for whose activities you have been and still are entirely and personally responsible. I intend to finish what I have to say, Morrell, painful as the recitation may be, and I have little doubt that this board will then instruct you –"

"*Instruct?*"

Sir Charles gazed at him coldly. "Yes, Morrell. It will appear in the minutes as an instruction. The minutes will as usual be forwarded to Mr. McLennan in New York, and to Mr. Laing. I hardly believe they, on whose support you count so much, would allow you to ignore –"

"Fortunately you won't have to put yourselves in the ridiculous position of asserting an authority you don't possess. You're not in a position to give me instructions, Sir Charles, and you know it."

"In this instance, Morrell, I consider the situation presents new aspects. We are considering the case of a man whom you yourself engaged and who was appointed to this board as an executive director on your recommendation. *Insistence* might describe it better. He is, I understand, a friend of yours, a personal friend of long standing –"

"Shipmates, weren't you?"

Morrell nodded to the Admiral. "We served together, yes. In the same flotilla."

"There's your answer, then, Briscoe. Can't serve with a feller at sea in wartime without knowing him. No better way to know a man."

"Thank you, Admiral." Briscoe smiled. "You won't dispute, Morrell, that you are personally and entirely responsible for this unfortunate appointment?"

"Why the hell should I?"

"Quite –"

"Pelly is a first-class engineer and since the war he's made his mark as an administrator. There isn't a better man I could have found for the job. That's why I hired him."

The Admiral frowned. "You said he drinks, Briscoe?"

"Many men drink, Sir Hartley. But this man's been incapable for days at a time. At one point, for an entire working week. And yet Morrell here still supports him as an executive director of our company! Now, gentlemen –"

"Wait, will you?" Morrell spoke quietly. "Before you make yourself look even more stupid, you'd better listen to me. Pelly's a damn good man. He's been on the booze, though, you're right about that. Where you're entirely off-beam is when you say he's been – what was it, incapable for long periods? That's rubbish. He started hitting the bottle – incidentally I know the cause of it, although it's nobody's business here – about a month ago. I went up there and read him the riot act. He pulled himself together, until last week –"

"And you suggest we should continue to –"

"Let me finish. The second point on which you're grossly in error is your statement that I – quoting your words, which you will now I hope feel obliged to retract – 'still support him'. I've fired him, and I've promoted his assistant, Bill Grant, to take over his responsibilities, at any rate for the time being. . . . Well, what else d'you want to tell us?"

Briscoe was blushing again. "You've deliberately allowed me to – Morrell, you know perfectly well you should have kept me informed. You kept this information to yourself –"

"Nonsense. I sent for Pelly the minute I knew he'd relapsed. He got here this morning, and I fired him. At that time you were much too busy thinking up ways to attack me at this meeting to listen to any reports of business that really matters to the company. Even if *you* hadn't been, *I* was busy – amongst other things, on the phone to Washington about a contract worth more than all the orders *you've* scraped together in the five years before I took over. No, you damn well listen to me, now! I've sat here listening to your Girl-Guide claptrap, your puerile attacks based on your own personal jealousy and ignorance of this company's affairs, nagging away like a neurotic old fishwife – I use that term, Sir Charles, advisedly –"

"Steady, Nick."

Morrell glanced at Valor. He read professional warning in the lawyer's frown.

"All right, I use it in anger. Because I'm angry – *damned*

angry. I've taken this company off the scrap-heap and made it work. McLennan Ridgeway is a highly organized, expertly managed group with the finest equipment in the industry, a high return on capital investment and the longest order-book in the business. Other yards are talking about merging, linking into bigger groups so they can survive and compete. We don't have to think of that, because we're operationally efficient and making profits. We're in this position because it's where *I* put us. Not you, Sir Charles, not this board collectively or any of you individually. *I've* done it, I'm not afraid to tell you so and I don't give a damn that you hate my guts. I'd be worried if you didn't. I started off here in a co-operative, friendly spirit, ready to play along with you so long as you allowed me to get on with the job. But I've done the job too well for your liking – mainly because the outside world knows I'm the man who's done it. Consequently, you'd like me out – and this morning's fandango was aimed at conditioning your fellow directors to the idea that the company would be better off without me. What you don't seem to realize yet is that it doesn't matter a tinker's fart *what* you think – I'm running this company for McLennans, not for you. Can I put it any more plainly than that?"

"What you're saying, Morrell, is that you are working for the Americans. You're an Englishman, we're all Englishmen here, but this doesn't affect you in the slightest. You have no natural loyalty, no –"

"I have several loyalties, Sir Charles. The first, in this context, is to my job – to do what I'm paid to do. And to the truth, which is something you tend to avoid. To America too – as the country that gave me a job and taught me enough about this business to put your neglected shambles into some recognizable shape. As for your implication that I've no loyalty to Britain, I'd say first that I resent the cheapness of the insult, second that when you were sitting on your arse in one of the ministries I was at sea fighting a war, third that this very morning I landed an export contract which will make headlines and please just about everybody *except* our American competitors. That includes McLennans – they won't love me for it. For the rest of it, the bulk of our orders in all three yards are for export –"

"You're still importing those American boats when we

could just as well make them here. You've completely ignored my own views on that –"

"I'm importing the hulls because it's cheaper to do that than to set up our own moulds. It reduces the capital investment and that improves the ratio of return. It also saves space which we're using to very good effect. We're importing the hulls, but every other damn thing that goes into the boats is British. And we're selling the finished product in every market in the world except the American continent and the Caribbean. The cost of importing the glass-fibre hulls is a tiny fraction of our income from hovercraft sales to America and Canada. All these things I've initiated myself without the slightest help from you. All right, we had a government grant to set up the hovercraft business, but I didn't need *you* to get that. You had a lousy little yard down there at Hamble living from hand to mouth on single orders for fishing boats, a tug or two, a yacht nobody wanted when it was built. Now the same yard's up to its eyes assembling powerboats and building hovercraft. There as well as on the Clyde we've been ahead of everyone setting a new pattern for labour relations, breaking down the demarcation barriers that made for restrictive practices, high costs, late deliveries, loss of orders. The Unions are playing ball with us and we're playing ball with them." He took a deep breath. "I could go on for hours. Shall I tell you what I want to do as the next step?"

Briscoe had been sitting stiffly with his eyes shut. He opened them, now, and blinked at Sir Paul Wyllie.

"If you have plans for new developments, I imagine it would be reasonable for this board to hear about them."

"You'd need to hear about this, certainly." Morrell smiled. "I know you love me already, but this is going to fill you all with a truly deep affection for me. It's long-term, mind you, an idea for the future more than an immediate plan."

Admiral Vaughan looked up. "Well, speak out, man!"

"There are five non-executive directors on this board at present. I would like to replace three of them with one representative from the labour force in each yard."

While Briscoe was walking out of the room, Wyllie and Scott-Ridgeway hesitating, undecided whether or not to follow him, the others all talking or shouting at once except for Valor who was smiling and shaking his head, he thought, I'd keep the Admiral. He's not a bad old stick, and he's always good for a laugh. And Valor – he's a damn good lawyer, and I like him. But the others – Hunstanly, Law, and Johnson-Hughes – they can go and be self-important dummies some place else. On a golf-club committee, perhaps.

He hadn't intended to mention his thoughts about appointing shipyard workers to the board. He'd told them about it on the spur of the moment because he was sick of Briscoe's attacks and the others' sycophantic support for them. He'd tried politeness, in the early days: then firmness, but still not the open contempt and defiance he'd shown them today. Today. Today he'd let them see his teeth.

Morrell pushed back his chair, and stood up. Perhaps, he thought, Briscoe will think twice before he launches the next assault.

Firing Pelly hadn't been pleasant. He'd had to do it; with Briscoe scratching around for any chance to put the boot in, he'd have been vulnerable if he'd kept a drunk who was also his personal friend not only on the payroll but in a key executive position. As Briscoe had said, when he'd still thought he was in a position to win one nasty little victory, even Gil McLennan couldn't have stood for that. The McLennan backing was real and powerful, but only while Morrell showed results and kept his nose clean. Assessment on performance was a McLennan criterion, and a perfectly sound one too. If a man slipped up, he wasn't a man to support.

Which was why he should have been ready to sack Pelly in any case, irrespective of his own position. Morrell thought, as he walked back to his own office, I shouldn't have had any doubt, any hesitation. The fact I've known him for years hasn't a thing to do with it. He'd shown he couldn't be trusted, so he had to go. The company is bigger than one man.

"Everything all right?"

He glanced at Priscilla as he shut the door.

"What?"

"The meeting go all right?"

"Oh, yes." He grinned. "Well, maybe that's not completely true. It was a brawl. The chairman walked out in a huff.... Priscilla, send down for two beef sandwiches and some coffee, will you?"

"Right."

"Mustard on the beef, please. I want Ed Swarthout on the line at exactly four p.m., and check on Sunday and early morning flights by BOAC and Pan Am. Don't book, just get the schedules."

"Stopping off in New York, or straight through to Washington?"

"Washington. When I'm through there I'll drop in on Gil."

He thought, Get it signed and sealed first. *Then* singe the fox's beard....

Priscilla, on her way out, stopped, holding the door open. She said as a warning to Morrell, "Oh. Mr. Valor. Good morning –"

"Afternoon, just." Chris Valor smiled at her, and came in. "I hope he treats you better than he treats us."

She laughed. "I've no complaints so far."

"Spare a minute, Nick?"

"Any time." Morrell nodded. "Sit down. You go ahead, Priscilla. Well, Chris, did you enjoy that?"

"Worth a guinea a minute.... But seriously, Nick – why go so far out of your way to antagonize them all?"

"I suppose they made me cross."

"You don't have to tell me *that*. But it's Briscoe makes all the running. You have him sewn up, why put the others on his side?"

"Because they're on his side already and I wanted them to know they're backing a bloody dummy, a non-starter."

Valor put a cigarette in his mouth and lit it. "Don't you think you'd have an easier ride if you won a few of them over?"

"Who wants an easy ride, from those creeps? They don't worry me, Chris. As far as I'm concerned they're furniture. So many holes in the air. I'm doing a job and getting results, and anyone who doesn't feel satisfied with that can go pee up a rope."

"I like the phraseology –"

"I'm not saying it for laughs. I spent a couple of years being nice to those bums, letting them feel important, explaining the difference between left and right, how it's easier to sell a product at a low price than a high one, how customers like to have the deadline met – wiping their bloody snots for them, practically – and where's it got me? Well, you saw, this morning. I'm sick and tired of being an Aunt Sally for those stupid, ignorant sods, so I showed them I can hit back when I'm attacked. Anything wrong with that?"

"You realize Briscoe'll fight you tooth and claw now?"

"What d'you think he's *been* doing?"

Valor smiled as he stood up. "I take it you're not joining us for lunch?"

Morrell laughed. "What do *you* think?"

"Only that it might be an idea to leave the quarrels inside the boardroom. You might do yourself some good by coming along and acting the life and soul of the party."

"I'd gag on my food.... But I've too much on here, anyway." He glanced down at his desk, saw that Priscilla had typed a notice about Pelly's resignation and Grant's new appointment: also Braithwaite's draft for a Press release on the subject of the American contract. He looked up at Valor, "What with this U.S. Navy job – and I'll have to fly up to Scotland and see Bill Grant before I can go to Washington – plus a load of muck to clear before I can do either – no, even if I wanted to I couldn't spare the time." He smiled. "But I do appreciate the concern."

"Don't mention it." Valor frowned. "There's one thing I wonder if you know about. These rumours of takeover – you heard any of that?"

"Takeover of this company?"

The lawyer nodded. "So one hears."

"Well, it's balls. We're in a very strong position, Chris. McLennans, I mean."

"I know. But it seems to be a fact someone's trying to scoop up any loose shares they can find. The rumour is it's some undercover operator out for eventual control."

"Is that so? Well, they won't get far."

"They say you're the man behind the buying, Nick."

"They say *that*?" He stared up at Valor. "Well, that proves it's a cock and bull story, doesn't it?"

"If you say so. *I'll* take your word for it."

"Decent of you."

"But there are people who wouldn't. Briscoe, for instance. How about McLennan – would he accept your word?"

"You think someone's trying to plant this on me, do you?"

"It could be. I wouldn't have any way of knowing."

"I suppose not. Well, thanks for the tip."
"Any time." Valor nodded. "But Nick –"
"Yeah?"
"Play it cool, will you?"

CHAPTER TWENTY

Morrell walked into the United Hunts Club at six fifty-two that same evening, and by six fifty-nine he was on a stool at the bar munching a handful of nuts while Johnny poured him a large whisky and water. Guy Davies, a City editor, was due to meet him here at seven. Whatever was going on, Davies was the man who'd know about it.

In a place like this, Morrell thought, looking up at the circular, decorated ceiling, you could look back at all the stages of your adult life. The war, in different ranks and on different ships: the end of it, still in the Service but wondering what the hell came next. Two visits from America – the second one that prospecting trip when he'd met Briscoe for the first time. . . . Let's not, he thought, give too much thought to Briscoe. But after each long interval, you'd come in here a different man. You'd gained in some directions, lost in others. On the surface, gains outranked the losses. It was as well to remember, though, he told himself, that in one currency or another you paid for every step along the way.

Who could have guessed, twenty years ago when he'd drunk in this very bar with a young R.N.V.R. engineer, that a time would come when he'd send for the same man – who by this time was not quite so young, and had a wife and children, the wife a girl to whom you'd introduced him in the first place – and fire him from his job?

Pelly had married Sue, the girl Morrell had taken along to join that party at the Orchid Room, back in 1945 – the night he'd seen Diana with the R.A.F. man. Diana: he wondered where she might be, now. Married, surrounded by half-grown children? Sue had told him that evening, he remembered, that she was expecting to marry some Army character who at the time had been in Burma. Someone called – Mike. He'd been killed out there, about the time the bombs dropped on Japan, and Sue had married Pat Pelly instead. Since they wouldn't have met if Morrell hadn't taken her along to the party, you could say he had some responsibility for their getting married. Every damn thing you did, however small, stood to having its effect sooner or later. Because of Sue, Pelly had taken to the bottle – well, that had been *his* story. They'd moved to Scotland when Pelly had joined MR, and Sue had disliked it enough to bitch things up. She'd told Pelly he could do what he damn well liked, but she was going back to London. He could get down for week-ends, couldn't he? Was he married to her or to the bloody company? Anyway, lots of men spent a good part of each week separated from their wives – what right did he think he had to make her live in this God-awful dump, marooned hundreds of miles away from all her friends?

Morrell thought, The answer is I shouldn't have hired him in the first place. He was qualified, all right, but he wasn't the man for the job. If a man's reaction to strain – domestic or any other – is to hit the bottle, he doesn't belong in that bracket. He lacked the strength, and I should have seen it: it's part of what I'm paid for. And if I'd left him where he was instead of giving myself the pleasure of hiring an old friend, he'd still be happy and so would Sue and so would I. So there it is – *I* did this to him.

"Your guest, Mr. Morrell."

The hall porter: and behind him, Guy Davies. Tall, balding, and immaculate. . . . Morrell slid off his stool.

"Thank you. Hello, Guy. Whisky?"

"I think a Campari and soda. You're looking well, Nick."

Morrell told the barman, "Large ones, Johnny." He said to Davies, "Let's sit over there."

Johnny brought the drinks to their table. Davies murmured, "Cheers. Well, now. Have you some State secret for me, or is this just a drink for old times' sake?"

Morrell put his glass down. "An exchange, I hope. I have something to tell you, and I think you'll have something for me. Here's mine first." He handed him a copy of the press release about the American contract. "We put this in the post this evening. So you're the first to get it."

Davies skimmed through the announcement. He whistled. "Well, good for you! My God, Nick, there's no stopping you, is there?" He looked up. "Mind if I phone this through right away?"

"Go ahead. Through there, and the little door under the stairs. Why not drink that before you go?"

While Davies was telephoning his paper, Morrell organized fresh drinks. The journalist came back smiling.

"I'm grateful, Nick. Thanks a lot. Now let's hear the tit for tat, eh?"

"By all means. Either you'll know the answer or you'll know where to get it for me. I gather there's a rumour going around that someone's trying to buy up MR stock. Have you heard anything about it?"

"More than a rumour. It's a fact."

"I want to know who's behind it."

Davies smiled at him. "What are you trying to pull, Nick?"

"Sorry. I'm not with you."

"If you could pick up another – well, say twenty per cent – you'd be in a very strong position, wouldn't you?"

"Why should I want that?"

"Insurance? Plus the instincts of a capitalist hyena?"

"I don't need insurance. I run the company for the American end – I'm a vice president of McLennans, you know that. What's more, even if I wanted a bigger holding I couldn't afford it. I'm not badly off, but I'm not a multi-millionaire either. . . . You think I'm doing this?"

"Five per cent of MR makes you a millionaire, I'd say." Davies lit a cigarette. "Millionaire plus. How did you get that much, Nick?"

"I bloody well bought it, that's how!"

"Not bad going, in just a few years."

"I don't know what you're driving at." Morrell frowned. "You think I have some private financial backing, the same person or people who're in the market now – that it?"

"Could be. Pure speculation, of course." Davies looked around. "I like this place."

"Yeah. It has the advantage one doesn't meet the sort of people one knows in business. Not often. Guy, I'll tell you how I got my holding in MR. First, I was damn well paid in New York for quite a few years. I couldn't have spent all I earned – wouldn't have had time to. Besides that, I had annual stock options in the American company. That stock doubled its value every six months or so. And with my cash I played the market, using very good advice. So it piled up. When McLennans wanted to send me over here, I didn't want to move. I liked living in the States, and I was doing damn well. Well, they were doing their nuts, just about, to get me to take this job, and – to cut the story short, I took it strictly on my own terms. One of the terms was five per cent of the new company's equity. I could afford most of it, and the rest was paid out of my salary as a McLennan vice president. That's all there is to it. I wouldn't mind increasing my holding, because you're right, we're really going places, now – what I have's already worth four times what I paid for it. But –" he looked Davies squarely in the eyes – "I'm not, have not been and will not be trying to buy any more. Nor do I have the slightest notion who *is* trying to. You might as well believe me, Guy, because it's the truth."

"All right, I believe you. . . . I confess I'm surprised, though. The story's all over the place, and it's strong. Would you like me to print a denial?"

"No. Not yet, anyway. What I want is to know who's trying to frame me."

"Frame you?"

"If the rumour's that strong, and it's a downright lie, doesn't it smell like a put-up job?"

"But who'd want –"

"Briscoe would be my candidate. He'd like nothing better than to push me out."

"Old Charlie Boy, eh? Yes, you could be on the right track, I dare say. You know, of course, he's a very close friend of the minister?"

"Hooper. Yes, I know that."

"He's very close to Mr. *and Mrs.* Elliot Hooper. Spends holidays with them, even. You should keep your eye on Charlie Boy, Nick."

"Not the most pleasant use for an eye."

"As you say. There was a story going the rounds that he was in love with Hooper's wife. Just a story – you know how these things get about. But –"

"I'd say it was unlikely."

"And I'd agree with you." Davies smiled into what was left of his drink, and Morrell signalled for replenishments. "Yes, indeed. There's something I'll show you, one day. Make you laugh your head off."

"I'll look forward to it. But right now, d'you think these

stories could be traced back to him? If I could do that, I'd know how to scotch them."

Davies closed his eyes. "Your theory would be, I imagine, that Charlie Boy is trying to get you in bad with your American friends?"

"That's about it." Morrell thought, And the bastard was laying the groundwork, or trying to, at the meeting this morning. Getting them ready and conditioned to pull the knives out the minute he exposes a chink in my armour – which is McLennan's support. "Thanks, Johnny. Guy, I'd put my shirt on it!"

"You could very well be right. The leg man in all this, you see, is Andrew Gaisford. I didn't know he was connected with Briscoe, but he's a protégé of Elliot Hooper's and that's as near as dammit to a direct link. Is he a pal of Briscoe's, d'you know?"

"Don't ask me." Morrell shrugged. "I never heard of him."

"Oh, come now!"

"What d'you mean?"

"Andrew Gaisford is a close friend of yours."

"I just told you, I don't know him from Adam. Never even heard his name. What *is* this, for God's sake?"

"Well, well, well." Davies sat back, stubbing out his cigarette. "The plot thickens! Gaisford swears he's your buddy. Great admirer of yours, and a close friend. And since he's the front man for whoever's in the market for MR stock, I imagine that's how the illustrious name of Nicholas Morrell creeps into the story. You *sure* you don't know him?"

Morrell nodded. "Certain. But I'd like to meet him. Could you fix that?"

"Nothing easier."

"Without him knowing I'll be there? Just spring it on him?"

"I'd enjoy it immensely, Nick. Tomorrow night?"

"I'll be in Scotland tomorrow. Could you manage it the day after?"

"Certainly. How about Claridges, six-thirty? I'll bait the line with some fantastic innuendo, and have him there so you arrive last. You bust in – I'll be surprised to see you, of course – and we'll watch his pretty face."

"Is he pretty?"

"Oh, very. People sometimes tell him he ought to be on the stage. He laps that up."

"What does he do for a living?"

"Sort of a contact man. Introduces finance to entrepreneurs, and so on. Helps set up mergers. Always ready with the inside dope. Two per cent of this and five per cent of that." Davies rubbed two fingers together. "You know? Come to think of it, I can't quite see him as a buddy of yours."

"That's a weight off my mind, Guy." Morrell grinned. "How about having one or two other people there, at Claridges? To witness the confrontation?"

Davies nodded. "I'll see what I can do."

When he'd first come back to England, his mind had been so full of Toni – in a strangely mixed way – that he'd had no time for any other women. He hadn't had much time anyway, for anything except the job – and twenty-four hours hadn't been a long enough day for that, in the first year or so. The mixture of feelings had been compounded of attraction, responsibility and resentment: the attraction he'd felt ever since their first meeting and which had been deepened by every more recent sight or sound of her, culminating in the marvel of those few days at Arrochar: the responsibility of knowing he'd planted his child in her belly: the resentment of the way she'd finally dismissed him, shut him out of her life. It seemed the only thing she'd wanted was the child: now she'd got it, and she'd made sure it would be hers absolutely. Hers and Gil's. He'd asked himself, Wouldn't a normal woman want to share her child with its real father?

One could, of course, rationalize the way she'd acted, interpret it as remorse for infidelity to Gil, wanting to make that up to him: as concern for the child, that nobody should know the circumstances of its conception, brand it with illegitimacy. One could construe that she'd wanted a child and that Gil, presumably, had failed to give her one, so that now she had it she was content to be Gil's wife and the child's mother. All these aspects fitted well enough to Toni's basically moral character, her dislike of intrigue or artifice: although, having weakened and then regained her strength, it was through the biggest intrigue of all that she'd reasserted her loyalty to Gil and to an unborn child.

Morrell had been in England about five months when Toni's child was born. A girl. She'd named it Alison, and he'd sent her a Georgian silver porringer for a christening present.

He'd sent presents, since then – dolls, teddy bears – on the child's birthdays and at Christmas. But Alison was three, now, and he'd never seen her. He'd made several visits to New York but he'd been only once to the McLennan home, and Toni had been away, on Nantucket with her daughter.

A year ago he'd been in Hamburg on a short business trip, and Karl von Mettendorf had said something about Seymour Laing and the Trust which Laing represented: it had started a new train of thought in Morrell's mind. He'd remembered the closeness of Toni and Laing: seeing them together in an out-of-the-way restaurant, deep in conversation over lunch. That, and other things. He'd written to a friend in Sydney, asking him to run a check on Toni Russell: the answer had come within the month, and it had been stunning in its simplicity. Toni Russell's grandfather had made a fortune in gold, land and sheep: he'd left a Trust worth nearly 250 million Australian pounds, and she'd inherited it, under trustees' control, at the end of 1945.

So he'd known, then, whose was the real financial power behind the dramatic expansion of McLennan's interests. As for his feelings towards Toni, it was if someone had pressed a switch and changed the lighting. That hardness in her eyes when she'd told him she wanted him to go to England, that whatever had been between them was finished.... He could see her eyes as they'd looked when she'd spelt it out. And when he'd asked her to get a divorce and come to England with him, she must have been thinking in terms of the company, pounds and dollars.... The girl with him in Scotland hadn't been Toni: it had been a Toni in some kind of delirium. Back in New York she'd straightened things out with Gil, and found she was having a child: so there was no further use for Nick Morrell. Except that the company wanted him to move to England. She had a private reason for wanting the same thing, and although he hadn't known it at the time, she *was* the company. A big part of it, anyway.

He'd sired a child who was flesh and blood, but he felt he'd done it by going to bed with a cash register.

He saw Guy Davies out to a taxi, then came back into the club to call Inge. It was nearly eight, he'd arranged to pick her up at the Dorchester at eight-thirty, and he needed time to get back to his flat and change.

He'd met Inge Hegardt in Hamburg, nearly a year ago. Since then he'd seen her in Stockholm, Paris and London – the trips abroad had been necessary business visits, but timed to coincide with her constant moves. She was a star, world famous now, and the premiére of her new film was to be at the Odeon, Leicester Square, tomorrow night. He wasn't sorry he'd miss that – through having to make this quick visit to the Clyde yards – because he'd have felt obliged to go along and Inge would have been tied up in the swirl of cinema people. But she'd come a day earlier than she need have, and she'd be here until Sunday: so he had tonight, and the night after tomorrow night –

Oh, God. . . . He remembered, suddenly, his date with Davies and the smart alec Gaisford. Well, six-thirty – he'd be through with that by eight. Possibly even by six-thirty-one. He breathed relief as the Dorchester switchboard put him through to Miss Hegardt's suite.

"Hello?"

"Inge?"

"Nick, darling – how lovely! But you're not here already?"

"No. Look, I've been delayed, I still have to go home and freshen up. Make it nine instead of eight – well, say eight forty-five?"

"Why don't I meet you at your flat? Save a little time?"

"Remember the address?"

"You crazy? I'll be there a little past eight-thirty. Okay?"

"Not sure I can wait that long –"

"Nor me. It's – oh, it's *bad,* Nick!"

"What's bad about it? It's bloody marvellous!"

"You can teach me some more idiomatic English over dinner. Where are we going?"

"Savoy Grill. That all right?"

"Oh, please, something a little smaller. Shall we discuss it later?"

"Okay. See you." Morrell hung up. In his flat in Eaton Square he flung his clothes off, showered and shaved, and dressed again: all the time he had her face in the front of his mind – her long, tawny hair, wide, grey eyes, that incredibly smooth skin. The figure that had cinema queues stretching for whole blocks in every city of the world. He told himself, knotting his tie, By God, I'm a lucky man! Then he heard her ring: his stomach tightened. and he thought, I'm like a kid, a youth facing his first date.... He ran, more than walked, to meet her at the door.

"Inge. You're beautiful. Every time I see you you're more lovely than the last time."

"Don't I get let in?"

He pulled her inside, and flung the door shut. "I mean it. I *know* you're beautiful – the whole damn world knows it – but *I* know it, I think about you and picture you in my mind in between the times we meet, and still when I see you again you – you stun me. D'you know that? I can't *speak* –"

"I suppose all that was on tape, then?"

"I can't take my eyes off you –"

"Now you must, because I need a drink."

"There's champagne in the frig."

"You want I should get it?"

"I want to kiss you."

This is the most beautiful woman, the most exciting woman, I ever met in my life!

He thought, suddenly, the question coming out of nowhere and hitting him almost like a pain, *More exciting than Toni? How to compare, or – Christ, if I have to think of Toni every time I put my hands or my mouth on another woman – even on this one –*

"Nick, more later, huh?' She'd pulled her head back.

"For such a big star, you're awfully small. I have a crick in my spine!"

"Perhaps we should give up kissing." She walked ahead of him into the living-room. "Perhaps you are getting old?"

"I'm old for you." He saw her shake her head, smiling at him in the mirror where she'd gone to fix her face. He told her, "It's a fact. When I was twenty-nine I was attracted to a girl of eighteen. I felt bad about it – I thought, 'She's just a kid. It'd be cradle-snatching'. Now I'm forty-eight and you're twenty-four – so I'm twice your age –"

"Mathematics bore me, Nick. It's people that count – not numbers." She turned from the mirror, and smiled. "Isn't it so?"

"I'd like it to be."

"For me, it *is*."

He said, "I'll get the wine. Then you can tell me what sort of place you'd like to eat at."

"I don't care where we eat. Here, if you like."

"No food."

"We could go out and get some, couldn't we?"

"Everything's shut by now."

"What a silly country!"

"Maybe. We're going out, anyway. Then back here to relax and talk. Every time we leave each other I remember a dozen things I meant to say or ask you."

They dined at *Au Père de Nico*'s: on the way back to his flat, she told him that when she left on Sunday she'd be flying to New York for a week of publicity appearances. She went on talking, and a few seconds after she'd said that, he realized what it meant: he laughed, interrupting her.

"You'll be in New York next week? I'll be damned! Like to guess where I'm going on Monday?"

"It *can't* be New York." She looked at him, smiling. "Can it?"

"Not quite, no. Washington. But then New York. I should be there on Wednesday at the latest. A couple of days – more, if you'll have time for me –"

"*Time* for you! Nick, did you just decide on this, when I told you?"

"Certainly not. I have to see people in Washington about a contract – we're going to build some ships for them – and while I'm on that side it's only polite to drop in on my New York office. My flight's already booked – hell, I'll change it, now! Make it Sunday, bring everything forward a day. So I could be back in New York by Tuesday. Now how's that for a bit of luck?"

"Oh, it's lovely! But I must warn you, they *will* be keeping me busy, you know, while I'm there."

"When they aren't, I will."

"All right. Just remember I have to sleep sometimes, Nick."

There was an answer that, a category of answer, but it was much too important a subject to be flippant about. Besides, it was too close to the front of his mind at this very moment: it mattered more than it ever had before. Not just for itself, but as part of a much bigger, wider thought he'd carried around with him in the last few months: an idea he wanted to discuss with her tonight.

"I suppose with this première tomorrow, you don't want to stay up too late tonight?"

"Oh, it doesn't matter."

"Good. Where do you go after New York?"

"California for two, three weeks. Then I hope some rest."

In the flat, he opened another bottle of champagne, put a stack of records on the stereo, and dimmed the lights before he sat down beside her on the sofa. He asked her, "Am I being obvious?"

"*Let's* be obvious."

"Inge – you know how I feel about you, don't you?"

"I think so. Like I feel about *you*. Only not quite the same, because I'm a woman and there must be some small differences."

"In that case, if I asked you, you'd sleep with me?"

She watched his face for a moment before she answered. "Not a very passionate approach, Nick, is it?"

"It isn't an approach. It's a question. Would you?"

"I think to get the answer you would have to try me. Not – interview me!"

"I suppose you've wondered why I haven't, too. Have you?"

She shrugged.

"I'll tell you. First because you're who you are – because all over the world millions and millions of men must look at you and think of bed. If I tried to get you into bed – which I admit I'd like to do – I'd be just one of the millions, wouldn't I –"

"I think you may be overstating it a little. I have had three lovers in all my life, not millions."

"I'd give everything I have to be the fourth and last. I'd like you to marry me, Inge. Will you, please? Inge, will you?" He kissed her, feeling her arms slide warm and soft around his neck. He felt he'd never in his life wanted anything this strongly. "Please, Inge?"

"But you're such a busy business man. I'm – this picture, that picture, the next one, publicity tours – how would you like it? A married life in week-ends here or there, miles and months between us –"

"You plan to go on with it for ever? Wouldn't it be nice to step out now, at the top?"

"Nick, how could I? All this money they're paying me, all the work – terribly hard work – to get to this –" she smiled – "top, you call it –"

"I've enough money for both of us. More than enough. For anything you want."

"It's not only money." She looked down at his hand cupping her breast. "Undo the zip fastener, Nick. On my back. . . ." She leant forward, resting her chin on his shoulder as he groped behind her back. "It goes right down. A long way. Nick, not only the money. If I said to you, Yes, I'll marry you if you leave your office and your ships and those things, I don't think *you* would – would you?"

"I'm a man, it's different. It's up to me to earn a living –" His fingers found the catch on her bra, and unfastened it. "I know you'll say *why* is it different, you're making a pile yourself and why should you give it up if I'm not prepared to do the same." He was peeling the dress off her shoulders, pulling it right down to her waist. "But you see, there *is a* difference. It's a man's job to make the living for himself and his wife and his family. It always has been, it's ingrained in us. Okay, so you're a great star, you have this fabulous career – I'm not belittling it, only –" he flipped her bra off: it dropped over the side of the couch. *"God, you're beautiful."*

She sat up straight, her breasts high and firm, naked above a waist so small that it made them seem larger than they were. She had the nipples of a young girl, small and pink, already partly risen although he hadn't touched them yet. He looked into her eyes: cloudy grey, half closed, their lids and lashes heavy, screening. One of her hands stroked the back of his neck: then it was pulling, pulling his head downwards and towards her breasts. He resisted that, moved his hands to them instead, stroking, gently lifting, the tips of his fingers feeling her nipples swell and harden at their touch. He asked her, "Inge, will you marry me? Say yes, sort the details later?"

"Let's think about it, Nick." She spoke in a whisper, slowly, her eyes drifting lazily about his face. "We don't have to hurry. Not all at once, no rush, is there? Let me think about it?"

"I suppose that's better than a straight *no* –"

"Of course it is." Her arm tightened, the hand pulling at his head. She murmured, "But no thinking now, Nick – Nick?"

He told himself, lowering himself to her, *That's right. There's been too much thinking. Now forget her: good-bye, Toni darling.*

CHAPTER TWENTY-ONE

Pelly had been back to his office at the Number One MR yard, cleared his personal possessions into a couple of brief-cases and vanished with hardly a word to anyone. At the other yard he'd done the same an hour later. Morrell spent half the day with Bill Grant, and left satisfied though not at all surprised that the young Scot had taken a firm grip on all current work and problems. There'd been no pause, no vacuum, and although there was naturally a lot of gossip about Pelly – everyone seemed to know the real cause of his abrupt departure – it was already a *fait accompli* which had left no backwash or bruised feelings. Grant, a popular man at all levels in both plants, had taken the wheel smoothly and without fuss. Morrell took him out to lunch, and over it they discussed progress and programmes for every job in hand and pending, and the shape of changes which would have to be made to accommodate the new minesweeper project. One of the first things on Grant's plate now was too arrange a meeting with Union representatives to clear the way for necessary transfers of labour between the two yards: that flexibility was already agreed in principle, but talks were still necessary to avoid snags cropping up over points of detail.

He spent an hour after lunch at Number Two yard: then it was done. He shook hands with Grant.

"I can see I needn't have come up. But any time you want me here, just give me a shout."

"Thanks, I'll do that. And I'm glad of this visit. It'll have done me good with the lads to've had you here just now. Back to London now, I suppose?"

"Yeah. And next week in the States. I'm going to call in on the Pelly family before I leave here, though."

"You'll find the birds flown, I reckon." Morrell's eyebrows rose. Grant nodded. "That's what I hear. Up an' away. Well, I wouldn't blame 'em. Can't be easy."

"It's bloody tragic." Morrell added quickly, "I mean for them personally. Not for the yard. I can see you have all this in hand. Keep it that way, Bill. And remember I'm only too glad of an excuse to climb out of that snake pit when you need any help up here."

"Aye." Grant's eyes smiled. "Sooner you than me."

Stopping his rented car outside the house which had been the Pellys', Morrell saw at a glance that the place was empty. There was a lifeless look about it: blank, curtainless windows, a group of overloaded dustbins outside the empty, open garage. To make sure, he got out of the car and walked up to the front of the house, rang the bell: he heard it ring in the sad vacuity of a deserted home. Through bare windows, sightless as a blind man's eyes, he saw empty rooms, walls marked where pictures which had hung for a couple of years had been taken down.

He walked slowly back to the car, loathing the entire situation and wishing more than ever that he'd never hired Pat Pelly. He'd imagined he was giving a friend a golden chance at the same time as putting the right man in the right job. He'd never been more wrong: and his mistake had wrecked a family.

He spent the night in Glasgow, and flew back to London on the first morning plane. He went to his flat to clean himself up, and while he was there he telephoned Inge. Getting through wasn't easy: half the world seemed to be using her telephone. The new film had opened to wild applause: he'd read glowing notices in the papers during the flight south. There'd been pictures of her, too, taken at the première. Now everyone who knew her and quite a number who didn't were calling with congratulations. And no doubt, he thought, offers .... He had to get the hall porter to send a message up to her, and he waited anxiously until she called him back on another line.

He told her he'd collect her at the Dorchester that evening at eight o'clock.

"Lovely. Where shall we go, Nick?"

"A joint called the Blue Gardenia. Sort of country nightclub not far from Maidenhead. We'll be out of the stink of London for an hour or two. All right?"

"Sounds good."

"Okay. Eight o'clock on your doorstep."

She giggled. "I think I shall run out with a coat over my head. Like a person being arrested – you know?"

"Wouldn't fool *me*. I'd know you under a pile of blankets –"

"I *must* go, Nick. 'Bye."

He put in a long afternoon's work at the office. Priscilla had switched his flight booking from Monday to Sunday, and called Ed Swarthout's office to say he'd be in Washington early Monday morning. Since he'd be away most of the week, there was a hell of a lot to do: he dictated letters for two hours, and then told Priscilla he'd like her to come into work tomorrow, Saturday, as well.

"Nothing arduous – just to clear up. Say ten o'clock, and we'll pack up at noon. Okay?"

She nodded. "Whatever you say."

"You can take things a bit easy while I'm away."

"I can't, you know. That's when I'm *really* busy."

"Yes. Yes, I suppose so." He looked at her, wondering why she put up with it. She was well paid, of course, but she could have earned just as much, and more, back in the States. And be working for someone less demanding. He asked her, "Priscilla – I make you work damned hard. Don't imagine I don't know it. Back home you could have an easier life and earn more, and be among your own people. What makes you stick it?"

"I suppose I'm happy here." She sat down, smiling at him. "I'm not in love with you, if that's what – if you've been reading serials in women's magazines."

"No, I wasn't suggesting anything like that. You're a very attractive person, you're a darned good secretary – well, a lot more than just a secretary – and we seem to get along together. But we're both here to do a job, and when I'm in this building it's the job I think about. I imagine that's how it is with you. I hope we're friends?"

"Sure we are, Nick . . . Well. I've worked for you a long time now, and I like it. The job's interesting, exciting sometimes, and by British standards I'm certainly not underpaid. I might get more in New York, sure, but I wouldn't live better than I do here in London. And I have just as many friends here as I had there – some Americans, but plenty of English too."

"Boyfriends?"

"Sure, I'm human."

"Think you'll marry one of them, one day?"

"Maybe. I've had my chances."

He thought of something. "Priscilla. On Saturday, if we

knock off here at twelve, would you like to lunch with me and Inge Hegardt?"

Her eyes widened. "The Swedish sexpot?"

"You read the *Daily Mirror*, or something?"

She saw the quick annoyance in his face. "I'm sorry." She shrugged. "I suppose that was silly. I didn't know you –"

"That's okay. Her publicity's to blame – it's all rubbish. She's a hell of a nice girl. I thought you might like to meet her, that's all."

"I would, I'd love to."

"Fine. If she can make it. Otherwise you'll have to risk being seen alone with me." He smiled. "It's quite a while since we shared a steak, isn't it?"

Priscilla nodded. "Too long. Well, it's a date. I'll look forward to it." She stood up. "Are you and Miss Hegardt – well, do you know her well?"

"Enough to want her to marry me."

"Wow-ee!"

"So what does *that* mean?" He didn't know if she looked pleased or just amused. "That Red Indian war-cry –"

"Cry mean good luck to Big Chief Nick Morrell. Him plenty brave guy, I guess."

He thought, when she'd gone back to her own office to start work on the stuff he'd dictated, Well, *that*'s all right. He worried about her, sometimes. Sticking with him as she had, getting very little out of it that he could see, he'd felt when he'd stopped to think about it that in a sense he was using up her life, trading on whatever it was – loyalty or friendship, whatever – to keep her with him while she became gradually less young, less likely to get married: that one day she'd wake up and find she'd missed the boat, spent half her life in dedication to a typewriter and a pay packet.

He buzzed through to her on the intercom.

"Priscilla. Tell Burton I want my car here at five-thirty. I'll be driving myself, so he can shove off then."

"Right. Is it the Swede, tonight?"

"Mind your own damn business." He heard her laugh as he switched off the box.

Morrell found a space for the Rolls in Brook Street, and got into Claridges a few minutes after six-thirty. He walked through the foyer and into the big lounge on its other side, and he spotted Guy Davies at once, at a table on the side with two other men. Drinks were on the table. One of the men was around thirty, darkly handsome: that, he realized, must be Gaisford, the one who liked to be told he should be on the stage. He was talking a lot, moving his hands: even if he hadn't guessed who he was, Morrell would have disliked him on sight. The other man had grey hair, thinning above a high forehead; he was lying back in his chair watching and listening to Gaisford's lively monologue. Davies had seen Morrell now: he looked away again at once, back at Gaisford, leaving it to Morrell to decide how he'd make his presence known. Morrell moved towards their table, walking slowly but purposefully, as if his destination was somewhere further down the room. When he was almost at the table, he allowed himself to notice Davies. He stopped, and smiled.

"Hello, Guy. Slumming?"

Davies glanced up. He seemed surprised.

"Well, hello!" He stood up. "Join us? D'you know –" his hand indicated the other two. Morrell shook his head. Gaisford glanced up at him rather peevishly, annoyed by the interruption. He gave no sign of recognition: only looked at Davies, waiting for the introduction.

Davies said, nodding towards the man with grey hair, "This is Jack Dunsfold. You must have –"

"Of course. In the *Financial Times*?"

Dunsfold smiled. "Fame, at last."

Davies looked from Morrell to Gaisford. "You two don't know each other?"

"No." Morrell shook his head again.

"But surely –" Davies looked puzzled as he glanced back at Gaisford. Then something happened to those smooth, even features: a flash of alarm, comprehension, covered quickly by an attempt at an easy smile.

"Nicholas! Long time no see!"

He frowned at him. "Why do you call me that? Who the hell are you, anyway?" He looked at Davies. "Introduce us, Guy."

"Damn it, I'm Andrew Gaisford –"

"I'm supposed to know you?"

"But of course you do!"

"Where did we meet?"

"All over the place. I mean –"

"Name one place and date that I can check in my diary."

"Now, really! How could I – just off the cuff –" He looked at Davies angrily. "What is this, Guy?"

"What d'you mean, what is it? I'd say *you* might explain that. You didn't recognize him, you didn't even pretend to, at first. Then you called him Nicholas –"

"His name – Nicholas Morrell."

Dunsfold, entirely relaxed, was watching the game with a faint smile of amusement. He asked Morrell, "Do your friends call you Nicholas?"

"When I first joined the Navy some idiots called me Nickle Arse. Since then, not a soul. And this punk was in nappies at the time." He sat down. "Guy, if you're buying, mine's a scotch and water."

"Of course." Davies beckoned a waiter. "I'm sorry. My manners as a host suffered from the surprise of learning that you two were strangers to each other. Well – Andrew Gaisford, Nick Morrell."

Gaisford, completely off-balance now, began to put his hand out. Morrell had moved his a little, by way of encouraging him to do that. Now he slid his own hand into his pocket and stared at Gaisford's.

"I rarely shake hands with a man I'm supposed to know already." The hand went back as if a snake had bitten it. Morrell added, "And I never shake hands with a bum who goes around saying he knows me when he doesn't."

Gaisford blustered, "Why on earth should I do that? I'm *certain* we've met. I know your face, I knew your name – how would I know that if we hadn't met before?"

"You let it be widely understood," Dunsfold murmured, "that you were a close friend of Morrell's. I'm satisfied you did it deliberately and that you never saw him before in your life."

"But –"

"Shut up, Gaisford –"

"Now look here –"

"I said, shut up." Morrell stared at him coldly. "All of us here know what you've been trying to do. I think I could probably sue you, if I wanted to. As it is, you can run along and play – on condition you do one thing for me. I'm right in thinking you're some kind of errand boy, aren't I? Well, you go right back to Sir Charles and tell him that if I hear another word of the lies you've been putting around about what I'm supposed to have been doing, I'll have something to say, – and witnessed, at that – about his sexual predilections. You got that message?"

"I'm afraid I've no idea –"

"You'll be afraid, all right, and so will he, if the slander doesn't stop." Morrell glanced at Davies. "Cheers, Guy. You can print that denial now, if you think it's worth the space."

Dunsford asked, "Mind if I do the same?"

"Thank you. I'd be delighted. And if I need to sue this creep, can I count on both of you as witnesses?"

Gaisford jumped to his feet. "I've had about enough of this –"

"Yeah. I expect you have. Goodbye, Andy Pandy."

The three of them watched Gaisford flounce away. Davies laughed. "Nick, I wouldn't have missed that for all the tea in China. What's this bit about your chairman's sex life?"

Morrell frowned. "Off the record?"

"My God, what do *you* think?"

"Well, to start with, you can tell at a glance he's abnormal. I've seen enough of him now to be certain he's as queer as a coot. Well, I don't want to insult any clean-living coots. And no proof – just observation. But the man he had doing my job before we took control – a very sound fellow, Norman Wilmott –"

"Oh, yes." Dunsfold nodded. "He went back to motorcars. First-class man, Wilmott."

"Sure. Well, he told me. That's why he was so pleased when McLennans bought in and he lost his job with something like a diamond handshake. Wilmott's allergic to pansies, and he reckoned old Queen Charles had taken a fancy to him. That may be true, because he tried to persuade us to keep Wilmott on the payroll." Morrell grinned, "Wilmott told me he was always damn careful to keep his back to the wall when Briscoe was around."

They were all three laughing when Morrell, whose chair faced the entrance to the lounge, started so badly that he slopped his drink.

"My God! It *can't* be. . . ."

Ava Baines swept towards them, trailing mink and shoulder-length copper-coloured hair. ' 'Nick, *darling*! What a *lovely* surprise!"

In the few seconds he had in which to take in what was happening, he noticed that she'd hardly changed at all. Perhaps her figure had become a little more voluptuous, but she still moved like a hungry panther. He found his voice.

"Ava! Surprise is right! Ava, this is Guy Davies, Jack Dunsfold. Mrs. Baines." He asked her hopefully, "Eustace with you?"

"Not with *me,* honey." Ava laughed. "He's with the Lord." She hooted again. "Or that other guy – who knows?" She told the three of them in a loud stage-whisper, "A week in damp sheets is all it took. . . . Nick, you married now?"

"Not yet. My God, Ava, you're a sight for sore eyes!"

"Think so?"

"Look around. Every man in this room thinks so."

"You darling! Say, what a cruise that was, huh?"

Davies murmured, "Cruise?" He and Dunsfold glanced at each other. Morrell looked quickly at his watch.

"Ava, I'm terribly sorry, but I have to rush away."

"Oh, the hell you do! All this time, now I've found you I'm not having you run out on me!"

"Honestly, I was just on the point of leaving when you showed up –"

"So now you darn well stay, instead!"

"I can't. I honestly can't. I've only a few hours, then I'm off to the States. I'm sorry, Ava, it's one of those things."

She pouted. "Most unfair thing I ever heard. Here's me just come from there, and here you are, and all you can say is –" she flipped one hand, then the other – "hello – good-bye! Why, it's downright –"

"Believe me, Ava, I can't help it. Think I wouldn't stay if I could? How long are you here for?"

"Coupla days. Then Paris, France. Nick, look – take another plane? God damn it, I'm a widder woman, well heeled and fancy free –"

"Guy. Jack. Look after Mrs. Baines for me? I really do have to hurry." He told Dunsfold, "I'm most grateful for what you've done. Perhaps you'd both lunch with me one day after I'm back?"

Dunsfold nodded. "I'd like to."

Davies pulled back a chair. "Mrs. Baines, do sit down. What shall I get you to drink?"

"A, my name is Ava, and B, this time of day it just *has* to be a champagne cocktail.... Nick, you really leaving me, you bastard?"

He spread his hands helplessly. "Breaks my heart, but I have to."

"You're darn lucky I don't break something else –"

"Yeah." He met the other men's startled faces. "Thanks again. I'll be in touch.... Ava, enjoy yourself –"

"You can count on that!"

Walking quickly towards the door, he heard Guy Davies ask her, "Do please tell us about the cruise you mentioned...."

"I like this place very much, Nick."

Inge clung to him: her soft hair brushed his chin. His right hand felt the gentle undulations of her spine as she moved against him, safe in the semi-dark, both her arms up round his neck. She was leaning back a little, but her breasts still pressed against his chest. She murmured, "You were a clever boy to find it."

"Shall we dance here the first night of our honeymoon?"

She laughed. "Perhaps by then we will be too old for dancing!"

"You can joke, Inge, but –"

"I can't just walk out on everything."

"You wouldn't have to. Not right away. We could work something out. Inge, nothing's impossible if you want it badly enough."

"All right – if you want it so badly, you could wait a year, even two years maybe –"

"No, I couldn't. If you felt as I do, you couldn't even *think* in those terms."

"Oh, Nick, now *listen* to me –"

"God, any time.... Your voice gets right into my bones. I hear it inside my skull even when you're a hundred miles away –"

"Nick, I am on this – crest. Like a wave, you know? Going this fast, I can't jump off –"

"I told you, you don't have to!"

"Even if we did get married, we couldn't be together more in the next twelve months than we can already. So what would be the point?"

"I'd know I had you."

The music flared, faded, stopped. They moved apart, holding hands, waiting for the crowd to melt on the dance floor so they could cross it to their table. One couple still danced on without music: the girl was crooning in her partner's ear. She was tall, slim: her partner older, shorter and thick-set. Inge watched them, smiling: at that moment the pair stopped dancing, and as the woman turned to leave the floor, heading their way, Morrell found himself face to face with Ava Baines for the second time that night. He was too late to duck: she'd seen him, and her smile had died in the moment of recognition.

"Well! If it isn't Mr. Nicholas bloody Morrell!"

"Hello, Ava." He thought, She's plastered. Stinking. And I'm supposed to be on my way to America. Jesus, it looks like trouble. . . .

"And who's *this*, now?" Ava peered drunkenly into Inge's face. She pointed a wavering finger. "Don't I know that sexy little kisser?" She asked Morrell, swaying and talking loud enough for all the room to hear, "Who're you corrupting now, you lying bastard?"

"Ava, I beg you –" Her partner had put a hand gingerly on her arm. She jerked away from him. "Now Ava, let's sit down, eh? Be a good girl –"

She rounded on him, furious. "Take off, buster, or by God I'll –" The small man backed away. Ava had the room's attention, now: out of the corner of his eye, Morrell saw the *maître d'hôtel* hurrying towards them. Up on the stage, the band had become a part of the enraptured audience. Inge tugged at his arm.

"Nick, we better leave."

"Not before I'm through with him, he won't!" Lights gleamed on Ava's skin-tight, gold lamé dress. She lunged forward suddenly, swung her arm: her palm connected with Morrell's face. Sharp and hard as a pistol shot.

"Cheat! Liar!"

The *maître d'hôtel* had grabbed her arm. At the same instant, a flash camera popped right in their faces. Morrell, with Inge clinging to him while Ava struggled and spat curses in the joint embrace of the *maître d'hôtel* and the chief wine waiter, was still blinking, stunned by the combined effects of Ava's stinging slap and the bright explosion of the camera: another went off, slightly closer. The photographer was scuttling around on his knees, trying to get the whole group in one picture: Ava just missed his head with a wild, swinging kick. The *maître d'hôtel,* grunting from the effort of restraining her, yelled "No pictures, please! I forbid it! No –" another flash burst in his face.

Morrell grabbed Inge. "Let's get out of this."

Ava screamed at Morrell's back, "Coward! Yellow four-flushing bastard!" Several diners cheered.

The head waiter intercepted them at the door, grinning from ear to ear. Morrell pushed four fives into his hand. "Keep the change, Mick. If you can get those photos stopped, it's worth another fifty." He and Inge ran to the Rolls. As he helped her in, she said, "He won't be able to stop them. At least one of them was paid to follow me about. That picture must be worth a little fortune to him." She collapsed into the car, and began to laugh, pressing both hands against her stomach. Morrell flung himself in and started the car just as a group of men burst out through the main door. Gravel spurted under the car's tyres: Inge covered her face with her hands as more cameras flashed.

On the M4, cruising at just under seventy, she asked him, "Who was that mad woman? Or would you prefer not to tell me?"

"Her name is Ava Baines. I knew her ten years ago in America. Tonight I ran into her in Claridges – I had to meet some men there, on a business thing, and she just walked in. I hadn't seen her for ten years, and then it was only for a couple of weeks – well, I'll tell you the story, some time – but she thought here's Morrell, let's have a ball. I had to get away fast, to get back to the flat and then pick you up, so I told her I was leaving for the States tonight. It had to be something like that or she'd have gone on pestering me. Anyway, it was the first thing came into my head. It was just damn bad luck. I'm sorry, Inge. I'm more sorry than I can say."

"It's no worry at all to me, Nick. They put on stunts to get much less publicity than that. We'll be on the front pages tomorrow – *all* of them –"

"Yes, I know it.... Well, we'd better not go to my flat, now."

"Why should we not?"

"Hell, they'll be waiting for us, six deep! They can't help knowing who you are, and they'll know who I am too, by now." He swore. "Oh, damn it! They photographed us when we arrived, didn't they? They have my name anyway. This may be fine for your publicity, but it's a real stinker for mine."

"You don't want to be seen out with me?"

"Not in a squalid brawl."

"But it's not your fault, is it? Just because that drunken fool –"

"It's a long, complicated story, but the short way to explain it is that my own chairman's already busy setting me up for a character assassination. He'll grab this with both hands – it's a gift for him. Now if they trace you back to my flat, just think what they'll make of it! You don't want *that* kind of publicity, do you?"

"You're taking me back to my hotel?"

"Wouldn't that be best?"

"No. I want to talk to you. Can't we just stop this car somewhere quiet?"

"Sure we can." They'd just passed Slough. He thought, I'll turn south in a minute, down on to the A4. Find a quiet turn-off after that. He told her, "Better get off this motorway first. "There's probably a posse on our tail already."

"But they'll be waiting at the hotel too, won't they?"

"Bound to be. That's hardly the same as catching you in a parked car or arriving at a bachelor's pad after midnight."

"I suppose you're right." He'd put his left hand out to her: she held it tightly. "Stop soon, please, Nick. What I want to talk about is important."

The press were waiting in strength outside the Dorchester. Cameras starting popping the minute he stopped the car. The doorman helped Inge to alight: a barrage of flashes exploded in her face. They began again as Morrell joined her and they walked inside together. The reporters were shouting questions, jostling to get in close. In the foyer, Morrell faced them, holding up his hands.

"Just a minute –"

Flash.

"Now wait, will you? Please? Miss Hegardt wants to make a statement. She'd like you all to come up to her suite to hear it. Just give her five minutes to straighten up – will you do that, please? Then she'll be ready to answer all the questions you want to ask. Okay?"

He told an anxious-looking hotel executive, "Don't worry. We'll make it short and snappy. Send up a dozen bottles of good champagne, please, and two dozen glasses – and hold this gang here five, ten minutes. Can you manage that?"

"Very well, sir. But it's late, and most of our residents will be trying to get some sleep. I hope you'll try to keep the noise down."

"Leave it to me." Inge moved towards the lifts. She was calm, unflustered, smiling at the Pressmen. Morrell said quietly, "The champagne's to be on my account, not Miss Hegardt's. I'll settle when I leave, or you can send the bill." He handed the man a card.

"As you wish, sir."

Morrell hurried after Inge. By the time the journalists assembled in her suite, he had the champagne poured ready for them. Inge came in from the bedroom: she looked radiant, as sleekly beautiful as if she'd spent the whole evening resting and just got dressed for a late party. Morrell handed her a glass: she took it, and linked her other arm with his.

Cameras were poised, pointing at them from all directions. Inge raised her glass.

"Gentlemen. I invite you to drink to my engagement to Mr. Nicholas Morrell!"

CHAPTER TWENTY-TWO

Morrell threw his briefcase into the back of the taxi and climbed in after it. He told the driver, "Empire State. If it's still there." The driver glanced at him over his shoulder, poker-faced: then he threw his cab into gear and set off from the airport terminal.

Morrell hadn't told McLennan he was coming, but Gil would be expecting him all the same. Any likelihood of surprising him with an unannounced arrival had been obliterated by the flash of cameras when he'd landed here from England a couple of days ago. They'd had the story about him and Inge on the Saturday, and when he'd flown in, an hour or so behind her own plane, the boys had been waiting for him. So

Gil McLennan would have read in his newspaper that one of his vice presidents had touched down in home territory to a blaze of personal publicity – without having either told him he was coming or contacted him on arrival.

It was just one more thing Gil McLennan wasn't going to like. And it would have had all the more annoyance-value for the fact that only the day before all the New York papers had carried pictures of the nightclub fracas, wired from London where they'd been spread across most front pages, linked with the pictures taken later in Inge's suite.

On that Saturday morning, Briscoe had telephoned him at the office and asked him brusquely if he'd seen the papers. Morrell had said just as brusquely yes, of course he had. There had been a pause, then, before Sir Charles asked, "Have you any explanation to offer?"

"What for?"

"For this highly unfortunate – er – exhibition –"

"If you want an explanation, you'd better get hold of the Baines woman." Morrell put his hand over the mouthpiece and winked at Priscilla. "Might do him a world of good –"

"You realize that this scurrilous brand of publicity is the worst possible thing for McLennan Ridgeway? You may imagine that your private life is your own affair, Morrell, but you will have observed that our company's name is mentioned in juxtaposition to – er – degrading photographs?"

"I can read, if that's what you mean."

"Morrell, I take the most serious view of this and of your attitude towards it in retrospect.'"

"Shouldn't you have started by congratulating me on my engagement?"

"Under the circumstances – no. I *deplore* –"

"Marriage wouldn't appeal to you, I dare say –"

"Will you repeat that, Morrell?"

"I'll make it clearer. I can understand your disinterest in marriage and therefore I am prepared to overlook your discourtesy on this occasion. But right now I have a lot to do, and if you don't mind I'll get on with it."

"We will discuss this further on Monday."

"Like hell we will. I'll be in Washington."

"Oh. Yes, I'd forgotten. On your return, then."

"I've no intention, Briscoe, of discussing my personal affairs with you at *any* time. Good-bye."

He banged the 'phone down. Priscilla coughed, and checked the place in her shorthand notebook. She murmured, "Letter to Grant. Your last paragraph was: 'In discussing these matters with the unions you should point out that agreements now on swapping labour between the two yards will be only extensions of their earlier endorsement of complete flexibility within –' " Priscilla looked up. "That's when the 'phone rang."

"Within the five established groups, namely engineering, metal working, wood working, finishing and ancillary. There is also agreement in principle for interchange between the groups, and you had better raise this with them at the same time . . . Right, that's all for him. What's next?"

He stopped work at noon, arranging with Priscilla that she'd come to the United Hunts Club at one-fifteen. He went straight to Aspreys, where he found Inge waiting: she'd already chosen the ring she wanted, and by luck it was a good enough fit. A big diamond, flanked by squarecut emeralds.

The salesman accepted Morrell's cheque: even in Aspreys, apparently, they read the newspapers. Morrell asked him, "Can you organize a taxi for us? The sight of Miss Hegardt out there's liable to attract a crowd."

"Of course, sir."

They got into it quickly, unrecognized, and drove to the Hunts Club. In here, they were safe: and Johnny was overjoyed at seeing them. Morrell introduced him to Inge. He told her, "You wouldn't believe how many times this fellow's saved my life."

"In that case I adore him too!"

Johnny was smiling so broadly he could hardly speak. Wrenching his eyes off Inge, he focused on Morrell and put his hand on the Martini shaker.

"Not that stuff, Johnny. This is a champagne morning."

They were well into the first bottle when Priscilla arrived, and by the time they went into lunch they were all three aware that this was a celebration. Morrell was pleased that the two girls seemed to have found a lot in common. Priscilla was telling Inge now, "Our chairman didn't much care for this morning's pictures." She glanced at Morrell, smiling. "He got a darn good earful in return, though!"

Inge asked him, "Is this the same man you told me last night was trying to make trouble for you?"

"Not trying to. *Is*. Not that it's getting him anywhere."

He'd said it lightly, but he was worried. After the showdown at that meeting, followed by the public crushing of Gaisford and the smear campaign, he'd thought Briscoe would have pulled his head back at any rate for long enough to lick his wounds. Now it was evident from that phone call, futile as it had been, that Sir Charles had no intention of letting up. So presumably he had another trick or two up his sleeves. Morrell thought, Well, there's nothing much he can do that makes more than nuisance value. I've stopped him so far: I'll go right on stopping him.

McLennan came out to the anteroom to meet him. He said, shaking hands, "Sure is nice to have celebrities drop in on us. When they feel they have a little time to throw away, that is." Morrell smiled, but didn't answer. The old principle was a good one, tried and tested: let the enemy loose off all he has, then go in and fix him. Well, this was no enemy. McLennan growled, "Come in my office. I guess you have a little explaining to do."

Morrell followed him inside. To his surprise, Seymour Laing was in there, lounging in a deep chair. Laing was sixty-four, now, to Gil McLennan's sixty-seven, but of the two he looked older. He climbed to his feet, and shook hands.

"Well, Nick. Congratulations."

"Nice of you to say that, Seymour."

"Goddam it, I clean forgot." McLennan held out his hand. "All the best, Nick."

"Thanks, Gil."

"Some looker, huh?" Morrell nodded. McLennan asked him, "How about La Baines busting you one, all that stuff? We had it in the papers here, Briscoe sent me a heap more – well, go on, tell us what happened, will you?"

"If you saw the papers, you know as much as I do. I saw her for the first time in ten years, I told her I couldn't manage a date with her, later she sees me with Inge and she's blind drunk. . . . She's a nut, that's all."

"You're really intending to marry the Swedish girl?"

"Sure I am."

"Why are you over here now – because she is?"

"Certainly not. I had to go to Washington –"

"Yeah. We heard about that. And since you're so busy stealing our contracts from us, from your own goddam company, you didn't like to show your smug puss in here until you had it all signed up. Right? In case I talked you into dropping out, huh?"

"Wouldn't have been a hope in hell of that happening, Gil. And my own company is McLennan Ridgeway, not McLennans New York. I've been doing my job, that's all. I had to get straight to Washington, because Ed Swarthout wanted it signed before his Committee started back-tracking. I'd have gone direct to Washington, except they haven't inaugurated that route yet. It'll be a help when they do."

"You're planning more, are you? Well, Nick, how would you feel if I flew into London and pinched a big job you'd been working on for damn nearly a year?" McLennan put a cigar in his mouth and held a match to its other end, but his eyes never left Morrell's face. "How would you like that?"

"I don't suppose I'd like it much. But your first question, how I'd *feel* – that'd be one, I must be slipping: two, *you* must be on the ball. Something like that."

"So I'm slipping. That's what you think?"

"Of course not. What this comes down to is you object to competition from your own British company. Do you have any reason to think you'd have picked up the contract if I hadn't been in the running for it?"

"We thought our chances were pretty good."

"Why don't you talk to Ed Swarthout, Gil? I'm pretty sure there were two or three more competitive tenders than yours. You check that. If it isn't so, I'll agree I've stolen some business from you. But as things are, the way I see them, I've won a contract from competition which didn't include you, and I've won it for *your* British company – and that's what I'm paid for, anyway. If there's anything about the situation which you don't like, you'd better spell it out very carefully because from my angle it's unlikely to make too much sense."

"I'll check with Ed."

"Good. But suppose you *had* been next in line? Have I ever had any instructions or requests not to compete in the American market?" He looked at Laing. "Would I have been doing my job if I'd held back?"

Seymour Laing shrugged. "In the general principle of the thing, you can understand Gil feeling a little uncomfortable. Can't you?"

"Certainly. I'm uncomfortable every time I fail to win an order."

McLennan scowled. "You're an uncompromising bastard, Nick. So maybe I didn't lose anything. But for the future, I want this kind of operation handled differently. We're closely associated companies, engaged in very similar activities and with joint marketing arrangements in many parts of the world. It's crazy we should knock our heads together. If you compete for a U.S. contract, or if I go after a British one, we do it from here on in consultation, each informing the other of what he's doing." He pointed at Morrell with his cigar. "*Before* – not *after*. Okay?"

"You mean if I was coming in with a tender you couldn't match, you'd stay out – and vice versa?"

"Maybe. Depends on circumstances."

"Dangerous. Suppose that happened, and they turned me down simply in order to keep the contract in the States? Then you wouldn't be in there to catch it. And another thing. Not only do I have a job I'm paid to do, but in the present state of the British economy I'm bound to look harder for export orders than home orders. Now I don't want to be beaten by, say, some Dutch yard just because you dream up a new system that ties my hands –"

"Who's tying your goddam hands, for Christ's sake?"

"An elaborate routine could delay a tender going in."

"What's so elaborate about letting me have copies of tenders you submit in the United States?"

"That's all you want?"

"I just said so, didn't I?"

"Well, that's fine." Morrell smiled at Laing. "No problems."

"Here's another thing. Seems to me we're cutting our own throats by shipping you our powerboat hulls. We used to sell completed boats in Europe, Australia, New Zealand, South Africa –"

"Not as cheaply as I can sell them now. I'm not taking anything from you, I'm *making* it for you. Don't you see it that way?"

"On the broad front, sure. But in this specific area, the pleasure-craft, I'm losing what you're making. Right here in the home market we have competition hotting up so much that in the last six months we sold fewer boats than we did in any three-month period in the preceding five years. Now, that's not good news."

"But your production must still be well up. I haven't just taken over those markets, I've trebled powerboat sales in them. Well, why not, when the product's cheaper and right on the doorstep? It isn't out of this pocket and into that one: it's a little less maybe into this one and certainly a great deal more into the other. Overall it's better business – and it's *your* business, Gil. . . ." He glanced at Seymour Laing. "Am I missing some point?"

"Hard to say, without the figures." Laing asked McLennan, "Gil, why don't we get a complete breakdown of sales and profits in that division over the past three years? Split into sales of our boats and sales of hulls to the British yard. If we could have that data while Nick's with us, I guess we could arrive at the right conclusion without too much difficulty?"

"All right, I'll put Selby on it right away." McLennan made a note. "How long you planning to stay, Nick?"

"I'd thought all week." Morrell smiled. "Well, it wouldn't be wasted time, and it happens Inge's here until the week-end. But the way things are going at home – particularly with Briscoe – I think I'd better get back as soon as I can."

"I'll have the figures we need tomorrow morning. Say ten o'clock, the three of us, in this office?" They both nodded. "You could take the afternoon plane out, if you want to. . . . Now, Nick, how about you and this chairman Briscoe? He keeps writing me, and from what he says you can't even be civil to him. Is that right?"

He nodded. "Close enough. The fact is, he wants me out. The company's in good shape now because thanks to the free hand you've given me, I've done what I went over there to do. All I've done is apply the lessons I learnt here. Now Briscoe would like to be seen to be running the show. He'd run it, all right – back into the ground. But for the moment all his peculiar talents are concentrated on getting rid of me."

Morrell talked for half an hour while McLennan and Laing listened, putting in an occasional question. He told them about the constant and now mounting attacks – accusations of fostering his own public image, the Pelly affair, and the Gaisford attempt to frame him.

"The object of all that was to discredit me in *your* eyes. Briscoe knows damn well he can't touch me while you're behind me, so he'd like to shake you and me apart. I'm confidently expecting further moves in the same direction – so don't be surprised what you hear."

Gil McLennan opened a large, buff file of letters, minutes of meetings and news clippings. He shook the contents of the file in a heavy shower into his waste basket.

"There you are. Ninety per cent of that is stuff about you. I get a drawerful of it every week. See where it ends up?"

Morrell grinned. "Where it belongs. Fine."

"Yeah. . . . Nick, if anything comes up that worries me or that I don't understand, I'll let you know." He patted the telephone. "I'll be on to you in a matter of minutes, when that happens. Meanwhile, Briscoe can write all the reports he wants. Unless you hear directly and personally from me, you can assume it's water off the old duck's back. . . . You free for lunch?"

"I think so. I'd like to call Inge first."

"Sure. Bring her too, why don't you? Hey, Nick – why not bring her out to Greenwich tonight? Toni'd just love to meet her – hell, I mean, she'd like to see you too, but –"

"I'll have to check with Inge. This is a publicity tour she's on, TV appearances and all that. She said they'd be keeping her busy."

"Yeah, I guess so." McLennan frowned. "How are you going to handle it, Nick? A wife with a career in pictures?"

Morrell shrugged. "We'll work it out." It wasn't his job to make any premature announcements about Inge Hegardt's intention to refuse any new contracts after she'd finished the current one. She'd be choosing her own moment to drop *that* bombshell.

McLennan was grinning at Laing. "Our boy likes to have it the hard way, I guess."

"There's nothing hard about marrying Inge."

"I'm glad to hear that. One more personal question, before we go to eat?"

"Go ahead."

"McLennan Ridgeway. Can't be too comfortable, with all Briscoe's crap. And you're not short of money now. You and this celebrity wife of yours could live off your fat for a hundred years. Or you could take a job where you didn't get shot at all the time. Right?"

Morrell nodded. "I suppose so."

"So why don't you?"

"Because McLennan Ridgeway's my baby. Like your pleasure-craft division was. I didn't want to leave New York, you know that. But you persuaded me to go over, and now this job's under my skin. I want to see it through." He met McLennan's stare: it was blank, interested in the answer but giving nothing away. Talking to Gil McLennan, he thought, was like feeding data to a computor: the facts were stored away for a reaction which might come years later at a touch on the appropriate key. He turned to Laing. "I'm enjoying it, I suppose, because I'm producing results. I've got my teeth in it and I don't see much reason to let go. Certainly not in favour of that bastard Briscoe."

They were looking at him, both of them, as if they were trying to see more in his words than their surface meaning. If there was more to it than that, Morrell didn't know it. He thought, If you throw a dog into a pond, it starts to swim. Put a man in a ring and punch him on the nose, he hits back.

He asked McLennan, "Mind if I use your phone?"

It was a lovely evening. They'd had dinner: McLennan had switched on the outside lighting and he was showing Inge the pool. Morrell and Toni stood on the terrace looking down at them, just catching the murmur of their voices in the still night air.

Toni slipped a hand inside Morrell's arm.

"She's sweet, Nick. Really a nice person. I hope you'll be very, very happy."

"Thanks." He looked at her, and smiled. "You seem a little bit – well, unfrozen, Toni. Is it me getting engaged to Inge that's done it?"

"Maybe." She watched the other two, strolling now beyond the pool. "Yes, all right, I'll admit it. I'll be glad to know you're settled down, raising your own family –"

"That's moving a bit fast, but I think I understand you. While I'm at large, loose, I'm some kind of threat – if not to you, to Alison?"

"Let's just say I'm glad things are working out like this. We can all be friends, now, without feelings of – oh, thoughts of any other kind of relationship. Nick, I was watching your face when you were playing with Alison earlier on. You're really fond of her, aren't you?"

"She's my –"

"Don't say it. Don't even *think* it. For her sake, Nick, make yourself forget all that. Think of her as Gil's daughter – like I do. *Believe* she is. Will you try to do that?"

"I'm not good at brain-washing myself. But don't worry, I can keep a secret."

"Will you feel you have to tell Inge?"

"No. I wouldn't dream of telling anyone. All I'm saying is I can't delude myself. You know the facts, I know them. So it stays with us. We *know* it."

"I'm determined Alison shouldn't know. Ever, or whatever happens to any of us. Will you promise me you'll never tell her?"

"If you believe such a promise is necessary." He patted Toni's hand. "Don't worry. I'm nuts about Alison, so I want what's best for her. Okay?"

"Okay. And thank you. Nick, I was a bit tough, wasn't I? A few years ago, at the time you left?"

He nodded. "A little. I'm over it now, though."

"I only acted as I thought was best for us. For Alison mostly, but for us too – you, me, Gil. . . . If I hurt you, Nick, I'm sorry. I can tell you it wasn't easy for me either – except I just knew that was how it had to be."

Gil and Inge had started to climb the steps back to the terrace. Morrell said quietly, "That's old history, now." He called down to Gil McLennan, "About time too, you brought my girl back!"

Later, driving Inge into New York, he asked her how she'd liked the McLennans. She told him she'd liked Toni very much; and the little girl, Alison, was charming.

"She has quite a look of you, Nick. Do you know that?"

"Of *me*?" He didn't look at her. "What a crazy idea."

"It's true. She could be your daughter."

"Well, she isn't. She's Gil's and Toni's. Hell, she looks like *Gil* –"

"I don't think she does. I can see her mother in her, but when she smiles her eyes go just like yours. I can't see him at all."

Morrell switched the subject. "Didn't you like Gil?"

"I don't *dis*like him. He's a charming man and a very kind host. But he is – well, I don't think I would trust him very far. He's too much like a fox –"

He laughed. "That's what the boys at the yard call him. The Silver Fox." He thought, I'll have to watch my step. This future wife of mine sees too damn much.

"How did he get to be so rich?"

"That's a long story and I still don't know all of it. He's been in a lot of things – and out of them. Lost all his money at least once. He got a big stake from the wife he had before Toni. She died – around 1946, I suppose it was. During the war was when he started to make good in a big way: I think it was Elizabeth's money he used to get the yard going, and he had some first-class brains working for him. He introduced welding instead of riveting – that speeds things up – and launching sideways instead of stern-first, which saves space in the yard. And he used his political connections to keep the yard in his own hands – otherwise it would almost certainly have been taken over by the government. From there on he's never looked back."

"He told me you did enormous things for him when you were working here."

"Nice of him to say that. Well, I put in my two bits' worth, as they say, but I learnt a hell of a lot in the process. I owe McLennans plenty. I didn't know a damn thing about anything, until they taught me."

Inge was silent, for a few minutes. He wondered if she was thinking about Alison: which would mean, of course, about him and Toni. But she didn't mention it when she spoke.

"Where will we live, after we've married?"

"Wherever you like. But we'll certainly need to have a flat in London – a bigger one than I have now, so we have room to entertain – and I've been wondering how you'd feel about a house in the country, down near the Beaulieu River. It's nice country, and we have a yard down there, at Hamble, which would make for convenience as far as I'm concerned. I have a boat of my own there too, so we'd have that to play with."

"It sounds lovely."

"Well, when you're back in England in three weeks' time –"

"Four, Nick."

"Okay, in four weeks' time – we'll go down there and look around. But I was thinking we might have some little place in the sun, too. Sardinia, perhaps – on that stretch of coast the Aga Khan's developing." He smiled at her. "That would give you one flat and two houses to find and furnish. You'd enjoy it, wouldn't you?"

"First I want time to enjoy just being married to you."

"Now *that*'s something I'm going to work at."

In the morning he met McLennan and Laing, as they'd arranged, in the Manhattan office. They went over the figures for the pleasure-craft operation, and the picture which emerged from the detailed analysis was both clear and happy. Sales in the American home market were certainly lower than they had been: but taking the Hamble yard into account and the business through both companies as one international marketing effort, world sales were considerably higher than before. And McLennan profits on sales of hulls to the British yard more than balanced the loss of sales on complete boats to European and other export markets.

Morrell sat back, looking at McLennan. Gil should, he thought, have been smiling: but he wasn't.

"Aren't you satisfied, Gil?"

"With this?" McLennan nodded. "Sure. Nothing wrong here at all. No, what's griping me is *this*." He picked up a letter from his desk. From halfway across the room, Morrell recognized the McLennan Ridgeway letterhead. McLennan said, "Came in this morning. From your buddy Briscoe."

"What's he trying now?"

"Seems it's not him, this time. It's your goddam Limey government. They've told Briscoe they intend to broaden and –" he glanced down at the letter, frowning – "yeah, *fully implement* their declared policy of shipyard mergers throughout the industry. Not only the unprofitable areas, but the whole lot – including McLennan Ridgeway. You realize what this'll mean, if they go through with it?"

"Can I see that letter?"

"Sure." McLennan passed it over. Morrell skimmed through it quickly.

"They can't do this –"

"The hell they can't." McLennan watched Morrell pass Briscoe's letter to Seymour Laing. "If it's government policy, we have to go along with it. Merge into some lousy great combine – 'rationalization' is the word they use, and it's a euphemism if there ever was one – so we'd lose our identity, water down the management, dilute the equity and f— up the whole goddam operation! We'd lose control! Well, I tell you – if this goes through, McLennans pull out first. I'm damned if I'll sink my profits into supporting lame ducks with half-baked management – d'you hear me, Nick? If this is true, it's the end of the road!"

"Gil, cool down. Relax. Sit back a minute – *think* ... I told you, they want me out. They've realized now they can't get me out while you're in control. So what's the next step? Easy – shake *you* out. And how do they set about it? I tell you. Briscoe runs round to the minister, Elliot Hooper, who happens to be his little friend. And they hatch this up. Well, it doesn't make sense otherwise. But they reckon you'll believe it and pull out – exactly the way you've reacted. So that gets rid of you – and believe me, now the outfit's running in top gear they'd be tickled pink to have it all back in British hands. In the process they lose me too, of course. They get a highly profitable company, and it's all theirs – clean sweep. Once you're out and I'm out, that's all they want – they can forget any merger. Gil, this is simply one more trick – and it's a bluff."

"If we sell out now, we'll be okay. If we take a chance and wait until the shares drop –"

"They won't drop. If they do on the rumour, who cares? They'll pick up again. Give me three weeks to call their bluff."

"How would you set about it?"

"Have I ever let you down yet?"

"No –"

"I won't now, either. Remember, Gil, I stand to lose too. Give me three weeks – even two. Will you, please?"

CHAPTER TWENTY-THREE

Priscilla knocked and came in. She said, "Mr. von Mettendorf is on his way up now. Shall I show him right in?"

"Yeah." Morrell smiled at her. He felt like singing: he could have jumped out of his chair and kissed her, he felt so good. He'd beaten not just Briscoe, but Elliot Hooper too.

He hadn't done it alone. The job had been done – that was what mattered, what made this a lot better than any ordinary, early summer afternoon. He told Priscilla, "Yeah. Bring him straight in, will you?"

She nodded, "I'm still trying to get that line to New York."

"Good. Keep at it."

He'd booked the call to McLennan, to tell him the good news. It was something he was looking forward to: the pleasure of proving he'd been right when he'd said it was a bluff, and the fact that he'd called it, drawn the enemy's teeth. And in ten days, not three weeks.

The first thing he'd done had been to drop in on Guy Davies at his newspaper: he'd shown him a photostat of Briscoe's letter to McLennan. Davies had expressed astonishment. When Morrell had explained the motives behind the threat, astonishment had given way to anger.

"They can't play ducks and drakes with the industry just to satisfy one man's ego!"

"That's what they *are* doing. No doubt they'll think up a lot of spurious justifications for it, but that's what it amounts to."

"If your guess is right." Davies glanced up. "Is it any more than a guess?"

"Maybe not. But I'm sure of it. It's part of a pattern, you see, which I've seen growing for some while. And if you can produce any other reason for it – a reason for serious intent to cripple a thriving company with a very high export performance – well, you let me know, because I'd like to hear it." Morrell shook his head. "There's no such alternative, Guy. It's what I say – a bluff, to force McLennans out. In the process, they'd cut back on all the progress we've made, but that doesn't worry them a bit. Well, possibly it would, if they had the sense or ability to see it straight. They don't know enough – either about the business or their own incompetence."

"Are you saying we British are incompetent?"

"Don't be wet, Guy. You know I'm not saying anything of the sort. I'm saying Briscoe and his gang are incompetent and ignorant. They probably imagine that now the show's rolling along so well, even they could keep it ticking over. Well, they couldn't. First thing would be that under Briscoe labour relations would go right back to square one. They hate him – and they've good reason to. The way we've been running the yards, they know their jobs are safe – that's why they can afford to co-operate with us. Once Briscoe's in charge again, *nobody's* safe. The orders'll dry up, jobs in hand will fall behind schedule – hell, the old vicious circle. Guy, these are facts I'm talking, I'm telling you what's just around the corner!"

"Not without a small axe to grind –"

"Sure I have. Not so damn small, either."

"It *could* be argued that British industry is best in British hands?"

"Claptrap. We need all the help we can get, and we need dollar investment too. You think it's unpatriotic to use American help to build a profit-making industry? If you do, you need your head seeing to."

"Tactful as ever." Davies smiled. "You really believe Hooper would have gone this far to help his friend Briscoe?"

"Well, he has, hasn't he? The proof of the pudding's in that letter. Maybe it'd be good for his rating politically to push the Americans out – I don't know, maybe there's some other reason."

"Perhaps there is." Davies stood up, crossed the room and unlocked a filing cabinet. "On the subject of Briscoe and Hooper, d'you remember a chat we had the other day – when I told you I had something you'd be interested to see? Well, here it is." He came back to the desk, and put a photograph face-down in front of Morrell. "Take a deep breath, Nick, then turn it over."

Morrell flipped the print right-side up. Davies murmured, "Taken in Capri, two summers ago. The photographer wasn't looking for Hooper – he was one of a whole bunch trailing a certain Royal person and her husband. Telescopic lens."

Morrell sat transfixed, examining the print. It showed Elliot Hooper in Bermuda shorts and a flowered shirt. Beside him, Sir Charles Briscoe white and skinny in a pair of bathing pants. They were walking across a lawn – grass, anyway – and they were holding hands.

Morrell looked up at Davies. "I suppose you couldn't ever print this."

"No." The journalist shook his head. "I couldn't. I've only kept it for its own peculiar fascination. You can have it, if you like. The negative's around here somewhere."

"Thanks." Morrell laughed, still looking at it. "What a repulsive pair they are. . . ." He slid it into his wallet. "Now listen. What I was thinking, about this McLennan Ridgeway business, is that you could perhaps report the story as emanating from New York, and then go on to tear it apart – if such intentions do exist, etcetera. Now if you could build it into something of a campaign, maybe get a few other papers to pick it up from you – stir the whole thing up as a scandal that has to be prevented and so on – export orders, jobs – you've got records of MR's performance over the last few years, and there can't be much more convincing argument than those figures –"

"All right, all right." Davies nodded. "I get the message. Jack Dunsfold'd join in on this, too. And he and I could have a talk to Don Tremloe – get the Opposition warmed up on it."

Morrell nodded. "Exactly what I was going to suggest. Bring the issue to boiling point, then –"

"Put Hooper on the spot by having Tremloe ask a question in the House." Davies grinned at Morrell across the desk. "How're we doing?"

The call to McLennan still hadn't gone through when Karl von Mettendorf arrived. Priscilla showed the German in, and Morrell greeted him warmly. Karl was one of his closer friends, these days: apart from anything else, it was he who'd introduced him to Inge Hegardt. Besides, Morrell was feeling well disposed to almost everyone, this afternoon.

"Surprise visit, Karl? You usually let us know a day or two ahead. Trying to catch me on the hop?"

Von Mettendorf shook his head.

"This is a private visit, Nick. I wanted to see you – well, personally. I have a little trouble on my hands, you see."

"You've come to the right place, then." Morrell grinned. "This room is trouble headquarters. I've just climbed out of a real sticky one myself."

"The government merger policy?"

"You know about it, then."

Karl nodded. "I read all your papers. They seem to be clearly on your side."

Morrell nodded, smiling. "They do, don't they?"

"You put them on it, did you?"

"Me?" He looked astonished. "Come on, Karl, you know me better than that. Anyway, the climax came this afternoon. Man called Tremloe –"

"Sir Donald?"

"Well, you *are* well informed." Morrell nodded. "You probably know also that in the Shadow Cabinet he's Elliot Hooper's opposite number?"

Von Mettendorf nodded.

"Tremloe got up on his hind legs and asked the minister – Hooper – whether in order to put an end to uncertainties in the shipbuilding industry he would either confirm or deny a government intention to force self-sufficient companies or groups, in particular McLennan Ridgeway Ltd., into mergers which in the view of the companies themselves and the industry as a whole were both unnecessary and undesirable. Hooper replied with a straightforward denial of there being any truth or basis for the rumours which had been reported in the press: he said the government's policy towards this industry was well established and there was no change contemplated. So that's us off the hook."

"I congratulate you. Have you told Gil yet?"

"I've a call going through now. . . . Well, Karl, let's hear *your* trouble. I gather you think I may be able to help, or you wouldn't be here now. That right?"

"I don't believe you can help." Von Mettendorf shook his head. "I've come here more to warn you than to ask for your assistance. You see, it affects you very closely."

Morrell closed his eyes. "Don't tell me I'm up the bloody creek again *this* soon." He opened his eyes. "All right. Let's hear it."

Karl took a long breath. He said, "I am going to have to sell my McLennan Ridgeway stock."

Morrell waited, watching him.

Karl continued, "I am under pressure to sell it. From my own board. We are a little over-committed: we have to find some money to cover certain – well, expenditures – and we have a buyer for the stock –"

"Presumably you'll offer it to McLennans?"

"Naturally that was my first thought. But Gil's not interested."

"Not *interested*?" Morrell's face cleared. "Oh, I get it. Well, maybe he will be when he hears my news. He was thinking of pulling out altogether – if Hooper hadn't backed down. I imagine he'll feel quite differently now we're in the clear –"

Priscilla buzzed. He flicked the switch. "Yes?"

"Your New York call. Mr. McLennan on the line."

"Thanks." He grabbed the phone. "You there, Gil?"

"Sure, Nick, I'm here. Nice work, boy!"

"You *know* about it?"

"Sure. Briscoe called me half an hour back. Like he'd fixed it all himself."

"The shrewd bastard –"

"Yeah. I congratulated him. Showered him with thanks. I also asked him to convey my appreciation to his friend at the Ministry."

"The hell you did. Well, that's taken the wind out of *my* sails, hasn't it?"

"He's a smart shit, all right. Makes no difference though: you pulled it off. I know it and he knows it and what's more he knows I know it. So who does he think he's fooling?"

"Keeping the record straight, that's all. So he can report what he's done to the board and take all the credit instead of being shown up for the creep he really is. Gil, there's something else."

"Shoot."

"I've Karl von Mettendorf here with me. He tells me you know about his little problem. Am I right in thinking you'll be feeling differently about that now we've fixed the other nonsense?"

"I'm not buying his stock, if that's what you mean."

"But Gil, for Christ's sake! If anyone else gets it – and I'll lay you ten to one this is another ploy from the same quarter – that'll put as much of the equity in outside hands as you own yourself. So where's the control?"

"With your piece of the equity –"

"That's a knife-edge position whichever way you look at it. And they wouldn't be doing this without damn good reason. Even if there's nothing more up their sleeves, it'll strengthen their position and weaken yours. Gil, won't you think again?"

"I'm sorry, Nick. I've got all the MR stock I want, and the last thing I need right now is to get in deeper. I'm getting a little sick of all this, Nick – besides, I'd have to go to the bank for it, and that's a hell of a lot of dough. I have plenty of use for money right here. Another point is there are new restrictions coming in on overseas investment, so even if I wanted to – which I don't – I'm not sure they'd let me. Anyhow, Nick, like I said, with your five per cent we'll still have the edge on them. And you don't know it's *those* people."

"I've a damn good idea it'll turn out to be. They simply aren't letting go – it's one damn thing after another. You say you're sick of it – well, so am I, but don't you see that's just what they want? All they need do is keep the pressure up until you're *really* sick, wait for you to drop off –"

"Nick, don't get all carried away. Nobody's dropping off. You tell Karl to offer his stock some place else. Hell, MR stock is as good an investment as you'll find. Tell him to try Zürich?"

"I'll tell him, Gil." Morrell glanced across the room at von Mettendorf. He felt tired, suddenly – like Gil McLennan, sick of the whole damn thing. "Gil, give it a little more thought, will you?"

"God damn it, no I will not! Now you have my answer, Nick. You look after your end of it, and tell Karl from me he should look after his. You can handle this, between you –"

"You're telling me we're on our own. Right?"

"Sure you are. Nick, about the other thing, the matter you called to tell me about – well done. I mean that. You did a first-class job."

Morrell hung up, with his eyes on von Mettendorf. He said wearily, "You were right. He doesn't want to help. What in hell's got into him? Just when we looked like winning –" Morrell slammed the desk with his fist. "I was thinking this was a *good* day!"

"What did he say you should tell me?"

"Oh, to look around and unload your stock somewhere safe. Zürich, he suggested."

Karl shrugged. "I could sell it anywhere. The difficulty is, you see, these people are offering a premium. The offer is well over the market price. That's why my board in Hamburg is so keen to take it."

Morrell's eyes had widened. "And that just about proves it's these – Karl, who's making the offer?"

"A company that calls itself Stanley Investments. A new unit trust company. Nick, I told Gil McLennan this, he knows it. The Stanley Investments chairman is a director on your board here. Lord Hunstanly."

"Well, well." Morrell passed a hand over his eyes. "Now we

really see the niggers in the woodpile. And you say McLennan *knows* this?"

"I told him yesterday. He said that didn't prove anything – a man like Hunstanly's on plenty of boards, there doesn't have to be any plot...." Von Mettendorf shrugged. "You see now why I felt I had to come and warn you. Not that there is anything much you can do about it –"

"The hell there isn't!" Morrell stared at him. "Can you stall Hunstanly and keep your board quiet for a week or so?"

"With what object, Nick?"

"To give me time to find an alternative buyer, of course. It shouldn't be all that difficult...." He felt, quite suddenly, a new surge of fighting spirit. "Give me a week, Karl. Two, if you can. But even a few days might be enough. Hang on as long as you can, will you?"

"I'll do my best –"

The intercom buzzed: Morrell saw the light burning above the slot marked *Chairman*. He pushed the switch up.

"Yes?"

Briscoe's voice said, "That danger would appear to have been averted, Morrell."

"It would, wouldn't it."

"A great relief."

"I was sure you'd be pleased."

"Quite.... I'm informed Mr. von Mettendorf is in the building. Do you know where he is?"

Morrell glanced at von Mettendorf. The German stood up quickly, and shook his head.

"He was with me, but he's left. Going straight back to Hamburg, I believe."

"Oh, really." Briscoe's tone was flat. "I would have liked a word with him. Pity." The light went out: Morrell switched off.

"You'd better scoot, Karl. I expect he knows damn well you're still here." Morrell stood up, and moved towards the door. Von Mettendorf picked his briefcase off the desk. Morrell asked him, "You'll give me a week to get something started?"

"I'll stall as long as I can."

"All I ask." They shook hands. "Keep in touch, eh?"

Priscilla knocked on the door, and opened it. She said, her voice edged with anxiety, "Sir Charles is –"

"Ah, Mettendorf, my dear fellow!" Briscoe came in smiling, holding out his hand. "I was afraid I might have missed you. This is a *great* pleasure, unexpected and therefore all the more – er –"

Briscoe glanced at Morrell as if he was surprised to see him in his own office. Morrell pointed at the briefcase.

"He came back for that –"

Karl nodded. "And now I have to hurry even more –"

"Oh, surely you can spare a minute? Just one minute? I've been looking forward to a little chat with you." The chairman's smile exuded charm. "Just one brief minute in my office?"

"Very well."

Von Mettendorf shook hands again with Morrell. Briscoe ushered him out: then, with the half-open door between himself and the German, he turned and looked at Morrell. He said, speaking so quietly that his voice was almost a whisper, "I'm told it's the last round that really matters, Morrell. And we haven't had that one yet, have we?"

The outer door opened and shut behind him and von Mettendorf. Morrell was still standing there, thinking almost entirely in four-letter words, when Priscilla hurried in. Her face was white.

"I'm terribly sorry. I couldn't hold him, he just –"

"That's all right. Wasn't your fault, Priscilla." He flopped into his chair. "Now I know what a man feels like just before he takes to the bottle."

She frowned her concern. "It can't be *that* bad –"

"You're right. It isn't." He looked up at her sharply. "Of course it isn't. And Briscoe's right too – we *haven't* had the last round yet."

"I'm afraid I don't –"

"I know. I'm rambling. . . . I tell you one thing I want to do. One day. I want, one day, to put the heel of my shoe in that man's face and just sort of grind it in."

"You've been doing it for the last three years, haven't you?"

"Bad as that?" It surprised him: but he realized that what she'd just said was true. Well, partially true.

Priscilla nodded. "If I were in his place –"

"Oh, don't try to work *that* out. It'd be like trying to imagine what a fish feels like on a hook. It's a different creature –

cold-blooded. . . ." He smiled at her. "You're a human being."

"Thank you –"

"Briscoe isn't. He's a *thing*."

She laughed. "I'm glad you're feeling better now. Have you anything urgent for me?"

"Yeah. Get Maurie Cohen on the line, will you?"

"Maurie Cohen?'

"Sure. The merchant banker. He's in our private book. If you can't get him, leave a message that Nick Morrell – say that, not *Mister* Morrell – Nick Morrell would very much like a word with him, at his convenience. Leave my home telephone number in case he decides to call me tonight. Okay?"

One had to admit that Briscoe was showing remarkable tenacity. Briscoe, or whoever was behind him. Elliot Hooper? Hunstanly, too – unless he was just a name on a letterhead. But it was one attack after another, even overlapping, and always from a new direction. Morrell wondered if they realized, Briscoe and Co., how close they'd come to success. Gil McLennan's "I'm getting a little tired of all this" was the first sign of a crack in the defences. Coming right on top of this afternoon's victory in the House of Commons it was all the more disheartening.

He told himself, as he poured a scotch and splashed in water, It would be disheartening if I let it be. I'll have to watch that: else I'll be getting tired, too. One weak member of the team was more than enough: he'd have to strengthen his own spine to make up for Gil's failing grip.

He sat down on the sofa, and swung his legs up. He told himself, Briscoe can't keep up the pressure for ever. We've trumped every card he's played: if I can head him off from the Mettendorf stock, he'll be running short of aces. In time, if I can go on blocking each move he makes, he'll give up the game. He'll have to. And once he knows he's stuck with me, he may even throw up the job. Perhaps I should aim for that now: go over to the attack, work up a case for a new chairman.

Well, who?

He thought suddenly, Chris Valor: he's the man for it!

I'd better have a talk with Valor. He'd be a useful chairman. He's sound, intelligent, already a respected public figure but alert, with his feet on the ground. And his political connections would be extremely useful. Now *that's* a thought: Sir Donald Tremloe. I owe him some expression of thanks, so I could ask him to lunch. Perhaps with Guy Davies. If there's a change of government soon, which is surely not unlikely, Tremloe will be the man who matters most to us. He could be a big help right now. I haven't done anything about politicians, and it's past time I did. Take a leaf out of old Gil's book.

What would they want, in return for sacking Briscoe? A contribution to Party funds? Well, they won't get a penny, not *that* Party, while Sir Charles is in the chair. Once he's out, it could be quite a different matter. Nobody'd need to spell that out, not to a man like Tremloe.

He'd finished his whisky. He got up, crossed the room to pour himself another. The liquor was doing him good, soothing the irritations of the day and helping to set his mind going on fresh, constructive lines. He thought, After this one, I'll eat. Inge may ring, this evening. And maybe Cohen –

Someone at the door. Now who the hell. . . .

He put his glass down, went out of the room and across the hall to answer it. He opened the door: Andrew Gaisford smiled.

"Good evening. Gaisford. Remember me?"

Morrell still had his hand on the door. He stared stonily at Gaisford. "What d'you want?"

"I'd like to bury the hatchet long enough to have a little talk. I've certain information –"

"I want nothing from you."

"You'd find it *extremely* interesting. And I want nothing in return. Just a few minutes?"

His first inclination had been to slam the door in the smooth, young face. Now he thought, I might as well hear what the next trick's going to be. The more I know of Briscoe's moves, the better: kicking this rat downstairs won't teach me anything.

He stepped back. "All right, come in. But make it quick. I'm expecting some calls and I don't want you here when they come."

"Well, that's frank." Gaisford stopped just inside the lounge. Morrell walked past him. The younger man said, glancing interestedly around the room, "That's very frank.

And since frank is how you like it, I'll come straight to the point." He smiled. "I'm afraid you may find this a bit of a shock. Wouldn't you like to sit down before I start?"

Morrell faced him with the length of the room between them. "Say what you have to say."

"All right. But you must realize this isn't a *message* I'm giving you. It's simply information which I think you should have. And I can't tell you how I've come by the information – only what it is. Is that acceptable?"

"Go on."

"Yes ... well, I understand there is to be a McLennan Ridgeway board meeting on Thursday morning. That's correct?"

"It is."

"Well, what I gather is – I dare say it'll sound odd to you, unless of course you know it already, which is unlikely – it's simply that at the meeting on Thursday you're going to resign from the company. Oh, yes – and you're going to agree to sell your personal shareholding to another company of which Lord Hunstanly is chairman." Gaisford shrugged. "Well, that's it. Sorry if it comes as a bit of a surprise, but I did think you ought to know."

Morrell watched him, thinking, He's not giving me information. He's come straight from Briscoe.

"Presumably you're going to tell me *why* I should do all that?"

Gaisford rubbed his nose thoughtfully. "Oh, yes. There *was* a reason. . . . Now what on earth – oh, yes." He frowned. "I'm afraid this is rather unpleasant. Of course, it has absolutely nothing to do with me –"

"Get on with it, will you?"

"Ostensibly you'll be doing it because of your intention to marry that *marvellous* looking Swedish girl –"

"Leave her out of it."

"Just as you like. But that's the official reason. The real one is that – well, you know that shindy at the Blue Gardenia about three weeks ago? All that stuff in the papers? Well, apparently it started certain people thinking about you in a certain way. To be exact, sort of poking into the past – your background, and all that. Here and in America. They came up with this quite fantastic story – please do understand I don't believe a word of it myself – that Gilbert McLennan's wife has a daughter named Alison – four years old, I believe, or nearly that? – and the child's father isn't Gilbert McLennan at all. They say *you're* the father. And they seem to think that if Gilbert McLennan were told of it there'd be the most frightful commotion –"

"Get out."

"What?"

"I said, *get out* –"

The one thing, he thought, which I can't fight. . . .

They've got me, finally, through threatening a little girl. One who, according to Inge, has a look of me. He's right: she'll be four quite soon, now.

How the hell did they find out? Who knows, apart from me and Toni?

Well that doesn't make much odds, not now. The fact is they *have* found out. And I can't fight them because that kid's whole damn life could be wrecked if I did. Quite apart from the fact that I promised Toni nobody would ever learn the secret. There's Toni's life, too. And Gil: he's nearly seventy and he's a tough old shit, but that's no reason to break his heart.

He thought, I'm glad Gaisford got out fast. There'd have been no satisfaction in roughing him up. Just a mess, that's all: and as I told him last time, he's only an errand boy. But Briscoe: that smooth, oily bastard, threatening me through a child: Briscoe I could happily kill with these bare hands.

His hand shook and the neck of the whisky bottle rattled on the glass. He told himself, I'll sit down now, think about it, work out the angles. But there still isn't a damn thing I can do. Except what they've told me I have to do. . . .

The phone rang, loud in the quiet flat. Morrell set his glass down on the table beside it, and picked it up.

"Morrell here."

"How are you, boy? Maurie Cohen."

"Hello, Maurie. Nice of you to call –"

"You wanted to talk to me?"

"Yes, Maurie, I did. I had something I thought might interest you. But in the last ten minutes there's been a change. I would have called you in the morning to cancel that message."

"Well, don't worry about it. Nice to have a word with you.

Are you all right, Nick? You sound a little down in the mouth."

"I'm okay . . . Maurie, thanks for calling –"

"So let's have lunch one day. How about – would Thursday suit you?"

Morrell winced. *Thursday*. . . . "Thursday's out, I'm afraid. Let me call you next week?"

"I'll look forward to hearing from you. Don't forget, now – it's been too long already. . . . Nick, I want to congratulate you. That's a very lovely girl you're going to marry!"

"Just for that you can come to the wedding."

Cohen chuckled. "Oh, you wouldn't want an old Jewish buzzard like me?"

"Nicest old Jewish buzzard in London –"

"Now I'll tell Miriam you said that!"

"Give her my love, Maurie."

"I will, I will. Nick, just out of interest, what was it you *would* have told me?"

"Well, you know Karl von Mettendorf?"

"I know of him. I know his business."

"He owns ten per cent of McLennan Ridgeway. He's ready to sell out, in fact he has to. There's a party waiting to buy that stock, and as things were early in the day I wanted to make sure they didn't get it. Now I don't care one way or the other."

"From my point of view, you think it would be a good idea?"

"An hour ago I'd have said yes, without a doubt. Now, I wouldn't advise any friend of mine to go near it."

He put the phone down slowly, and picked up his whisky. He thought, Even if all the friends I have in the world got together with all the money in the world, they couldn't help me out of *this* one.

CHAPTER TWENTY-FOUR

Morrell sat alone in his office. He'd told Priscilla and the other two girls out there that he didn't want any calls or callers. There was an hour to go – almost an hour – before the meeting. He felt that if he had to talk to anyone, he'd be sick.

The pressure felt like that inside him. Pressure in his brain, a fist balled tight in his guts. He kept thinking, *to be so damned helpless....*

Completely on my own. Gil McLennan's here in London – according to Briscoe, and for some reason best known to himself – and Karl von Mettendorf has been calling from Hamburg, wants me to ring him back. Neither of them can help me, though, or affect the situation in any way: and whatever they may want, I can't help them. I can't even talk to them – certainly not to Gil. Of *all* people, not to Gil McLennan. Karl will be ringing about his MR stockholding: and I suppose I should warn him to unload it, fast. But if I do that, the cat's out of the bag: and it's not Karl's money that's involved, it's his company's, and it's the other members of his board who want to sell out to Hunstanly. They must know how doing that would affect us here, because Karl will certainly have told them the score on that: but they still want to do it, so why should I worry about *them,* for Christ's sake? They're out for a quick profit and the hell with what happens to us: so let them make an even quicker loss.

He looked up at the photograph of *Wildoak* in that Atlantic storm. It was taken, he remembered, by *Dunnock*'s captain, Tony Hart, and on the very next convoy after that one *Dunnock* was fished and Hart went down with her.... The opposition had been Kraut, then: Karl von Mettendorf had killed Tony Hart. But the fighting had been more honest than it was now when the enemies were one's own compatriots. He thought, suddenly, I'll get out: maybe back to America. But anywhere out of England, wherever Inge wants to live *except* this bloody island which I and several million others were once so ready to defend.

What was that *for*, for God's sake?

Perhaps the war is close to the root of the trouble. Perhaps we lost too many natural leaders. So the scum – Briscoes and Hoopers – has floated to the surface through the gaps they left.

But this – he told himself, staring at the picture on the wall above his desk and forcing himself to recall the atmosphere of war, the spirit and resilience they'd needed and had – this is only one single defeat. It feels all the worse for being such a personal attack, vicious, underhand: but it is only one defeat, the first I've seen: I've won all the battles, until this one. That's another reason why it feels so bad.

A knock on the door: Priscilla came in quickly. He glanced at her, frowning his surprise.

"I thought I told you –"

"I'm sorry. First there's this from Sir Charles, marked 'immediate and personal', and now there's –"

"Me, I guess." Gil McLennan came past her into the room. He held out his hand. "You can't lock the old man out, Nick. Not when he still owns most of the goddam company."

Morrell glanced at his secretary. His eyes asked her, *What the hell's the matter with you? Can't you follow a simple instruction?* She stared back at him apologetically: he noticed suddenly that her eyes were damp.

"Priscilla – you all right?"

She nodded. Gil McLennan patted her arm. "Run along, now. I'll make the excuses to your boss." She went out quickly: McLennan dropped into a chair as the door shut behind her. "Nick, she was crying her heart out. She tried to stop me getting in to see you, but I'm a hard man to stop. Now what's this damn nonsense she told me out there?"

"It's all quite personal, Gil. I'm resigning, that's all." He glanced down at the chairman's "immediate and personal" letter. "Mind if I see what's in this?"

"Go ahead."

Morrell opened the envelope. It was the letter he'd asked for: a formal undertaking, signed by Briscoe and witnessed, to buy Morrell's total MR stockholding at this morning's Stock Exchange quotation. Morrell folded the letter and slid it into his pocket.

"Gil, from what you said when we spoke on the telephone just a few days ago, my leaving won't make much difference to you. You said you were getting tired of hearing about our troubles. Well, how the hell d'you imagine *I've* been feeling? I'm sick to bloody death of it, that's how! So I'm getting out."

"Without a word to me before you do it? Don't I own this heap?"

"You did. I don't know what developments there may have been in Hamburg in the last few days, but by now it's possible you don't own any more stock than the opposition has. I warned you about it, and you weren't prepared to take any kind of action, so –" he shrugged – "so here we are. This is how it is."

McLennan said, lighting a cigar, "I just came from Hamburg, Nick. Didn't Karl call you, this morning?"

"He tried to. I was supposed to call him back. Under the circumstances, there didn't seem much point in doing so."

"You should have. Might have brightened you up some."

"Have you bought his stock?"

"No, But Seymour Laing did. He's right here in London – he'll be along for the meeting. He bought about half of the von Mettendorf holding in MR, for that Trust of his."

"Of Toni's, you mean."

"You know about that?" McLennan looked surprised. "How'd you get on to it?"

"I checked in Australia – had a friend of mine look into it. No special reason, Gil. Wanted to know who I was really working for, I suppose."

McLennan frowned. "You're working for *me*, damn it –"

"I have been, sure. For darned near twenty years. You realize it's that long? Well, I'm sorry, Gil. Our association has about twenty-five minutes to run. Unless of course you'd like me to come back to the States."

"I wouldn't want that if you're letting me down here."

"I can understand you feeling like that. Unfortunately –"

"We'll discuss that angle later, if we have to. Now about this stock. Karl's ten per cent, I mean. The Trust has half of it, and an old coot named Maurie Cohen has the rest."

"Maurie Cohen?"

"Sure. He has a lot of time for you, Nick." McLennan nodded. "And he told me you'd put him on to it. Is that right?"

"I'd intended to. Then this other thing cropped up, right in my face like a – well, by the time I got to talk to him, I told him not to touch it. You realize the market value of McLennan Ridgeway is likely to be something like halved by this time tomorrow?"

"That's what you're trying to do to me?"

"Don't be stupid, Gil. Damn it, I *warned* Karl –"

"You didn't warn *me*, though –"

"You'd made it plain you weren't touching it anyway. You know that's true – we both know it. But I don't understand Cohen ignoring what I –"

"Maybe he reckons he knows better than you do. Well, he did it, anyway, so who cares? Nick, isn't this a load off your mind?"

"It would have been – if things were just as they were when I phoned you." He saw McLennan's frown. "The way things are, I'm only sorry you got in deeper. It doesn't help my position now, my personal situation –"

"Now about that, Nick –"

"Wait a minute. When I phoned you about Karl's stock, you weren't interested. What changed your mind so quickly?"

McLennan shook his head. "Nothing. Wasn't a change of mind, and it wasn't a case of *disinterest* to start with. It happens I'm extended to the limit: I'm expanding some more, and – well, I'll tell you about that some time, but the fact is I couldn't have done a thing myself about that stock. Doesn't mean I wouldn't have *liked* to. Hell, I thought about it, you had me good and worried, believe me. So I talked to Seymour, then we went out to Greenwich together and he talked with Toni. He could see the danger to the Trust's investment – he's no fool, you know –"

Morrell smiled. "I know."

"Sure. Well, he had Toni seeing it the same way. And the other difficulty, restrictions on new oversea investment, he knew a way round that, too. When it's to protect an existing investment, you can get around it. Seymour knew he could, and who he could get to in a hurry for a provisional okay." McLennan shrugged. "So that's how the picture changed. Now, Nick, you give *me* some information. What's this new thing that happened so quickly and I don't know about?"

"It's personal." Morrell frowned. "I'm more sorry than I can say, Gil. You and Seymour and Maurie Cohen have done all this, and I'm in a spot where I have to let you down. But I can't help it, Gil. I just can't."

"Sounds crazy to me. Not only you're ready to shake us down for millions, you're pulling out just when we get where nobody can damn well touch us! Funny time to chicken out."

"Gil, tell you what I'll do. I'll see Briscoe – he knows I'm resigning today – and fix with him to delay it a couple of days. Give you time to sell whatever you want to sell –"

"You think he'd be that much of an idiot?" McLennan's smile had broadened. "Nice of you, Nick. I appreciate it. But

I won't be selling a single share. What's more, you won't be resigning."

Morrell sighed. "It's already in writing. I'm going to hand it to Briscoe at the meeting this morning."

"Been trying a little blackmail, has he?"

Morrell looked away. "I can't discuss it, Gil –"

"I can, though. . . . Nick, you must think I'm a stupid old man who can't see the end of his nose or make four out of two and two. Now, for example. This has to be something you can't talk to *me* about. Otherwise you might have invited some kind of assistance. So it's personal to you and to me. Right?"

Morrell didn't look up. His hands were flat on the desk and he seemed to be examining the backs of them. He tried hard to keep his surprise from showing in his face.

McLennan went on, "You don't have to answer. Now, Nick, I'm going to tell you something very, very personal. You won't mention it to any other party, I know that. That's how much I trust you, Nick. It's like this. I've known since I was maybe thirty years of age that I couldn't ever contribute effectively towards the birth of a child. I mean, make a woman pregnant. I found that out after the first time I got married, and they ran tests on me. I'm not impotent, Nick, I wouldn't want you to have a wrong idea like that. Just my seed's not fertile, for some damn reason. Now you see where *that* takes us, don't you?"

Morrell was watching him, now.

"Toni told me all about it. She had to, you see – she and I both knew it couldn't have been me, we knew that. But hell, how could I blame her? I never told her my trouble before I married her. I guess I was scared she wouldn't have said yes. You could say I played a trick on her, to that extent. And a girl like Toni needs to be a mother. Well, she's settled for just the one." McLennan frowned. "I still love her, Nick, and I love my daughter, and I have no quarrel with you either. So now, you punk, you can forget about Sir Charles bloody Briscoe, can't you? I'm going to let him know how things are, Nick. I'm going to tell him I've heard this story and if anybody so much as breathes a hint of anything I don't like about me or you or Toni or my daughter, why, I'll sue them for every goddam cent they ever had or ever will have. I'll sue the goddam pants off 'em!"

Morrell was still mentally pinching himself. This could be the sort of dream from which you woke up to find everything as it had been the night before. He asked McLennan, "Tell me how you guessed all this?"

"I told you, it had to be something personal, some matter you couldn't discuss with me –"

"I wonder why Toni never told me you knew about it –"

"Kind of my secret, wasn't it? But answering your first question, how I guessed – there's another thing. How they got wind of this. Now can you guess who I heard *this* from?"

Morrell shook his head.

"Martha Scotland, that's who. Nick, I was a little bit naughty, at one time. That's another reason Toni – well, it was when Toni was over here. That trip out to Australia, and all. . . ." He frowned. "When she got back home, we kind of sorted it all out. I had to tell Martha how things stood – you know, lay it on the line, the payoff. Maybe I told her a little too much. It had to be convincing."

"But how did these bastards get to Martha?"

"They hired enquiry agents to look into everything you ever did. Even went down to the yard and fired questions at Hank Smith – got a short answer from him, I can tell you. . . . But the first thing these guys do is find out who your friends were – that's how they operate. It's not difficult, especially with women. Well, everybody likes talking about old times, folks they knew once, old gossip. . . . So they got on to Martha – and afterwards she came running to me. Scared maybe she'd get into trouble – you know how they talk, they don't realize what they've said until they see it in some damn newspaper –"

Morrell nodded slowly. "When was this?"

"Four, five days ago. Martha's a bit of a kook, these days. The TV networks dropped her, her face isn't so damned good now, she never could act, and she never stayed with one man long enough to marry him. So when this snoop comes along with a big play and a case of scotch, Martha's not holding much back." McLennan shook his head. "Can't blame her, I guess." He looked sharply at Morrell. "You still want out, Nick?"

Morrell smiled. "Jesus, *no*!"

"Now that's music in my furry ears! Leave it to me to break the news to Briscoe?"

"Oh, Gil, I'm going to *fix* Briscoe, now –"

McLennan looked disappointed. "You don't want me to tell him?"

"Sure, have your fun." Morrell found his letter of resignation, tore it to shreds, and dropped the pieces in his wastepaper basket. Then he tore Briscoe's letter to him once across, into halves. "Gil, will you give the old darling this, at the same time?"

"What is it?" McLennan dragged himself to his feet, and took the two halves of the letter.

"An undertaking to buy my stock at this morning's price."

McLennan frowned. "Looking after yourself, weren't you?"

"Sure. You weren't interested in buying more MR stock, Gil. Remember?"

"Oh." He nodded. "Yeah. I guess that's right. Nick, are you happy with the way things have turned out?"

"Of course I am." Morrell stood up. "I'm sorry, I'm – a bit numbed. It's been a very tough couple of days – then you walk in like a fairy godmother –"

McLennan laughed. "You have that wrong, Nick. It's the fairy godmother I'm going to walk in on *now*!"

Morrell laughed with him. "Kick her in the crutch for me, will you? Just as a little something on account?" He put his hand out. "Gil – thanks. I mean – well, *total* thanks. There's no way of putting it –"

"So forget it. D'you think I'd want to lose all that nice money? Or see this company go down? I'm not here out of brother love, Nick."

"I'm still grateful."

"Okay, *be* grateful. What are you aiming to do to Briscoe, now?"

"Let me tell you when it's done." He opened the door. "Priscilla, get on to the Ministry, see if you can get Elliot Hooper personally for me. If you can't, get as close to him as you can, tell them it's urgent, personal and confidential and very much in his own interests that he and I should meet some time today. Do that before anything else, will you?"

"Right." With one hand resting on the phone, she looked up at him. He found himself wondering if her lashes were real. She said, "You sound more cheerful –"

"I am. And I'm –" He jerked his head. "Here. Come in here a minute." He shut the door behind her. "Priscilla, forget all I said earlier on. I'm staying here, and so are you."

"That's *marvellous*!"

"It is, isn't it?" He grinned at her. "It *is* good –"

She reached up, suddenly, kissed him on the cheek. "Nick, I'm so *happy* for you –"

"Don't I get one of those?" McLennan stooped, offering her his cheek. He pointed with the tip of one finger. "Right there, please. While you're in the mood?" She kissed him, and he winked at Morrell, "Guess I should come over here more often. You get all the –"

"How long are you staying?"

"We'll fly home tomorrow, probably."

"Will you and Seymour join me tonight, then? Do the town?"

"I don't know, Nick." McLennan glanced at Priscilla. "I don't want any of those crazy women hitting me over the head in nightclubs –"

Morrell told Priscilla, "Go and put that call through to Hooper, will you?" He turned to McLennan. "I'll pick you and Seymour up at the Hilton at seven this evening. Can't make it before that because Inge's due to call me from Los Angeles at six-thirty. Seven all right for you?"

"Fine. Is Inge okay?"

Morrell nodded. "She'll be here in a couple of weeks. How about you and Toni buzzing over for the wedding?"

The lift, undoubtedly an antique, clanked to a halt on the second floor of the Ministry building. It was the slowest lift he'd ever ridden in: the noise of the machinery which had hoisted its cage slowly and shakily from floor to floor suggested that the motive power might be steam. Now at rest, it was hissing, ticking from the exertion of the long, slow haul.

The ancient gates clanged back. A tall young man in striped trousers smiled dutifully, holding out his hand. "Mr. Morrell?"

"Yeah."

"The minister's ready to see you at once. Will you come this way, please?"

Morrell thought, following the lad, Hooper will have heard from Briscoe by now. He'll know the cat's among the pigeons. And Sir Charles will know I've made this date to see his buddy. Well, they'll both be out of their misery soon. In far worse misery, if I have anything to do with it.... Following the black jacket and striped trousers through a hundred yards of passages, he noticed old men pushing trolleys loaded with files and bundles bound in tape: angles of passages filled-in with filing cabinets, wooden cupboards bulging with heaps of dusty paper. They turned in a heavy door, across a large, carpeted office, and the guide knocked on an inner door. A voice called "Come in!"

The lad stood to one side. "Mr. Morrell, sir." Elliot Hooper rose behind an enormous desk. A tall, grey-faced man with thinning, mousy-grey hair. His eyes were deep-set, shadowed, perhaps even a little frightened. A surgical scar ran vertically from his left ear to the top of his collar. A white collar, fixed to a striped shirt: an entirely Briscoe-type uniform. Morrell found himself shaking a thin, soft hand.

"Mr. Hooper. Nice of you to spare the time. We've met twice, but neither time long enough to talk much. This is a great pleasure."

"It is for me as well. Won't you sit down?" Hooper subsided into his own chair. "I've heard about your work at McLennan Ridgeway, and I've had no real chance to express my appreciation of it. Let me make up for that now, eh?" Hooper smiled. At the same time, he threw a glance at an unusually ugly clock. "Unfortunately, I only have about eight minutes. But you mentioned a degree of urgency?"

"Right. I'll make it as brief as possible." He thought, Gently does it. Cool and calm. I know he knows as much as Briscoe does, but he doesn't know I know that. He doesn't *have* to know, either: I need co-operation, not more enemies. Even if I have to scare him stiff to get it.

"Mr. Hooper. Since the British government is still a large shareholder in MR, I believe you should first know what's going on, and second use your influence as necessary in the company's affairs –"

Hooper leant forward, smiling slightly. "I think I'm quite well informed, Morrell, most of the time."

"By Sir Charles Briscoe –"

"He is of course our own appointee –"

"Yeah, he is. I'll get round to that. First, however, I want to tell you about two things that have happened to me recently. First there was an attempt to frame me: to make it look as if I was trying to buy MR shares to increase my personal standing as a shareholder –"

"You were not doing so?"

"No, I wasn't. A bum named Andrew Gaisford, who is a friend of Briscoe's and I believe known also to you, was doing the work and letting 'em all think he was doing it on my behalf. I'd never met him in my life. I gave him a counter-threat to carry back to Briscoe, and the smear seemed to stop immediately. Funny, that."

He smiled at Hooper.

"You're suggesting that Sir Charles Briscoe had some part in – in what you say was going on?"

"I'm not *suggesting*. I know it. I could even prove it. The most recent attack on me – again through Gaisford, and emanating beyond question from Sir Charles – has been dealt with only today. It was plain, ordinary blackmail – a criminal offence, as you know. It was also, I'm glad to say, based on a lie."

"Why on earth should some person wish to – er – blackmail you?"

"Not *some person*, Minister. It was initiated by your appointee, Sir Charles Briscoe. His reason is partly personal jealousy – he'd like to be cock of the roost and he can't while I'm there because I won't damn well let him – and partly a desire, which for all I know you may share, to push out the American control now they've done the job you couldn't do for yourselves."

"No. I assure you, such a desire couldn't possibly form any part of my policy."

"It would be unethical, you're right –"

"And I find it impossible to believe that Sir Charles, of all people – a highly respected member of the Civil Service as he was for many years –"

"Life's full of surprises, Mr. Hooper. Did you know he's a pansy? Homosexual?"

"Briscoe?" Elliot Hooper had coloured, just a little.

"I'm afraid so. My predecessor, as one instance, was *very* glad to leave the company. That's why he made no fuss about it. But you know, Minister, these smears do get around. The things they were saying about me – well, damn it, that kind of thing sticks. No matter *what* you say or do. You can kill a story at source, but it goes on spreading, mouth to mouth, for years afterwards. Eventually *everyone* believes it – it's split up into a dozen different stories by then, all pointing at the same message, and – well, you know, people say 'no smoke without fire', and so on. I don't have to tell you that men in positions of authority and responsibility can't afford that kind of thing being said about them. Let me give you an example – purely by way of illustrating my point, and between ourselves, of course. . . ."

Morrell went through a show of searching his pockets.

"Where the hell did I – oh, I know!" He smiled pleasantly at the minister as he pulled out his wallet and extracted from it the photograph which Guy Davies had given him. The one of Hooper and Briscoe holdings hands. He slid it across the desk.

"Summer before last, wasn't it? In Capri? Personally, I'd accept that it could have been just some trick of the camera. You *look* as if you're playing sticky hands with Briscoe, but I dare say it's possible you were only passing him a box of matches: you can't see any matches or anything else in the picture, but – well, anyway, some people, may be less charitable, might swear black and blue that you and Sir Charles were holding hands. When you add that to what one knows – what a lot of people know, about Briscoe –"

Hooper was tearing the photograph into small pieces. Morrell nodded, watching him. "When I next see a print of that snapshot, I'll tear that up too. I'll make a point of doing it whenever I'm shown one. Of course, there'll be a negative around somewhere –"

"What do you want, Morrell?"

Eyes definitely frightened now in the camouflage of flushed, angry face. . . .

"I wanted to show you how unpleasant it is to have stories, smears, lies and so on, spread around the place. It can happen to anyone – just as it's been happening to me –"

"You want some kind of protection against future attempts –"

"A very definite and effective kind of protection, Minister. I've told you what Briscoe's been up to. There's plenty more, but those are recent examples. He's not alone in it: he has the support of several other directors who are quite useless in any directorial capacity. So I want Briscoe sacked. Now – today."

Morrell wasn't bothering to smile, now.

"I want Briscoe flung out on his ear. I also want Hunstanly,

Law, Wyllie and Johnson-Hughes removed immediately from the board. I want Christopher Valor Q.C. appointed chairman, and in the course of the next few weeks I'll arrange with him to appoint three new directors from our shipyards. They'll be working directors and representatives of the labour force. Do I have your agreement on all those points?"

"You most certainly do not. You come in here with an allegation of homosexuality against a man of impeccable record in the public service, and you imagine I'd –"

"Just a minute. Briscoe's private life isn't my concern. The only relevance of what you choose to call that *allegation* is that the man's waspish nature, his jealousy and so on, make him totally unsuited to running a big, busy company where the work's done by *men*. Give him a dress-making business, let him design costumes for the ballet, but for God's sake get him off our board. It's the *effect* that concerns me. If it didn't obtrude into the conduct of our business, I wouldn't give a damn – he can sleep with a Tibetan yak, for all I care, so long as he leaves the bloody thing at home. All I'm asking for are conditions under which I can get on with my job."

Hooper raised one forefinger. "Allegations of homosexuality against Sir Charles Briscoe." He raised the middle finger. "A barely disguised attempt to blackmail me on the strength of a trick photograph. . . ." Hooper's voice shook. "Have you played all your cards now, Morrell?"

Morrell smiled, and shook his head. "Hardly started. In any case, I don't know what on earth you mean about blackmail. *I've* been blackmailed –"

"With some cause?"

"None, as it happens. But would you justify blackmail if there were some basis of fact behind it?"

"Of course not."

"The man you're sticking up for has certainly been blackmailing me. Well, trying to. You still support him?"

"You've proved nothing –"

"But I can, and if I have to I'll do it in the open. Do you recall an incident recently which culminated in a question in the House about whether or not it was to be your policy to merge all shipyards, forcing them to merge with larger groups even when, like McLennan Ridgeway, they were already self-sufficient?"

"Certainly I remember. There was never any truth in that

suggestion. It was a political gambit started by Tremloe purely to create embarrassment."

"The hell it was. It was a necessary campaign started by me to make you change your mind or at least withdraw the threat. I have Briscoe's letter to Gilbert McLennan in which he quotes you directly as warning him about the extension of the merger policy."

"There was no such extension of policy, and I issued no such warning. I can't be held responsible for letters which Sir Charles Briscoe may elect to write – no doubt, I may add, in the best of faith, perhaps from some misunderstanding –"

"But Briscoe is a close friend of yours. That photograph is surely just one proof of it. Even if you weren't holding hands, look at the way you're – oh, you can't look at it now, can you. You tore it up. Well, if you want one to keep, I'm sure I could lay hands on a copy.... Minister, now this isn't anything but a statement of fact. If I have to mount a full-scale attack on Briscoe, using newspapers to do it, journalists who already know the score, there's going to be a lot of fur flying, and it won't be only his. The effect will be the same in the long run, because you won't be able to hold out against the pressure and he won't dare show his face in public. But there it is: if you won't dismiss him, I've no alternative. I'll do it my way."

"I thought you disliked blackmail, Morrell?"

"I detest it. Who's talking about blackmail? I'm simply pointing out to you the likely results of a course which it seems you're forcing me to take. I stand for the progress and efficiency of McLennan Ridgeway. That means getting rid of Briscoe. There's no justification whatever for him, or Lord Hunstanly or Sir Paul Wyllie or that oaf Johnson-Hughes continuing to gum up the works. And Briscoe deserves nothing less than summary dismissal. Either you do it – it's your job to do it, we both know that – or I'll achieve the same result the hard way. My way, there'll be repercussions and a lousy stink in all kinds of places. But if you tell me that's the only way to do it, I'll set the ball rolling within half an hour of leaving this building. It's as simple as that, and perfectly straightforward."

Hooper flipped up the lid of a silver box.

"Do you smoke?"

"No, thank you."

The minister put a cigarette between his lips, and lit it. He said, taking it out of his mouth and staring at it, "Nobody wants scandal. Unless you do. Why not agree to wait, let me do something quietly –"

"No, I've told you the only course I'll accept if you're doing the job. Inform Briscoe he's dismissed, with immediate effect. Sack the other three with him – this afternoon. Then ask Christopher Valor if he'll accept the chair. Maybe you'll feel he should have a knighthood to go with it."

"Perhaps you'd like that for yourself too?"

"Let's keep this conversation to the point –"

"I'm perfectly serious. For services to industry." Elliot Hooper smiled. "Morrell, there's no reason why you and I shouldn't be friends."

Morrell thought, I could give you a dozen damn good reasons. . . . He said, "All I want out of this is what I've told you, and then to be left alone to get on with my job."

Smoke trickled from Hooper's mouth. He seemed more composed, now, and thoughtful. As if the two of them were working out a plan together, a matter of mutual interest.

"I agree with you to the extent that public scandal, even smoke without fire – which such a scandal would be – is better avoided. I take it that you yourself would accept the fact that there is no truth in any of the – the allegations at which you've hinted, those aspects which might titillate the cheaper breed of journalist?"

"I don't know any journalists of that kind. Personally, I've no interest in washing other people's dirty linen in public, if that's what you mean. But you see, I *can* prove what Briscoe's been up to. I can prove it up to the hilt. I can also prove he's something less than obviously heterosexual. With all that, and the position he holds as the result of a government appointment, you must see that responsible newspaper editors would regard his continuance in office as contrary to the public interest?"

"I suppose –" Hooper stubbed out his cigarette only half smoked – "I suppose if the case were trumped up well enough –"

"Trumping up doesn't come into it. But if all this came out, don't you think a lot of people would want to know how and why you yourself, you personally, Minister, should have wished to support him, keep him in his job, hush it all up?"

"Now you look here, Morrell –"

"I haven't finished." Morrell managed a friendly smile. "I'm only trying to make you see this as the public would see it. If anyone asked me why should Elliot Hooper, a respected politician with his country's interests at heart, want to stifle the facts or ignore them, keep this unseemly creature in a highly-paid job – well, I don't know about you, but I *wouldn't* like the job of explaining it. Minister, I haven't come here with demands. Still less with threats. You may have misunderstood me, a few minutes ago. I've simply been telling you what has to be done, in one way or the other, and why. You could do it simply, quickly and effectively – even comparatively quietly. If you won't, then I'll have to, and the effect will be rather like using a nuclear weapon to clear a potato patch."

Hooper nodded slowly. Morrell thought, He must realize a lot of this is bluff. But he also knows he can't risk seeing the other half in print....

"Will you do it, or shall I?"

"I suppose, to avoid a great deal of unpleasantness –"

"You might say, 'for the good of the industry'?"

Hooper snapped, "I suppose I can choose my own words?"

"Of course. So long as the sacking is summary."

The minister blinked once or twice. He said, "You've opened my eyes, Morrell. I had no idea what's been going on. I'm afraid the picture I've had from Briscoe has been quite different...."

Morrell thought, fascinated, *We're allies, now. Me and Elliot Hooper!*

"It's still set me an extremely nasty job –"

"I know. But then, Sir Charles has really been very nasty to me, lately. I wouldn't mind him being just plain nasty – wouldn't mind it so much, anyway – if he was the slightest bloody use to anyone.... Now, Minister, I want to see the sackings announced in tomorrow's papers. If they aren't featured prominently in all the morning news, I'll go to town on Briscoe *my* way."

Hooper stood up. "I thought I'd told you, I'm accepting your advice. Now I'm afraid I'm late for a very important conference –"

"Sure." Morrell pushed himself up from the chair. "Sorry if I've overstayed my welcome, but thanks for listening to me." He shook the minister's hand. "Believe me, you're doing the right thing."

He thought, as he walked over to the door, *and that's one man I'll need to watch out for, from this moment on. . . .*

Inge's voice, all the way from California, was as clear as a bell.

"Is everything all right with you, Nick?"

"Except you aren't here yet, everything's wonderful. When d'you think you'll be finished?"

"Ten days, I hope. You miss me?"

"That, Miss Hegardt, is a *crazy* question."

"But you can wait ten days?"

"Only if we get married the minute you arrive. Soon as you land, let's rush straight off and do it?"

"Do what, Nick?"

"That too –"

"How about a licence?"

"I'll fix one. Send me a copy of your birth certificate, will you? They can't need more than that. Ten days, that'll make it the twenty-fourth. I'll book a session at the Caxton Hall."

"To be sure, make it the twenty-fifth?"

"Well, all right, I'll double book, if they'll let me. Inge –"

"I'm still here –"

"I love you."

"Well, I should hope so! How is that horrid chairman?"

"Fired. I fixed him. Gil McLennan came over and helped do it. Complicated story, though – tell you when I see you."

"So now you have everything you want?"

"I will have, by the twenty-fifth."

Morrell thought, hanging up, This whole situation is just too good to be true. Everything, as the song says, coming up roses. . . . Better watch it now, Morrell – any minute, you may hit the bloody thorns!

Well, it's up to *me,* now. The only thorns could be of my own making, home-grown. I've got to let Inge fill my mind, I have to do that in order to measure up to all the things I've promised her, all she's going out on this limb for. No harking back: all that's over, and the past mustn't wreck the future. I love Inge: there's no room for anything but that solid fact.

But now, I'd better get cracking, over to the Hilton.

The telephone rang again.

"Morrell here."

"Nick, Guy Davies. You've been holding out on us, haven't you?"

"How's that?"

"This statement from Elliot Hooper saying he's sacked Briscoe and three other government nominees from your board. No reasons given, just that bare announcement. You never mentioned this was brewing, Nick. What's it all about?"

"Guy – this is off the record, now – it's come up so fast I haven't had time to sit down and think about it. In any case it was Hooper's job to make the announcement, not mine. We had a fairly thunderous board meeting this morning, I saw Hooper this afternoon, I've just had Inge on the blower from California and now this minute I'm off to the Hilton to pick up our two American directors. So you see –"

"McLennan's over here?"

"Sure. And Laing. They're at the Hilton, if you want to talk to them. But all that was just between us, Guy. If you ask me about what Hooper's announced, my answer's that I can't comment. Those four men are government appointees, so their dismissal – if that's what it is – is the government's business. I certainly won't express regret, but for any further information you'll have to get in touch with the Ministry. Okay?"

"I can quote you as saying you can't express regret?"

"Why not? Call me in the morning, Guy. We might meet later in the day."

"Right. Who's to be your new chairman, Nick?"

"Ask Hooper. Government appointment."

"You mean you don't know?"

"I mean it's Hooper's job to tell you. Look, I have to run now –"

"I think I might meet you at the Hilton. D'you mind?"

"Of course I don't mind. See you, Guy."

There was still some whisky in the glass at which he'd been sipping while he changed and waited for Inge's call. He knocked it back, slammed the glass down, and headed for the door. He thought, Elliot Hooper certainly hasn't wasted any time. I wonder how Briscoe's feeling now? Now he's down and out, licked, I could almost feel sorry for the swine. But only *almost*: he'd have shown *me* no sympathy. He'd have danced on my face with hobnailed boots. Well, his boy friend will look after him. He and Hooper are probably crying on each other's shoulders right at this minute.

Morrell opened the front door of his flat. At the same moment, Christopher Valor stepped out of the lift.

"Ah. Just in time. Glad I caught you, Nick."

"Chris, I'm sorry, but I'm already late –"

"Let's make it short, then, but I want to know what's happened. What, and why."

"Did Hooper call you?"

Valor nodded.

"Have you accepted?"

"Not yet. I wanted to talk to you first. This is important, Nick. However much of a hurry you're in."

"Come with me." Morrell half dragged his new chairman into the lift. "I'm on my way to the Hilton to meet McLennan and Laing. Come and have a drink with them, and we'll talk this over. Have you got time?"

Valor glanced at his watch, and nodded. "I can spare half an hour. I promised I'd ring Hooper at his home tonight."

"Half an hour's plenty. And you can call him from the Hilton, if you want to."

The lift stopped. Morrell's car was right outside. As they crossed the pavement, Burton jumped out and opened the rear door. Morrell said, "In you go, Chris. . . . Harry, take us to the Hilton, then shove off home."

"Sir." Burton snapped the door shut. Morrell looked at Valor.

"It was my idea, Chris. You're not Hooper's choice."

The Q.C. expelled a long, slow breath. "Well, that's all right, then. All I needed to know." He nodded. "Thanks. I'll accept. I think we'll work pretty well together, don't you?"

"Damn right we will." Morrell grinned. "And what a pleasant change *that's* going to be!"

Burton eased the Rolls out into the stream of evening traffic. Morrell leant back, consciously relaxing all his muscles, watching the passing flow of homebound Londoners. His own words echoed in his ears. He thought, Count-down . . . lift-off! *Now*, by God, we'll show them!

THE FAMILY 40p
Leslie Waller

Truly great novels about the Mafia are few and far between. *The Family* is not only the most recent but one of the very, very best. The *New York Times* called it "a jumbo entertainment, full of everything" and drew attention to the book's shattering combination of big business, violence, raw sex, protest and comment on the richest society in the history of the world. It is a dramatic and engrossing story that exposes a new breed of gangster less concerned with strong-arm tactics than with financial manipulation. Woods Palmer, chief executive of America's biggest banking empire, becomes the pawn in an operation of a naked ruthless power that only the Mafia's mighty, complex machine can wield with such effectiveness and shameless brutality.